RE
D0339961
NOV 2010
BALLARD LIBRARY

the DEMON'S PARCHMENT

The Crispin Guest Novels by Jeri Westerson

Veil of Lies

Serpent in the Thorns

the DEMON'S PARCHMENT

A Crispin Guest Medieval Noir

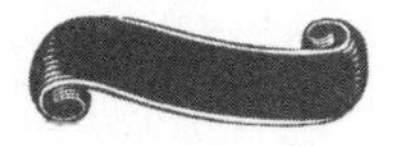

Jeri Westerson

MINOTAUR BOOKS NEW YORK

This is a work of fiction. All of the characters, organizations, and events portrayed in this novel are either products of the author's imagination or are used fictitiously.

 Printed in the United States of America. For information, address St. Martin's Press, 175 Fifth Avenue, New York, N.Y. 10010.

www.minotaurbooks.com

ISBN 978-0-312-62104-9

First Edition: October 2010

10 9 8 7 6 5 4 3 2 1

To my personal knight,
Craig, who slays all my demons

Acknowledgments

There are always a great many people to thank, particularly when research is involved. It's not something you can accomplish alone. Thanks go out to Gillian Pollack and the late Reva Brown for helping me with post-expulsion Jewery; to Henk T'Jong for the French translations; to my Vicious Circle of Ana Brazil, Bobbie Gosnell, and Laura James for helping me whip the plot into shape; to my ever patient husband, Craig; to my agent, Joshua Bilmes; and my editor, Keith Kahla. Thank you all.

the DEMON'S PARCHMENT

I

London, 1384

"HE'S STILL OUT THERE." Jack Tucker leaned his head and shoulders out the window.

"Close the damn shutters," growled Crispin. "It's too cold in here as it is."

"Sorry, Master," said the boy, doing as bid. His ginger hair was dusted with snow. "It's just that that man is still out there, looking up at us. Makes me a bit shivery."

"The cold will do that." Hunkered by their meager fire, Crispin held one hand toward the flames. The other was curled around a bowl of tart wine.

"He might be a client, sir."

"He might be."

"Why don't you go look?"

Crispin drank the bitter liquid. Winter did not seem to bring him as many clients as the warmer months. Perhaps fewer crimes were committed in the winter and a "private sheriff" was not in the family finances when it came down to it.

The small room offered little comfort. Its few bits of rented furniture—a chair, a stool, a rickety table—stood in the center of unadorned walls. Crispin's pallet bed was shoved against the wall near the hearth, and on the opposite side of the small fire lay a pile of straw, the place Jack tucked in at night. Four strides would take him to a chest by the door, which held Crispin's change of stockings and braies and his few writing implements. He was lucky to have two windows, one facing the back garden and the one Jack had been leaning out of facing the Shambles. But "luck" was a relative term. Today, with London chilled like a frozen lake, two windows only offered more opportunities for an icy draft.

"Let me see, then." Crispin rose with a bone-weary sigh and set the empty bowl aside. He joined Jack by the window, but instead of throwing open the shutter, he peered down through a crack in the wood that he usually kept stuffed with a rag.

Below, in the snow-painted street, stood a man in a long black gown. His dark beard was salted by time as were his bushy brows. His head was covered by a tight-fitting felt cap with flaps that covered his ears. And he was looking up at Crispin's window expectantly, ignoring the occasional passerby in the street.

"He certainly seems determined about something," said Crispin.

"Then why don't he come up?" asked the boy, twisting his cloak across his chest.

"A very good question. Why don't you go down and find out."

"Me?" Suddenly the mystery did not need solving so urgently. "He might be a madman. He's been there a straight hour and he hasn't moved."

"All the more reason to see what he wants. Go on now, Jack. If apprentice you wish to be, then you had best obey your master."

"I knew that would bite me in the arse," he grumbled. Securing his cloak, he marched toward the door. He took a firm grip of his knife sheath and looked Crispin in the eye. It was moments like these that Jack seemed so very young. Of course it was true. At twelve, his cheeks were still plump from childhood, and though his voice cracked a bit, it hadn't yet deepened. "If I don't come back, it's your fault."

"Shall I keep watch? Is an old man so much of a threat to you?"

"I'm going!" he replied sullenly, and slipped through the door.

But Crispin did keep watch through the chink, and saw Jack appear cautiously below. The man tore his gaze at last from Crispin's second-storey window and stared at Jack. The creak of cart and hiss of wind made it impossible for Crispin to hear their quiet exchange, but he could well tell by Jack's pantomime what he told the man. He appeared to be entreating him upstairs, but the man shook his head. It seemed that he was content to stand in the snow and merely gaze up at the window.

Crispin studied the man anew. "Hmpf. Now *I* grow curious."

Footsteps at his door told him Jack had returned. The door opened. "Bless me," said Jack, shaking the flakes from his cloak and stamping at the threshold. "He *does* want to talk to you, sir. But he will not come up."

"Oh? Does he say why?"

"No, sir. He seems most stubborn about it. I told him that the Tracker was not in the habit of meeting strange men in the cold streets instead of his warm lodgings."

No, indeed. He had no wish to leave the feeble warmth of his room, but the larder was decidedly bare. "It seems I have no choice but to humor this miscreant. Tell me, Jack. How did he seem to you? What was his character?"

He knew the boy liked to show off his growing skills, and on cue, Jack puffed up and hooked his thumbs in his belt. "Well, now. He is a man of middle years, well-spoken, neat and clean."

"London or foreign?"

"Foreign. French, I think. His speech has got a light touch, if you get my meaning. He seems like a gentleman."

"Then he'll have the coin. Very well. I shall meet this mysterious man on the street." Crispin buttoned his cloak tight, pulled his chaperon hood up over his head, and yanked open the frost-bitten door.

He trotted down the narrow stairwell, mindful of the icy last step, and when he reached the lane, he studied the man with steel-gray eyes. The man turned and measured Crispin but did not approach. Instead, he bowed. "Do I have the pleasure of meeting the great Crispin Guest?" The accent was soft but unmistakably French.

"'Great' is a matter of perspective. But Crispin Guest I am. And you, sir? You find your occupation by staring at my window. To what end?"

The man took a step closer. Crispin eyed his gown, a dark woolen robe cut in solemn lines and trimmed with black fur. His skin was pale and his beard grew past his chin but was not long enough to graze his chest. There, on the breast of his gown, Crispin observed something unexpected: a round, yellow patch carefully stitched into place.

The man saw Crispin eye it but did not comment. "My name is Jacob of Provençal." He stepped closer. "I am a physician. From the continent."

Crispin said nothing, waiting.

The man continued. "I have heard others speak of you, of this 'Tracker.' You find things. Lost things."

"Indeed. It is my bread and butter." His stomach took that moment to growl. The tips of his ears warmed.

The man smiled. "*En effet.* I am looking for a most important object. A dangerous one. It must be found before, well, it simply must. I beg that you come to my lodgings and we shall discuss it there."

Crispin turned an eye to his window, knowing well Jack was spying on them. "And where are your lodgings?"

"At court."

He hadn't meant to, but Crispin stiffened. The man watched him with a judicious eye. "I . . . have also heard," the man said carefully, "that you may not be welcomed there."

"An understatement. It would be difficult my going to King

Richard's palace. But I know of another place that might suit. Someplace closer. Will you permit me to lead you to an alehouse?"

The man hesitated. He pressed a pale finger to his lip and glanced up at Crispin's shuttered window before he lowered his head. He muttered something under his breath and lifted his face. "Very well, then. Lead me."

Crispin tramped through the slushy snow with rag-stuffed boots. He did not wait for the sound of the man's footfalls behind him, though they came anyway in a faint and reluctant step.

He tried to tread into the already dark hoof marks carved into the snowy streets, but his stride was not as long as the draft horses, and his boots were soaked and cold by the time he made the turn at the corner to Gutter Lane where the Boar's Tusk cast its weighty shadow across the road. When he came to the door he waited. The man approached and Crispin opened it, gesturing him through. Crispin followed him in and the warmth, which his own humble lodgings lacked, clapped his cold cheeks hard. He felt his bones thaw as he moved into the dim room to find his usual seat near the fire, his back to the wall and facing the door. He gestured for the man to sit opposite him.

Jacob gathered his cloak and gown around him and sat gingerly on the bench.

It wasn't long before a plump matron came to their table with a sweating jug in one hand and two clay bowls in the other. "Crispin," she said with a wide smile.

"Eleanor." Seeing her warm and friendly face touched off a spark of warmth within him. She and her husband, Gilbert, owned the Boar's Tusk. They were the first to befriend him since he came to the Shambles some seven years ago.

"Will you share wine with me, Master Jacob?" said Crispin to the wary man.

Jacob shook his head and squinted at Eleanor's expression. "I mean no offense to this good woman here, or to her establishment. But I may not partake of anything . . . here."

Crispin's eyes flicked to that yellow rouelle on the man's breast once more before settling on his lined and drawn face.

Flushed, Eleanor merely poured a bowl for Crispin and left the jug before she scooted away. Crispin surveyed the room of uneven wooden tables with their hard-worn benches and stools, scouting for familiar faces or eavesdroppers. Some tables were lit with candles, their greasy odor lifting and blending with the smells of toasting logs, roasted meats, and sweaty woolens. There were few patrons this afternoon. It was too cold to venture forth other than to earn one's daily wage. Yet Crispin usually found himself in his favorite tavern each day. Little wonder his funds were low when he insisted on his wine.

He took up the bowl, silently saluted his companion, and drank. The wine was slightly bitter, but it didn't matter. It warmed him and dulled the ache in his heart when he considered his empty money pouch and the depths he had to plumb to fill it.

Jacob hunkered in his robes and surveyed the other patrons with a wince of disdain. "We are quite alone, Master Jacob," said Crispin between quaffs. He poured more into the bowl and set both jug and cup on the table, turning the cup slowly with his fingertips. "What is it you wish to tell me?"

Jacob canted closer to the table and placed both arms on its surface. He clasped his long, pale fingers together. "*Maître* Guest, I have heard many rumors as concerns you."

"Could any of them possibly be true?" He smirked and drank another dose.

"I come from afar, *Maître.* But even I have heard of the Tracker . . . a man who was once a traitor."

Seven years had passed yet still he hated the term. He gripped the bowl. "Traitor I was, sir, though I do not boast in it. I am alive.

I do not boast in that either, for that circumstance can surely change with the season."

The man eased back. His eyes darted about the room, wary.

Crispin's gaze fell again to the yellow patch on the man's chest and could not help the welling of mistrust in his breast. "May I ask?"

Jacob sat very still. Robes gathered protectively about him, he seemed more chrysalis than man.

Crispin did not mince words. "Why is a *Jewish* physician called to England's court?"

The man smiled cautiously. His gaze rested steadily on Crispin's. "Why indeed? To a place where Jews are unwelcome? In fact, so unwelcome that your king made it illegal for Jews to reside here generations ago."

"Yes." An unnamed discomfort flushed Crispin's body. The Jews of England were exiled well before his time and he had been spared congress with them. It was said they had lived in Camden, but if they had, there was little trace there now. What remained was the old Domus Conversorum on Chancery Lane, the place where the converted Jews lived under the grace of old King Henry of Winchester, the father of Edward Longshanks, who expelled them at last. Jews were outlawed from entering England and it was a just law, although there was the occasional new inhabitant to the Domus, those traveling Jews who had come to their senses.

Crispin had been to the Holy Land, seen Saracens and Jews, and their ways were too foreign, too disturbing to his Christian sensibilities. To be sitting with a Jew now in his favorite tavern made him itch to leave. Even so, the man's demeanor was respectful and cautious. He seemed to know well how he stood and was almost amused by it. "And so," Crispin pursued. "Why are you here? At court, no less?"

"My specialty was desired. If I may be bold," he said, his white hand pressed to his breast and his head bowed. "My services are well known far from France. Your king has permitted me passage here to serve the queen."

"Eh? I was not aware that our queen was ill."

The man merely blinked. His rosy lips pressed closed and would divulge no more.

Crispin poured more wine, took up his bowl, and drank it down. The warm buzz he sought had settled pleasantly into his head. "And so, our King Richard allows a Jew to live in his palace." *And not me* was the unspoken thought. He chuckled to himself. "I've no doubt that your services are more valuable," he muttered. He put the bowl aside and squared with Jacob. "Then tell me. What would you hire me to do?"

"Your fee is sixpence a day?"

"Plus expenses, if I must travel."

"Of course, of course." Jacob stroked his beard and stared into Crispin's wine bowl. The light flickered on its ruby surface. "Your discretion—"

"Have done with this," Crispin growled. "You say you know me and my reputation. Then get on with it."

The man nodded deferentially, a skill learned, no doubt, from the lessons of subservience. "Very well. Valuable parchments have been stolen from my apartments. They must be returned."

"Valuable in what way? Deeds?"

"If only they were so mundane. But they are important, nonetheless. Can you help me?"

"Recover lost parchments? For sixpence a day, I will see what I can do. But it might help to know what they are."

"Oh . . ." He waved his hand and quickly hid it again under the table. "Texts. In Hebrew. You would not find them significant."

"But clearly someone did. And you called it 'dangerous,' if I recall." Jacob said nothing. He merely blinked, his papery lids folding over hazel eyes. "Some scholar who wished to examine them?" Crispin offered to the silence.

"Perhaps." Jacob tugged on his beard again before he seemed to realize the habit and lowered his hand to his lap.

Crispin sighed. Lost parchments seemed more trouble than they were worth, especially for a Jew. But coin was coin. "I shall have to see your apartments. And to do that, well, it will be difficult. I must raise my fee and charge one shilling a day for my trouble."

The man seemed startled. "Why must you see my apartments?"

"To examine the place from which they were stolen. From this I might garner valuable information." He studied the quiet man and his stooped posture. "Out of curiosity, why have you not gone to either of the sheriffs with this theft? Or complained to the king, since you have his ear?"

"No. I have come to you."

"That you have. But it does not explain—"

Jacob rose abruptly. "Come to the palace gate, and I will meet you there at nightfall."

Crispin rose more slowly. The meeting was apparently over. "Very well. There is the warrant of my fee . . ."

Jacob's eyes widened and he wrestled with his robe for a moment before producing a small leather pouch. He placed it on the table between them. "There is four shillings' worth of silver there. Till nightfall, *Maître* Guest."

Crispin took up the pouch and clenched it in his fist. "Master Jacob," he said with a curt nod of his head.

He watched the man hurriedly leave and looked again at the small pouch. He pulled out one coin and left it on the table for Eleanor. At least he had been able to pay his way today.

UPON RETURNING TO HIS lodgings, Crispin explained it to Jack, who had been glad to hear that Crispin was hired but was not as pleased to hear that the man was a Jew.

"You're taking money from a Jew? Ain't they the ones who crucified our Lord?"

"So says Holy Scriptures."

"Then they aught not to be in England. The law was made ages ago."

"You will find, Jack, that laws and kings are rarely to be met within the same sentence."

"Eh?"

Crispin snorted. "Whatever King Richard desires, he gets. The man is a physician to the queen. I've no doubt he is here to discover why she has not gotten with child."

"Oh." Jack looked out the window thoughtfully. "But you're to be at the palace gate at nightfall."

"Yes. Have you objections to that?"

"I don't trust him."

"Why?"

Jack shrugged. "I just don't. He loses papers he says are not important yet he won't go to the sheriff. What are those papers about, then?"

"I was wondering that myself. He called them parchments of Hebrew texts. I was trying to think what might be important about that."

"Scriptures?"

"If so, why did he not say so? Perhaps they are for his physician's art. Yet he did not admit that either. It makes no matter. I will find them, and I will make a pretty penny from it."

"I don't like it."

"You are not required to like it," he snapped. "I must take employment where it comes!" He didn't like to bark at Jack but the boy had little concept of his place. Yet when he turned to Jack and studied the boy's threadbare coat and hood, he suddenly remembered that Jack did know it. Hadn't the boy spent the best years of his childhood on his own in the streets as a cutpurse? Jack was lucky to have survived at all.

Reluctantly, Crispin softened. "Do you wish to accompany me?"

Jack's head snapped up. His brown eyes rounded, catching the firelight. "Me?"

"You are my apprentice. How are you to learn anything hiding out here? And I can keep a sharp eye on you. Keep you out of mischief."

"I don't get in no mischief," he grumbled. And as if to prove it, he grabbed a broom from the corner and began furiously sweeping the clean floor.

THE SUN BLED IN streaks of faded color between slashes of heavy gray clouds. Crispin and Jack set out and walked for nearly half an hour down long, snowy lanes toward the city of Westminster and the palace. As they entered each parish, they heard the echoing timbre of church bells even above the howl of wind, each tower with its own characteristic sound. The deep tones of St. Paul's, whose shadow hovered over the Shambles, soon dispersed and they entered into the domain of the tinny jangling of St. Bride. A few more streets and then St. Clement Danes' urgent claxon gave way to St. Martin-in-the-Fields' timid pealing before even that sound was finally overshadowed by the rich resonance of the bells of Westminster Abbey.

Charing Cross stood rigid in the icy cold of the crossroads. Its cross and steps were snowcapped and solemn. Jack's admonishment kept preying on Crispin's mind: *You're taking money from a Jew?* Was he that desperate? The answer came swiftly. His rent was due in a few days and he had no money with which to pay it. Martin Kemp, his landlord, was kind to him and often did not demand the rents on time, unlike his shrewish wife, Alice, who enjoyed constantly harrying Crispin on that very point.

Money. It had never been an issue before. Not before his ill-fated decision to join with those conspirators seven years ago, at any rate. There was money aplenty then. Shameless amounts of it. Wasted on trinkets for foolish women and wine with dubious friends. Where were those friends now? And where the women? He had tossed coins so carelessly to bards and beggars. He sunk sackfuls of it on gardeners for his estates in Sheen. His former manor was not far from the royal residence and appearances had to be maintained. If the king wished to stay at the Guest Manor, then it must be as well appointed as the king's own. He recalled one year when he harassed the tenants for their rents early in order to supply his kitchens for the king and his retinue. There was many a time he had nearly paupered his own household in order to feed and house all of court. But he had not complained, for this had been for the old king, Edward of Windsor, King Richard's grandfather. For the old king, he would have done anything. Even commit treason so that his son John of Gaunt and not his grandson Richard could sit on the throne.

Alas. Those days were long, long gone. His lands had been taken along with his knighthood, and the loyal tenants on the Guest estates called another man their lord. Crispin knew not who, nor did he care to know.

He glanced down at his own seedy coat and the sturdy cloak that hid its shabby appearance from view. Yes, that was a long time ago.

Flurries arrived with the waning sun and Crispin quickened his step to keep warm. They followed the Strand now, heading out of London toward the palace. The shops and houses did not seem as crowded and the street opened onto a wider avenue where the spindly trees of gardens could be spied beyond the rooftops.

Crispin set his mind to the task at hand. What papers could a Jew value so much that he would seek him out? He must be desperate to venture from court, knowing that he would not be welcomed outside of it. He almost laughed. And to seek a man who was not allowed *into* court! A fine pair they were.

It was a simple theft, no doubt. Someone inquisitive about the Jew. Perhaps it was stolen as a simple prank. That made one of two possibilities: The papers were long gone, destroyed. Or someone thought them valuable enough to try to sell to a third party. If the latter was the case then they still might yet be recovered. If the former, well, he'd take his money from this Jew and be troubled by him and court no more.

The freezing wind was angry, whipping off the white-capped river, and shrieking down the alleys, whirling through the lanes and taking with it the last brown leaves of an autumn that was just a memory. Ice pelted Crispin's face like tiny shards of glass. He squinted into the weather, head ducked down and encased in a hood that he wished for the thousandth time had been lined with fur.

But even above the baying wind and the churning foam of the river hissing against the stony embankment, Jack and Crispin heard it at the same time. A plaintive cry from the direction of the Thames. Crispin paused, wondering about it when the sound lifted up into the cold afternoon a second time. People on the street near the embankment stopped and moved toward the edge. Crispin watched as some men scurried down the bank and disappeared from view. Others took up the cry and Crispin found himself running.

Men with poles were trying to pull something in. The Thames wrestled with them, spitting icy water up into their faces, dampening their stockings and boots with freezing water. It wasn't until Crispin pushed some onlookers out of the way that he saw what it was the men were heaving onto the shore.

Hurrying down the embankment, Crispin helped pull up the small form.

A boy. About Jack's age.

Naked. Bruised. Dead.

2

THEY LAID THE BOY on the rocky shore. Men with wet stockings knelt beside him. Everyone crossed themselves. Women wept and many went running. Crispin knelt and looked over the boy's body. "Has someone gone and fetched the sheriff?" he inquired, his voice hoarse.

"Aye," said a man beside him, shivering. His shoes were soaked through. He was one of the men who had plunged into the freezing Thames to bring forth the body. "My boy went to get him. Was it an accident, you think?"

The body had not been long dead, Crispin decided. No bloating, no nibbling from fish. It was recent. There were bruises on his arms and wrists and a deep bruise around his neck, so deep that whatever had strangled him left a profound indentation. A slice up his abdomen was done neatly with a knife. It was deep. "This was no accident," said Crispin.

"Shall I call the hue and cry?" asked the man.

Crispin nodded, his gaze never leaving the wide-open eyes of the boy. Eyes that had been blue, their cloudy whites webbed with broken blood vessels. Eyes that would see no more.

The man left their side and began to shout to the nearest shops and houses. He was joined by others. Crispin did not know whether such a move would prove useful. The boy might have been killed last night, the culprit long gone. The cold of the water left the time of death in question. Why he had not sunk to the bottom was also a mystery . . . and a blessing.

Crispin removed his cloak and covered the boy's nakedness. He shivered. He did not know if from anger or from cold, or which was the greater.

He noticed Jack beside him. Jack was shivering more than he. "God help us," the lad murmured.

Crispin stood and, for the first time, eyed the crowd surrounding the boy. Some were standing quite near while others were perched up on the embankment, leaning in. His gaze roved over the faces, those in quiet despair and sympathy over the loss of one of God's innocents, and those with prurient curiosity glowing from their cold-etched faces. Did anyone look particularly guilty, he wondered. Did anyone look overly interested? It was possible that the devil was there among them, watching as his victim was discovered, taking hellish delight in the misery dropped like a stone into their midst. But even Crispin's sharp eye could not see into men's hearts. No one within his vision seemed to fit his ideal of such a monster that would kill a child.

The men about Crispin kept their vigil, murmuring prayers quietly beside the stricken boy. Crispin uttered no prayers. He could not. He found it hard to ascribe to a God who would allow mere men to debase such innocence. Who would murder a child? And in such a way? Not out of sudden anger with a blow to the head to teach him better, an accident perhaps. But in a deliberate act of cruelty and barbarism, for surely such steady strangulation, looking into the eyes of the child as he struggled to breathe, was not the act of a man. Not a man who walked the earth among other men. No one who breathed the same air, ate the same food, watched the same stars ebb and flow across the sky.

And the knife cut. What did that mean? With only a cursory

glance, Crispin had noticed the hollowness of the boy's gut. Had his entrails been taken by animals? But no. There was no tearing, no scratches from beasts. If there were no entrails, then they had been deliberately removed from the boy.

Crispin shivered again. If God was not present, then Satan surely was.

Hoofbeats. Then the shout of two men commanding their sergeants.

"Thanks be to God," Crispin murmured.

Simon Wynchecombe was no longer one of the sheriffs of London, hadn't been since September. Strangely, Crispin found himself missing the arrogant man. At least he was efficient. But the roles of sheriff were now played by the lanky fishmonger Nicholas Exton and the squat mercer John Froshe, both of whom were dismounting from their horses.

They liked being sheriff no more than had Wynchecombe, but they, too, knew that such a position could only lead to better appointments. Crispin knew Wynchecombe's sights had been set on the position of Lord Mayor, and these two were no exceptions to the ambitions of a London alderman.

Nicholas Exton was as tall as Wynchecombe, which made him a head taller than Crispin. His face was long and morose with a hooked nose and lazy brown eyes. He wore a gown whose hem reached his ankles and he was fond of poulaines with exaggeratedly long, slender toes that came to a point. He picked carefully over the rocks and crab-walked down the embankment.

John Froshe was short and thickset, with a round belly braced with a low-slung belt. His cotehardie was trimmed with ermine and his red stockings carefully conformed to his fat legs, giving them the look of sausage casings. He, too, wore poulaines of fawnskin, definitely not designed for trotting down to the river's edge. He stood at the top of the embankment with a curious expression on his jowled face, clearly wondering whether he should bother. But when

Exton had reached the spot where Crispin stood he wouldn't allow himself to be outdone.

Crispin watched as Froshe clumsily made his way down. His servants only belatedly followed, picking him up when he fell, and apologizing when he cuffed them.

"By God, Guest," said Exton, wrinkling his considerable nose at the proceedings. "Must you always be here before us?"

"I came upon him by chance, just as the others had." That was the only explanation he would offer. It was the only one the sheriffs needed.

A wheezing cough behind him and Froshe arrived. He brushed unsuccessfully at his velvet cotehardie. "You stupid oafs! I fell at least three times!"

The servants tried to look contrite but Crispin knew them better than that.

"And so," said Exton. "What have we here?" He looked past Crispin at the small form under the cloak. His face a mask, he pushed past Crispin and knelt, lifting the edge of the covering. He quickly dropped it back in place and ticked his head. "The Coroner is on his way." He stood again and turned to Froshe. "What do you make of it?"

"Bless me. It looks to be a dead boy, Nicholas."

"Indeed." He wiped his hands on his cloak. "And you, Guest. You are the man with all the answers, I hear tell. One cannot take but a few paces in London without someone mentioning the Tracker. As if you invented the very notion of Justice. Our predecessors spoke of you often but in less than glowing terms. Are we to believe all that is said of you? Shall you be declared a saint next?"

Bristling, Crispin scowled. "Hardly, my lord."

"Then what, pray, is your assessment? My learned colleague has declared the boy dead. I concur. What do you say?"

"I say he is murdered, my lords. Most foul. It turns my stomach." He said the latter in hopes of bringing the conversation around to the proper comportment and it seemed to have done the trick.

Froshe waved his hand in front of his face, as if shooing some unpleasant aroma. "The Coroner is on his way."

"And then we will move the body to Newgate," said Exton.

Crispin wondered if he were to be included in the "we."

THE CORONER HAPPENED TO be in London and came forthwith, examining the body and questioning the townsfolk who were present. His clerk took meticulous notes. The Coroner questioned the men at the houses and shops nearby and by then night had fallen. After he was satisfied, he nodded to the sheriffs, whose men surrounded him with flickering cressets on poles and their clouds of breath. The Coroner was no longer interested in the body. This was now the province of the sheriffs to take matters in hand. They would use what they learned from the Coroner to question the locals, but Crispin had his doubts it would yield anything. He wanted to inspect the corpse for himself.

He helped the sheriffs' men carry the light bundle up the stony embankment to an awaiting cart and laid him upon the straw within. The Fishmonger Exton whipped off Crispin's cloak and returned it to him. He covered the little corpse with a threadbare blanket.

The driver snapped his reins and the cart jerked forward. The wheels dug two dark lines in the snow, pointing the way back toward London. Silently, he and Jack walked behind the cart. As the dark cloaked the city, the cold crept in with deeper fingers, seizing Crispin in an icy grip that had as much to do with weather as with the coldness of murder.

It was more than half an hour later that the solemn procession neared the duel towers of Newgate. The portcullis creaked upward until the way lay open like a soundless maw, delivering them to the sullen mews below the prison where the boy was to be laid. The sheriffs' retinue carried the cressets in and mounted them in their sconces, but even that fiery light could scarcely illuminate the dank recesses of stone and shadows. The boy was laid on a table and then the sheriffs' men left them. There remained only Crispin, Jack, and both sheriffs, though Froshe looked decidedly ill at ease.

Crispin did not wait for permission. He flipped the blanket away. Jack turned his face from the sight of the pale figure. "Bring a light, Jack," said Crispin quietly, but even as quiet as he was, his voice reverberated in whispering echoes, hissing into icy, darkened corners.

Jack's shuffling steps added more echoes but soon he brought the light. With a shaking hand, he held it where Crispin needed it.

Crispin closed the boy's eyes, not wishing for their fishlike stare to consume him any longer. He studied the neck again. A dark ring surrounded the obvious indentation in the flesh. He looked lower. The boy's pubes were not yet grown with hair. He must be ten or eleven. Delicately, Crispin touched the cut edge of flesh where the skin had been slashed with such brutal accuracy. He pulled the flap of skin aside. No entrails.

"*Guest!*" The Fishmonger's tone was harsh and shocked. "By our blessed Mother! What are you doing?"

"Examining the body, Lord Sheriff. This child has been eviscerated."

"It was fish."

"No. It is cut cleanly. Look here."

"No! I shall not. It is an abomination!"

Crispin looked up at him. Froshe stepped back and was having none of it. He looked at Exton as forlornly as Jack had done.

"This *murder* is an abomination!" said Crispin. "We must examine *all* the evidence to determine the scope of this fiend's crime."

Exton gritted his teeth. He did not bother to look toward Froshe, who seemed bent on warming the stone wall with his back.

As a fishmonger, Exton was used to gutted creatures, but a boy was a different matter, to be sure. He seemed to suck up his courage and leaned over, peering into the cut Crispin indicated. He could not look long before his lips paled and sweat pebbled his brow.

"Heinous. Blasphemy." He staggered toward the lamps in their niches, away from the little corpse.

"Yes." Crispin continued scouring the boy, down his legs to his feet. His ankles had been bound. The marks of ropes were still there. He lifted a pale hand and examined the nails. Bitten and broken down to the quick. The cuticles were torn and there was dirt still embedded under the nails. Calluses were clearly evident on the pads of his fingers and palms. The boy himself seemed scrawny, underfed, with the evidence of protruding ribs under stretched skin. Crispin pushed the yielding lips open and saw teeth chipped and uneven.

Turning the boy over, he gasped at the bruises on his buttocks and hips. His suspicions provoked, he examined more carefully, ignoring the outraged cries of the sheriff.

"Sodomized," he said quietly. He vowed silently in that moment to find this murderer, this slayer of the innocent, and utterly destroy him.

"God in heaven!" cried Exton. The lamplight grew even shakier until Jack could stand it no more.

"Let us leave this place, Master Crispin! Please!"

He took the light from the boy and replaced it in its sconce. Standing silently in thought, he finally raised his face to Exton. "He was strangled with something. Not with hands. There are no finger bruises to his throat. I believe the cut to his belly was done after death, else the stroke would not have been so clean. It is too precise. As for the absence of the entrails . . ." He shrugged. "I am at a loss. If he were dead, what would be the use of it? His hands show hard work. Hence he was a servant or a child of the streets. A shopkeeper's child might not have such old calluses. And lastly, his being sodomized. We are therefore looking for a man."

"No," said Exton. He stood against the stone wall. The malicious play of torchlight hid his eyes in shadow.

"No?" asked Crispin, perplexed. "We are not looking for a man?"

"These things you have said. I do not believe them. I do not believe the boy was . . . was . . . sodomized. Nor that his bowels were removed. These can all be explained. The river. A jagged root or a piece of wreckage could have torn him and fish did the rest."

"Lord Sheriff!"

"Perhaps he was caught in a net while fishing and strangled."

"Naked? In winter?" He strode up to the man and tried to catch his eye. "Master Nicholas. You know what I am saying is the truth."

"I have heard of all your tales from Sheriffs John More and Simon Wynchecombe, Guest. You fabricate these wild stories to make yourself important in the eyes of your fellows. I don't begrudge you that. But I will not have it in my parish! Maybe Wynchecombe bore it but not I—"

"Nor I!" said Froshe weakly from the back of the room.

Exton nodded toward him. "I declare that this boy died in some sort of accident—"

"God's blood!" Crispin swore. "What ails you? You can plainly see the evidence for yourselves!"

"Leave it be, Master Guest! This was a beggar at best. What does it matter?"

"What does it *matter*?" He could not help a darting glance at Jack, who cowered in the shadows. He drew his shoulders back. "A citizen of London was *raped* and *murdered,* my lord. That is reason enough to concern you."

Exton hissed a curse and spun away, shuffling toward a dim corner before pivoting and returning to the spot he started. "You show an appalling lack of respect for this office, Master Guest." He sighed and Crispin heard the tremble in it. Finally, Exton approached Froshe who looked at him with pleading eyes. He bent his head toward him and they whispered furtively for a moment. By the expressions on their faces it did not look as if they had come to an agreement, but Exton turned to him anyway, despite Froshe's vigorous head-shaking. One of Exton's eyes twitched. "This . . . is not the first," he said.

Crispin felt his stomach flip. "God's blood," he whispered.

Exton looked ill. The bulbous knot on his throat bobbed as he swallowed. "I rue the day I was elected to this post. I thought"—he shook his head—"I never dreamed we'd . . ." He glanced at Froshe who was all but cowering in the corner and licked his lips. "What a pair of fools are we, eh, John?" Froshe did not raise his eyes. His fat cheeks were colored a ruddy blush. The shadows seemed to want to swallow him, but there was too much of him to do so. Crispin said nothing. He merely watched as Exton's face wrestled with something he would not voice. Finally, after an interval, he said, "Let us to the sheriff's chamber where we may talk. There is wine," he added. As if he needed to.

Crispin and Jack followed the men out of the mews and up the familiar winding staircase to the sheriff's chamber. The clerk, who usually sat outside at his desk and who often eyed Crispin with disdain, was absent.

A servant arose from an alcove and scurried to stir the coals in the hearth and added wood until it burned well. Exton slowly lowered into the chair behind the desk and Froshe wandered toward the shuttered window. Crispin stood by the chair opposite the desk and waited. The servant finished his chore and hurried out, closing the door. When Exton looked up and saw Crispin standing before him, he seemed surprised. He waved him into the chair as Jack took his place behind him.

"Your servant may pour wine," he said with a grand gesture.

Jack did not need Crispin's urging. He rushed to the sideboard and poured two goblets, bringing the first two to each sheriff with a sloppy bow. He returned to the sideboard and poured another for his master.

Crispin lifted the goblet to his lips in relief, knowing that soon the wine would take the sharp edge from the proceedings.

Exton drank as if he had not drunk in ages. He stared into the fire and hugged his empty goblet to his chest. "Unholy business, this."

For the first time, Crispin felt a splinter of empathy for these men. "You say there were others. How many?"

"Three more. All boys."

"The same manner?"

"Yes. To almost every detail."

"Since when?"

"Since Michaelmas. Just as we had taken office." He said the last bitterly, as if it had been the fault of those electing them. As if they had all colluded with one another.

Two months. Crispin took in a long breath. "Have you any clues? Any suspects?"

The sheriff slowly shook his head. "I have never"—he inhaled a trembling breath—"I fear it is the Tempter himself in our midst." He crossed himself. His voice cracked. "Such desecration. Such insidious acts. Master Guest"—he shook his head—"I cannot stomach it. It is sin that rends this place. Such dreadful sin. We've not enough priests to purge the city of it."

"Purge the city," echoed Froshe, cradling his goblet. He had not drunk any of it.

"Sin it is. Grave sin," agreed Crispin. "But a man did this."

"Enough. What can one man do against this? These are strange times. I fear another plague is coming. And rightly so."

Crispin never thought he would think it, but the sheriff's defeated tone disturbed him. It was plain these men preferred the status quo and these murders did not fit well into the carefully delineated view these merchants held of the world within London's walls.

"Hire me," said Crispin.

Exton raised his eyes and glared. "What?"

"Hire me. I will catch this murderer."

A harsh bark of a laugh erupted from the sheriff's lips. "We were warned of you and your tricks, were we not, John? Look how Master Guest would manipulate us. Wynchecombe warned us—"

"Oh be still, Nicholas!" Froshe spread his hand over his face and rubbed, rubbing the sin away. "What choice have we got?"

Exton shot to his feet. "Fool! Can't you keep your mouth shut? Or at least your cowardice to yourself."

But color had returned to Froshe's face and he tossed his goblet aside and reached for his sword, though he did not draw it. "Churl! Do you dare call me a coward!"

"My lords." Crispin rose slowly to his feet. If this was the way of it, then he might well manipulate these two jackals. "Please, do not fight amongst yourselves. I have offered you my solution." He leaned on the table and looked Exton in the eye. "Hire me."

"The devil take you."

"He may very well. But not before I have brought this particular devil to justice."

The man hedged. He slid a sly gaze toward Froshe who glared daggers at him. "Suppose," he muttered, slowly. "Suppose we *were* to hire you. No one must know, of course."

"It will be more difficult making inquiries."

"I see. And so you back away."

"I said nothing of the kind, Lord Sheriff. It is only more of a challenge. And there is one thing you must learn about me, my lords. I have never balked at a challenge."

Exton twisted the stem of his goblet in his thin fingers. He chewed in his thick lips and looked toward Froshe. "Well?"

"I fear we are signing a pact with the devil." But in the end Froshe reluctantly bobbed his head.

"It is as you wish, Lord Sheriff. May I be privy to the Coroner rolls?"

Exton nodded and finally set his goblet aside. "We shall send copies to you at your lodgings on the morrow."

The silence pressed between them again and Crispin, too, set his empty goblet down. "I will take my leave, my lords. Unless you have more to tell me."

"If there were more, I would tell you, Guest," said Exton with a sneer. He did not look at Crispin but into the hearth flames. "Report back to us as soon as you discover something. The king has not yet heard tidings of these deaths. But when he does, even though they be beggars, he shall make our lives miserable. And if our lives are made miserable—"

"So, too, is mine made." Crispin bowed. He swept out of the room with Jack scurrying behind him.

The night was cold, but it kept its cold to itself without the winds from earlier. They trudged quietly in the dirty and hoof-trodden snow back down Newgate Market to the Shambles. Once they entered their lodgings, Jack quickly laid a fire from the smoldering ashes and lit the candle on the table as well. Crispin understood the sentiment. As much light as possible to chase away the nightmares.

Crispin dropped his weary body onto his chair and Jack knelt, pulled off Crispin's boots, and laid them beside the hearth to dry. "Master," he said softly. "We have forgotten to meet with that Jew."

"Yes." It seemed so unimportant now, yet he did have the man's silver in his pocket. "It makes little matter."

"Begging your pardon, sir. But the rent is due and the sheriff didn't give you aught—"

"Damn." Yes, he would still have to meet this Jew if he were to pay his rent, for to ask the sheriffs for funds now would earn him little but aggravation. They seemed no more generous with the king's coffer as was Wynchecombe.

"I will think about it on the morrow, Jack. For now, have we any food?"

Jack did his best to cobble a meal from their meager pantry and once they had cleaned away the leavings and settled into bed, Crispin on his pallet and Jack in his straw in the corner, Crispin fell into a fitful sleep.

WHEN MORNING CAME, IT brought not only the sun's brightness through the stagnant cloud cover, but a renewal of his strength to face whatever lay ahead. Fortified with gruel and small beer, Crispin and Jack set out again toward Westminster and reached it by mid-morning.

Leading the way, Crispin edged down the embankment and studied the shore that had been so difficult to see last night. He saw nothing helpful. Only the thought that the body, if newly killed, had not sunk to the bottom of the river as might be expected. He could have been pushed along the shore by the current, or the lithe boy could very well have been dumped nearby. What could be nigh that would lend itself to secret doings with young boys?

He raised his eyes from the rocky shoreline, up past the dark-timbered houses and shops. King Richard's palace rose above him, its spires and high walls the very testament to secrets. But was this the origin of such heinous crimes?

"What are we looking for, Master?" asked Jack, shivering in his cloak.

"I don't know." And the damnable thing of it was, he didn't. The boy himself was the greatest clue, and three others like him. Not just a death, but something more. Raped, yes. But the slice to his belly intrigued and horrified him the most. What was the meaning behind this evisceration?

"Do you recall, Jack, which houses the Coroner visited?"

"I . . . I think so, Master."

"Then we will ask our own questions. I do not wish to wait to read the Coroner's notes." Crispin allowed Jack to lead the way and the boy pointed to the first shop, a goldsmith. He peered through the open shutter, through the diamond panes of a glass window, and saw a man bent over a table close to his sputtering candle. Crispin knocked upon the door and the man looked up. He watched him approach through the wavy panes and the door was pulled opened.

Squinting, the man pulled his gold-embroidered gown close over his chest. "Good master," he said to Crispin with a bow. Crispin returned the courtesy.

"I have come to inquire about the boy yesterday. The one pulled from the Thames."

The man's brows rose. "The Coroner already inquired of me and I gave my testimony."

"Yes. But I am here to dig deeper."

As expected, the man looked Crispin up and down, no doubt noting the frayed hem of his cotehardie and the patches on his breast. Crispin endured it with a clenched jaw.

"And who are you?"

"I am Crispin Guest—"

"God in heaven!" the man gasped. He grabbed the door and tried to shut it but Crispin was quicker and blocked it with his hands.

"Clearly my infamy precedes me," he said with a sneer. He shoved the door hard and the man fell back.

"Please!" cried the goldsmith, stumbling to his feet. He searched wildly in his shop for a means of escape. "I run an honest business. I wish no congress with you, Guest."

"We're not posting banns, man. This is a murder inquiry. Get a hold of yourself."

"You . . . here . . . near the palace . . . ?"

"Yes, the palace. I am here on the king's business. Surely you have heard of the Tracker? I am he."

"The Tracker?" He blinked and Crispin could see his mind whirring behind his fluttering lids. Crispin gestured to the chair. Gingerly, the man sat. "I . . . have heard of the Tracker."

"Then you know what deeds I have done. I am here to ask about the dead boy."

He looked from Crispin to Jack. "Yes. Yes. But I already told the Coroner—"

"Did you know the boy?"

"No. He did not sound familiar."

"Did you hear anything, see anything?"

"Nothing. Only the hue and cry last night."

"Have you heard a rumor regarding this boy or . . . others?"

"Others?"

Crispin looked quickly at Jack. "Other . . . mayhem," he corrected.

The man shook his head. "No. As I said. But there are many alleys, many shadowed lanes, even near the palace. Such things might occur there."

"Indeed." Crispin rocked on his heels, studying the shop. "You are a goldsmith?"

"Yes, sir. My name is Matthew Middleton. I have been a goldsmith on these premises for nigh on twenty years."

"Then you have seen much. Have you ever seen such a murder?"

"The death of a child?" He toyed with his beard. "Alas. Too many, I fear." He glanced at Jack. "A city is a harsh place, at times. Death takes his own by way of sickness and poverty. Surely you have seen with your own eyes the plenteous beggar boys in the streets. There is not enough charity to protect them all. They do not last long. The Thames has claimed its share, I'll be bound."

Crispin felt Jack's presence most keenly. "And lately?"

"I have heard of none of late. But I do my duty and give to the queen's charities. I give my share in the alms basket."

"I do not impugn your generosity, Master Middleton. I merely inquire." He walked slowly around the shop. Neat. Good order. Rich, of course. A trader in gold did not starve nor would his children or servants. He looked last at the man himself. "Have you perchance heard of an errant apprentice or servant? Someone who has gone missing?"

"No. Nothing."

"If something should occur to you, I can be found on the Shambles in London."

The man rose and bowed. "If something does, I shall so do, Master Guest."

Crispin nodded and with a tilt of his head at Jack, they departed.

Looking out to the broad street he sighed a cloud of cold into the day. The smell of the Thames was strong here, but at least they were upwind of the privies. "Jack, I fear that questioning these shopkeepers will not yield anything of substance."

"Are we to ask anyway?"

"Of course."

But as Crispin suspected, the others they questioned did not know the boy nor had they heard anything untoward in the evening. The murder did not happen on the street, but in a private place where screams would not be heard.

Jack had not spoken all day unless addressed directly, and even then his replies were grunted and sullen. Crispin understood. He had never asked Jack how he had managed to survive for his many years on the streets as an orphan. He had not felt it his place to ask. He knew Jack was a clever thief, but cleverness could only take a boy so far.

"Jack," he said kindly. "When you were . . . before we met . . . you must have known many such boys on the streets."

Jack raised his head, squinting from the cold. Those amber eyes looked Crispin over. So clever, those eyes.

The boy pushed his palm over his reddened nose and sniffed.

"Aye, Master," he said slowly. "You know well what I was. A beggar and a thief." He crossed himself. "I am not proud of that," he said mulishly, as if by rote. "But it kept me alive for four years since me mum died. A sister run off, a father I never knew. What did you expect?" The last was harsher than Crispin anticipated, and it seemed more than Jack wanted to convey. He gusted a sigh through his freckled nose and stood, feet planted, waiting for Crispin's backlash.

But he did not strike out at the boy. Instead, he ran a thoughtful finger over his own lips. "Surely you were old enough to get work on your own. Why did you not stay with your master?"

"I didn't have no master. Me mother worked as a scullion for a merchant. I kept the fires. When she died they threw me out. Didn't want no part of me."

"Could you find no similar work?"

"No. I was too angry for it. Those sarding masters. Flung me out like the dregs of a pissing pot."

"And so you found yourself on the street. Can you tell me what a typical day was like?"

"Why?"

Jack had never looked so angry and Crispin furrowed his brow at him. "Why do you think, boy? Do you think I wish to know out of prurient curiosity? Do you forget who you are speaking to? Do you not recall that I spent many a day on the streets myself, begging for *my* meals?"

Jack's toughened expression softened. He kicked at a dirty lump of snow, wetting the toe of his patched boot. "I . . . I reckon so." His glance darted away from Crispin again, hiding his many secrets. "You . . . you want to know what a day was like?"

"Yes. It will help, perhaps, to follow in the footsteps of the dead child. I know what *my* days were like. But it must have been quite different from that of an eight-year-old boy."

Jack gnawed uncertainly on a finger until Crispin dropped his hand on Jack's shoulder. "Let us to an alehouse, Jack. We will warm ourselves and share wine. Maybe some bread will help you decide whether to speak or no."

Jack allowed himself to be steered toward a nearby tavern. When Crispin opened the door, the noise spilled out with a cascade of raucous laughter. The sharp tang of a reed and a drum bleated out a tune that some were singing to. It looked to be a better kept place than the Boar's Tusk, but, to be fair, this tavern was in the shadow of Westminster Palace and the clientele were apt to be wealthier than the patrons of the Gutter Lane's alehouse.

Crispin guided Jack to two stools by the hearth and waved to the alewife.

"Aye, good masters," she said to them.

"Good wife, please bring a jug of wine." Crispin handed her the coins. "And a loaf of bread, if it is not too dear."

She examined the silver and nodded. "A loaf and wine," she said, and left them. Alone again, they measured their surroundings. Jack said nothing, staring at the men nearby in their fine fur-trimmed gowns and long-sleeved houppelandes. From under low lids, Crispin observed Jack's nervous movements.

At last, the woman returned, placing the round, day-old loaf on the hearth beside them, poured the wine into the bowl, and left the jug at Crispin's feet.

He handed the bowl first to Jack, who looked up with surprise. "Go on, boy. Take it."

With dirty fingers, Jack took the bowl and lifted it to his lips. He took a long quaff and, wiping his mouth on his sleeve, handed the bowl back. Crispin drank what was left and reached down to the jug to refill it. "Have some bread, Jack," he said, nodding to the loaf and taking his own quaff.

Jack tore a hunk from the bread and raised it to his lips. He chewed openmouthed, staring at the floor.

"Do you wish to tell me?" asked Crispin after the boy had eaten a bit and drank another bowl.

"In truth, Master, no. But . . . because you are my master, and a good and kind one, it is fitting to help you. And so I will tell you what I know." He clutched the hunk of bread in his hand, fingers curling protectively around it. "Before I met you, life was hard. If I was lucky enough, I found a place to spend the night. Sometimes it was a stable or sometimes a sheltered doorway. I even spent the night in privies."

Crispin nodded into the bowl Jack passed to him. "Yes, as did I."

The lad looked up at him in wide-eyed awe before he nodded. "Aye. Winter was the worst, but they wouldn't keep that strict an eye on things in winter when it was cold. Keeping themselves inside all safe and tight, mostly."

Crispin nodded again, remembering.

"In the morning," Jack continued, "me first order of business was to find food. Church steps were crowded with men who'd just as soon slit your throat as let you beg alongside them. So I found the best place was outside alehouses. Men leaving the taverns with scraps of bread and cheese and their own bellies full would see fit to toss the rest to me. When I got good at it, I could cut a purse or two when crowds of men went in or out, but that meant I was done at that doorstep for the day. Many a lad got himself carted off to Newgate 'cause he stayed put, got greedylike, and wouldn't move on. They were the cod-pated ones. Wouldn't listen to nobody." Jack tore a piece from the hunk of bread in his hand and chewed it thoughtfully. The more he talked the more relaxed he seemed to be.

"There were lots of boys," he went on. "Some were apprentices caught stealing and tossed out by their masters. They were the worst, as they thought they was better than the rest of us and wouldn't listen to reason."

"Did you help one another?"

Jack shook his head unapologetically. "I ain't no saint, Master. If'n I was to stay alive, it weren't no charity I could be giving. I had to look out for m'self."

Crispin nodded. He, too, had tried to band with the others. In numbers there was safety and strategy, but they had not trusted his palace accent nor his unfamiliar ideas.

"And so?" Crispin urged.

"Well, some boys were worse than others. They became more animals than men. I'd see them sniffing along the shore near the fishing boats and they'd eat the leavings. Fins and tails. They'd eat them raw like a dog. I can't say that I blame them. Hunger is a powerful sin."

"Yes," murmured Crispin, taking a delicate bite of his bread, but leaving the majority for Jack.

"I . . ." Jack lowered the piece of bread to his thigh. "I was hungry enough . . . to do the same at times. The hunger can gnaw such a hole inside of you." His voice broke and he took a bite, taking a long time to chew. Crispin looked away to give him a moment. "I— There were times, Master Crispin," he whispered, "when I would have eaten *anything*."

Crispin grunted his affirmation.

"There were times," he said in that same low, pitiful voice, "that I *did*."

He touched Jack's sleeve.

The boy swallowed. "There were other boys . . ." He shook his head and blinked his eyes. His voice trembled, whispering. "There were other boys . . . they couldn't find no way. They couldn't steal enough to keep them fed. Everyone knew them. They'd let men . . . *lie* with them. There were secret stews of them. In Southwark."

Crispin clenched his jaw. Men who would pay panderers for the use of boys. Yes, the Bankside on the opposite shore of the Thames housed all manner of filth and degradation. He knotted the hem of his cloak. He wanted to ask, but did not have the heart for it. Who was he to judge a man? If Jack had sinned, then he had done it as a necessity. Crispin reckoned the boy had paid many times in penance—more than the beads of a rosary—if he had to stoop to such evil to keep alive under the shadow of London's cathedrals.

"Then it is possible," said Crispin tightly once Jack had fallen silent, "that this boy could have come from those stews?"

Jack's pale humiliation gave way to thoughtfulness. He clamped his jaw as he ruminated and eventually shook his head. "No, Master. I do not believe that boy came from the stews."

"And why not?"

"Th-the boys who were tied up, as this one was, they were also beaten. Not to punish. But for sport. That boy at Newgate. He wasn't beaten."

Crispin recalled the pale, dead flesh of the corpse in the bowels of Newgate. The boy had bruises around his neck and on his hips, but nowhere else, neither old scars nor new. "Have you . . . ever heard of the rest? The cutting? The strangulation?"

Jack shook his head. "No, Master. Sometimes a boy was lashed so badly he was no good for the house no more and was left in the streets to die. But I ain't heard of aught like we saw."

Crispin handed Jack a full wine bowl. "Thank you, Jack. I— It was surely difficult to tell me."

"No one should die like that," he said softly, almost dreamily. "That ain't no way to die. That ain't no way to live."

"Indeed not. I will find this killer, Jack."

"I know you will, sir. And I'll be right there beside you."

The color had come back to the boy's freckled cheeks. Crispin was glad to see it.

He was about to offer Jack a word of encouragement when a shadow lanced over the boy's face. Jack looked up and Crispin turned.

"Bless my wretched soul, but if it isn't Crispin Guest."

Crispin stiffened. These encounters were few, but when he did come upon an acquaintance from his past, he did not usually bear it well. He rose to hide his discomfiture and because the man was a lord and it would not do to sit in his presence, even though once upon a time he was perfectly within his rights to do so.

"Giles," he said with a rigid bow.

"My Lord *de Risley*," the man corrected with a smirk. "At least in front of these—" and he motioned to the room. Giles smiled warily. His beard followed the curve of his jaw in a thin, tight line as did his neatly coiffed mustache.

Crispin's cheeks burned. "Of course . . . my *lord*." And he bowed again. Jack scrambled to his feet and looked from Giles to Crispin worriedly.

"Crispin," he said, ignoring Jack. Giles looked Crispin up and down not seeming to notice Crispin fisting his hands close to his sides. "It has been many a day since I've seen you last," said Giles. "When I heard the news of your arrest all those years ago, it tore at my heart."

Crispin nodded. What could he say?

"But I am glad to see that you live." He offered a warmer smile. "How fare you? Are you well?" Without waiting for an answer, he sidled closer, looking around at the crowded tavern. "But Crispin. So close to court? Is that wise? The king . . ." The smile was back. "But of course, you were always a bit wild, weren't you? Never one to hide. To take the easy path. Was it not so in our jousting days? You were the one who always took risks, always getting hurt—"

"Always besting *you*." It was Crispin's turn to smirk.

Giles's expression tightened before he released a laugh. "I suppose you did win most of our contests. But not the fair Margaret."

It was Crispin's turn to lose his smile. Did Giles have to remind him of those days? Margaret had been Crispin's lover and she had left his bed for Giles's. It wasn't Giles's fault, of course. She was fickle. And Giles flaunted his wealth, giving expensive gifts. Margaret was a fool for it. But it had stung, nonetheless.

Giles moved toward Jack's seat and took it, paying little attention to Jack struggling to get out of his way. The man sat wide-legged on the stool and warmed his hands at the hearth. "Sit with me, Crispin. God's eyes but I am glad to see you. May we share wine?" Giles leaned forward and rested his arms on his thighs. He took up the empty bowl and waited. Crispin shot a glance at Jack and the boy quickly filled it. "When was the last time we met? Do you recall?"

"Nine years ago," he said, sitting. "A tourney at Aquitaine, I believe. I unhorsed you and we fought on foot."

Giles smiled and drank. "Yes. I think it was a draw."

It wasn't, but Crispin let it lie.

"Yes," Giles went on. "What a bitter opponent you were. You had an unusual style. Learned at the knee of some Frenchman."

"My Lord of Gaunt taught me, my lord. All that I learned of warfare and swordsmanship came from the duke personally."

"Well, we all know Lancaster has devious ways."

Crispin scoured the room quickly. No one had caught their intimate conversation. If they had, many more would have come to the aid of the duke of Lancaster's honor. As it was, Crispin was hard-pressed to defend it himself these days.

He had bested Giles in all their endeavors, save the one with Margaret, but it was mostly on the lists, where cleverness often won the day over brute strength. If de Risley had ever bothered to learn that lesson, he could have won over Crispin in their many tournaments or even on the battlefield. More often than not, Crispin had captured several knights to ransom, where as Giles de Risley had killed his prey, thus leaving him with nothing to earn. Too impatient was Sir Giles, looking for the easy way rather than the better part.

He drank more of Crispin's wine and studied him. "The lists are not as merry since you left them, Crispin," said Giles, mirroring Crispin's own thoughts. "I enjoyed riding against you."

"I, too, miss them, Giles."

"Alas," he said. "A pity the king did not see fit to restore your knighthood."

"Ah, but he did."

Giles sat back with surprise. "When was this?"

"When I saved the king's life from an assassin. Surely you must have heard—"

"It seems I did hear something of the kind," he said, cheered. "But then, something must have gone wrong." He looked him up and down again.

"Indeed. The king's offer balanced on a task I could not perform."

"Oh? And what was this chivalrous deed he implored of you?"

Crispin straightened his shoulders. "I was to beg for it."

Giles burst into peals of laughter. "And that—" he said between gasps, "you certainly would not do!" He slapped his thighs. "Crispin! You have always made me smile. Such youthful vigor! But I am certain that your refusal of the king was warranted. You must be doing well, then. A comfortable existence here in London? Am I right?"

Crispin endured the man's laughter silently.

Giles prodded with his elbow. "Tell me, Crispin, for truly I wish to know. Tell me where it is you live."

"I do live in London."

"Yes, yes. But where?"

"I live . . . on the Shambles. I thought everyone knew that."

Giles's laughter stopped abruptly. "Oh. You aren't jesting? Oh, Crispin." He lowered his face and shook his head. "I thought—

Ah, I see. Tell me. Is there something I can do, something I can say?"

"No. Thank you. I have learned to earn my keep here. And I am"—he tested the word in his head before he said—"content."

Giles offered a weakened smile. "You were always so stoic, Crispin. When I married Margaret, well . . ." He drank from the bowl. "I thought you would hate me after that."

"No, Giles. I did not hate you. I suppose it was for the best. After . . . everything."

"Yes." He leaned over his thighs and turned the now empty bowl in his hands. "After Margaret died all those years ago—"

"I was sorry to hear of it."

"Ah, so you did hear? Well. The child died as well. That was a sorrowful time. And do you know, the one man I wanted to talk to, to gain some comfort from, was you? But, of course, that was impossible then. Now you seem to move about more freely." He grinned. "I am glad of it. We were often rivals but it was never personal. I'd like to think we were friends."

"We were." Crispin looked away into the fire.

"Yes. Well. After Margaret died, I decided to move on."

"Have you remarried, then?" Crispin did not realize how starved he was for court news. It never seemed to matter before.

Giles looked embarrassed. "No, not remarried. But . . ." He turned the bowl in his hands. "In fact, I suppose you should know that I have recently acquired . . . that I have purchased— Dammit, Crispin. I do not know if these are good tidings or not."

"Tell me, then."

"A manor house along the river in Sheen, not far from his Majesty's lodgings. I have only moved into them a few months ago—"

Crispin froze, a cold feeling slipping around his heart.

"I am taking good care of them. After Margaret, the house seemed too empty. A change of scenery. And when his Majesty offered it, I—" He looked at Crispin's face and abruptly rose, his own expression stricken. "Maybe this isn't the time. I'd best take my leave. God keep you, Crispin. I'm certain we will meet again."

He set down the empty bowl, but in his haste to depart, his foot caught it and kicked it toward the hearth where it clinked against the clay jug and cracked it, spilling its wine like blood.

3

"THAT MAN," MURMURED JACK when they had escaped to the street. He trotted after Crispin's hurried steps. "Who was he, Master?"

"Giles de Risley," Crispin grunted. "A peer of the court. An old friend."

"Aye, I reckoned that much. But what did he mean about all that talk of a manor in Sheen?"

Crispin whipped around and bore down on Jack. "He was talking about *my* house, Jack! *My* ancestral home! The king sold it to him for some godforsaken favor."

Jack blinked. "M-maybe he was lying—"

"No." Would that he were. But Crispin knew it in his bones to be true. He couldn't begrudge Giles, and if it had to be so, a friend within those walls was better than an enemy. Still, with the house lying empty it had almost seemed as if it were waiting for Crispin's return. The last hope of his old life, the last gleam of redemption. But with his manor gone to Giles, his past was now forfeit.

Despair closed over Crispin like a dense fog, and all he knew was to get back to the Shambles as quickly as possible.

Jack followed but Crispin turned on him. "Go back to our lodgings, Jack. Await the messenger from the sheriff."

"But Master Crispin, what of that Jew—"

"Go, Jack! I am in no mood."

The boy knew when to flee and flee he did. Crispin watched him go with only half an eye. He wanted drink and plenty of it. Only this, he knew, could numb the approach of life's many failures steeling upon him.

AFTER A LONG WALK, he returned to London, back to Gutter Lane and the Boar's Tusk. He pushed open the door and sat hard in his usual seat. Ned brought him a drinking jug of wine without a word and Crispin set to drinking himself blind.

He was nudged awake by the proprietress, Eleanor, some hours later. The jug lay empty on its side mere inches from his lax fingers. Still feeling the indentations of the wooden table impressed into his cheek, he wiped a bit of spittle from the side of his mouth. She looked a little blurry to his wine-soaked eyes but he could tell her displeasure right enough.

"Go home, Crispin. This is no inn."

He didn't argue. He drew himself up—feeling as if he were a sack of rocks—and staggered toward the door. Drunk he was, but not as numb as he would have liked to be.

The cold slapped his cheeks hard. He shook out his shaggy head, trying to stay awake. Clumped flakes of snow fell about him, wet blossoms landing and sticking to his dark cloak. He let them. Above him, a cluster of dark clouds and a washed-out sky added to his sense of despair. There was little relief in the landscape of London. White smoke curled from every chimney, and shutters were tightly closed, allowing only splinters of light to streak across the opaque streets. What did it matter? Go home, Eleanor had told him. To the Shambles? That wasn't his *home*. It was just the place he lived. Giles de Risley lived in his *home*. His *home*, goddammit! He was raised there. His sister and brothers were born there. Born and died in that same manor house. As a young man, Crispin had kept safe the Guest household with the help of his mentor, John of Gaunt, the duke of Lancaster. But kept safe to what end?

Did Lancaster know? What did it matter if he did? He could no more save Crispin's home than he had saved his miserable life. Oh, yes. He had been saved from the gibbet, right enough, but was this *life*?

Crispin leaned heavily against a wall, the roughened daub, pilling the threads of his cloak. His lover gone to Giles, his home. It seemed like too much. True, it hadn't belonged to him in some seven years, but still the thought of it, lying fallow all this time. The friendly halls of his youth, the warm solar, his rooms with the embroidered bed curtains. How many nights had he spent staring at those horsemen galloping across those curtains and dreaming that this would be him someday, on a steel-gray charger, sword drawn, hacking the heads from infidels? And it had been. He had been a noble and valorous knight. He had proven himself time and again in battle and on the lists. Crispin had been a force to be reckoned with. He had become everything he had wanted to be. Lancaster had been proud. Crispin was pleased to make him so.

And then it all fell apart.

Pushing himself away from the wall, he trudged on. Shops were closing early from the fading light and the heavier snowfall. The aroma of stews competed with the sharp stench of the Shambles as he turned the corner. A fishmonger was sliding the slippery remainder of his basket of eels back into an urn filled with water. His apprentice mopped fish scales from the doorstep into the frozen gutter.

Crispin reached the dark, narrow stairwell squeezed between his landlord's tinker shop and a butcher's house. He stepped onto the creaky bottom step and dropped his key into the slush twice before Martin Kemp opened the door of his shop to see what the noise was. He looked Crispin over with a shake of his head. Crispin ignored him and staggered up the stairs. He never got a chance to fit the key in the lock. Jack yanked the door open, his face awash with worry. "At last!"

He shoved Jack aside and stumbled into his chair, which Jack had positioned in front of the fire. A peat fire. Not the large logs of oak that Crispin had enjoyed at the manor in Sheen. He barely noticed Jack kneeling at his feet to pull off his sodden boots, or pull his cloak free of his shoulders. He did raise a brow when Jack stood uncertainly next to his chair with the jug and bowl in his hands.

"Think I've had enough?" growled Crispin.

"Truth be told, sir . . . yes."

"Bring it here."

"Master. You've been in the Boar's Tusk all afternoon—"

"How the hell do you know that?"

"Mistress Langton sent a message."

"Eleanor should mind her own business. As should you. I said bring it here."

Jack hesitated. His fingers curled tighter around the jug's handle.

"God's blood! Can I not expect to be obeyed in my own house!" But then the words sunk in. It was as far from his "own" house as could be imagined.

He lumbered up from his seat, lunged at Jack, and grabbed the jug. He sloshed most of its contents when he pulled it free from the boy's grip. He didn't bother with the cup. He planted his lips on the jug's rim and knocked it back, spilling more down his neck, shuddering at the cold of it. But only when he had drained it did he set it aside.

"I'm hungry," he growled.

"W-we have pottage, sir."

"Well then?"

Jack timidly pulled the iron arm from the fire from which a small kettle hung. He picked up the bowl from the floor where Crispin had tossed it, and carefully ladled the thick soup into it. He handed the bowl to Crispin with a quivering hand. Crispin took it without thanks and drank the liquid without tasting. Pottage again and again. Peasant food. Where was the meat he deserved? Where the sweetmeats and honeyed fruit?

When he finished he made noises about having more. Jack shuffled forward. Crispin had not noticed whether Jack had partaken or not. "If you have more now, sir, there will be nothing for breakfast." Jack's eyes glanced toward the pantry shelf. Crispin did not need to look. He knew how empty it was.

He hunkered down in his chair and pulled the blanket from the bed over his legs.

The room was dark except for the fire. Jack said nothing, merely added more peat and small sticks now and again to urge the timid flames to life. He coughed a few times at the smoke and darted a wary glance at Crispin occasionally, but the creaking rafters and the flicker of fire were all the sounds in the room for a while.

Until Jack finally spoke.

"Master Crispin," he said quietly. "Forgive me. I don't always understand courtly ways. But . . . did you not lose your family estate some years ago when you was . . . was banished from court?"

Crispin's curt *"Yes!"* cut knife-sharp into the room's stillness.

"So why does it fret you so now?"

The wine was heavy in his belly but it did not muddle his mind as much as he had hoped. "Of course it was the king's to dispose of as he would. But . . . my *home,* Jack!"

"I know, Master. It is a sour thing. But . . . so long ago."

"For generations, the Guests have lived there. The barony, too, was granted to my ancestor by King Henry II and each generation has been knighted in turn—" His broken voiced unmanned him and he shot from the chair. But the wine had addled him more than he realized and he stumbled. Jack caught him with a surprisingly strong hand.

"Go to bed, Master Crispin. It will be better in the morning." He pulled Crispin toward his small bed and pushed him down. "Shall I help you with your clothes?"

He waved him off. He fell back against the straw-stuffed pillow and closed his eyes. Yes, perhaps sleep was what he needed. God grant him a dreamless sleep. For once.

HE WOKE BADLY. HIS head was pounding and his tongue felt thick and dry, his belly queasy. A pot rattled against another, sounding like the gong of a bell. "Stop that godforsaken noise!" he bellowed.

The pot crashed hard into the hearth. Crispin cringed and squinted at it. Jack stood with fists dug deep into his boney hips. He was scowling.

"I must care for you, drunk or no, or whether you suffer from its ill effects, because you are my master. But you must stop growling at me! I'm doing me best. If you didn't drink so much . . ." He let the sentence linger, never finishing it. He grabbed the pot again and hoisted it with a grunt onto its hook over the flames, nudging another smaller clay cauldron sitting on a grate, the flames licking its bowed sides. Crispin watched the steaming water slosh into the pitiful fire, hissing as it met orange coals.

Vaguely, he thought of apologizing, but he was still awash in too much self-pity to utter the words. "Hmpf" was what he managed instead, and threw his legs over the side of the bed, wrapping the blanket around his shivering shoulders.

"Now then," said Jack, standing over him and thrusting a steaming bowl toward his face. "I've made peas porridge. It ain't much and it's a bit watery, but thank the saints we have something to eat."

He waited as Crispin stared at it. Finally, he lifted a hand and cupped the bowl in his fingers. Porridge again. He brought it to his lips and drank. Jack was right. There was more water than grain and meat, but it warmed and managed to still his belly.

"Thank you," he grumbled.

Jack nodded and poked at the fire. "The water for your shave will be ready anon."

Crispin sighed. It was times such as these that he realized how much a luxury it was having Jack at his side. A man in his present position could surely never afford the likes of a servant. Though he had not thought so at the time, saving Jack from the sheriff all those months ago and finding the boy in his service had been fortunate indeed.

A knock on the door made them both jump. Jack was on his feet, the poker in his hand like a weapon. He looked at Crispin to see whether he should answer it.

He nodded to him. Dropping the blanket, he stood unsteadily on his stocking-clad feet.

Jack timidly opened the door, hiding the poker behind it, and then pulled it opened wider.

A man wearing the livery of the Sheriff of London stepped into the threshold and looked around, a dubious expression on his face. "I seek Crispin Guest." The tone of his voice seemed to convey that he would not find such a person on these premises.

Crispin straightened and mustered as much dignity as his mussed hair and slept-in clothes could impart.

The man frowned. His eyes flicked toward each corner of the modest room; from ramshackle bed, to chest, to table. "Very well," he muttered. He pulled the pouch slung over his shoulder toward the front and threw open the flap. Reaching inside, he withdrew several scrolls. He looked first at Jack and then at Crispin, not quite knowing to whom he should give them. He settled on placing them on the table. "From the sheriff," he said unnecessarily.

Crispin and Jack stared at the man a moment longer before he seemed to decide his presence was no longer needed. He bowed and backed out of the room, rumbling down the rickety stairwell.

Jack closed the door and Crispin fingered the scrolls. His head was still unsettled but the face of that dead boy in his mind did much to sober him. Sitting, he reached for a scroll and unrolled it. Jack pulled up beside him on his stool and peered over his arm, staring at the tight scrawl. Crispin had begun to teach Jack to read Latin, French, and English, and though the boy was a quick study, he had little patience for his lessons. But Crispin supposed that crime was more intriguing fare, and he watched out of the corner of his eye as Jack's lips worked over the words.

Crispin read for himself. These were copies of the Coroner's rolls: the people he had questioned, the answers they gave, the Coroner's conclusions based on these questions and answers. It was plain that the Coroner did not know who the dead boy was and was no closer to finding his killer than was Crispin.

He grabbed another scroll, leaving the last in the hands of Jack, who was still mouthing his way through it, ginger brows furrowed deep into amber eyes.

Another dead boy. Not the one Crispin had seen. This corpse was found two months prior, though not in London. Again, he had been fished from the Thames but more upstream. Perhaps, then, the murders were not committed in London after all, but further afield.

But the body Crispin had seen was not waterlogged. It could not have traveled down the Thames too far, not as far as this other one. When he read the accounts of the other dead boys, they were found even further up the Thames. It seemed the killings approached London slowly over the course of a few months. Where had this killer been? And why had he come to London?

"It's the Devil," whispered Jack, his face pale. He was reading over Crispin's shoulder again. "Unspeakable."

"Yes." These boys were all Jack's age or younger and none of them seemed to be notable sons of noble families. It was possible they were the sons of merchants, but no one had claimed them. Crispin suspected they were lowlier than that. They were the invisible. Beggar boys, possibly. Wayward apprentices. He felt Jack's warmth at his side. The thought that a similar fate could have befallen Jack Tucker made his skin crawl.

He rolled up the parchments and set them aside. Staring into the fire, he tossed the cold facts inked on those parchments back and forth through his brain. "Four boys. Dead. Spaced apart in a matter of months. What links them, Jack? What did they have in common?"

"It does not say, sir."

"Nor would it. But there is something that is common to all of them. And through this knowledge, we shall come close to finding their killer."

A knock on the door drew both their heads swiveling sharply. The sheriff's messenger again? Perhaps a client? He nodded to Jack's questioning eyes, and the boy hurried to the door, opening it.

A boy, a page, shifted uncomfortably on the landing. "I . . . I seek Crispin Guest."

This is the day for it, thought Crispin. "I am he," he said, rising and approaching the door.

The boy looked Crispin over with an air of disappointment. "I bear a message from the physician Jacob of Provençal. He wonders where you were two days ago and entreats you to come to the place he advised previously at the same appointed time."

Crispin clenched his jaw. Yes, he must see to this. For the rent and his belly. "Yes, boy. Tell him I will come tonight."

He bowed to Crispin, flicked his eye at Jack, and scurried down the steps.

There was little to do for the rest of the day except to study the Coroner's rolls. Jack made a trip to the poulterer's at the other side of the tinker shop and returned with an old, tough pullet that he roasted over the fire, filling the small room with the aroma of sweet, cooked flesh at last. With a stew of turnips and leeks, Jack fed them well. He produced an apple at the end of the meal and Crispin was so glad to see it that he refused to question how Jack acquired such a treat.

By late afternoon it was time to make the trek back to Westminster. They bundled in their cloaks and headed out along Fleet Street where it became the Strand outside the city walls. It was cold but not snowing. Merchants were still out in full force, calling their wares before the day was spent. Many sat bundled in their stalls, large fires glowing in their shop hearths or in iron braziers outside, while their apprentices labored in colder back rooms.

Crispin kept half an eye on Jack, who was alert and observing the activity of London with acute ears and wide-open eyes. The boy was no fool. He was clever. But what of these other boys? Were they snatched from the streets without a fight? Had they been in stews, selling themselves to perverted men? Crispin thought of the things he had done to earn a crust of bread once he had been cast from court. Mucking the privies had seemed an insult to his character but he had endured it. He had to. But a boy with few choices had either to beg, steal, or service men for coin. Such was one's lot. Jack could have no more chosen his way in life than had Crispin.

They moved without speaking, each deep in their own thoughts. They stopped once at a meat pie seller and shared half a pie as they continued on. The bells tolled for None by the time they reached Charing Cross, though little could be seen of a sun hidden behind a dull expanse of cloud cover.

Crispin stood again at the place they had found the little corpse. He skidded down the embankment and walked along the muddy shore while the tide was out. Seagulls pecked at rocky crevices and waddled awkwardly over the stones, lumbering to stay a few paces ahead of him. Along the river, skiffs and other small boats carried fishermen or ferried workers and goods to and from each bank. He watched a dirty-faced boy sitting at the stern of such a craft, clutching the boat as an older man beside him forced the tiller into the waves. The sail flapped as it caught the wind, and the boy shivered, watching Crispin. They disappeared around a barge, heading upriver toward Westminster Palace.

The wind swept up the Thames and battered his hood, trying to pull it away from his whipping hair. "Somebody must be missing these children," he murmured.

"Not if they was like me, sir," said Jack beside him.

Crispin started. He had been so engrossed in his thoughts he had forgotten Jack. He looked up at the sky. Still light. Nightfall was still some hours away. He carefully climbed back up the embankment and stood with his hands at his hips, staring down the muddy streets, with their frosty rooftops and slithering smoke. "You take this street, Jack. And I shall take this one."

"Er . . . 'take' it, sir? For what?"

"To question the merchants, of course. Ask them if they have heard of any boy who had gone missing. Even if it is a rumor."

Jack gnawed on his lip and shuffled his muddy shoes. "Beggin' your pardon, Master Crispin. But they won't be answering any fool questions from me."

"Hmm?" he asked, distracted. "Why not?"

"Well, look at me, sir. I ain't in no fit state. They'd think I was a beggar."

Crispin turned and measured young Jack, from his torn stockings to his beleaguered hood that he kept closed by pinching it tight at his chin. "Tell them you are on the Sheriff of London's business—"

Jack guffawed, showing a chipped tooth. "Go on!"

With a sigh of resignation Crispin nodded. "Very well. Tell them you are an emissary of the Tracker. No doubt they have heard of me even on these streets."

"Aye. That *might* do. But if they box me ears for impertinence, it's on your head."

Crispin smiled. "I shall gladly carry the burden."

Jack nodded once and was off, looking back warily.

With a snort at insolent servants, he headed to the first shop on the street he had chosen. These were further in from the Thames; shops and houses that the Coroner had not questioned.

Crispin repeated the exercise all the way to the end of the street, where Jack met him, rubbing his arms to keep warm. The light was slanting toward the horizon now. The sparse trees in back gardens were becoming dark silhouettes against the sky. Slushy flakes began to fall, speckling the lane. "Have you yielded anything?" he asked the boy.

"No, Master. No one remembered a boy gone missing, servant or beggar."

Crispin's eyes adjusted to the darkening night and measured the many lanes ahead of him. "There are many more houses and shops to ask."

"We can't ask them all, can we?"

Crispin's sigh created a curling mist around his face. He looked down the lane and scanned rooftops disappearing into the night. "The city is a big place. I do not see how we can ask them all. There must be another way."

"In the meantime, we must go to meet this Jew, then."

Crispin wound his cloak about him. Yes. He must.

The streets were becoming deserted. The merchants' stalls had been folded up and shuttered. Even the sounds of commerce had softened from the day. The muffled fall of hoofs tramping in the new snow and the squeak of a cart pushed back to its resting spot were the only sounds left from another busy day in Westminster.

Crispin led the way to St. Margaret's Street toward Westminster Hall. An icy mist rose from the Thames and every sound seemed to dampen beneath its heavy governance. The disquieting stillness sent a shiver down Crispin's spine. It fell heavily around him, this sensation. He found himself stopping and looking around, bewildered. He touched Jack's shoulder to stop him as well, and listened. It wasn't so much something that he heard as it was something he felt. Jack looked up at him questioningly. Crispin beseeched those steady, tawny eyes, asking silently if Jack felt it, too.

The world seemed to hold its breath.

Crispin spun.

For only a moment, with the light of a shopkeeper's brazier filling the misty space behind, Crispin spied . . . *something* . . . against the snowy fog. A large, hulking silhouette. Broad shoulders supported a tiny head and large arms hung like hams at its sides. An unspeakable fear like none other suddenly seized Crispin's heart. His first instinct was to grab Jack and drag his surprised form to him. His second was to draw his dagger.

He blinked. And suddenly the alley was empty.

"Master! What—"

"Be still." Crispin trotted down the narrow lane, looking for the . . . *man,* for want of a better word.

The flickering brazier toyed with the shadows, sending them running in long, dancing shapes along the walls of shuttered houses. Crispin listened with all his might, stilling his own straining breath in order to hear.

Ahead. Something like footfalls.

He ran, snow flying from his heels. The quiet, narrow streets seemed to close in on him, their crowded structures twisting toward the middle, towering above Crispin's head in their need to consume the sky.

Before he turned a corner he scoured the ground under the fitful moonlight. Large indentations in the snow could have been footprints, but they were quickly filling with new flakes.

He ran to the rhythm of his own beating heart for several more paces before he slowed to a stop. He listened again.

Nothing.

Jack came up behind him, beating the ground, skidding in the snow to grab hold of Crispin's cloak. "Master!" He panted, eyes wide disks. "What *was* that?"

Crispin rolled the dagger's handle in his sweaty hand once before sheathing it. Baleful apprehension would not allow his heart to slacken. "Jack, by the Holy Rood, I . . . do not know."

4

DISTURBED MORE THAN HE could say, it was after some minutes of searching—for what he knew not—before Crispin allowed them to return to the Great Gate. He took careful measure of the sounds and sights on the street, and when they backtracked, he tried Jack's patience by keeping his eyes to the ground and even returning to the street where the pursuit had ended.

Jack thumbed his dagger and kept licking his chapped lips. Crispin continued to look over his shoulder.

When the gate was in sight again, Jack crossed himself for the hundredth time. "Let us hurry and meet this Jew, Master. I would be home in me own bed."

"Yes," he answered distractedly before shaking it off. What was the matter with him? This business of dead boys was touching his mind. That was only some man going home to his warm lodgings. Some large man. Perhaps a blacksmith or a mason. How the shadows can make the ordinary sinister! He almost laughed at himself, but the lingering sense of disquiet would not allow it. He merely led Jack to the Great Gate and when they walked silently across the vast outer ward, they stepped up to an arched portico at the front steps. Under the arch, a porter warmed his hands over a brazier with several pages standing beside him.

Crispin approached, breaching the light cast by the brazier. The porter spied him and turned, grabbing his pike. "Hold there!" he warned.

Crispin bowed. "I have a message for Jacob of Provençal. I was to meet him here."

The porter glanced at the pages, who looked reluctant to move.

"I can send my servant if you do not wish to fulfill your obligations," said Crispin, gesturing toward a scowling Jack.

A page, with hair as black as Crispin's, straightened and pulled at his tabard. "I shall go to the Jew. Whom shall I say is at the gate?"

Crispin smiled. "He will know."

The pages shared a look with the porter, but the dark-haired one soon trotted to do his business.

Unfortunately, the brazier was within the stone portico. Crispin and Jack were obliged to stand in the snowy courtyard without benefit of a fire. Jack trotted in place to keep the cold away. Crispin stood stoically under his cloak. He had long experience waiting in all manner of weather for a battle. This was no different.

In time, the page returned with the physician. The man looked none too pleased and quickly scampered into the courtyard to meet Crispin in the shadows.

"You are tardy, sir," said the man in a severe tone.

"I am here now. How am I to get into court?"

Jacob looked back at the porter and pages and drew Crispin and Jack deeper into the shadows of the courtyard's wall. "We will exchange cloaks." He showed Crispin his. On it was the yellow rouelle designating him as a Jew. "Your servant and I will enter at the Queen's Bridge, while you return this way."

"A feeble ruse," said Crispin, eyeing the man's full beard while rubbing his own clean-shaven jaw.

"Keep your head bowed. I am all but ignored. No one sees me unless they must."

Crispin digested this even as he unbuttoned his cloak. He handed the garment to Jacob just as the old man passed his to Crispin. Crispin allowed a wave of discomfort before he spun the cloak over his shoulders and lifted his hood, hiding his face.

"The corridor by the Painted Chamber," said Jacob before he hastened out of the courtyard. The Painted Chamber? That was in the royal quarters, by the king and Lancaster. Crispin's heart thrummed in his chest. But he turned to Jack and urged him without words to follow the man. Jack grimaced his distaste but nonetheless followed.

Keeping his head down, Crispin walked like an old man, striding under the gate arch without the porter or any of the pages questioning him.

Glancing back, he snorted. So, the old Jew was right. He wasted no more time and headed down the familiar corridors toward the southern end of the palace. Crispin had managed to slip into the palace on other occasions, but after the latest incident with the king, he doubted his presence would be greeted with much joy.

Iron cressets burned, lighting his way, and there was occasional laughter muffled behind closed doors as he passed apartment after apartment.

He waited in the shadows, his hood heavy over his face.

A scuffled step. Crispin raised his head and saw both figures approaching; the older man and a reluctant Jack Tucker close behind him.

"This way," hissed Jacob, and Crispin and Jack followed his quick pace.

Crispin had been curious as to what the apartments of a Jew would look like. A certain uneasiness warred within his gut. Would it be odd and foreign like the homes of Saracens in the Holy Land, full of exotic smells and strange furnishings? His heart quickened when the door opened, but as his eyes adjusted to the dark, the fact of a normal room melted away his apprehension to disappointment.

The hearth burned low. Jacob took a poker and urged the flames to life, adding a log. Crispin sneered at the wood in envy. He had no logs for *his* fire. Only peat and the meager sticks Jack bought from the wood sellers or managed to scavenge.

Jacob used a straw to light several candles. As the room glowed, Crispin glanced about. Bright drapery hung on the walls, giving the plaster a cheery appearance. Shadowed alcoves pricked Crispin's curiosity, where tables with various beakers and bowls stood ready. Except for the numerous bottles and canisters and the odd smells emanating from that direction, the room looked to be as any ordinary physician's parlor. A door to the left must have led to a bed chamber. *Not bad for a Jew,* mused Crispin grudgingly.

The chamber door opened suddenly.

Crispin's hand reached for his dagger. A young man, thin and pale, stepped through the opening. At first Crispin thought him to be a page, but the yellow rouelle on his dark, ankle-length gown soon snuffed that notion. He wore a scarlet sash about his waist and from it hung a gold chain with a key, a money pouch, and a small dagger. A thick, gold chain on his chest seemed an attempt to hide the rouelle. The youth glared with narrowed, jewel-green eyes. "*Mon père.*" His voice was harsher than Crispin expected from his slight features. It was almost hoarse. His brown hair hung limply on either side of his cheeks down to the jaw. A dark cap perched on the crown of his head.

Jacob nodded toward the lad. "This is Julian. My son."

The boy did not acknowledge his father, but continued his mistrustful stare at Crispin.

Jacob frowned. "Is this how I taught you hospitality? How do you treat guests?"

Julian gritted his teeth and shuffled to a table near the high window. He poured four shares of wine into bowls, bringing the first to his father. When he settled his own to his chest, he leaned against the wall and studied Crispin from afar.

"Qui sont ces mendiants?" Julian asked derisively.

Exasperated, Jacob hissed at him, "English!"

Crispin stiffened. *"Nous ne sommes pas des mendiants,"* he answered. His lips curled into a lopsided grin when Julian drew back sharply, spilling his wine.

Jacob smiled. "Many Englishmen speak French. That will teach you to better guard your tongue."

Julian recovered and sipped his bowl, eyes wandering toward the dark window. His cheek was still pink.

"I apologize for my son," said Jacob with a sigh. He gestured Crispin to a chair. "He is often quick to judge and slow to change. It is the fault of youth, I am afraid."

"I would rather honest hate than useless flattery," said Crispin over his wine. " 'People generally despise where they flatter.' "

Jacob chuckled, noting Julian's discomfiture at their speaking about him. "You quote Aristotle. How interesting."

Crispin lowered the wine from his lips. "I am surprised you would recognize the words of a pagan philosopher, Master Jacob. I was not aware that your . . . people . . . would read such men."

Jacob waved a hand vaguely. "It was Jewish scholars who rescued the words of pagan philosophers from obscurity." Crispin narrowed his eyes at that, but Jacob went on, despite Crispin's obvious skepticism. "I have learned many things from many sources, *Maître* Guest. Though the Scriptures and the words of the ancient rabbis resonate in my craft, I realized quite early in my schooling that not all the wisdom of the ages belongs to the Jews . . . merely most of it."

Julian snorted a laugh but hid his expression in his bowl.

Jack hovered behind Crispin's chair, gulping his wine before Crispin twisted around and took the bowl from him. "Master Jacob," said Crispin tightly. "Perhaps if we can get to the business at hand . . ."

Julian grumbled. "I do not know why you had to bring this Gentile into our suite, Father," he muttered. "Who cares if something is stolen from a Jew, after all?" Julian fixed his glare on Crispin. The boy had an evil glint in his eye. "A man who does such work for money. Is that not why there is a sheriff?"

Crispin stood. "Then call in the sheriff. Here." He reached for the coin pouch and dropped the offending bag onto a table. "Take back your coin, Master Jacob."

Jacob looked beside himself. He touched his forehead and groaned. "You see what you have done?" he hissed at his son.

"I do not care! We do not belong in England. Their laws are a disgrace. We defile ourselves by being here! We belong in Avignon where a Jew is treated with dignity."

"You know nothing!" he hissed at the boy. He turned entreating eyes to Crispin. "*Maître* Guest, I implore you. I need your help. *London* needs your help."

He gave Julian a stern look. "I would counsel your son to keep his arguments to himself from now on."

Julian pressed forward, opening his mouth as if to speak, when Jacob wheeled on him. "You will be still!" Surprised, the boy blinked rapidly and clamped his lips shut. The fist at his side trembled.

Jacob nodded. "*Maître* Guest. I apologize for such an unruly household. My wife died when he was only an infant. I fear that he did not receive the benefit of Patience from a mother's touch as perhaps he should have done. Please, sit. Have more wine. Julian, bring a stool for the servant boy."

"You are enigmatic, sir," Crispin offered as Julian did as bid. "At first, you tell me that something dangerous has been stolen from you. And then you tell me your theft involved mere parchments. And just now, you intimate that London is in danger. I think it might be best to get to the point."

The firelight painted Jacob's white face with deeply etched lines of age and worry. Julian had eased into a folding seat and watched his father with pursed lips and glittering eyes.

"I am certain, *Maître* Guest, that you have been schooled in the sciences. You seem to be a well-educated man."

"My education would be beside the point."

"Oh no. I do not think so." Jacob settled himself deeper into his cushioned chair. "It is the very point. Have you ever heard of your Englishman William of Ockham?"

Surprised that the Jew had, he did not show it on his face. "Indeed. It is part and parcel to my personal philosophy. *Lex parsimoniae. 'Entia non sunt multiplicanda praeter necessitatem.'*"

A slight clearing of a throat behind him. He raised a brow toward Jack. "It means 'entities should not be multiplied beyond necessity.'"

"'The simplest explanation is the best'" offered Julian.

Crispin glanced at the young Jew, who gave him a triumphant smirk. He almost returned an admiring smile. Turning his metal wine bowl in his hand and feeling the raised designs under his fingertips, Crispin added, "Aristotle also coined: 'A likely impossibility is always preferable to an unconvincing possibility.'" Julian wore an approving expression before he seemed to remember himself and lost it again. "I have learned that truth is truth, Master Jacob," Crispin continued, "no matter the age, no matter the philosopher."

Jacob's chapped lips curved into a brief smile. "You are an interesting man, *Maître*. But there is still much to tell. I asked about your studies in science because it is so appropriate to our discussion. Great scholars of the age—Thomas Aquinas, John Duns Scotus, Roger Bacon, Gersonides—bear the one truth, the one we all hold dear. And that is that the Lord Almighty, blessed be His name, is the architect of our universe, of all that we can possibly understand and conceive. That the Lord holds every answer to every mystery. Is this not so?"

Crispin ran a tongue over his lips, tasting the last of his wine. "Yes."

"And to these few scholars, He opens the door but a crack, allowing in a mere candle flame of light. There is so much more to know."

"Someone has stolen your research, then," Crispin offered, trying to hurry him along.

"*My* research? No, not mine."

He turned to the youth. "Yours, then?"

Julian seemed startled to be addressed and opened his mouth to comment when Jacob jolted from his chair and paced before his book-laden table. He pondered the books for some time before pouncing and rummaging through them. Piles of parchments tied together with leather covers. Scrolls with unfamiliar writing, at least unfamiliar to Crispin from the brief snatches he saw of them before Jacob discarded one to pick up another. "Astrology tells us much; our personalities, our humors. Divination through numbers and patterns—"

"Father!"

Jacob stopped his furious searching and looked up.

Julian gritted his teeth. His eyes were wide and furious. "You trust this Gentile with too much!"

Crispin had begun to assess the young man as intelligent and worldly, until he opened his mouth again.

"He has my silver in his purse," said Jacob.

"And do you truly think that is enough to buy his silence? I implore you! Make him leave. Forget about those parchments—"

"No! The damage that has already been done! It grieves my heart to think—" He shook his head and leaned against the table. "*Maître* Guest, if you give me your word, I shall trust you. Can you give me your word and your oath that you will not use this information against me?"

Crispin wriggled in his seat. "Master Jacob," he said carefully, mindful of the venomous stares from Julian to the back of his head. "It would be difficult for me to swear before I know all." The man seemed sincere enough. But he was a Jew, and Crispin had little experience with such people. But the coins were needed. Dammit.

"I give you my word," said Crispin slowly. "If you will have me swear, then I shall."

Jacob smiled. "No need, sir. I believe you." He looked toward his son. "You see, not all men are false. Some, though they be English, can be relied upon."

"You tread on dangerous ground, Father. We are here by the grace of the king, but that grace may not extend to . . . to this."

Jacob sighed deeply and raised tired eyes to Crispin. "*Maître* Guest, have you ever heard of the Kabbalah?"

The Kabbalah? Vague impressions of half-remembered stories whispered through his mind like wisps of candle smoke. "Jewish magic," he answered warily.

Jacob shook his head. "Not magic, sir. But theology. The spiritual nature of—"

"Christ's toes! Jewish *magic*? I risked life and limb to creep into court for Jewish *magic*? The devil take me for the greedy fool I am!" He snapped to his feet and headed straight for the door. Pulling it open he looked back at Jack.

Scrambling up, Jack snatched Crispin's cloak from the fire and scurried to catch up.

Crispin heard Jacob's frantic steps behind him but kept going, only slowing and bending slightly so that Jack could drape his cloak over his shoulders.

"*Maître* Guest! *Maître* Guest!"

He suddenly recalled where they were and how loud Jacob was. He wheeled and clamped his hand over the old man's mouth, pulling him into an embrace. "Be silent!" Crispin glanced quickly about the long corridor but saw only the flicker of torchlight.

But then, hot stabbing pain pierced the arm he had wound about the man's neck and he released him at once. "*God's blood!*" He looked down and saw red darkening his right sleeve.

Looking up with murder in his heart, he stared into the eyes of the lad, Julian, his bloody dagger still raised in the air. "Get away from my father, you dog!"

"Damn you to hell!" He rushed the boy and slammed him and his wrist with the dagger against the wall. The boy cried out with the suddenness of the attack and the dagger dropped with a thud to the wooden floor. Jack snatched it up and held it tight. His teeth ground his lower lip and he was clearly itching to use the weapon on Julian.

"What have you done?" cried Jacob, grabbing at Crispin's arm.

Crispin yanked it from him and stepped back.

Everyone turned and froze at the sound of a door unbolting.

Without a second thought, Crispin dashed back into the Jew's chamber and felt like smiting himself for having to cower behind a door.

"What goes on here?" A woman's voice in a thick, foreign accent. Crispin spied the corridor through the crack of door and post. She had emerged from the queen's chamber. One of the queen's Bohemian ladies, no doubt. She took in the scene: Jacob reaching for his son who was still flush against the wall and Jack, standing with a bloody dagger, face like pale cream. "Physician?" she said, her voice tinted with fear.

Jacob assessed his surroundings and bent in a faintly obsequious posture. He put a hand to his breast and bowed to her. "Mistress, the lad here is a patient but he is reluctant to receive my care."

"Shall I call for the guards?"

He shook his head. He was the model of calm. "No need. You will come into the chamber now, won't you *garçon*?"

Jack looked from Jacob to the woman and slowly nodded. "Aye." He lowered the dagger and tried to hide it behind his back. "I, er, hurt m'self. With me knife. The good physician here offered to help."

"Does the queen need me?" Jacob asked, trying to look past the broad woman into the candlelit chamber.

"No. We heard the noise and I was sent to investigate."

"All is well, and you may tell her Majesty so." He took Jack by the arm and steered him toward his chamber. With a backward tilt to his head, Julian followed after him. The woman continued to glare in their direction even as Jacob closed and bolted the door, resting his forehead against it.

He took a breath and faced Crispin, gesturing toward his arm. "Let me dress that."

Crispin glared at Julian who sneered back at him.

"You attacked my father."

"I was merely silencing him. He announced my name in the corridor. Do you know what would happen to the lot of you if I were discovered here?"

Julian's eyes rounded. "What have you wrought upon us, Father?"

"Have I not told you at least a thousand times, Julian, to be still! We need this man. And for the moment, he needs our protection."

Julian sunk to his chair with a look of despair shadowing his face.

Jacob took Crispin's good arm and led him back to his chair by the fire where he pushed him into it.

Crispin squeezed the wound shut, scowling at Julian who was slowly shaking his head. He supposed he couldn't begrudge the youth for protecting his father. Jack might have done the same for him. In fact, Jack was still holding the bloody knife and he was trembling. "Jack," he said softly.

The boy turned. His brow was stepped with worry lines.

"Put the knife aside. I am in no danger."

Jack looked toward Julian, but Crispin shook his head. "No, I am in no danger."

With care, Jack lowered the knife to the sideboard and snatched the jug. "Master?"

"Need you even ask?"

Jack found Crispin's bowl, refilled it, and handed it to him with a shaking hand. He took it with his good hand and downed the bowl.

"I should take care with the wine, *Maître* Guest," said Jacob returning to his side. "A dose is good for the blood, but too much . . ." He took the bowl from Crispin and handed it to Jack. He took the wounded arm and tucked the hand into his side, cradling it there with his elbow. Jacob rolled back the sleeve of Crispin's cotehardie to his elbow and then did the same to his bloody chemise. Once the arm was revealed, Crispin got a look at the wound. Not deep, but it was still seeping blood.

Jacob clucked his tongue and murmured something in an unrecognizable language. Crispin tried to draw his arm away, fearing some strange Jewish incantation, but Jacob held it firm. "Worry not, Master Guest. I have been told I have a light touch."

"It is not your touch I worry over," he growled.

This made Jacob look up and meet his eyes. "I was saying a prayer, sir. In Hebrew."

"Limit your prayers to English from now on."

Without a change to his expression, the man lowered his face to his task. "Shallow but not ragged," he said, turning the arm and examining, allowing the blood to trickle out. "My son is usually a fine surgeon when not wielding a knife in anger," he muttered. "I will not need to sew it. But I will dress it with a poultice and wrap it tightly in linen."

"I do not want your poultice. Just tie it off."

The bushy brows rose. "But the poultice will help the healing, soothe the pain, and prevent scarring."

"Did you hear me? I do not want your poultice."

He shrugged and opened his hand to his son. Julian reluctantly dragged himself to the table of herbs and jars, retrieved a roll of linen strips, and handed some to his father.

Still cradling the arm, Jacob wrapped a length of linen over the wound, winding it tightly and expertly before tying it off with a firm knot over the cut. He began to roll the sleeves back down but Crispin yanked hard and freed his arm, doing it himself.

Jacob sighed and stepped back.

"I thank you," said Crispin as caustically as he could. "Jack, let's go."

"Wait," said Jacob. His face implored. He scrambled back to the table where Crispin had dropped his coin pouch and snatched it up. He held it out to Crispin with his white hands. "The parchments. I need them back. They must be returned. Please. Take the silver."

With one hand on Jack and the other on the door, Crispin turned back. "We are a danger to each other, I fear. Go to the sheriffs with this."

Crispin pulled open the door and scanned the empty corridor, wondering how he was to sneak out of the palace right outside the queen's own chamber.

"There will be more murders," said Jacob.

Crispin froze. Slowly, he turned back. "What did you say?"

"The murders," Jacob whispered. "The boys. I have heard of the murders." His tongue scraped his dry lips. "I know who is responsible."

5

"FATHER," WARNED JULIAN.

Jacob made a tight jerk of his head, closing his tired eyes.

"Explain yourself," said Crispin.

"Please." Jacob gestured toward the chair by the fire. "Sit."

Cursing under his breath, he felt a twinge in his wounded arm, and finally stomped back to the fire. He sat hard on the chair.

"I know you find this distasteful, *Maître* Guest." Jacob sank wearily onto his own chair. "Forgive me. But the help I need will not come from the sheriffs nor from the court. I sought you out in particular because of the rumors that you often deal with objects of religious significance. Is this true?"

Crispin felt the warmth of the fire at his cheek. It did little to warm the coldness creeping within him. "It is my curse," he said, half-jesting.

The man did not take it as a jest. He edged forward. "Then you are no stranger to the hand of the Lord."

He laughed unpleasantly. "Of this I know not. Relics, such as they are, are only relics to those who deem them so. They bear little significance to me." He swallowed the half-truth with the toss of his head. "Are you saying these parchments are relics? That they have to do with murder? By all the saints, I am at my wits' end, old man! Say your peace and have done!"

"I fear, *Maître* Guest, that the monster has been released."

Jack sprang to his feet. "God blind me!" he shrieked. "Monster?"

"He . . ." Crispin steadied himself and shook his head. "He does not mean that literally, Jack. He speaks of the monster of inhumanity—"

"I speak of it *very* literally, good *maître*. It is the missing parchments. They contain the words of Creation." He shook his head sadly and fingered his beard. "And I let them slip through my fingers. I'm a fool. I cannot forgive myself."

Crispin felt the tension in his body drain away. He saw in his mind a dark shape receding into the misty night. Heavy footfalls. Fear. "What . . . what is this . . . monster?"

"But we *saw* it, Master!" cried Jack. "We saw it!"

Jacob gasped. "What did you see?"

"This is utter nonsense," muttered Crispin. He ran his fingers into his shaggy hair. "It was a man, surely. Tall and very broad. A . . . a small . . . head . . ."

Jacob covered his mouth with his trembling fingers. "The Golem. He has been animated. We are dead." He reached for his robe and ripped the seam.

"Father!" Julian was kneeling beside him, staying his hand from doing more damage to his robe. "No! It cannot be. This man is lying."

Crispin raised his chin. "I am not lying. That is one sin of which I am not guilty." He glanced back at Jack to confirm it but Jack appeared too frightened to speak. Damn this! "Harken to me, all of you. There is no monster. There is only Jewish superstition and odd circumstances."

"The murders—" said Jacob.

"The fact that you know about these murders makes me *very* suspicious."

Jacob shook his head. "When they first happened, I was the

only physician nearby. They called me forth. I have since heard of two others. I saw the dead boys. Who but a monster would commit these horrible crimes?"

Who indeed? "What are you implying? That this . . . this *Golem* . . . has murdered these children?"

"I saw what was done to those boys."

"How did you know that I am investigating?"

"One hears things. But that was after I had decided to seek you out."

Crispin narrowed his eyes and looked across the room, peering into the shadows of the alcoves, trying to discern the strange beakers and jars from the shapes of alchemic apparatuses. "What is a . . . Golem?"

Jacob rose and returned to his table, unrolling a scroll with shaking hands. "This, *Maître* Guest, is the *Sefer Yetzirah*: The Book of Creation."

Curious, Crispin strode across the room and looked over the man's shoulders. He gritted his teeth when he beheld the page of strange symbols interspersed with Stars of David. "These *seguloth*," said Jacob, pointing to the symbols, "explain the book. Our Father Abraham was given the divine revelation of these pages by the Lord—blessed be His name—and the rabbis of old have discussed it and analyzed it for centuries. This," he said, spreading his fingers over the tan parchment, "is the understanding of Creation itself. How the universe was created through the *Sefirot*, the Ten Sacred Numbers—"

"Enough!" The room felt close suddenly. This talk of Jewish magic made Crispin's skin crawl. "This monster. This Golem. What is it? Did you make it?"

"Me? Oh no! Never! Only in extreme circumstances and only with the counsel of many wise rabbis would I attempt it. You see, *Maître*, the word 'Golem' means a 'shapeless mass.' It is made from mud or clay. The Golem is created to protect the Jewish people from harm. It is a sacred obligation. A man who has a Golem as a servant is naturally imbued with much wisdom and piety. Wisdom in being able to choose the right path, and piety in order to discern the Almighty's will. If he does not possess these traits, then there is no controlling the servant. No, *Maître* Guest, it was not me. But someone else. Someone who wanted the power of the demon."

"So it is a demon."

Jacob opened his lips as if to explain, but shut them again, his brows working over his eyes. Like a tutor speaking carefully to a pupil, he began. "Adam, the father of Man, was created from mud, from clay. From this clay, the Lord breathed life into him. And so it is similar with the Golem. He is made of clay and can be animated by reading the words on the *Sefer Yetzirah* and placing the word for 'truth' on its body. It is a soulless being with no emotions, no pity, no mercy. A man who uses a Golem for unholy purposes"—he shook his head—"is himself a monster."

"What makes you think this Golem of yours committed these murders?"

"The strangeness of it. The cutting along the abdomen. The taking of the entrails." He seemed to notice Crispin flinching and nodded. "As you noticed yourself. I do not think a Golem needs to feed, but there is so little we know of these creatures. The blood and entrails of a youth would be horrible nourishment, but nourishment just the same. If the Golem's creator wished it, these things would be done. A Golem is only a shell. He does what he is told."

"And so," said Crispin, walking slowly toward the alcoves. They seemed to compel him with their strange smells and instruments. "And so these papers were stolen from you. When?"

"It must have been two months ago. That was when the first murder was discovered."

"Months? Why did you wait so long to say something?"

"I did not want to believe it. I *could* not. But then, when the murders happened again and again . . ."

"This is a matter for the sheriff, then."

"But *Maître* Guest, you yourself said you were investigating these murders. Surely you could keep it quiet."

"A monster on the loose? Should I not warn the populace?"

"Oh no! That would be disaster!"

"For whom? You?" He said the last nastily and meant it.

Jacob drew himself up. "I am not afraid of your Gentile mobs, sir. Lives are at stake. It is more important than the life of one Jewish physician."

"Noble, I suppose." Crispin scowled. "Why should I believe any of this? How do I know you are telling me the truth?"

Jacob lifted his arms in an exhausted shrug. "You have no good reason, *Maître.* I am merely a Jew. I only thought, that if anyone would, *you* would believe me."

"Christ!" He thumbed the stubble on his chin and stared at the floor. "Who knew you had such papers here?"

Jacob thought a moment. "I do not know. But I do know that my rooms have been plundered before."

"Oh? When?"

"Many times since I arrived. My privacy here has been . . . less than private. Understandable when I am so close to their Majesties."

Crispin mulled this. "These parchments of yours. Are they written in Hebrew?"

"Yes."

"Then this culprit must surely be a scholar of some sort to be able to read it."

"Yes. That must be so."

"Who in this court can read Hebrew?"

"This I do not know. But there are astrologers, alchemists, and the like at court. I could not guess at how many."

"Do you lock your door, Master Jacob?"

"Of course. I bar it each night and lock it each time I go out."

"And you, boy." He turned to Julian, who rousted himself to glare anew. "What of you? Are you as assiduous at locking doors?"

"Of course I am! I do not trust these English Gentiles."

"Many would have a key, though," Crispin mused to himself.

"Master," said Jack, looking desperately at the window. "That is the bell for Compline." He had not noticed the distant deep clang until Jack mentioned it. "It will be curfew soon. And the gate to London must already be locked. How are we to get back home?"

"I have my ways, Jack, never fear." But he did not relish traveling after curfew. He wondered bitterly if it was snowing again. He stared at the curtained window. "When did you arrive to these shores, Master Jacob?"

"Two months ago."

"And the murders started then?"

"Much to my regret."

"These are Christian children." He pivoted and fastened his steely gaze on the physician. "The explanation could be far simpler than a supposed monster. '*Entia non sunt multiplicanda praeter necessitatem.*' "

Jacob's eyes widened and for the first time, he did look frightened. "You . . . you accuse . . . *me*?"

"You whoreson!" growled Julian. "I should have slit your throat rather than stab your arm."

Crispin spared him a cold glance. "I have not discounted your guilt in this, Master Julian." He was satisfied to hear the boy's gasp of outrage.

Jacob braced himself against the table behind him. "I . . . I can well see how your Christian sensibilities could accuse me of such deeds, *Maître* Guest. But I assure you—I swear on my physician's oath—that I cannot kill. And to kill a child . . . Never! *Never.*"

A disquieting sensation crept over Crispin as Jacob pled his case. No. The physician seemed far too sincere, too compassionate.

Julian, on the other hand . . .

"I must think on all this, Master Jacob. These tidings are disturbing."

"But—"

"I will inform you when I come to any conclusions." He swept Julian with a spiteful look before he signaled to Jack.

Now, how the hell were they to get out of the palace unseen?

He opened the door cautiously and stuck out his head, staring into the gloom of the corridor. This chamber was near the king's. God's sense of humor failed to tickle.

Crispin flipped his hood up and tugged it low over his forehead. Taking a deep breath he plunged into the corridor with Jack close behind.

"Master, what—"

"Be still, Jack," he whispered. He cocked his head to listen. It was late. Most of court would be abed or perhaps playing a late game of chess or tables.

He stepped into the all-too-familiar corridor, hearing the soft click of the door shutting behind him. That was that. They were certainly on their own now.

Crispin walked carefully, keeping along the walls and listening before he proceeded. He cast a thought back toward Jacob and his parchments. This was damnable. If that Jew was responsible for those deaths, Crispin certainly did not want to appear to be helping him. He recalled the stories he had heard of Jews murdering children. But this had been more than a murder. It had been rape and mutilation, which sounded to him like some sort of sorcery. The man admitted to the use of magic with those damnable texts. But Jacob's appalled expression did not appear to have been faked. Was he being entirely sincere?

He turned a corner. The wooden floor groaned under his step and he stopped, measuring the empty corridor. When the small noise failed to raise an alarm he continued his steps and his musings.

What of Julian? A sour lad. There was something secretive in his eyes, something Crispin did not trust. Was that boy capable? His distaste for Crispin's country was palpable. When Crispin shoved him against the wall the boy felt pathetic beneath his crushing grip. Such a slight youth might wish to prove himself stronger over smaller, weaker boys. Was he monster enough to have raped and killed? Maybe his father had no stomach for blasphemous experiments, but what of his son?

And Crispin had neglected to search the bedchamber. Foolish! He had been so concerned with getting out of there that he failed to do the most rudimentary of investigations. A child's mistake. He would not make that mistake again.

And yet. How was he to investigate at all? It would certainly involve those of the court. He would have to return and make inquiries, but how was he to do that when the king's mandate still stood? After Crispin had foolishly refused to beg for his lands and title Richard had screamed it to the court that Crispin was not to return. He had even refused the king's gold. *That* had been foolish indeed.

He noticed Jack was not as skittish and had graciously accepted Jacob's pouch of silver when the physician had pressed it on him in the chamber. At least one of them had a head on their shoulders.

But for how much longer?

Crispin was about to inquire of Jack what their next move should be when the door beside him opened. Before Crispin had a chance to react, a hand reached out, grabbed him by his hood, and dragged him inside.

6

CRISPIN SCRAMBLED FOR HIS dagger, but his arms were trapped in his twisted cloak. It had all happened so fast. The door, the man. Jack somehow followed, almost crying out but stifling himself.

When Crispin wrestled away he turned an angry expression on . . . the duke of Lancaster! "Damn you, Crispin!" shouted his former mentor. "What, by the mass, are you *doing* here?"

Crispin clamped his open jaw shut and straightened his disheveled coat. He smoothed back the hood from his face and stood bareheaded before his lord. *Former* lord, he reminded himself.

John of Gaunt glared down at him with dark brows and a dark beard. Being the king's uncle, his apartments were close to Richard and his queen, Anne.

"Your grace," said Crispin, bowing with as much dignity as he could muster. Jack sloppily parroted his master. "How did you know I was here?"

"I heard the commotion in the corridor and I lay in wait for you. How could you be such a fool as to come here?"

He cast his eyes to the floor, feeling like a child chastised by his sire. "A paying wage, my lord. I must go where the business takes me," he muttered.

"And it takes you to that Jew physician? What are you *doing*, Crispin?"

He looked up at the man who had nurtured him, saved him, and ultimately betrayed him. He knew not how to feel anymore. Instead, he let his eyes grow cold and leveled his gaze with that of the duke's. "I am earning my keep, my lord," he said with more passion. "May I go now?"

"No, you may not go!" Lancaster crossed to the enormous hearth and paced, his hands holding so tight to one another behind his back that they whitened. "Stubborn. Willful. Obstinate."

"All my patron names," said Crispin.

Lancaster flicked his head and glared at him. "Do not dare be flippant with me, Guest."

Crispin sighed. How was he ever to get out of the palace? Worse. How was he ever to get back in? Perhaps . . .

"My lord, I urgently seek your counsel."

"Ha!" He stood with legs wide in front of the fire. His red houppelande was fringed by golden firelight and his face fell into shadow.

Crispin took a cautious step forward. Lancaster could easily strike him for his insolence as much as help him. He wondered which was more likely. "My lord, there have been . . . unseemly murders. I have been sent to investigate them."

Lancaster's eyes glittered and steadied on Crispin. "Murders? Which sheriff sent you? That ineffectual John Froshe? Or that fish-faced Nicholas Exton?"

He hesitated. After all, he wasn't supposed to say.

"Never mind," said Lancaster. "I can see you are loyal to one of those fools. More misplaced loyalty, Guest?"

That stung. Why use Crispin's loyalty against him? "All of London knows I am trustworthy." It was no mere boast and Lancaster knew it.

The duke said nothing to that. He glared at him for a moment longer before slowly pivoting toward the fire. "You were told not to return to court," he said quietly. "How much is this physician paying you? Is it worth your life?"

"It is not merely the money." *If you knew me better you would know that,* he longed to say. "The murders," he said aloud. "I could not let it lie—"

"You could never let it lie." He shook his head. Crispin stared at that straight spine, the sword-roughened hands behind his back.

The room was too familiar. Crispin refused to take comfort in it. He shoved the memories back, memories of sitting before this very hearth with Lancaster, while the duke's children careened through that archway.

"Not when murder is concerned, my lord."

"So you say. Well, Crispin. What boon do you require this time?"

A hard stone settled in his belly. He gritted his teeth. "I must investigate this murder. I need to inquire at court."

"Godspeed to that. You well remember that the king specifically forbade this very thing." His eyes roved up and down Crispin's form. "And I see how well you obey. For coin, Crispin? Oh, very well. Because of *murder,* then. Yet you are still here and still forbidden. Is it your deepest desire to earn the king's wrath? Don't answer that. I would rather not fall prey to more of your impudence."

Crispin rolled his shoulder. His arm began to throb where that cur Julian stabbed him. Maybe he should have allowed the Jew to put on his wretched poultice.

Lancaster sighed and shook his head. Raising a hand to his temple he lowered himself to one of the chairs before the fire. "Crispin, Crispin." Gaunt's back was to him and it was only that dark head of hair over the top of the chair's back that Crispin could see. "How did we get here, you and I?" he asked softly.

He grasped his wounded arm and cradled it. "Because you are right," he replied, just as quietly. "I could not let it lie."

Lancaster raised his hand and motioned him to the other chair.

He hesitated. Would Lancaster help him after all, or was there more lecture to be endured?

In the end it didn't matter. Crispin wanted to sit beside him, wanted to soak up all the time he could with his former mentor. But he was not so much of a fool to let his guard down. Warily, he made his way to the other chair and gently sat. He stared at the man's profile for a long time. The hearth glow wove a pattern of dark and light over his pallid cheek, tipping the mustache with gold.

"Have your servant serve us wine, Crispin. It's chilly."

He turned to where Jack cowered in the corner and the boy suddenly stood to attention, looking for the flagon. He found it on the sideboard and filled two cups, serving Lancaster with a trembling hand. Crispin took the other from Jack and drank a bit of it before setting it aside. He had already had too much in the physician's chamber. He needed a clear head with Lancaster.

He watched the older man drink as he slowly sipped the fragrant liquor. Dammit, but he missed living at court! He missed the intrigues, the news, the day-to-day minutiae intimated to him in shadowed corners and even darker bedchambers.

He missed . . . this.

Crispin cleared his throat and asked the question he'd been trying to forget. "Yesterday . . . I heard that the king granted my . . . my lands to Giles de Risley."

Lancaster's face did not change. He blinked slowly. "That is true."

"Why?" He knew his voice sounded petulant but he could not restrain himself. "Why give it to him?"

"To punish you for refusing his benevolence," he said. "All of court knows that you and de Risley were rivals of a sort. Richard thought this meant that you were enemies. His hate of you is deep. I can only guess that he knew you would somehow discover it. You should be pleased that it is at least in the hands of a friend."

Crispin slumped, eyes distantly watching the flames. "But after so long. My *home,*" he murmured.

"Come now, Crispin. It has not been your home for some time. No use weeping over the past. You are the last man I expected of that. You had your chance when the king offered to give you back your name *and* your lands. Why did you refuse?"

He wouldn't look at Lancaster. "You know why."

The man huffed a sound and sat back in his chair. "Yes, I know."

They sat in silence for a time until Crispin sighed. "I need a way to get into the palace."

"Don't you rather need a way to get *out* of it?"

"God's blood!" he swore softly. "That, too. But my lord. I will need to return. I . . . I am loath to ask for your help—"

"No you're not. You're no fool, after all. Much evidence to the contrary."

Silence again.

Lancaster sighed. "By the saints, Crispin. How you put me in these situations I'll never—"

A knock on the door made them both swivel their heads.

"Uncle John?" came the all too familiar voice that stilled Crispin's heart.

"The king!" hissed Lancaster.

Crispin shot to his feet. Lancaster motioned to an alcove where an arras hung on an iron rod before it. Crispin rushed behind the tapestry just as the door opened. He tried to make himself as small as he could. God only knew where Jack was.

"Uncle John?" said Richard, coming into the room. "I heard you talking." He stopped.

Jack, Crispin thought with a curse. Crispin heard someone scrabbling across the floor and a shorter form tossed the arras aside, nearly revealing Crispin. Jack looked up at him with fear rounding his eyes.

Wonderful. This day was getting better and better.

"I wanted to discuss the move to Sheen for Advent, Uncle," said Richard. "I favor arriving on the Feast of Saint Nicholas." Crispin couldn't help himself. He very carefully moved the arras aside just enough to spy the room beyond it. Richard sported a wispy beard and mustache, not quite fully formed on his seventeen-year-old chin. He moved to the chairs by the fire and, with sparkling rings, fingered the second cup of wine.

Damn.

An eyebrow rose and Richard lifted his face to his uncle, eyes darting about the room, but he said nothing. Crispin let the arras fall back just as Richard cast an eye to the alcove. He cringed behind it wondering what he should do now. He could fall on his own dagger, he supposed. Dash his head against the stone wall, perhaps?

"Mayhap it is too late in the evening to discuss this now," said Richard. His voice was coming closer to Crispin's alcove. Crispin braced himself even as Jack traced a cross over his own forehead, eyes firmly shut, lips moving silently.

"You seem to be otherwise occupied," Richard continued. "And I thought your lady wife was elsewhere this night."

"She is, your grace."

"Oh?" By the sound of his voice, he was standing directly before the tapestry. Crispin expected it to be whisked open at any moment. He held his breath. He could not reach for his dagger as he itched to do. This was the king, after all. He would have to submit to anything Richard demanded.

The king made an impatient sound. "I do not approve," he said quietly, "of that Swynford woman."

Gaunt sputtered but said nothing. Crispin well knew why. It was an open secret that the duke had had an ongoing dalliance with Katherine Swynford for the past decade. She had been the governess to Gaunt's daughters, and when her husband died they had grown close. Crispin had even talked with Lancaster once about it in disapproving tones. He could still feel the lump he received on his head for his trouble.

"The sanctity of the marriage bond must not be compromised," said Richard in a courtly tenor. "The Lady Constance deserves better."

"Forgive me, sire," said Gaunt, his voice tight. "But this is not the crown's affair."

"Is it *your* affair, Uncle? Of course it is. But any form of scandal in my court cannot be tolerated. May I suggest," he said walking away from the arras, "that she not accompany us to Sheen for Christmas."

There was a long pause until Gaunt finally said, "As you wish, sire."

"Well then." Crispin heard Richard take a seat and settle in. God's blood! Was he *ever* to get out of the palace this night?

"I want my barons there. But I do not wish to discuss any weighty matters while in residence, Uncle John. I rely on you to keep my counselors at bay. I want the queen to enjoy herself. And she cannot do so when my brow is furrowed. No, this is the season for joviality. And with God's blessings, we might at last have an heir to look forward to. I've paid enough for that damnable Jewish physician. Let us hope he is worth his salt."

Lancaster still said nothing. Richard must have gestured for his own wine, because Lancaster tugged at the arras, showing his reddened face to Crispin and Jack. "Boy, serve the wine."

Jack gave Crispin a desperate look before he was dragged from the alcove by the duke. Crispin heard his stumbling steps as he retrieved the wine for the king.

"God's wounds, Uncle John. Where by the blessed Mother did you get this wretched child to serve you? He looks like a beggar."

"Hmpf," said Lancaster. They fell silent as they drank.

"Come, boy," said Richard. "More wine. And do try not to spill it on my shoes this time. I could have you skinned and made into my slippers."

Crispin cringed when he heard wine splattering on the floor. Jack choked out a sob.

"Now, now, Nephew. You're frightening the child. There, there. I'll take that. Go back to your cot."

Jack scurried around the tapestry, his hands over his face. He was trembling, and Crispin put his arm around his shoulders to calm him.

"An unusual locale for your beggar servant, Uncle John. I do not recall a cot being there before."

"My lady wife often changes the arrangements in these lodgings, sire. I can barely keep up."

"Hmm. Perhaps you should keep the tapestries open. After all, *you* rule your household, do you not?"

"I prefer them closed, sire."

"Do you? Are there more servants you would shield from me, Uncle?"

"Not at all. I have no secrets from you, Nephew."

"No? Then open that tapestry."

Crispin flattened himself against the wall. He and Jack exchanged grim expressions.

Steps approached and the duke grasped the arras. Crispin held his breath. He stared at the flat, smooth nails on Gaunt's fingers, the golden rings gleaming with a cold light.

Fingers tensed on the thick cloth, ready to throw it back when Richard said lightly, "Never mind." The duke's hand stayed. But Crispin saw the merest tremble in the cloth. "It's late," Richard went on in a satisfied tone. *Did Richard never tire of games?* thought Crispin. But even as the king scowled at the heavy drapery, he confirmed Crispin's judgment of him when he said, "Unless you care for a game of chess?"

"Is the queen abed, then?" asked Lancaster, voice steady.

As expected, he heard Richard rise immediately. "Perhaps I should get back to her. She does hate these English winters. She is convinced there is a draft in her chamber. I can find no evidence of it. But women can be foolish."

Lancaster remained silent.

The king's steps retreated to the door. Lancaster walked in longer strides to head him off and opened it for him. Richard paused. "Good night, Uncle. And heed my advice. Do not soil your marriage bed with a momentary dalliance. Take heart from my example. I dote on my wife and she is ever loyal to me. Never give your spouse cause to betray you."

"Yes, sire. That is good advice. God give you rest."

The door whined wider for an instant before it closed with a solid thud.

Crispin waited. He knew Lancaster would need a moment to compose himself. With a racing heart, Crispin realized he needed a moment as well.

The arras was cast aside and Gaunt glowered down. "Get you and your miserable servant out of my sight!"

"Gladly, your grace. And what of my return?"

"Damn you, Crispin. Don't you know when to surrender?"

He shuffled his feet. "The murders, my lord, of innocent children. They were found floating in the Thames. Defiled and mutilated. I cannot let it lie. I won't."

"Children? You never said anything about children. When? How?"

So now you ask. "I would have mentioned it before, my lord, but you seemed reluctant to talk to me."

"And so I am. But this is a different matter. Children, you say?"

"Yes. Four since Michaelmas."

"Four?" He seemed genuinely appalled. Crispin heartened. He knew he had won. "Why have I heard nothing of this?"

"I am . . . surprised you did not know."

"These sheriffs keep their tongues cleaved to their mouths." Lancaster stroked his mustache. His eyes wandered and landed on the tear-streaked Jack. "I suppose . . . you will need a way back in."

Crispin stood before him, his hand still firmly pressed to Jack's heaving shoulder as the boy tried to master his emotions.

"Perhaps," said the duke, eyes toward the fire, "I shall send livery to you. Do you still reside . . . where you did before?"

Crispin snorted. The man could not even bring himself to say "the Shambles." "Yes, my lord."

"Good. Then we shall send it to you there. Handle it with care, Guest. You see how close the king is."

"Indeed."

"Then go. Take your boy and begone." Crispin bowed and Jack followed suit, still trembling and sniffling. He reached the door when the duke called out to him. "Crispin," he said. The hearth flared behind him, throwing his shadow across the floor toward the door as if it were fleeing. His voice met Crispin at the doorposts. "Be careful."

He looked at Lancaster, thinking for not the first time that this might be the last instance he set eyes upon him. He bowed again. "Always, my lord."

He opened the door a crack and looked out, wishing that the cressets were extinguished. Darkness would have helped. He pushed his hood up, pulled Jack's up over his head, and yanked the dazed boy with him into the corridor.

He kept his head down, his cloak tight around him, and nearly dragged Jack through the long corridors. A guard stood at one archway but there was no one by the door of St. Stephen's chapel. Since the way to the Great Hall was effectively blocked, he decided that the better part would be to go through the chapel and out the cloister.

They slipped in. The chapel was dark and only the merest moonlight shined on the tall, narrow bands of stained-glass windows in the apse. Stealing across the checkered floor, Crispin stumbled into the frozen form of Jack, stalled in the center of the nave.

When he looked down, he saw the boy's eyes slowly rise up the tall columns to the vaulted ceiling with its painted stars, the rows of shields on either side, the jeweled stained glass giving color to the dark gray of the chapel. His shiny lips hung open, jaw slack as his gaze rose and rose. Though at any other instance Crispin might be pleased to give Jack a tour, now was definitely *not* the time.

He pushed at his shoulder. "Come along," he whispered, just enough to urge the boy's feet and set him to moving again.

They escaped into a passage between the cloister and the chapel that led to an outer door and they crept into the shadows of the gardens along the banks of the Thames until they reached a wall and climbed it to the outer courtyard. They walked brusquely to the main gate and down the lane toward Charing Cross. No one stopped them. No one questioned them. No one raised the alarm.

He remembered to breathe once they passed the Cross and he stood in the snow momentarily to regain his bearings. It was late. The curfew was now in force and the gates of London were surely locked tight for the night. But this did not trouble him. He knew ways around that.

"Do we *have* to return to the palace, Master?"

He looked down at the boy. His voice was a pitiful murmur of sniffling and whimpering. "Yes, Jack. At least I do. If it frightens you too much, I will not demand it."

The boy wiped his nose with his sleeve several times and peered up sorrowfully. His lashes glistened in the pale moonlight. "You can't go alone."

"I have been alone a long time, Jack. Never fear."

"But . . . what if you're caught? I'd never find out until it was far too late."

"Too late for what?"

"For me to rescue you!"

A warm sensation bubbling in his chest surprised him, and he smiled at Jack's sincerity. "That may be so," he said gently. "Then perhaps, if you will, you should come along to keep watch over me."

Jack sighed heavily with the exasperation of the put upon. "I think I'd better, then. I'd never forgive m'self if something happened to you, sir."

Crispin clutched the boy's shoulder affectionately before dropping it away. He filled his lungs with cold air.

The curtain of clouds above had opened, revealing a painfully clear night of tight stars and black sky, reminding him a little of St. Stephen's vaulted ceiling. The recent snow dampened the sounds, if sounds there were, for most of Westminster had gone to their beds. The Thames lapped the stony banks, and boats rose and fell with creaks and groans, but all was still.

They began their long walk home back down the Strand.

After a time, Jack raised his head. Beneath his hood, his cloud of breath lifted into the night. "Master, why does France have Jews and England does not?"

"A fair question, Jack. How am I to answer it simply? Our King Edward I exiled them from England."

"Why?"

"Because of usury and other despicable acts."

"Oh." Silence for a time, until . . . "What's usury?"

"Money lending at interest."

"What's int—?"

"Paying a fee for taking a loan."

"Why would—?"

"Jack, just understand that it caused a great deal of trouble."

"Oh." A pause. "But that physician seems like a kind man." His brows furrowed at that, as if not quite believing his own words. "Though I ain't saying the same for his dog of a son." His face was more at ease at this justified sentiment. "Yet the father *seems* fair enough. Maybe it ain't all Jews what caused the trouble."

Crispin said nothing. How to explain to the boy that men deceive, even the ones who seem benign? And yet . . . He relied on his gut instincts to carry him through many a difficult situation. And his gut told him that Jacob was the man he seemed to be. Jack's innocent assertion was more pointed than the boy could have imagined. Crispin had dealt with Jews before in the Holy Land. Suspicious merchants and obsequious money lenders. He had naturally seen them in France in Avignon, as there they were free to do what they liked. He had assumed they were all as he imagined, all he had been taught.

He didn't like the direction his thoughts were taking. He preferred, instead, to cast his thoughts on the murderous Julian, for it was easier to find evil in that narrow-eyed youth. He was more like the Jew he pictured in his mind's eye. That lad was the one Crispin could not trust. His wounded arm throbbed with the thinking of it.

The quiet settled around them as they trudged back to London. The soft sounds of ice crunched beneath their boots. They passed Temple Bar and headed up Fleet Street before they could make the turn northward. They'd have to enter London by Newgate, and though Crispin hated to do it, he knew it was the only—

Wait. What was *that*?

He halted and reached out to grasp Jack's cloak and pulled him to a stop.

Jack didn't speak, only looked up from his shadowing hood, puzzled. Crispin held up a hand for him to listen. They both did, cocking their heads.

A steady thud coming their way. Hard, heavy footfalls. The Watch? Perhaps a man carrying a heavy burden. That would certainly have slowed his steps. Or it could be someone injured . . .

The chill at the familiar sound rumbled up his core. It sounded like . . .

Out of the shadows emerged a large figure. Jack gasped and Crispin froze, staring. The figure stopped where it was, standing between two close buildings. A narrow band of moonlight limned one edge of the hulking man but not enough to reveal his face. He had unnaturally wide shoulders and a seemingly small head.

They stood staring at one another for several heartbeats, little more than a stone's throw apart.

All at once, the man turned and slipped quickly back into the shadows.

It seemed to break the spell and Crispin took off at a run. But when he got to the spot the man had stood, there was no sign of him at all.

A dog barked somewhere in the distance. The lonely sound only enhanced the isolated feeling of the empty street.

Jack was behind Crispin clutching his cloak. "Where'd he go?" His voice was breathless.

"I don't know."

"Was it . . . was it the same man from before?"

"It . . . might have been." Crispin truly wasn't certain.

"God blind me!"

And if it were, what did it mean? Crispin peered deep into the shadows, willing his ears to hear any faraway footsteps, anything that could yield a clue. He barely noticed Jack dropping to his knees into the shadowy snow.

The lad scrabbled about and gasped. Crispin could not see in the dim light what he was up to, but he could detect the boy trembling.

"What is it, Jack?" The boy didn't answer right away but he had something in his hand. He leaned over him, trying to see. "Jack? What is it? What have you found?"

Slowly, he rose. He was looking into his hand. In the darkness, Crispin tried to make it out. Was it a stone?

Jack was still trembling. "Holy Mother protect us," he whispered. He lifted his hand for Crispin to see but the dim light made it impossible. "M-master," he said.

"What *is* it, Jack?" He grasped the boy's hand and yanked it higher.

"See, Master Crispin. Clay!"

7

IMPOSSIBLE. YET HADN'T CRISPIN witnessed many impossible things in the last few years? Was this not merely one more?

This was madness. There was a perfectly logical explanation for the presence of clay. His mind was simply having difficulty coming up with a plausible reason. He motioned for Jack to clean the clay from his hands.

"It's the *Golem*!" rasped Jack, voicing both their thoughts and pushing his soiled palms down his cloak. "Holy Mother of God!" He began a litany of poorly mouthed prayers.

"It is no such thing!" Crispin blew a cloudy breath, one hand on his dagger hilt, the other holding his cloak closed. He peered again into the darkness, up the street and down. If he had not seen the man for himself, Crispin wouldn't have believed he had been there. Except for those droplets of clay upon the snow like blood. That damnable clay.

"Let us get back to London, Jack. We need our beds."

He pressed ahead but Jack still shivered in the snow, looking behind.

"Jack! JACK!"

A flicker of light sputtered to life in a window and its shutter opened a crack. Crispin grabbed Jack by his hood and dragged him into the shadows. A figure leaned out of the window and looked about before shivering and shutting it again.

"Come along!" he whispered.

He tramped heavily over the crunchy snow. After a time he no longer had need to drag Jack. The boy cleaved tight to him and they walked within the same shadow under the disappearing moonlight.

When they reached London's walls they headed north to Newgate. Jack cringed on seeing the rigid towers crawl up into the sky, frost gleaming in pale patches across its stony surface. "Master Crispin! We ain't going in there, are we?"

"It is the only gate I am certain to be able to pass through."

"But can we pass out of it again?"

A good question. One he did not wish to ponder.

Without thinking further on it, Crispin raised his hand and knocked on the heavy wooden door. After waiting an interval he knocked again. This time he heard footfalls and a small door opened in the larger iron-clad portal. A man, face dented from sleep and wearing a skewed leather cap over scruffy hair, squinted at him. He held a clay oil lamp and pushed it forward. "Mary's blessed veil," he swore. "Master Crispin? What would you be doing here this time of night? And on the other side of the gate?"

"Trying to get in," he answered curtly.

The man shook his head. "The sheriffs have gone home, Master. They wouldn't like being sent a message at this hour."

"I do not need to speak to either sheriff. I merely have need to pass through to London."

The man scowled. "It's past curfew." But Crispin was ready with a farthing. The man's face brightened when he saw the disk in his lamplight. "Aw now! Maybe it ain't so far past!" His dirty fingers closed over the coin and snatched it from Crispin's hand. With a mocking bow, he stepped aside. "Right this way, Master."

Crispin urged Jack in ahead of him. He stumbled over the stone threshold. Crispin took the lead after that, trying not to think of what lay above him in the towers or below in the murky cells.

They reached the London side in a matter of moments. There, the sleepy porter gave Crispin a cursory glance before he grunted to his feet. "It's past curfew," he muttered.

"I know," said Crispin. He waited while the man seemed to sample almost every key on his ring before opening the small door. "Mind the Watch," cautioned the porter and gestured into the black hole.

Crispin looked and saw no one along the dark avenue. No lantern that would indicate the Watch, no footsteps, and definitely no hulking figures.

Jack poked his head out and looked, too, likely wondering the same thing.

Crispin motioned him to follow and they hurried through the battered snow down Newgate Market to the Shambles.

ONCE HOME, JACK STOKED the fire until they were warmed through, then he banked it and they settled down for the night, but a disturbed sleep followed. When morning finally crept into the small room with gray light, Crispin rubbed the exhaustion from his crusty eyes. A quick glance into the straw-piled corner told him that Jack was not there. *Where did that boy go?* he wondered. A kettle hanging over the fire bubbled with something smelling like food and he threw his legs over the side of the bed and curled the blanket over his shoulders to lean toward the hearth and peer into the pot.

Turnip porridge. He cursed and rose, reaching for the spoon and the wooden bowl that was waiting for him by the hearth. He tipped the damnable porridge into it, blew on it, letting the steam warm his face, before he took a tentative sip. Awful. He downed it quickly.

Crispin heated some water for his shave and quickly finished his toilet, thinking all the while how he was to approach asking his questions at court.

With these murders somehow tied to those missing parchments, they seemed to be beyond his ability to solve. He knew from past experience that without reliable witnesses, murders often passed without justice. A murder in a parish happened when two angry individuals fought. Or one party tried to cheat the other, or some other misfortune that was well known to all the inhabitants. It was easy for someone to point the finger on well-known circumstances.

But the secret murder of children . . . This had gone unremarked for months! If witnesses there were, they were silent on it. Perhaps they lived in fear of retribution. Or had to protect someone.

This theft, on the other hand. Now this was something else, something Crispin could possibly sink his teeth into. A man invariably boasted about the thing he stole, giving himself away. But even if the thief did not boast, *someone* surely noted that another party was in possession of such a thing. A servant, perhaps? Yes, he would have to find servants and speak with them. And if indeed this theft was tied to murder then he would nab the miscreant himself.

Crispin waited impatiently for either Jack's arrival or the servant from Lancaster. But when neither made an appearance by late morning, he grabbed his cloak and headed out. He could still talk to someone who might have seen something down by the river, someone he had missed before.

He trod quickly down the narrow stair and walked out onto the muddy street, heading toward Westminster.

He pulled his cloak closer. Damn but it was cold! Saint Nicholas' Feast was close and that meant that another Christmas would come and go. Another solitary Christmas. Gilbert and Eleanor had asked him on more than one occasion to celebrate a humble Christmas dinner with them at the Boar's Tusk. He had always declined.

The memories were too dear of warm feasts in the company of his fellow barons and lords. The Yule log would burn bright and hot in those impossibly large braziers set all about the Great Hall in Westminster. The warmth and camaraderie would keep the winter at bay. Roasted boar's heads would be served to one and all, along with cheese pies, pasties dripping with gravy, loaves of warm, white bread. Bittern and quail swimming in rich broth. And puddings with Spanish raisins along with honeyed cakes.

He was certain the fare that Gilbert and Eleanor served would be delicious. But it would be small portions of goose and cheese and perhaps coarse bread and a crumb pudding along with their sharp tavern wine, never tasting quite as good as he recalled from casks he had enjoyed from Gasconne.

No. He could not bring himself to go.

It began to snow. Not gentle, lacy flakes, but melting blobs of ice, smacking his cheek like a challenge from an opponent. He almost missed the carriage as it lumbered along the road in the opposite direction. A fine draft horse, a driver, the flaps secured tight on the windows to the barrel-shaped conveyance. Just another rich lord or lady taking a shortcut down Newgate Market.

The carriage slowed and then stopped. Crispin passed it without a second glance until out of the corner of his eye, a window flap rose.

"You there!"

Crispin kept walking, ducking into his hood so that the leather would take the brunt of the slushy flakes.

"You there!" said the voice more sternly.

A shadowy figure through the window beckoned to him. Crispin looked over his shoulder just to check that it was, indeed, himself the man wanted, and then he stopped. He stepped forward but kept a decent distance. "You called me?"

"Are you . . . Crispin Guest?"

Like a cloak, a sense of caution enveloped him. "Who asks?"

A chuckle, deep and melodious. "May I offer you a ride?"

Crispin eyed the driver, who stared straight ahead, never looking down at him. He wore no livery, gave no clue as to the inhabitant of the carriage below him.

The doorway of the carriage lay open, a dark rectangle offering nothing. Were there more men within? An ambush, perhaps?

He studied what he could see of the shadowy face in the window. "You are not going in my direction," Crispin offered.

The chuckle again. "We can circle about. Whither do you go?"

"To Westminster."

"Mmm. Get in."

Crispin stood his ground, the snow piling around his feet. "Who are you?"

"I would never have guessed that the great Tracker was so cautious."

"Nor so foolhardy." The man was baiting him. Was it worth it?

The gloved fingers on the sill tapped a drumbeat before gripping the side. "Get in," he said again, sternly but still somewhat friendly.

Swearing under his breath, Crispin edged toward the doorway, hesitated one moment more, and then climbed in.

As soon as he sat, the carriage jerked and started again. He saw no one but the man. There was no attendant. No guard, save the driver.

The carriage's shadows covered most of him, but as Crispin's eyes adjusted to the darkness, he detected more of the stranger. A man perhaps younger than Crispin, bundled in a black, fur-trimmed gown. A high collar came up under his clean-shaven chin. Blue eyes considered him under lazy lids. A felt cap covered his fair hair. He seemed small in his clothing, as if he were made of sticks, not flesh. He said nothing as Crispin studied him. The carriage pitched and rolled over the rutted street. It wasn't a comfortable ride by any means, but it was better than walking. Just barely.

Crispin clutched the seat and sighed. "Well then? I am here. As you bid."

The man leaned back and regarded Crispin leisurely. He smiled. Even as the carriage bounced and he along with it, he didn't look ruffled. "You're a strange man, Guest."

Crispin shifted on his seat, looking for a comfortable spot on the scant cushion. He couldn't find one. "As you say."

He chuckled again. "And you don't even bother to deny it. You don't think that strange?"

"What is strange is this conversation. You have not yet introduced yourself, sir. Or is it 'my lord'?"

A gloved finger traced down his chin. The ring on it bore no signet.

Crispin waited. He glanced out the doorway and saw that they were now headed for Westminster. He sat back. "Clearly there is something you want of me."

"Clearly."

Amused silence emanated from across the carriage. He clenched his jaw. If there was one thing Crispin couldn't stomach, it was the playing of these games. He shifted again, making a show of impatience. But the stranger appeared to have all the time in the world.

Crispin started when the man spoke again even though he had been waiting for that very thing.

"I believe you are one of the few men who can appreciate order."

Games, then. "I doubt I am one of a few. Most men crave order. God in his Heaven. The king on his throne. His lords around him. Even the lowliest villein appreciates order knowing that all is well."

The man drew his hands together like a prayer, touching his lips with his fingertips. But he said nothing.

"I know you find this strange coming from the likes of me—" Crispin began, trying to bridge the unhelpful silence.

"No, I do not. As I said, I knew you could appreciate . . . order."

"And be wary of the lack of it?"

"Indeed."

Their exchange was rather like moves across a chessboard; nothing to be revealed too soon.

Crispin watched the face that did not change. Perhaps his questions needed to be couched like chess moves. "And what lack of order, pray, must I be wary of?" he tried.

The smile was back. "A lack of order can be very bad. For a parish, for a kingdom. Those who do not follow the order defy God. Would you not agree?"

"The Almighty molds our lives. Those who rule over us are anointed to do so. Those who defy this order . . ." Crispin offered a wry smile, "suffer."

"Indeed, Master Guest. You know this well. A pity you could not have reminded yourself of that fact before you committed treason." Crispin's smile faded, but the man went on. "It is no matter. You have served London well in the years following your appalling disgrace."

Much thanks, thought Crispin with a sneer.

"We must have order," the man went on. "Without it, we are like a castle whose walls are undermined. The foundations crack, the walls topple, and the enemy rushes in."

Crispin waved a gesture of agreement. He tried to surmise the man from his clothes, but there was nothing to indicate his affiliation or family name. Nor did his person boast of any parish fraternity. His pouch was simple, his girdle nondescript, his dagger plain. He was wealthy enough to own a carriage, but why not the usual display of his family's arms all over it? Why was the driver not liveried? And why were there no other servants abroad with him?

The man also wore no sword. He did not feel the need to arm himself then. In a land where even the king wore a sword, this man had none. What manner of man did not carry a sword? Surely he could afford it, unlike Crispin who felt the lack of a sword daily as if a limb had been hacked off. The man was also young, though his age seemed indeterminate. He was younger than Crispin, older than Jack. At times, when he turned his head just so, he seemed quite young indeed, but at other times, when the dim sunlight caught his eyes, the intelligence there would seem to mold him into something a great deal older.

"At any rate," said the man, "I want you to continue to do as you are doing."

"As I am doing?"

Those blue eyes continued to stare. "Yes. Your investigation." He polished the stone on his ring with his other glove, studying the effect. "Of the murders."

A spike of something hot lanced through Crispin's chest but his face remained cool. "What murders?"

The man threw his head back and laughed. Crispin crossed his arms over his chest and waited for the laughter to subside. "I was told to expect that from you," said the man. "I am pleased to see you do not disappoint." He smoothed out the cloth on his lap. "And the missing parchments, of course. I expect that you shall find them soon. And when you do, I shall be most grateful if you return them to me instead of the old Jew."

The man seemed to know far more about Crispin's doings than Crispin was comfortable with. "Forgive me." Crispin leaned forward and rested an arm on his thigh, keeping a steady eye on the man. "I think it best you tell me who you are. Now." It was a risk. The man was obviously wealthy. And his accent was not lowborn as so many rich merchants and alderman were, though it was distinctly foreign. From the north, perhaps? If the man were a nobleman, Crispin's tone might get him tossed out. Or worse.

Instead of some angry retort, the man merely looked out the window. "Oh. We are here."

Crispin twisted his neck, looking out the bright doorway. The carriage stood at the gates of the palace. "How did you know this was my destination?"

But the man's face was now closed. The finger ran softly over his lower lip.

Crispin snorted and rose, keeping his shoulders bowed for the short ceiling. He waited. The man was as tight as a portcullis. The whole matter annoyed. He was being manipulated and he had had quite enough of that. "Well," said Crispin sullenly. "I thank you for the ride at least."

"Not at all. I suppose you will need a surety from me." He reached for the bag at his belt, took out a small pouch, and tossed it to Crispin. Crispin caught it one-handed and felt the many coins within. But before the man could blink, Crispin tossed it back. The man stared at the pouch where it landed in his lap.

"I know you not. Nor your reasons for hiring me. When you wish to make that clear—as well as your name, sir—contact me again. I can be found on the Shambles."

The man smiled. "I know well where you live." The phrase unexpectedly chilled. The man took up the pouch and stared at it, still smiling. He did not look toward Crispin when he dismissed him with a chuckle. "Fare you well, Crispin Guest. God keep you."

"And you." He stepped out of the carriage. He turned to ask one more time, but it jerked ahead, rambling back down St. Margaret's Street toward London. *What the devil?*

Who was that man? And how did he know of the murders when even the duke of Lancaster had not? And how the hell was he privy to the missing parchments? Did he, too, wish to make his own Golem . . . or had he already?

Briefly, he considered following the carriage, but gave up the idea as fanciful. What could he discover if the man would not even deliver his name? Besides, the broad-shouldered carriage driver did not look to be one who would allow such liberties.

He tugged at his cotehardie to straighten its creases and scanned the streets. Did this man in the carriage know Jacob of Provençal? A chill rippled over him as he recalled where he had spotted the strange figure from last night. The physician was certain that this was his fabled Golem, but in the light of day, Crispin wasn't convinced. True, he had seen the figure with his own eyes, but eyes can be deceived or misdirected. It had been late, cold. One's imagination can thrive in the fertile ground of shadows and anxiety. What they had seen was not what they had thought. But Jacob was convinced it was. Why? He held much store by his Jewish magic, of course. Crispin shook his head at it. Gullible. His thoughts fell again toward the son, the one who could not be as trusted as the father.

Crispin swore, causing a young boy carrying a basket of eggs beside him to turn to give him the eye. *Idiot,* Crispin told himself. He should have searched their room! Well, there would be time for that once Lancaster made good on his promise to send that livery. If the duke could be trusted.

He sighed. Intrigues. They bedeviled him wherever he went, it seemed. The only thing worth trusting was facts. Facts stared you in the face. They did not try to deceive. Yet even facts could be twisted. It took a judicious eye to winnow out what was fact from lies.

So the facts of the case were these: four dead boys. He could only make a judgment about the fourth boy, having witnessed the body for himself; he was a beggar or a servant. The other three he did not know, for the Coroner's notes did not take such details into account. No child had been reported missing, which meant that these boys were alone and unwanted. But *was* that the case? Might it be that these boys came from afar and would not be missed for some time? If this were true, then their identities may never be known. Facts.

Second, Jacob of Provençal claimed that stolen magic parchments unleashed a murderer into their midst! At this, Crispin scoffed.

From the Coroner's rolls, he knew about the incisions on the abdomens of the boys and the removal of their entrails, though not all the same ones were missing. It seemed to Crispin that someone for some reason wanted these prizes. Someone very like a physician. Someone like the peevish Julian. A would-be physician. An angry young man with a purpose.

Surely their deaths were to hide sodomy. A would-be physician might use their deaths as an excuse for vivisection. And for other nefarious reasons. Crispin grimaced at the thought.

And now this nobleman in the carriage. What did he know of the murders? Too much.

A sick sensation swam in his gut. Had Crispin been entertained by a vicious murderer?

Many facts. None of them made the least bit of sense yet. But they would. He swore they would.

First things first. Jacob and his Jewish magic troubled him. It might be the root of all their ills or it might be only a foolish diversion. There was one person who could give him some perspective and some proper information on that troubled people, and that was Nicholas de Litlyngton, abbot of Westminster Abbey.

Crispin turned on his heel and headed toward the church.

8

WESTMINSTER ABBEY LAY ACROSS a snowy expanse of courtyard, spiny with peaks and arches, as prickly as a hedgehog. The white snow drifted into the mason's details of carved stone, ledges, and trefoils, defining their textures and curves.

Crispin debated with himself whether he should enter the church at the north entrance or back by the chilly cloister. The idea that the church might be a bit warmer won out, and he trod up the snowy path toward the Norman portico. Inside was dark, but the large rose and clerestory windows offered pale, colored light as if through the iridescent wings of a mayfly.

The nave was not empty. It teemed with men of all stripes. Though there were some kneeling by the distant rood screen, others paced across the shining stone floor. Business was flourishing. Clerks, scribes, and lawyers eager for employment from merchants and nobles, wore away the tiles in their quest. One clerk looked up hopefully before his eyes shadowed over Crispin's threadbare cotehardie and flicked away again.

The air smelled of old incense and must. A draft made the open nave cold, flickering the candles, but the interior was not as cold as the naked world without. Crispin's eyes adjusted and then searched the arched nave for a cassock.

The columns were surrounded by scaffolding. It seemed every great cathedral in England was being reworked and made anew, a caterpillar sloughing off last year's skin in hopes of emerging as a butterfly. Crispin supposed the money was well spent, but there seemed to him to be the same number of beggars at the almsdoor. Funny how he never gave it much thought before, when he was donating his coin purse for a chapel to be built at Sheen. A chapel in which others, Giles de Risley among them, now prayed.

The columns and pillars of stone shot up into the dim, vaulted ceiling. Taller than any forest, it was a feat to be admired. The mason's art was more than craft. It was too bad Crispin had not been apprenticed so. *I'd never be out of work if I had been.*

His eyes scanned again down the nave and peered past the pillars into the wooden choir with its own carved spires. There he saw a monk lighting candles, and headed toward him.

"Good Brother," he said, delaying the monk as he raised his silver candle lighter. The monk turned to him. He was young, perhaps little more than a boy. His hood was drawn low over his brow. Brown eyes glittered with surprise that he should be addressed. He said nothing, but waited for Crispin to speak.

"I need to see Abbot Nicholas. Could you take me to him?"

The monk's eyes widened. Crispin expected it. He interrupted what would surely have been a sputtered excuse. "My Lord Abbot and I are old friends. He will see me. I will tarry here if it please you. Tell him Crispin Guest awaits."

The monk could not seem to argue with this. He closed his mouth and blew out the wick at the end of his lighter. Scurrying down the aisle toward the south transept, he looked back once. Crispin followed, knowing that the young cleric would return this way. He strolled to the door at the crotch of the south transept. Three large quatrefoils within circles of stone reared above the arched entrance, upheld by lancet arches. The door would be barred. He would wait. He had no doubt the youth, or another monk, would be back.

It didn't take long for a familiar face to unlock the door and approach. Brother Eric smiled from under his cowl. "Master Crispin," he said. "*Benedicte.*"

"Thanks be to God," Crispin replied and took his hand in welcome, hiding a wince when his wounded arm flexed. "May I speak a few words with the abbot?"

Brother Eric nodded and gestured for Crispin to follow. They entered the cloister and ambled down the colonnade, walking side by side. Their steps echoed back to them and bounced from carrel to empty carrel. The cloister garden was a tangle of dead sticks and twisted, brown vines. All lay dormant now that winter was upon them, though the stillness faltered under the flitting of bramblings that rustled the branches and pecked at the wattle fences, their orange breasts lending a bit of color to the lifeless undergrowth.

The way was familiar to Crispin and, shoulder to shoulder, they trotted up the chilled steps to the abbot's quarters.

Brother Eric drew ahead of Crispin and knocked lightly on the abbot's door. A soft reply later, and the monk opened the heavy oak, allowing Crispin in before he shut it after him, leaving them alone.

"Crispin!" The old abbot's face lit and he made a move to skirt his worktable, but Crispin motioned for him to remain. Instead, he met the man with the table between them and extended his hand. "My Lord Abbot."

"It is good to see you, friend Crispin. Shall we have wine?"

Eagerly, he retreated to the sideboard where he knew Abbot Nicholas kept French wine in a flagon. He poured two goblets of the golden liquid and returned, offering one to the abbot before they both sat. Putting the metal goblet to his lips, Crispin closed his eyes and inhaled the sweet fruit before his mouth tasted. When he opened his eyes again, the abbot was smiling at him. "Good, eh? I just received this shipment from Spain. I favor the sweetness of this variety."

"Quite good," said Crispin, savoring the flavors exploding on his tongue.

They sipped at their goblets for a few moments before Abbot Nicholas sat back in his chair and sighed. "I have not seen you in some time, Crispin. Our chess game awaits."

The tall windows showered a rainbow of light onto the chessboard, illuminating chess pieces that they had left a month before. Slowly, Crispin sat in his chair on the black side and Nicholas seated himself opposite. The abbot took a short quaff of his wine, set it aside on a table, and rubbed his hands. "I believe it is your turn."

Crispin smiled. "This game will be over in nine moves."

Nicholas chortled. "Indeed? Pride, Master Guest, is one of the Seven Deadly Sins."

"It is not pride, my Lord Abbot, but the truth. 'Plato is dear to me, but dearer still is Truth.'"

The abbot's eyes sparkled. "Your Aristotle seems more dear to you. It is not wise to put your faith in one voice, and a pagan one at that, Crispin. 'Beware the man of one book.' So says Saint Thomas Aquinas."

Crispin gave him a sidelong look before reaching over the pieces to move his knight.

"Always you move the knight," muttered Nicholas, his watery eyes scanning the players.

"The knight is an enterprising fellow."

Nicholas quirked an eyebrow before returning his gaze to the board. "No doubt." He dithered his hand over several pieces before deciding on his bishop. "But I fear you did not come here to simply play a game of chess with me, much as it would cheer me to think it."

Crispin could not help the frown that shifted his mouth. "No,

Nicholas. Would that I had the leisure." He moved his knight again, keeping his eyes downcast. He felt the man staring at him.

"What then, I wonder?" Both hands clutched at the board's edge until he started to tap each finger randomly. "I wonder what you are up to?" The idle conversation seemed to be more about the board game than Crispin's presence. He smiled when the old abbot finally moved a piece.

Crispin took his knight and slid it into place. "Grave matters, Nicholas." He leaned forward and said quietly, "Have you heard of the murdered boy found in the Thames a few days ago?"

Nicholas crossed himself. "It grieves me to hear of it. But it does my heart good to know that you are investigating. You are, are you not?"

"I am. But there are . . . other considerations. I came for information about matters I know little of."

"God grant that I can give you the right and proper information you need," he said before moving a pawn.

Crispin stared at it and gauged the board again. "Just so. What can you tell me about Jews and Jewish religious customs?"

Nicholas drew back as if burned. "*Jews?* What tidings are these? Do you think Jews are to blame? But there are none left on these shores."

"That may be true, but I have reason to believe the murder might involve these people nonetheless."

Nicholas took a deep breath, but his otherwise pale skin blushed in agitation. "All of the Jews did not leave with King Edward's exile, you know. Many took up Christ in the waters of baptism and were allowed to remain. They live in the House of Converts. At least, the newer converts do."

"And where do they come from?"

"The occasional traveler and merchant. Those who stay must convert." Nicholas frowned. "There have been rumors," said Nicholas almost to himself. "Well, what does it matter? It was so long ago. Even so, there are those within the Church who—" His brows rose and he appeared to remember Crispin's presence. He resettled himself and offered a brief smile. "There are even things I am not at liberty to discuss with you, no matter how you use your wiles on me."

"Wiles, Nicholas? Have I used my wiles on you?"

"Many a time, you fox."

But Crispin now pondered what Nicholas had not said, trying to ferret out what it might mean. He kept his features neutral.

"You wish to know of their customs," said the abbot. "But to understand that, you must understand why they were banished from these shores in the first place. I can assure you, it was wholly justified. Have you never heard the tales of Saint William of Norwich or Saint Hugh of Lincoln?"

"These saints are familiar to me," said Crispin vaguely. He pushed one of his pawns forward. "But I confess, I do not recall the details."

"I shall enlighten you, then. William of Norwich was a very devout boy, singing the praises of our Lady both night and day. He was a tanner's apprentice and was forced to frequent the Jews' Street in Norwich. His holy praises angered the Jews and they rose up as one and slew him, tossing his body upon a dungheap. But even in death, he continued to sing the *Alma Redemptoris Mater.* This was his first miracle. The Jews were accused of his torture and murder and many were slain that day in just retribution." He toyed with his castle and, finally realizing it was in his hand, set it back on its square.

Crispin frowned at the board. He could well see how the townsfolk would be angered by such an act, but it was not well to rise up as a mob. Best to let the authorities handle the situation. The crown was, no doubt, unsettled by the affair. "And what of this other, this Saint Hugh?"

"Little Saint Hugh. Another child, an innocent. Slain by a

Jewish child who confessed that it was the custom to crucify a Christian boy once a year at the Passover."

"I thought Little Saint Hugh was found in a well."

"Perhaps he was crucified and then tossed into the well."

"If this was so, then why were there not more stories of Christian boys crucified?"

Crispin watched Nicholas move his castle. "What makes you think there were not?"

"Because I have never heard of such."

"I am certain the stories are somewhere." Nicholas shook his head. "Those were difficult times, Crispin. I am not sorry they are over. It is best that Jews remain exiled from England so the taint of usury and godlessness can no longer thrive here."

No, indeed, thought Crispin with a scowl. *Godless murder and thievery certainly do not thrive in London*. But Abbot Nicholas had gone on, heedless of his guest's discomfiture.

"The edict gave them ample time to prepare, to sell their lands and gather their goods." Crispin could well imagine. Selling their land to Englishmen who could demand any price, knowing the Jew *had* to sell and *had* to leave. What bargains there must have been that summer of 1290.

Not that he was sympathizing. He, too, found the matter distasteful. The image in his mind of the greedy Jew and now the blood-lusting Jew ran deep, even though, he admitted grudgingly, it did not complement the portrait of the benign physician who had hired him.

"In Avignon, the Jews thrive," Crispin heard himself saying.

Nicholas shrugged. "Yes. But ways are different in France."

"Would you send them packing again to some other place or simply slay them all?"

"I do not like to speak of death. And our venerable Saint Bernard of Clairvaux once said, 'Whosoever touches a Jew to take his life, is like one who harms Jesus himself.'"

"Hmpf," said Crispin. "Do you believe that?" Nicholas shrugged again. "A bitter potion, then. One cannot slay them and one cannot live beside them. What, then, should one do?"

"Allow the crown to deal with it, as it has."

"Let it be someone else's problem?"

"Precisely."

Grunting his reply, Crispin moved his knight, grasped the goblet into his hand, and took a sip before he declared, "Check and mate."

"What?" Nicholas's head swung back and forth as he studied each piece scattered upon the board. His frown wrinkled his forehead up to the feathery gray hair and down again to his thick brows. "Bless me!" he breathed at last. With a finger, he tipped his king and it fell to the board, rolling into the bishop and nearly toppling him. "Bless me. That was well played." He snatched up his goblet and comforted himself in the wine.

"Facts, my Lord Abbot," said Crispin and set his goblet aside. "Not pride."

Nicholas shook his head and began to replace his pieces into their proper starting points. "The oddities of their Jewish customs," he continued. "We cannot reconcile it. Do they not see that they condemn themselves for their demon ways? That they crucified our Lord was enough to tie the millstone about their necks. But to continue this atrocious sin of killing innocent boys—"

And more, thought Crispin, but he was unwilling to discuss it. "My Lord Abbot, have you ever heard of a Golem?"

"A goblin?"

"No, a *Golem*. Part of their Jewish magic."

The old man shook his head. "No, no. Best stay clear of that, Master Guest. It is unwise to mix yourself in their monstrous ways. We can little understand the mind of the Jew let alone his magic."

Frowning, Crispin agreed. Ultimately, he was not interested in their rituals. Only if such things were possible. And then he chided himself. He had never believed in its like before. Why should he toy with the notion now?

"You have given me much to contemplate," said Crispin. "These rituals of crucifixion. I wonder if any *other* torture might have been mentioned."

"I have the text of Thomas of Monmouth who related these and other tales. Would you like to borrow it?"

Crispin stood. "Very much so."

The abbot lifted himself from his chair and bustled to his shelves, looking over the leather-bound manuscripts before he found the one he wanted. Carefully, he lifted the book from its place and returned to Crispin, handing it to him. Crispin grasped it in both hands, feeling the weight of it. He missed having books. He had gathered a fair few in his library at Sheen. Many of them had been given to him by the duke of Lancaster. He knew how precious such a thing was and how much the abbot trusted him. He bowed to the old monk. "I am deeply grateful, Abbot Nicholas."

Nicholas waved him off. "Anything to find the murderer of that child." He laid his hand on the leather cover. The etched designs were dark from age. "Thomas was a contemporary of those events almost one hundred years ago. His writing is very clear."

"Thank you, Nicholas. I will take good care of this."

"I know you will. Here. Let me give you a scrip." The abbot retrieved a leather pouch hanging by its strap near the door. Crispin slipped the book inside and slung it over his shoulder, the strap cutting diagonally across his chest. "Until next time, Crispin. And perhaps I will best you on the chessboard."

Crispin glanced at the board with all its players carefully arranged to begin a new match. He smiled as he bowed again. "You can certainly try, my Lord Abbot."

* * *

ARMED WITH THIS NEW information, Crispin left the abbey and stood on the snow-pocked square. And so. There was precedent for the ritual blood-letting of Christian children by Jews. He hefted the book, thinking. Jews no longer lived in England. He didn't hold much store in Abbot Nicholas's rumors. It wouldn't be easy for Jews to hide themselves, the food they ate, or their houses of worship. Londoners lived too close together. Each parish knew the doings of each of its citizens. But Jews did live in certain areas of France and Lombardy, and Crispin had frequented those places in his travels with Lancaster. He had never heard of such murders before and certainly there would have been an outcry.

Still, his mind seized on images of the sour Julian. A ritual murder. Yes, the boy was angry enough. But if only one a year was needed, why had there been four deaths? And there was never a mention on the Coroner's rolls of signs of crucifixion in these murders, even if other unspeakable acts had been committed.

He adjusted the strap across his chest and surveyed the street. Westminster Palace lay ahead but he could not enter without the duke's livery. He had to wait for that disguise in order to speak to the servants within about any stolen parchments.

How he hated waiting.

"By the rood," said a voice behind him.

Crispin turned. A man in a splendid houppelande of rich velvet sat astride his mount, speaking to another man beside him.

"What is Crispin Guest doing so close to the palace?" said the man, staring into Crispin's narrowed eyes.

He had the presence of mind to bow to these men he did not recognize. "I was just—" he gestured toward the abbey, but never finished his sentence.

The man dismounted and the other man followed suit. His

mocking smile faded and a scowl replaced it. "You have no leave to be near the palace, Traitor Guest. For any reason."

Crispin's guard was up, his senses now attuned and sharpened to every sound, every movement around him on the street. How he hated these encounters! He didn't even know this lord's name, but it made little difference. Every knave with a shield on his arm knew that Crispin was as vulnerable as a deer. It was their little game to take a stab at him from time to time.

The man strode up to him, flanked by his amused companion and his horse. The man was dark with a close-trimmed beard, a scarlet rondelle hat with a ridiculously long liripipe tail, draped across his chest and over his shoulder, not once but twice.

His companion was young and clean-shaven like Crispin. He had the air of one who was a servant or steward, not quite the equal of his companion. His hair under his hat was the color of wheat in the rain. He was diminutive and delicate, with thin limbs and long fingers. He had the blush of an accent when he spoke quietly to the dark-haired man. Flemish?

The dark-haired lord stood toe to toe with Crispin, looking him up and down. "What mischief are you perpetrating now, Guest? Hmm? What trouble do you cause?"

"Trouble, my lord? I swear by God himself that I am after no trouble."

"Yet you've found it nonetheless." He leaned into Crispin and snarled stale breath into his face. "Traitors should not have leave to walk the streets." He shoved hard and Crispin fell backward, splayed into the muddy snow.

The man stood over him, laughing quietly, dangerously. His blond-haired companion lost his amusement and suddenly looked anxious.

The lord drew his blade. Crispin felt his heart battering his chest. Flaring his nostrils, he inhaled his own sharp sweat and the wretchedly cold air that filled his lungs until they felt as heavy as wineskins. His eyes darted from one man to the other. Was he to be killed in the street like a dog? His fingers scrabbled in the mud, clutching at nothing.

Crispin watched the sword point approach his face and hover over his nose. He pressed himself into the mud to keep as far away from the steel as possible. The blade moved down his neck, hovered over his chest, tucked into the edge of his mantle, and, with a flick, cast it aside. "What a disgusting coat, Guest. Filthy. Are you not shamed to be seen in the streets thus?"

Crispin held his breath, pressing himself into the mud.

"You chose badly, Crispin. You did not plot and plan. You did not prepare. God did not smile upon you. No, indeed. He turns away from the weak. The strong find the power—"

"My lord!" hissed the wheat-haired man.

"Master Cornelius. Worry not. I can say what I like to this cur."

The blade continued, slowly edging down Crispin's body until it drifted over his scrip. The point poked it and then flitted away. "What have we here?"

The man leaned down and untied Crispin's scrip, throwing the flap aside. He reached in and pulled out the book the abbot had given him only moments before.

He opened the cover and read a moment before looking down at him again. "Thomas of Monmouth? Where did you get this book? Did you steal it?" The blade was back, aiming at his chest.

"No, my lord," he said between gritted teeth. "The Abbot of Westminster loaned it to me—"

"You lie," said the man, sounding bored. "For why would the Abbot of Westminster have aught to do with you?"

"He's my friend!" said Crispin more harshly than he intended.

"Your *friend*?" The man made sport of the word through his malleable features. "Loaning you valuable books? You?" He looked at his companion. A small crowd began to gather just outside their circle. "Another lie, Guest. So many lies. So many secrets. It is a wonder that no one has put you out of your misery before now." His face contorted into an unpleasant leer. The blond man glared at him, but his warning look went unheeded.

For the first time in a long time, Crispin genuinely feared for his life. This man clearly outranked him. It was impossible for him to defend himself. He was very nearly above the law. Above any law that would see them punished for finishing off the likes of Crispin on the naked street.

And Crispin didn't even know his name!

He glanced desperately at the hooded faces surrounding their little tableau. Dull-witted workmen with slack mouths, frightened shopkeepers, and men passing by on horses. Spectators only. There was absolutely no one who would step forward to save him. No one of sufficient rank, at any rate, who would care to try.

The man smiled. "Guest," he said, bringing the blade closer and pressing the tip into his neck. He felt the tip pierce the flesh with a sharp twinge. "Shall I? Take you out of this workaday world and send you to a far greater reward? Unless, of course, you think Hell awaits. Which is the greater punishment, then?" He pressed deeper. Crispin choked, trying to keep his neck taut. "Beg for your life and I will be generous."

That was the wrong thing to say. Crispin clenched his jaw. If die he must, this was as good a way as any. He almost spit at the man but he could not move his head without spearing his own throat.

"Radulfus!"

The dark lord turned. Giles de Risley scrambled off his mount, grabbed the man's arm, and pulled him back. "What, by the saints, are you doing?"

"Just a bit of sport, coz. I saw this traitor close to the palace and thought to waylay him."

Giles looked horrified. "You fool!" He turned to Crispin but before he could make a move to help him up, another pair rode up to the back of the crowd.

"What goes on here?" A voice Crispin never expected to hear. Nicholas Exton and John Froshe appeared when the crowd parted. The former was mounted on a gray horse and the latter on a white one. They both tried a glare at the proceedings with little success.

"Lord Sheriff," said Radulfus mildly with barely a glance behind. He shouldered Giles aside and pressed his blade to Crispin's throat again. "I am merely disposing of a rodent. London is so full of them."

"So I see," said Exton, licking his fish-lips. "What was this man doing to warrant such swift justice?"

He displayed the book before he let it drop to the mud. "This, Lord Sheriff. I caught him red-handed with stolen property."

Crispin tried to swallow, but the blade in his throat made that difficult. His eyes rounded trying to watch the proceedings.

The sheriff shifted his mount forward. He eyed Radulfus first and then cast his glance to Giles, who was shaking his head vigorously. When he next turned to Crispin, there was hint of hysteria in his eyes. "What have you to say for yourself, Master Guest?"

"It was not stolen," he rasped. "It was a loan from Abbot de Litlyngton. Go ask him yourself."

"Perhaps I shall. And to do that properly—" he turned to Giles, "I will need the accused, Lord de Risley. If you would be so kind as to tell your friend, my lord."

Giles grabbed the man's arm again. Crispin's heart had not stopped its clamor and it stumbled once when he thought that Exton's brief reprieve was only that. Would the man run him through anyway? Defy the sheriff and Giles just for spite?

Exton didn't press the matter. He waited, expression vacant. His horse impatiently tamped the courtyard.

With a sigh and the tilt of his head, Radulfus pulled back his blade and very deliberately sheathed it. Crispin coughed a breath, which only tore the skin at his throat. He felt the hot blood dribble down his neck.

De Risley helped Crispin to his feet, but Crispin shook him off, flushing darkly. That Giles should witness his moment of weakness!

The sheriff pointed to the slushy snow. "Pick up the book."

Crispin cursed under his breath. The precious book that Abbot Nicholas had entrusted to his care was now wet and muddy. He leaned over and raised it from its mire, shaking off the excess water.

"I have this now in hand," Exton prompted, a little surer of himself.

Giles seemed in no hurry to leave the scene. "Crispin, I—"

"My lords," Crispin said with a bow, dismissing them.

Radulfus laughed and Giles glared at him and at the sallow Cornelius, who looked nervous near Radulfus.

Finally, the three mounted. They reined their horses about and looked back at the sheriff over their shoulders. "I trust you know what to do with lawbreakers, Lord Sheriff," said Radulfus.

"Indeed I do, my lord." He bowed to the men before Radulfus and Cornelius trotted away toward the palace gate. Giles looked back with an apologetic expression.

Exton watched anxiously until he saw the back of them and turned angrily on Crispin. "Master Guest. Your behavior is untenable."

Froshe edged forward at last. "Just what is it you did to prick his ire?"

Crispin rubbed his neck, wiping blood across his palm. "I did nothing, my lords. Nothing but cross his path, the bastard. I never set eyes on him before today!"

Exton whipped around, glaring at the crowd. "Disperse! All of you. Unless you wish to be arrested for disturbing the peace."

The milling people quickly fled with none looking back, hiding themselves in shops or into alleys.

"You might wish to speak more quietly—" warned Exton.

"And cautiously!" piped Froshe.

"Yes. *Much* more cautiously if you intend to insult courtiers in the streets. Whether you know their names or not!"

"He *is* a bastard. And more." The bleeding would not stop and he stooped to gather snow to press it to his sore neck. "And what I said was the truth. My mere existence seemed to compel him to violence."

"I am beginning to know just how he feels! Need we go to Westminster Abbey to prove what you said about that book?"

"Of course not!" The skin at his neck was numbed by the cold snow, feeling like a corpse's skin. He let the crimson snow fall and brushed uselessly at the mud and sticky snow at the back of his cloak. "The abbot loaned it to me. I'd swear to it on my sword, if I still had one."

Exton scowled. It was beginning to resemble Wynchecombe's. He glanced along the street again. No one was close enough to overhear them. He leaned over the saddle pommel and said quietly, "I take it you are here to investigate the . . . you know."

Crispin stretched his neck tentatively. The numbness was still there but no amount of snow could temper the humiliation that still flushed his cheek. "Yes."

Froshe leaned over. "Are you making any headway?"

Crispin scanned the street himself and his eye fell on a familiar and gratifying sight. "No. But if you leave me to it, I can carry on."

They both straightened. The scowls they cast at him could melt ice. "That's the thanks we get for saving your wretched life?" said the Fishmonger. "I should have let him stick you to the ground."

Crispin composed his features and faced Exton. In his best courtly posture, he bowed low to him. "I am deeply grateful, Lord Sheriff."

"Hmpf. I'll wager you are. My advice? Stay away from de Risley and his ilk. Just do your job," he added with a harsh whisper before looking at the crowd again. "Report to us tomorrow. If we are to spend coin on you, Master Guest, I want to see results!" He wheeled the horse and trotted away with Froshe following quickly behind him. The retreating hoofbeats drummed hollowly in Crispin's chest.

Out of the corner of his eye, he saw the ginger-haired boy approach, wearing the tabard of the duke of Lancaster. "Master," he said tentatively. "Master Crispin . . ."

Jack's face was a feast of sorrow. Clearly he had witnessed his disgrace. He clutched tightly to a bundle, his teeth worrying his chapped lips.

Crispin felt ill at ease under the boy's scrutiny. He tried to shirk the memories of the last few moments but it stuck to him as tenaciously as the mud that was ground into his cloak. He turned away on the pretext of surveying the square. "Jack" was all he said.

"The livery," said Jack. He raised the bundle slightly. "I've got one for you, too."

"Good." Across the street there was a narrow close. He headed for it, motioning Jack to follow. The walk was good for him. It allowed the clammy humiliation to slip from his shoulders. He left it back there in the street, discarded like chewed bones. When they'd reached the shadows, Jack handed him the bundle and Crispin shook it out. Another tabard with the Gaunt arms. Unbuttoning his cloak, he slipped the livery over his head, fitting it over his shoulder cape and over the scrip, keeping it safe. He whirled the cloak back over his shoulders and buttoned it again. He glanced down at Jack. "How do I look?"

Jack shrugged. After all he had seen, it didn't seem as if he knew what to say.

Crispin laid a reassuring hand on his shoulder. "You stayed out of the way. That's as I would have it."

"I didn't protect you! I was . . . afraid."

The vehemence and the words from so small a source stunned him. He took a moment to collect himself, mulling the sentiments. "Jack," he said quietly, his grip firming on the young shoulder. "You do your best. But in such an instance, it is wisest if you stay clear of me."

"But—!"

"No, Jack. No arguments. It's my command. And my wish."

Jack blinked rapidly, his eyes glistening. With mouth clamped tight, he gave a curt nod. Crispin gave him one in reply before he turned to the busy street in front of them and set out for the palace.

9

WITH HIS HOOD OVER his head and Lancaster's arms painted across his person, Crispin and Jack slipped unquestioned through the great portico, past guards and pages. Jack spoke not a word. Crispin sensed his fear. He was not beyond a little healthy fear himself. At every turn he was in dread of encountering Giles and his wretched cousin again. What would the man make of Crispin's new livery? Would he be accused of stealing it? There would be no sheriff to stop Radulfus's vengeance then.

The great hall was bustling with people, talking in small groups, citizens hoping for an audience with certain nobles, pages milling near their lords, servants trying to stay out of the way.

But it was the servants Crispin wanted to question. He headed toward a door he knew led to a narrow passage through which the workers often passed. Jack was at his heels, sticking close, like a calf to its mother.

Within the passage they encountered many liveried pages, and Crispin decided to try them first.

"You there!" he called, stopping a blond boy wearing the arms of some minor noble.

The boy paused and looked Crispin up and down. "Aye?"

"Can you point out the servants who serve the Jew's quarters?"

The boy's eyes scoured Crispin and Jack a second time. "And why would you be wanting to know that?"

Crispin straightened, showing off the colors across his chest. "My lord wishes to know. Why else?"

The boy seemed little impressed. He shrugged and looked around. When he lifted his arm, his finger pointed out a man of middle years with a round face, squat brown hair streaked with gray, and hard black eyes. "That is Bill Wodecock. He would know." Having discharged this information, the page slipped into the shadows. It didn't matter. Crispin was now focused on the man. He wore the king's livery and Crispin suspected he might have sway over some of the other servants.

"Master Wodecock! I would speak with you."

The man in question turned. The cogwheels of his mind seemed to be turning, trying to come up with a name to the face he seemed to recognize. If he were in the employ of the king some seven years ago, he might well remember Crispin. That meant Crispin had to work fast. "I would speak with you regarding a matter of some import. Is there a place to talk?"

"I cannot tarry now," said the man, continuing to walk at a quickened pace. "If you would ask a question of me, you had best do it on the run."

"Very well," said Crispin, matching his pace to the older man with Jack bringing up the rear. "I seek the servants to the Jew physician."

"Why?"

"I must ask them questions."

The man's gaze flicked once to the tabard and the duke of Lancaster's arms. "I ask again. Why?"

"It is not for me to know. It is for my master's sake."

They reached a corridor that was empty but for themselves and a guard stationed at the other end, far from them. Wodecock stopped at last and gave Crispin a hard look. "I know you are lying. You are

Crispin Guest. Give me one good reason why I should not hail yon guard."

Crispin sighed. Jack edged behind him that much more. "I suspected you knew me. And I also suspect you know something of why I am here."

"I don't pretend to know anything. It is unwise for a servant to presume." He looked back at the guard and scratched his broad chin. "I know what you do now, Master Crispin. I have ears, haven't I? But there are some here who won't talk to you no matter what you are investigating. It is too dangerous."

"Then I need to talk to those who do not fear it."

The man gave him a wary smile. "I see the king hasn't killed the pride in you. God help you."

He turned to go but Crispin grabbed his arm. "This is no mere whim, sir. I need your help to prevent more mayhem."

He shook off Crispin's grasp. "I am not *your* servant, Master. No matter who you *once* were. And I care little for what you think you are doing here. Be grateful I have not cried out for that guard."

"I beseech you. I am here to save lives. Whatever you may think of me and my character has nothing to do with my mission now."

Wodecock sighed loudly and tapped his foot. "By my Lady," he grumbled. "You are just as imprudent as ever, Master Guest." He shook his head, his flattened hair moving not at all. "Very well. I do not do it for you. I do it for my wife's nephew whom you saved from the gallows nigh on two years past. Not that he hasn't deserved the gallows since." His next words slid from him reluctantly. "Go to the Jew's corridor as close as you may. I will send someone anon who *might* be willing to talk with you. More I cannot promise."

Crispin offered the man a brief bow. "I thank you, Master Wodecock."

"Hmpf" was his reply, before he whirled on his heel and hurried on his way.

Crispin caught Jack's eye. "Let us hasten to the queen's chamber."

"I don't like this, sir," said Jack, following. He was as skittish as a cat in a kennel. "It don't matter what livery we wear. Going back to that corridor is cod-pated. The king could appear."

"He could appear anywhere, Jack. This *is* his palace."

They wended their way carefully through the corridors and found a guard at the archway to the corridor where the queen's chamber lay. It was also the corridor to the duke of Lancaster's apartments and Crispin took courage from their livery that they would not be stopped. With head down, he approached the guard with Jack at his side and released his held breath when they passed him unmolested.

Would lingering in the corridor arouse suspicion? He realized he knew little of the life of the servants who waited on him since birth. Though he served as a page for Lancaster, his life was far different from the likes of Wodecock and lesser servants who stoked fires and changed linens. Many slept in their masters' chambers in cramped alcoves.

As they waited, a master of wardrobe exited the queen's chamber, urging two female servants forward, their arms full of linens. Crispin turned his face away but he felt the man's questioning eyes on him. The footsteps receded and the corridor fell to silence again.

"How long can we tarry and not bring forth that guard?" whispered Jack into Crispin's sleeve.

Crispin turned his head slightly and eyed the guard . . . who was eyeing him back. "Not long, I fear. I pray that servant arrives soon."

Crispin was barely done speaking when a man in a quilted dark blue tunic carrying a bundle of fuel pushed past the guard. His head was covered in a leather cap with ear flaps whose ties swung freely as he lumbered. He was built more robustly than Crispin but of the same height. His eyes snapped up and captured Crispin's gaze, keeping it as he approached. His shuffling step was hurried and he did not pause as he whisked by them. But a rasped "Follow!" hissed from the side of his mouth and Crispin and Jack joined him as he opened the door to the Jew's quarters with a rusty key.

The shadows swallowed them and the man turned swiftly, his back to the doorway. "Master Wodecock bid me speak to you," said the man in a roughened voice. He looked older upon closer inspection, perhaps ten years Crispin's senior. His eyes looked out from darkened hollows. The skin on his spotted face was stretched taut with an unhealthy pallor.

"I will mince no words with you then," said Crispin, eyeing what he could see of the corridor through the opened door. "The Jew physician claims that he is the victim of thievery. Parchments were stolen from him."

The man's eyes widened a fraction but he said nothing.

"Might you know of such a theft?" Crispin pressed.

The man licked his lips. His pale blue eyes flicked over Crispin's livery. "A theft?"

Crispin measured his expression carefully. Something was dancing behind those troubled eyes. "Yes," said Crispin. "Or perhaps . . . not so much a theft. But if, say, a nobleman requested such a thing. Perhaps even paid a servant to open the door for him . . ."

The servant's eyes shifted toward the floor. He licked his lips again.

Aha.

Crispin dropped his own gaze from the man and absently stroked the blazon on his tabard. "It is such a little thing, in the end, isn't it? Open a door for a lord. Is this not the house of the king? Are these lords not the king's minions? And what is this Jew but a servant of the king?"

The man's jaw muscles tightened on his stubbled jowl.

Crispin fingered his money pouch. "I might have a halpen for a man who would share this information. Money well-earned, I may add. And with my being as discreet as a priest, no one would know that such a man told me aught."

Those eyes darted back to Crispin and traveled over him efficiently like a shuttle in a loom.

"Well then?"

The man opened his mouth to speak when a sound in the corridor startled him. He whipped his head around and glared through the archway. A scowl set his mouth. Hurrying with his bundle, he dumped the wood and sticks into a box by the hearth. He wiped the loose bark and woodruff from his garments and returned to the door. Opening it a crack further, he peered out and kept a white-knuckled grip on the door. "I might find my way to earning that halpen. Meet me at Charing Cross. At Compline."

"Can you not tell me now—"

"No time!" he rasped. "Later!" With that, he slipped out the door and threw it closed behind him.

Frustrated, Crispin glowered at the closed door. It seemed a simple question. But perhaps it was not simple at all. Yet the fact that they were in the Jews' apartment suddenly swelled to the forefront of his thoughts. Would this not prove a good opportunity to spy?

Jack was already at the door with his hand on the ring when Crispin whirled away from it to go to the closed inner chamber he had not had the opportunity to examine before. He reached for the door's latch when Jack was thrown aside by someone entering the room. A slender silhouette pierced the archway, a dagger in hand.

Crispin yanked Jack out of harm's way before the door closed again and the figure made its way to the fire. "What is the meaning of this?" The voice of Julian made whole the shadowed stranger. His knife flashed in the fire's glow. Face still in shadow, the heat glittered fiercely in his eyes.

Crispin made certain Jack was behind him. "We were speaking with a servant."

"So I saw. Why in our rooms?"

"This is an investigation of a theft. Surely you expected me to look at your chamber."

"You are a liar!" The blade rose but Julian made no move toward them even as he vibrated like a psaltry string. His nostrils flared.

Instinctively, Crispin raised his empty hands in appeasement, but it was only a ruse.

He lunged. One hand closed around the wrist with the knife while the other clasped Julian's throat. He shoved the young man hard into the wall, tightening his grip on that slender throat and slamming the hand with the knife into the plaster until it fell from his fingers and clattered to the floor. Crispin heard Jack scrambling to pick it up but his eyes were solely on Julian's face. He leaned closer, their eyes fastened on each other. Julian's green eyes were wide as he struggled to breathe.

"You are quick with that knife, boy," he growled into his face. "What is it you are hiding, I wonder."

The youth gasped, his face reddening, eyes bulging. Crispin leered into his cheek. "Not so nice a thing to strangle to death, is it?"

"Master!" cried Jack behind him.

"Maybe you have something to do with the death of these boys, eh? I cannot abide a murderer. And a murderer of children. Tell me. How does it feel to be helpless?"

"Master!" Jack tugged on his coat.

Without tearing his eyes from the frightened Julian's, Crispin sneered, *"What?"*

"Stop, Master. How else can he answer you?"

The arm that held the boy's throat still throbbed from its knife wound, but Crispin could see the sense in Jack's plea. But how he enjoyed putting that whelp in his place! He gave the trembling youth one last look, sweeping his eyes up and down his person, before he slowly released his grip on that throat. He was satisfied to see the red marks from his hands clearly visible.

Julian put a trembling hand to his neck and coughed. His eyes were still wild with panic and he slumped against the wall. "You are mad," he choked. And then muttered words that Crispin only guessed were Hebrew.

"None of your magic, Jew. Keep your incantations to yourself."

"It is a prayer, *Gentile*! I would not expect an ungodly man like yourself to recognize it as such." He shoved Crispin aside and staggered toward the hearth, gasping.

Crispin watched him dispassionately. He wished he could drag out the Thomas of Monmouth text now and shove it the lad's sour face.

Julian was still huffing into the fireplace. He wiped at his eyes and grabbed a straw from the mantle. He leaned in and lit the tip, cupping it in his hand as he lit a nearby candle. With the glowing straw he lit more until the shadows shied from them and flitted into the dim corners.

Julian scowled and turned to Crispin. Crispin merely sneered in reply and set about examining the alchemy on the tables in the room's alcoves, touching anything he could, eliciting a further snarl from the livid boy.

Small burners, strange glass vessels, broken quills, scraps of parchments. There was something dark burned at the bottom of a crucible smelling of sulfur. He looked at Jack, who was still holding tight to Julian's dagger, before he walked to the other alcove and surveyed that messy table.

More of the same. A milky glass canister held some slimy substance, and when he pulled off the glass lid, it smelled faintly of lavender.

"A poultice for soothing the nerves," said Julian acidly. "Perhaps you should try some."

Crispin did not answer. He strode next to the door of the

mysterious inner chamber and pulled at the ring. Locked. He turned toward Julian. "Give me the key."

The boy stiffened. "No."

Crispin straightened his shoulders. "Perhaps you did not hear me."

"Perhaps you did not hear *me*. I said no."

It took only three strides for Crispin to grab the young man's collar. He hauled him up to the balls of his feet. "Give me the key to that door or I shall bash your head through it."

The boy's lower lip trembled and his eyes suddenly glistened, but tears refused to fall. *"Bâtard! Vaillant, fort chevalier!"*

The words bored into Crispin's pride. He could force his way in, yes. Even be pleased to do so should this lad prove to be a murderer. But it did not sit well with him. Technically, these Jews were his hosts. And though the son deserved his ire, the father did not.

He slowly lowered the boy and unwound his fingers from the fabric.

"You are an English brute," Julian gasped, choking on a sob even as he raised his proud chin. "That is our private chamber. Why would I ever allow the likes of you to soil it?"

Julian wiped at the tears on his reddened face, pretending they were not there. A swath of guilt slithered up Crispin's spine, but he would not apologize. The boy disturbed him deeply. There was something that he could not identify about the lad that put Crispin in an odd mood.

With only suspicions and without proof Crispin could not force the issue. He could not tackle the youth and snatch the key from him. Much as he wanted to.

God's blood! He wanted the boy to be guilty. But wanting a thing did not make it so. Perhaps the answers were behind that chamber door. Or on the tongue of a servant whom he would meet at Compline. Whatever it was, he suddenly felt too close in the dark room.

He drew himself up and headed steadily toward the front door. "This is not over, Master Julian."

"Would that it were, *Maître* Guest." He spit the words after Crispin, rubbing his sore neck. Crispin paused at the threshold. He looked back and felt a flutter of guilt. The lad was headstrong, to be sure. Protective of his father and of his faith. Grudgingly, Crispin recalled acting in a similar vein when he was that age.

But it didn't mean he had to treat the boy as if he were made of glass.

"Be assured, I will be back," said Crispin firmly. "And I will look in that room. And you will have nothing to say about it." He yanked on the door ring. "Jack."

Jack tossed the knife and it landed with a harsh clatter on the table. "That is the second time I have disarmed you," he said to Julian. "Do not pull it on my master again or you shall suffer the penalty."

Julian sneered and made a false charge toward Jack. Jack hadn't expected it and startled backward into Crispin. Julian laughed. "Go away, little man. I am not afraid of you. Or of *you,* Guest."

Crispin slammed the door behind him. He suddenly felt winded. It was the easiest course, finding the physician's son guilty, but the easiest was not always the wisest. Or the truest. Was he banking on William of Ockham's the simplest explanation is the best? Yet the boy was hiding something. That room. He had allowed his own pride to sway him from forcing the youth to relinquish the key. What was the matter with him? Going soft?

Crispin hurried through the corridors, wishing that servant could have told him at once what he wanted to know. He could be using his time to search the palace, but looking at the solemn-faced Jack beside him, he knew he could not risk overstaying his welcome. The palace was full of spies, full of people both servant and noble who would recognize his face and call the alarm. He was surprised he had made it this far without being stopped. Yet Gaunt's livery might buy him a needed reprieve. It might be assumed that the king allowed him the life of a page again. But he could not count on this thin assumption.

They ducked into St. Stephen's chapel in order to leave secretly again. A few people knelt in prayer in the sacred space. A woman in a moss green gown pressed her forehead against her clenched hands. A man, obviously a merchant, murmured words while looking upward at the rood screen.

As he crossed the floor to the other side a shadow came up behind him. His reaction was instant.

Spinning, Crispin drew his dagger but nearly dropped it when he encountered blue eyes and a slight form. The stranger from the carriage smiled and watched each of Crispin's careful movements as he sheathed his knife again.

He looked Crispin over, noting the new addition of his tabard. The smile broadened. "Master Guest."

Crispin was used to hiding Jack behind his back by now. "Yes, my lord." He bowed perfunctorily. But then the thought suddenly occurred to him. "Are you . . . following me, my lord?"

"Following *you*?" He smiled, his eyes taking in Jack before dismissing him. "How goes your mission, Crispin?"

The idea that this man was following him was bad enough. But that Crispin had not noticed was worse still. What had he seen? What had he heard? "As well as can be expected," he answered slowly. "For whatever it is I am doing." He managed a half-smile.

The man nodded in acknowledgment.

"My lord," asked Crispin, "I am certain it was an oversight, but you neglected to tell me who you were when last we met. And since you are making it your business to know my doings, perhaps a gesture in kind from you would be mete."

But the man seemed in no hurry to divulge anything. He slipped his hand into his scrip and withdrew a familiar coin-filled pouch.

"I am still willing to pay for your services, Master Guest. Those parchments are preying heavily on my mind. It is imperative that I have them. And soon. What say you?" He swung the pouch in a tantalizing arc.

"If parchments there were," he said casually, "what would you do with them?"

Slender fingers closed over the purse. "This amount of silver does not grant you my every thought, Crispin. It is only a fee for a job well done. I insist you take this."

Crispin stiffened. "No."

"No?"

"I choose my own clients, my lord. Little is left to me as it is. And so this small freedom is my own."

"But coin, Crispin. Much more than your feeble sixpence a day. I could double it. Treble it."

Jack whined behind him, but Crispin swung a foot, connecting with the boy's shin to shut him up.

"An undeserved boon, surely, my lord."

The man stared at him. Clearly, he was a man unused to being refused. He shook his head. "A very unusual man," he muttered and dropped the pouch back into his scrip. "But there will come a time, my dear Crispin—soon, perhaps—when you will regret this decision."

Crispin's stomach growled. He already regretted it, but not quite enough to change his mind.

A servant Crispin recognized as the man's driver approached. Ignoring Crispin, he bowed to the dark-gowned stranger. "Your Excellency," he said, the rest of his words lost in whispers.

Excellency? An honorific for a bishop. But the man seemed young to be a bishop. But if he were, it might explain why he rode in a rich carriage and wore no weapon. Why then did he not wear his vestments and enjoy the full honors of his title?

The man inclined his head toward his minion and, after

listening for a moment, finally straightened. "I must take my leave, Master Crispin. Forgive me for my haste."

Crispin bowed. "Of course . . . *Excellency*."

The man's eyes narrowed slightly before their edges crinkled with amusement. He said nothing, and followed his servant out. Crispin watched them depart, waiting just long enough before he began to follow him with Jack in tow. They made it outside in time to watch as the man and driver strode across the gravel courtyard.

Crispin slipped the scrip out from under his tabard and turned to the boy. "Jack, take this and go back to the Shambles. I have other work to do."

He started after the man when Jack tugged at his coat. "But Master! Surely there is more I can do."

"You can go back to our lodgings where it is safe."

"But Master Crispin—"

"I do not like repeating myself, Jack." He strode ahead, keeping well away from his quarry, too distracted to register that Jack had not turned in the direction of the Shambles.

CRISPIN ALLOWED HIS TARGET to forge ahead. The man's servant walked with him and led him to the carriage. The strange lord climbed inside while the driver swung himself up to the seat where he took the reins from an attendant. The carriage moved unhurriedly, pausing for traffic across the busy avenue before joining the throng of carts and wagons laden with wares.

Crispin kept pace. There was something dangerous underlying the man's character. One did not give cryptic warnings without reason.

And Crispin especially did not like the idea of this unnamed man following him.

They moved steadily out of the bounds of Westminster Palace and toward Charing Cross. At a trot, Crispin tracked. They traveled a long way down the broad avenue. He soon found himself pinned behind a man moving his swine toward London. On foot, there seemed no way around the many donkey carts, wagons, and travelers. The carriage lay far ahead and he feared to lag too far behind. Though it was clear to Crispin that they were heading toward London, they could easily be swallowed by the traffic the closer they got.

Crispin looked down at his tabard. He did not wish to appear obvious. Whipping off his cloak, he slipped out of the livery, turned it wrong side out, and tugged it back over his head. No sense in losing the extra bit of warmth it allowed. With his cloak back in place, he continued his stealthy pursuit.

At last, the man with the wayward swine moved toward the river, and Crispin was free to move past him and his squealing charges. But instead of the carriage bearing toward London's gates as Crispin expected, it veered northward.

The carriage rolled into dim alleyways. Crispin worried that the diminishing crowds would make him noticeable, but the driver's attention lay before, not behind. He kept to the walls just in case, pressing himself into the shadows and was almost relieved to see the dusky outline of fog rolling up from the river. It swept slowly beyond him up the road like the Angel of Death and shrouded the carriage, painting it a ghostly shape with only the sound of creaking wheels and clinking harness anchoring it to reality.

At Chancery Lane the driver stopped and waited at the end of the street.

Crispin leaned against the wall of a shop, his shoulder resting against a closed shutter.

In time, the man emerged from the carriage, yet he appeared as only a gray spirit in the enveloping fog. A small boy, another ghostly figure, carried a bundle across the lane, dropping one of his packages. The stranger paused and appeared to be merely looking at the boy. After another pause, he moved forward, stooped to retrieve the package, and returned it to the stack in the boy's arms. He spoke and the boy listened attentively.

Crispin's senses prickled. The driver stood as a lookout, effectively barring the street's entrance with the carriage's girth. No one but the boy and the mounted man could be detected on the hazy street, now clouded with fog. The stranger seemed to engage the lad with a friendly air. He pressed a hand to his scrip and after a moment, took something from it—a flash of silver. He held it forth. The boy stepped closer, and every nerve in Crispin's body had the sudden urge to scream out a warning to him. They became one silhouette, man and boy, against the gray. The horse turned its large head and chuffed an icy breath before shaking its head. The jangle of his harness was the only sound to travel so far, not the soft tones the man spoke to the boy, who moved closer as if under a spell, transfixed by the offered coin.

The boy reached up, his arm extending in a soft arc. The momentary tableau could have been the mirror of a sacred carving. A shepherd boy entreating his lord; the child Jesus speaking to the men in the temple.

But the gentle picture suddenly shattered.

The man's hand shot forward, capturing the boy's wrist. Another clamped over his mouth. The packages flew. The child was only able to squeak out one surprised sound before he was dragged toward the waiting carriage.

Crispin's dagger was in his hand and he was running before he could gather another thought.

The driver turned and got a fist in his jaw for his trouble. He wheeled back, falling into the horse. The horse whinnied and pulled on the harness, jostling the wagon.

Crispin wasted no time on the fallen driver. He lunged for the boy and grabbed a flailing arm. "Release him!" he shouted.

The bishop turned white-rimmed eyes toward Crispin. Gone was the haughty expression he'd worn for Crispin's benefit. He scowled and pulled harder on the child, thrusting his foot onto the carriage step.

Crispin clamped a death grip on the boy and raised his dagger. He plunged it deep into the man's thigh with a meaty sound. He screamed. The boy fell from his grip. The knife bobbed in his leg as he struggled, half in, half out of the carriage. Crispin pulled hard on the child's arm, wrenching him back and flinging him away into a snowy bank. Crispin spun back toward the man when a booted foot caught him in the chin. He staggered back, stars exploding in his vision.

The fog thickened about them. Cold. Deathly cold. The man's features were lost in gray. Still lingering in the carriage doorway, he pulled the dagger from his bleeding thigh and pitched it to the ground. He slid painfully to the bottom step and came at Crispin again with a snarl.

Crispin recovered and swung, his fist hitting solid flesh. He heard the man grunt and double over, but he wasn't down long. He exploded upward and slashed out with his arm. Crispin detected the flash of a blade and leapt back, his body flexing and scrambling.

A slice of silver and Crispin jumped back again. How he wished he had not left his knife in the man! Only God knew where it was now.

He chanced a look behind him for weapons or defense and saw nothing in the swirling mist. He felt the man swinging before he turned and nearly caught the blade arcing toward him. He flung his foot upward and connected with a wrist. The knife went flying and Crispin reared back, his fist ready.

The man was faster and sank a punch deep into Crispin's belly. Dropping to one knee, Crispin's breath whooshed away, and he raised his arm in defense, feebly trying to ward off another strike.

He never saw the driver rush up from behind. When that blow fell, the world slanted, and the wet street came up to meet his face.

* * *

CRISPIN DIDN'T WANT TO awaken. Clearly it would make the ache in his skull that much greater. But with someone bathing his forehead in a cold cloth and cooing softly to him with a whispered song, he could not seem to help himself.

He blinked, his eyes feeling hot even for the cold cloth. When they focused, he did not expect the knot of people surrounding him. And then fear made him jerk to a sitting position. "The boy! Is he safe?"

A gentle hand pushed him back, and his pounding head was more than grateful for it.

A small voice at his side said, "I am, my lord. I am safe. Because of you."

"I am not a lord," he replied automatically.

"You are to me, good sir."

"And to me," said a woman's voice, the one who soothed his brow with a cool hand.

The small feeling of satisfaction was offset by his bewilderment. He had been embroiled in a violent encounter with that vile stranger. Once down, he had not expected to rise again, but obviously, he had somehow come out the victor. "Where is that man? The would-be abductor?"

"Gone," said the woman at his side. "Once you fell, he and his man made off."

A mercy, then. His head felt an ache like an ax slowly wedging further into his skull. A small mercy.

"I do not suppose there is such a thing as wine?" he asked hopefully, closing his eyes against the throbbing pain.

Not long after his plea, something was pressed against his lips. He gulped it gratefully before it was pulled away. He opened his eyes carefully again and tried to make sense of his new surroundings. The room looked to be a workroom of sorts, with shuttered windows through which dim light filtered in angled, pale shafts. Heavy beams held up wide rafters. Benches lined one wall.

"What . . . is this place?"

Glances were exchanged above him. Worried brows told him he would not receive the truth. He looked them over: men, women, children. Wardrobes of every stripe, from that of servants to the rich in furs like a merchants' garb. What the devil? Could this still be Chancery Lane, or had he been brought elsewhere? His eye snagged on a man who immediately slipped behind another, ducking his face. Even Crispin's pounding head could not hide the fact that he recognized that face. But from where? His muzzy mind would not allow him to sift out the answer. He dropped his forehead into his palm, trying to squeeze away the pain. He'd give up all the gold in the world for relief from the splitting ache in his poor head . . . wait. Gold? Goldsmith! He raised his head again and speared the man with a narrow-eyed stare. "I know you. You're—" What was the name? "Middleton. Matthew Middleton."

Accusing faces turned toward the hapless goldsmith trying to become smaller behind a man with a broad hat.

Crispin rose and rested back on his elbows. "Days ago I questioned you. About the dead boy. You're that goldsmith."

The man eased away from the others, his hands placating gently. "Aye, good sir. I am he."

"What are you doing here? What is this place?"

Middleton looked to the others and cautiously approached. "A place of safety, Master Crispin. We are indebted to you for saving the boy. Surely when you are well enough you can be on your way."

Crispin pushed the soothing hand away and sat up, throwing his legs over the side of the pallet. It was a mistake. His head swam but there was nothing for it.

It also did not go without Crispin's notice that the crowd blocked his way out.

He gripped the pallet and slowly rose. "I thank you all for this kindness. . . ."

"It is we who thank you, sir," said the woman who had ministered to him. Probably the lad's mother. From her apron she brought forth Crispin's bloodied knife. She offered it hilt first.

Crispin took it and sheathed it. Apparently he was to be released after all. He moved unsteadily forward and the crowd parted for him. But their desperate faces, their furtive looks toward one another, were an uncomfortable mystery. There was more to this gathering than the relief of a boy's salvation. He looked again at the long, rich gowns, the tattered tunics. "Tell me who you are."

"Master, please," said Middleton, the reluctant spokesman. "It is best you leave and think of us no more."

"This I cannot do. I have sworn to protect those in London. So, too, am I compelled by my knightly vows. And protect you I shall. If you fear retribution for your actions, do not. I am your witness to an attempted abduction. I have the ear of the sheriff." Which was not strictly true but could be managed.

Minutely, those near the exit shouldered closer. Something was definitely amiss. In one instant, they seemed to be ushering him out and the next, preventing his departure. "Am I being held against my will?"

"No, good sir," said Middleton. His anxious expression and beaded forehead did little to allay Crispin's anxiety.

"Then explain yourselves. You would do well to tell me now. Did you know that man who attacked the boy?"

As one they shook their heads. Some cast their eyes to the polished wooden floor.

"I see," said Crispin. "How can I help you if I cannot get the truth?"

"Master Crispin," begged Middleton. "Please. Just leave us in peace."

"And I would if my way was not barred." He glanced again to the men at the door. They seemed confused as to what to do.

"Shall I bring the law on this place?"

"No!" Middleton pressed his hands into fists.

"Master Crispin!" The boy was at his side.

He looked down at the earnest child tugging at his coat. He had freckles across the bridge of his nose and cheeks, much like Jack's. He couldn't be much younger than the cutpurse. "You mustn't bring the sheriffs," the boy went on. "They're not to know—"

"John!" cried the mother. She reached a trembling hand for the boy.

"No, mother. I can tell *him*. He's the Tracker. He protects good folk. I've heard the stories."

"John," said Middleton urgently. "Listen to your mother."

"Let the boy speak," said Crispin slyly. He knelt before the boy and took his shoulders gently. "Go on. What is it you would tell me, lad?"

"You mustn't tell about us," said the boy. His grave expression reminded far too much of Jack Tucker.

"I cannot promise until I know your meaning."

The boy licked his lips. His dark eyes blinked rapidly. "But sir," he whispered. "We could die."

As much as Crispin wanted to, he could not look away from those earnest eyes. Against his better judgment, he said, "Then I promise, child. I will keep my own counsel."

The boy sighed with relief. "I knew you would, good sir. You are like the knights in the songs." Crispin felt the air in the room fall still. No one seemed to breathe. The boy leaned forward and whispered as if they were the only two present. "Because we are Jews, sir. It's to remain a secret, you see. Now you understand why you mustn't tell?"

10

CRISPIN FELT HIS MOUTH fall open. He had no need to confirm the boy's pronouncement. The collective breaths of the crowd were still held, the tension taut in the air.

But the boy seemed satisfied that his deadly secret would be safe with Crispin. He smiled and nodded his assurances. Crispin wished he could be as certain.

Slowly, he straightened and finally raised his eyes to the gathering of men and women. But surely these were Englishmen! They couldn't be Jews. The edict that had banished them had been clear. The scourge was vanquished from the land almost a hundred years ago.

He looked down at the boy again. The discomfort he had felt in Jacob's company could not now be summoned. He found it difficult to call the boy before him a "scourge."

Maybe this was the Domus Conversorum, the House of Converts. These were all converts, then.

But with another search of their anxious faces and John's confident one, Crispin rather thought not.

"God's blood," he breathed.

"M-master Guest," ventured Middleton.

Crispin flicked a wary gaze his way.

"You have sworn an oath to the boy. We have all heard it."

Crispin barked a laugh. He couldn't help it. He was well and truly caught. It could have been a headache-induced illusion. People who should not have existed on English soil were here, right before him. It was laughable.

"How has this remained a secret?"

Everyone seemed to breathe again. The men at the doorway eased back. Someone poured more wine into Crispin's bowl and he didn't think twice about taking it. He drank it down and sank to the pallet. Middleton, whom the others had urged closer, sat beside him. Crispin felt no distaste this time. Funny. Was it the wine? Or perhaps the blow to his head had been harder than he thought.

"Master Guest. I know this is difficult. But if you let me explain then surely you can see, surely you will have mercy."

"You, all of you, trespass on the king's law."

"We are London born and raised, sir. Just like you."

About to object, Crispin spied the boy, who was looking at him with that damned air of certainty. These people mocked the king by their presence. He had a duty to inform the sheriff at the very least. But the boy's eyes threatened any sense of his duty to the crown.

John took Crispin's empty bowl from his hand with a curt bow.

"Very well, Master Middleton. You had best tell me and quickly."

Middleton clenched his hands together. "It began with the Edict of King Edward." His voice was tinny, small. "All Jews were to convert or to leave. You can imagine the uproar. The heartache. Land that our families had held for generations suddenly snatched from our hands. Our homes, sold to others." Crispin squirmed. "We had to leave the bones of our ancestors behind. We paid heavy fines to the king, paid our own passage to France and to whatever country would take us. We carried what was left as well as our faith to other places. But there were some who took the waters of baptism and lived in the Domus Conversorum, not far from here. The

House of Converts. These were our grandsires and great-grandsires. Many became devoted to the Christian life. But still many others lived as best they could as Christians outwardly, but inwardly, where none could see, lived as our forefathers, preserving the traditions of our faith."

Middleton paused, gauging Crispin's reaction.

But Crispin did not know what to think. Not a man of deep faith, he felt only mild distaste at false Christians, but the uneasy feeling in his belly might just as easily be attributed to the other things Middleton was saying. He had never thought about the details before, never imagined uprooting children and families for places unknown with little but what they could carry. Yes, he had seen such an exodus after battles and thought little of it. These were the conquered. It was right that they were sent away. In the Holy Land, were not Christians exiled by the pagan Saracen?

The faces before him were not as he expected. They did not reek of evil or evil intentions. They did not sneer derisively as did the petulant Julian. They seemed like Englishmen.

His neck hairs bristled.

When Crispin had been exiled from court, he had at least been allowed to stay in London among the familiar. But to be exiled to a foreign kingdom . . .

His head hurt. That was it. That was why these revelations were turning his stomach.

Either that or the Jewish wine.

He said nothing, waiting for Middleton to continue. The man looked as if he could use some wine himself. "And so . . . you see us here." His gesture included the assembled. "One hundred years later. We make no trouble. We respect where we live. Though we have no rabbi, no spiritual leader, our parish leaders read the Torah in Hebrew to the assembly. At least as much of it as we were able to acquire. We keep the traditions but we keep out of the way. It is always all we ever wanted."

Crispin glanced at the boy again. The young face was serene, fresh in the knowledge that his savior, Crispin, would also be his champion. He wetted his lips. "Have . . . have you been missing any boys, Master Middleton?"

He shook his head. "No, Master. And we are grateful that John was spared today."

Crispin considered. Boys snatched from the streets. Was the man who wanted the parchment responsible for the other four deaths? Was John to be the fifth?

Or are there *two* men abducting boys?

And where did this Golem fit in?

Exhausted, Crispin sighed. "Then this man who tried to abduct the boy. I ask again. Do you know him?"

"We do not," said Middleton.

"Did any of you know the missing boys?"

They all shook their heads. This was getting him nowhere. He rose—a little more steadily this time, though his head did not hurt any less. What was he to do? How could he keep something so grave a secret? Was he not in enough trouble with the crown? Yet he had given his word, and if he had not his word, then he had nothing at all.

He glared at these faces. These *Jewish* faces. And the thought, dark and sticky, finally occurred to him. Oh they were benign, weren't they? They with their humble spokesman and innocent-looking boy with a face like Jack Tucker. But this Golem, this demon, came from the minds of people such as these. A Golem would do the bidding of its maker, so said Jacob of Provençal. The missing boys had not been Jewish. So then this Golem was snatching good Christian boys for its mischief—

Wait.

What was he thinking? He rubbed the back of his aching head. He did not believe in this Golem. No, he did not! Despite what he thought he saw, he could not believe in such an outlandish thing.

And yet, if *they* believed it . . .

"I have one more question." He took in each solemn face, each studied expression. "Have any of you ever heard of a . . . Golem?"

There was a gasp and the faces around him broke into wide-eyed fear.

"We do not speak of such things," said a man with a rondelle hat.

"Indeed," said Crispin with a sneer. "Well, I *am* speaking of it. Who amongst you knows how to make a Golem? You already admitted to knowledge of Hebrew."

The gathering fell to silence. No one so much as breathed. Even young John was hauled against a hip and hugged into silence.

"No one, eh?" Crispin walked a slow circle, staring into each face. Eyes fell away from him with something like guilt. "These things can be discovered. Who amongst you has access to court?"

Again, silence.

Crispin scowled. "If none of you will talk, it will go badly for all of you. Speak. I will not hold responsible the entire community if you give up the one."

But Crispin slowly realized that this was the wrong thing to say. Middleton raised his chin and stared defiantly. Others lifted their faces and soon Crispin found himself surrounded by a wall of rebellious people.

On the one hand, he was furious with them for their defiance. But on the other, he admired their fortitude.

"I have seen it," said Crispin.

A woman holding and jiggling a baby over her shoulder shushed her companion who tried to hold her back. "What is your meaning? You saw . . . the Golem?"

There were sounds of protest, and a grouse or two about women holding their tongues.

"Yes," said Crispin in a strong voice. "I have seen the Golem. He was large, broad-shouldered, with a small head. There was clay. . . ."

Whispers rumbled through the crowd and more than one gaze fell from Crispin's.

They know something. A quick glance toward Middleton revealed his startlement. And something more. Recognition?

"I tell you now," warned Crispin. "If you are harboring this thing or concealing its whereabouts, I cannot be held responsible as to what happens to you. Speak!"

But the whisperings ceased and Crispin was right back where he started. Stubborn, these Jews.

He settled one hand on the hilt of his dagger. "For the time being, I see no reason to inform the sheriff of your . . . little community. But I cannot promise complete anonymity. Should it prove relevant to this case, I do not see how it can remain a secret."

Middleton licked his chapped lips. "But if it is not—"

"I cannot speculate. *Everything* is relevant." He pushed forward and the people stumbled out of his way. "I thank you for your assistance," he tossed out. He felt unaccountably stifled and needed air. The crowd allowed him through the door into a smaller parlor where a servant was lighting a candle on a sideboard. The room was plain but clean, with a tapestry of a leaf and vine pattern hanging above the sideboard. Blank walls, walls devoid of crucifixes or saintly portraits. The image chased him out the door to a courtyard of pruned rosebushes and brown, tangled vines. It was a perfectly normal courtyard. But the absence of shrines or of statues suddenly stood out like a green leaf on the white snow.

He walked backward, looking at its darkening shadows from behind as he drew further away. What to make of this! The London he thought he knew was becoming more foreign by the moment.

Crispin trotted across the lane and propped himself against a post. A nearby brazier warmed his left flank. Night had fallen during the time of his convalescence and he was glad for the wrong-side-out tabard that helped to keep him warm.

He surveyed the street from where he had come. Chancery Lane. It had been known as the Jews' Street long ago and was even vaguely referred to as such in disparaging tones. No one was on the street now. The fog had thickened and shrouded the avenue in gray mist. The dark shapes of houses rose above the street like sharp-steepled gargoyles, looming near one another in some iniquitous coven. Yellow light limned shuttered windows and the occasional spark let loose and flew from a crooked chimney. But all else was dark and cold and lonely.

On the one hand were these Jews, who seemed aware of a Golem. But it was no fabled Golem whom Crispin had witnessed snatching a boy from the street. He had seen that nameless man with his own eyes, fought with him and saved the boy from some horrible fate. It would explain an anonymous carriage when a horse would do. Unspeakable acts could be accomplished in a closed wagon drawn through deserted alleys. But why then had the man entertained Crispin within it? To taunt him? He thought of Giles's cousin and knew the answer to that. Such men needed to taunt, to prove themselves in ways that could not be achieved on the lists or among men of character.

If this so-called bishop devoured these boys then what was his purpose?

And what, by the mass, did it have to do with Hebrew parchments? Did this bishop want a Golem to serve his disgusting habits or . . .

Crispin stopped, his thoughts overwhelming him. Perhaps the old Jew was lying. Perhaps he *had* made this Golem but lost the means to control it when his parchments were stolen. Then who has the parchments now?

Wait, wait. That would imply that such a creature as a Golem existed.

"There is no Golem!" he barked. A man trudging down the lane and carrying a heavy sack over his shoulder stopped and stared at him. Crispin glared back, his hand lying on his dagger hilt in warning. The man's gaze flicked to the gesture and he moved on without a word, shambling through the gray snow.

Crispin watched him disappear in the gloom. *But what if the man in the carriage was* not *a bishop,* he thought. The honorific "Excellency" was freely wielded, might even refer to one of those astrologers Jacob spoke of. It was not uncommon for physicians to consult star charts. Divination played just as important a role as the use of purges and potions. Yet some astrologers were only in it for the money. Those could be found in wealthy households, making good coin from their signs and scratches and burning twigs, like some Greek priest in an ancient temple. Crispin had even known a few generals who would not set foot to stirrup until their astrologers had told them it was wise to do so.

He did not recall these generals being particularly successful.

There were indeed astrologers at court. It was rumored the queen favored one. But a woman desperate to produce an heir to the throne might be inclined to all measures at her disposal. Including hiring a Jewish physician.

Missing Hebrew parchments, he mused. If an astrologer didn't read Hebrew, might he know where to go to get someone who did? Perhaps through abduction of a Jewish child?

Crispin shook his head. He couldn't go round and round like this. Something had to make sense. And a Golem did not.

"I'm weary." His voice sounded strange and alone on the deserted street. What hour was it? And just as he thought it, the slow tolling of bells from Westminster chimed Compline. All to rest. The end of the day where silence reigned.

But to Crispin, it meant finally meeting with that servant and avoiding the Watch. Curfew was now in force.

It was time to leave these meandering thoughts for a brief while and concentrate on his rendezvous at Charing Cross. He reluctantly pushed away from the glowing brazier, and moved by feel toward Westminster through the thickening fog. It was a long way made longer by the shrouding night and mist. He looped through dark, narrow lanes to Temple Bar and veered right along the wide avenue of the Strand, guided by the warm threads of light ringing the shuttered windows.

The road curved, following the bend of the Thames, and by this he knew he was drawing closer. Hidden by the fog he hoped the servant would find him before the Watch.

The stone cross of Charing Cross suddenly rose out of the darkness. It did not offer a traveler's comfort but instead stood more like a disapproving nun, blocking his path.

Of course he did not spy the servant. That would have been far too easy. No, instead, he was to stand out in the cold and await him. He patted his arms and stomped a bit in the slush. Well, the man served at the pleasure of others. He couldn't begrudge him too much for his delay.

He cast his eyes toward Westminster Palace but could not see beyond the dark rooftops before him. He began to speculate what the man would tell him, which lord he might implicate, for if he were hired or coerced into stealing those parchments, then he was hired or coerced by *someone,* and that someone might well be guilty of murder. Could it be as simple as this? No mysterious Golems? No sinister lords with dark carriages?

A cynical laugh tried to climb up his throat.

Crispin expelled a warm breath into the cold air. This seemed to be taking a long time, or did the cold just make it seem so? He marched in place for a bit before he decided to pace around the cross itself, warming his muscles by constant movement.

His stomach growled. He couldn't recall the last time he had eaten. Was there any food at home? He hoped Jack was cooking something. Something other than turnips. "God's blood, but I hate turnips."

He circled the cross a few times, stomping at a marshaling pace.

"Where is that damnable servant?" He scowled in the direction of the palace as if by its nature his scowl could roust out the man from wherever it was he was hiding.

Impatiently, he climbed the cross's steps to get a better vantage and peer farther down the lane, even if it were possible to see through the fog. He didn't rise but a few steps when his foot jammed into something soft.

He glanced down. At first it looked to be a pile of clothing. Strange, his mind said, but his strident heart seemed to know better, and he reached down on instinct and encountered the form of a person huddled on the steps.

"This is no place to sleep," said Crispin to the curled figure. But even as he reached, he knew. He knew.

II

HE COULD NOT SEE the corpse without a torch, and though he was reluctant to do it, he had to call the hue and cry and rally a messenger to retrieve the sheriffs.

When Exton and Froshe arrived, he saw by their expressions that they were learning the extent of their relationship with Crispin. Their faces were pinched and white. And the fact that they had, no doubt, been called away from their suppers, pleased them even less.

"Why is it, Master Guest," said Froshe in a sharp, low tone as he dismounted his horse with a great grunt, "that when you are set to a task to solve one murder, you garner more?"

"It is my poor luck showing itself, Lord Sheriff."

"No, *your* luck appears to be good. It is the luck of the poor souls around you that plagues us all."

Crispin said nothing as the sheriff motioned to his man William to bring a torch.

William was a wall of a man with a flat face like brickwork. He was a servant of Newgate and had served gladly under the brutal Simon Wynchecombe, but he looked a little warily at his two new superiors.

Nevertheless, William pointed a sneer in Crispin's direction as he lumbered forward, tilting the cresset and its sputtering flame over the body. The erratic patch of wavering light confirmed that this was the servant whom he had planned to meet, who was going to implicate someone. And now the man was dead and his information with it. Even if anyone else in the palace knew something, this would certainly silence them.

Grimly, the three leaned over the corpse. It was Crispin who knelt first and when the sheriffs followed suit, William lowered the cresset at last.

The golden light passed over the dead man's face. His eyes bulged like a frog's, mouth slack and tongue lolling. But there was no froth at his lips, no indication that he had been poisoned. Crispin took a breath and reached forward. He thought Exton or Froshe would stop him, but the sheriffs said nothing. Better Crispin soil his hands than the sheriffs, he assumed.

His fingers curled at the neck of the man's tunic and pulled open the laces. "Lower the torch," he said, and was surprised that for once the combative William complied. The light revealed a dark welt ringing the man's neck. But not merely a welt. It was an indentation so deep that the skin had welled red around it. Something had pulled so tautly about his neck and throat that it might have severed his head were it sharper. His neck looked the same as the strangled boy from the Thames.

Crispin cocked his head toward Exton and silent confirmation was written clearly in his eyes. Yes, Exton had recognized it, too. He joined Froshe in an unspoken exchange.

Crispin looked his fill and was leaning away when his eye caught on something at the shadowed edge of the groove in the skin. Closer. He plucked a thread from the folds of skin and lifted it out. A thread that did not match the man's garments.

"What have you there, Master Guest?" The Fishmonger was so close his breath huffed against Crispin's hair.

"It is the murder weapon, Lord Sheriff."

"What? *That?*"

"Or should I say that it is *from* the murder weapon. He was strangled with a length of cloth."

"A length of cloth?" said Froshe, pushing his way forward. "What do you mean?"

"A strap, a drawstring, apron ties. Some sort of cloth. Then a stick or a knife might be used to twist it tight. A garrote. You see the severity of the strangulation. A garrote would be the thing." He tried to distinguish the reddish color in the flickering light. He'd have to wait till morning to get a good look at it. He pushed his tabard out of the way and tied the thread carefully around the straps holding his money pouch to his belt.

"Who was he, Master Crispin?"

Crispin stared again at the face. "A servant in his Majesty's court. He had information for me relating to this case."

Exton straightened and stared down at the corpse. "Alas."

Their silent commiseration continued only for a few moments more before Exton motioned to William and Froshe. It was clear to Crispin who was the dominant man in this office.

"Get the cart," said Exton. He swept away the audience of bedraggled folk, dwellers on the skirts of Charing Cross who had been summoned from their beds by the hue and cry. No one had seen or heard anything. Crispin searched beyond their shivering shoulders outside the halo of torches and candles, but the fog still hung too thick about them.

Exton mounted and Froshe soon followed. Crispin watched him and wondered if he should mention the secret enclave of Jews. But measuring Exton's irritated features and the inevitable explosion to follow such an unexpected pronouncement, he kept silent.

Besides, he thought with a bit of malice, *he had given his word.*

The sheriff leaned down toward Crispin. "Except for the strangulation, this death is not like the others."

"No indeed," concurred Froshe.

Crispin cast his eyes toward the body William was hefting into the back of the cart like a carcass of beef. "No. This murder was hasty. Needful. The other deaths seemed to take some time."

"This death brings you no closer to finding the murderer, Master Guest."

"On the contrary, Lord Sheriff. Someone is frightened enough at how close I am. They knew why I wanted to speak with this servant and what's more. . . ." Crispin paused, his thoughts landing where they suited best. "They saw me make my appointment."

"Eh?" Exton leaned so far forward he looked as if he might fall. "You know who it is?" He carried the expression of a man about to receive a prized gift.

Crispin rubbed his chin, feeling the first raised bits of beard. "I might."

"Tell us, then."

Both sheriffs bristled on the edge of their saddles, clutching the reins tightly in gloved fists. "I will catch him, my lords. Never fear. But you must be patient. There is more to discover."

"What?" Exton's voice cracked the brittle silence. He whipped his head around and then scowled. In a harsh whisper he said, "You will bring this culprit in immediately, do you hear me?"

"I cannot, Lord Sheriff. I ask your indulgence."

"My indul— Master Guest! You are treading on very thin ice."

"As always, Lord Sheriff." Crispin gave them both a courtly bow before sweeping hurriedly away, listening to their stifled rants behind him. He chuckled to himself. It wasn't often he could get the better of a sheriff and he knew he would likely pay for it later with the fists of their sergeant William, but he had to return swiftly to court to see if he could catch Julian, the only one who could have overheard him with the servant.

CRISPIN WAITED. THE GUARDS at the Great Gate were relieved by new men, and while greetings were exchanged and feet crunched over the icy gravel, Crispin slipped into the shadows near the wall. Months ago, Lancaster told him of a passage into the palace. He steeled himself and moved.

The night fell silent like a corpse dropping to the snow. No one stirred. The bells had long ago fallen silent and would not stir again until dawn. The cold fog still lingered like an unpleasant stench in the courtyard and beyond its walls, and so even Crispin's breath was not detected as he made his stealthy way in the darkness.

He wrestled his way over an icy garden wall, slid across the sharp stone pinnacle, and dropped down noiselessly to the other side. Ahead lay the large blocky shape of the palace. He touched a buttress, running his hand along its cold surface. Using it as his compass in the shrouding gloom, he found St. Stephen's chapel. The right direction.

More garden walls, more climbing. The repetition served to warm his stiffening limbs, but not the fear of capture. He counted the gardens. He knew where each chamber lay, knew which window he needed. Of course, if it was barred, he'd have to break in. The thought made him chuckle. Breaking into the king's palace? Richard's expression would be priceless . . . before the guards bore down on him, of course.

There ahead. The Jews' apartment. He reached up to the window and wedged his booted foot on a stone plinth, pushing upward. He grabbed hold of the decorative stone and peered within. The heavy drapes had not been entirely closed and so a slim strip of the room was visible. All dark. A red glow from the hearth changed the shadows in the room and he saw the outline of a four-poster bed. The bed curtains remained open. The Jews were not yet abed. Good.

Crispin inched his hand up the casement window, and found the seam. It was latched, but there was enough room to slip his blade through the thin opening. Hoisting his dagger out with a grunt, he gripped tighter to the decorative stone surrounding the window. The blade skittered off the glass. He paused, listening.

No footsteps.

Holding his breath, he wriggled the steel through, found the latch, and lifted.

The metal latch flipped with a whisper and the casement creaked open. Crispin grabbed it, pulling it wider.

Just then, a window several rooms down opened, spilling candlelight onto the snow-whitened courtyard. A man leaned out and turned.

Crispin froze, hoping against hope that the darkness and fog hid his burglary. But eyes met eyes and Crispin was shocked to see Lancaster staring back at him. And here was Crispin, with one leg already hoisted onto a window ledge that was not his own.

Lancaster's eyes widened for a moment. When his lips parted it was not to shout, but to swear an oath that Crispin could not hear. The man shook his head slowly, his expression stunned. Finally, he looked pointedly in another direction—perhaps thinking it was better to feign he had seen nothing—and slowly withdrew back inside.

Crispin waited, eyes darting, ears pricked. No sound. No alarm. Just the soft spitting of the fire in the grate and a distant splash of the Thames kissing the shore.

"God's blood," he whispered, blinking hard. He gathered himself and slipped inside, lighting on the floor in a crouch. Swiftly, he turned and closed the window again, sheathing his knife. The shock of warmth unsteadied him for a moment, but he quickly recovered and stepped nimbly to the wall nearest the door. At last, he was in the inner chamber! He leaned over and pressed his ear to the door, listening for movement without. Nothing. The physician and his son must be attending the queen, even at this late hour.

Crispin felt safe enough to take a straw from the small canister near the hearth, enflame the tip, and light a nearby candle. Taking up the candle he raised it and looked about the Spartan room. It was not merely a bedchamber, but an extension of the physician's workroom. A trestle table was set up in a niche on the other side of the bed. Glass jars with lids and parchments covered it. His eye immediately fell on the closest jar. Floating in some clear liquid was a grayish mass reminiscent of the offal sold by the butcher. Leaning close, he peered at it, a grimace growing. What *was* that? Its vague familiarity raised his gorge. Could it possibly be human?

His anger rising, Crispin longed to sweep it from the table and send it crashing to the floor. What was that physician doing with such a dreadful thing? He looked at the notes in a leather-bound journal lying open on the table beside it and paled. In French, Crispin read the details of experiments with entrails and offal. These were from young creatures but the nature of the creatures was not mentioned.

He lifted the journal and tilted it toward the candlelight, squinting at the tight, careful script. After a bit of reading, he realized that the journal did not belong to the physician, but to the boy Julian, and his anger threw his pulse into a vigorous thrumming.

Flipping pages back, he read the earlier entries, trying to discern what the youth had been up to and liking it not at all. Experiments involving poking the internal organs while they were exposed to the air, the abdomen being sliced open, the poor creature bound and helpless to resist. It explained how long it took the creature to expire and all the abominable note-taking in a dispassionate tone.

He slammed the book closed and panted. Murderers he had known, but *this*!

He searched the rest of the room, looking for other evidence, other horrific things he did not wish to find. More books and scrolls, some in the physician's hand and some in the youth's. There was a wooden pail by the bed and when Crispin inspected it, he saw a twisted mass of discarded rags smeared with dried blood. They *could* have been used for the physician's art, but when he looked back at the table and its gruesome contents, he could imagine only the one thing.

A door fell shut and he swiftly pinched out the candle flame. His dagger was in his hand, ready.

A key turned in the bedchamber lock. Its pins fell and the latch lifted. With a hushed whine, the door swung open. A figure, haloed by the firelight from the outer chamber, passed the threshold and reached for a candle.

Crispin's knife met the small of his back. Julian stiffened with a gasp.

"Master Julian," growled Crispin close to the young man's ear. "I would not move if I were you."

"Y-you!" he whispered. He began to tremble. His voice was choked with anger. He tried to turn around but Crispin could see him struggle not to. "You . . . you vile, hideous man! What do you think you are doing here? This is our private chamber!"

"Light the candle."

"What? I—"

"Light the damned candle!"

The lad swore an oath in French and reached for a straw. He echoed Crispin's movements of only moments ago and lit the same candle that Crispin had moved to the trestle table. Slowly, Crispin stepped back, his knife still visible. He motioned toward the journal with it. "What is this abomination?"

Eyes darted, narrowed, then looked up at him with hatred. "You could not possibly understand."

"Try me," he said.

"How can I explain to a man unfamiliar with the medicinal arts? It would be like explaining the nature of the Almighty to a simpleton."

Crispin reached back without looking and tapped the glass jar with his knife blade. "What is *that*?" he demanded.

"That?" Julian frowned at him, his brows contracting to an unpleasant "v." "It is a spleen. It is one of the organs—"

"Who is it from, whelp?"

"*Who?* You must be jesting. It is from a goat."

"Prove it."

Julian tore away from the nimbus of candlelight. His face fell into darkness. "I can't. I won't. These are important experiments. They might save lives someday. But what would you care with your brutish ways and clumsy oafishness? You break in here without a by your leave and expect answers from me at knifepoint. I am not afraid of you. I am not afraid of anyone!"

Crispin's anger bubbled. He had met murderers aplenty. It seemed in London they came a penny a dozen. But the young corpse that he had seen with his own eyes was beyond murder. He dismissed the idea of a Golem. That was a distraction, a cheap conjurer's trick to fool the eye. Whatever that thing was, if it existed at all, did not perpetrate these atrocities. The body was handled in too calculated a way, too clinical, too careful. The crime was committed by a man, to be sure. And he was beginning to be certain that the culprit stood before him.

"You *should* be afraid of me. And afraid of the hangman's noose. You are a murderer of a most foul nature. To do the things you have done—it disgusts me to even think of it."

"How dare you! I am no such thing! I *save* lives. It is against the code of the physician. It is against the code of my faith."

Crispin proffered his knife again. "You will tell me *exactly* what you have been doing here. And I will examine the evidence for myself."

Julian stepped into the candlelight. His face was contorted with frustration. His hands, those long-fingered hands, gestured at him. "I murdered no one. What do you accuse me of?"

"Very well. If you must play this game. Four boys were discovered murdered. They were found naked with evidence that their limbs were bound. Their bowels were skillfully ripped from their bodies. And they were sodomized."

If actor he was, Julian showed superb skill. His pupils dilated until the irises were a mere pale green ring against the whites. At last his lips trembled and a hand came up to press upon their whitening pallor. "No," he whispered. "Almighty Lord, no." His hand groped for a stool and he found one behind him. Sinking down, his taut body fell limp. From the hearth light and the candle, Crispin noticed the sash around the boy's waist. Such a thing could easily be used to strangle.

"You accuse me of this," he said with a husky voice. And then, any amount of sympathy the youth might have engendered was lost as he raised his head and snarled an ugly laugh. His eyes gradually cleared and he gritted his teeth. "Get out."

No more of this. Crispin grabbed his shoulder and yanked hard. The youth stumbled to his feet. "Explain it to the sheriff."

"What? No! Unhand me!" The boy wrestled, wriggling like an eel until he slipped from Crispin's grip and ducked away from him, melting against the wall. "I am not a murderer! What will it take to convince you?"

"Do you conspire with those other Jews? Is this an elaborate plot to kill Christian boys?"

Julian stared at him. "*Other* Jews? You are mad. What are you talking about?"

"Do not play the fool with me, boy. I know of the secret Jews in London. And I also know of the plots to kill Christian boys. Is this part of a larger scheme?" Crispin's hand hurt. He realized he'd been gripping the knife hilt tighter and tighter.

Julian's green eyes darted to both of Crispin's. "You make no sense. There are no Jews in England. Your own king saw to that."

That was enough. Crispin lunged and grabbed the boy by his

gown, pulled him forward, and shook him. "Do not *play* with me! So help me, I will flay you alive—" The blade speared toward the young man's face and those green eyes contracted, staring down its tip.

"*Maître* Guest!"

Crispin's attention slid for only a moment toward Jacob staring horrified in the open doorway. But it was enough for the slippery youth to escape again. This time Julian's blade was free and in his hand. His chest heaved as he inched toward the door.

"Father! Back away! This man is insane. He speaks nonsense and of horrible things."

Jacob looked from one to the other, searching for some sense between them. Crispin sneered. "It is this son of yours whose sin you should fear, Master Jacob. His 'experiments' are an abhorrence to God. And these *things*"—he gestured toward the table—"should be destroyed."

Jacob entered and curled a taut hand around the lad's wrist, pulling him none too gently behind him but not allowing him to leave. "Have I not warned you of this abomination?" he hissed at him. "We are not butchers. We do not need to have such filth in our midst."

"But Father—"

"No, Julian! I have allowed it for too long. These things must go."

Crispin was unmoved by the physician's rhetoric. "All very well, Master Jacob. But surely you are aware that these are *human* entrails."

Jacob did not loosen his grip on the boy's arm but his attention now lay fully with Crispin. "Human? No! They are animal entrails, *Maître*. Animals! We examine these organs to understand their functions. Surely you can see—"

"I accuse your son of most foul murder, Master Jacob. That which you ascribe to some mythical Golem. It is your son who stands accused of murder, disembowelment . . . and sodomy."

Crispin expected much, but he did not expect the curiously stagnant expression on the physician's features.

Jacob merely shook his head and chewed his lip. "No. No, *Maître* Guest. You are mistaken. On all counts."

"I am not! This is the proof of it! These foul canisters! Can you deny it?"

"I do," said Jacob firmly. "Julian might have been in error harboring these forbidden things, these *animal* things, but he means well." He turned to his son, still holding fast to his arm. "Your notes are sound. Your conclusions scholarly."

Julian beamed at his father's praise, forgetting Crispin's denouncement.

"Damn you both!" That snapped them out of it satisfactorily. The two turned toward him. "I am speaking of murder. Are you deaf?"

Jacob released the boy's wrist and calmly set his hands before him, crossing those weathered fingers one over the other. Julian stood slightly behind his father, glaring. "I am far from deaf, *Maître*. And you are far too loud for the hour," he said, his voice lowering. "I submit to you that you are mistaken about my son. He is no murderer. Nor is he capable of the other things you accuse him of."

"Forgive me, Master Physician," he said tightly, "but I have seen what lesser men are capable of."

Frustratingly, Jacob shook his head again. Crispin dearly wanted to wrench it from his neck. "He is an apprentice physician. He stays at my side, learning. These things you accuse him of, and horrific though they may be, are not possible. We do not kill. We save lives. Further, *Maître,* the touching of blood is against our faith. True, I must bleed patients to revive their humors," he said, raising a hand to Crispin's openmouthed objection. "And in cleansing wounds." He sheepishly nodded toward Crispin's arm. Crispin felt a twinge where Julian's knife had breached him. "But we are assiduous at purification," said Jacob. "Some sacrifices must be made for our art. The Lord hears our prayers and our pleas for forgiveness. Julian has made his experiments, it is true. But to learn. These horrific tokens"—his hand swept over the table—"will be disposed of and shall not be spoken of again."

"*Mon père*!"

Jacob closed his eyes. "They shall *not* be spoken of again." He waited for Julian's silent submission before he opened his eyes and went on. "Julian is always at my side, as I said. Simply, he would not have had time to do the things you would accuse him of."

"And yet he was here alone with me," said Crispin.

"For a mere few moments. Tell me, *Maître* Guest, in your expert opinion, would a man have time to do that of which you accuse my son and still have time to erase the offal and blood that would surely follow such an abomination? From the room and from himself? You are a man used to combat. You must realize the amount of blood that would be produced from such doings."

Crispin gritted his teeth. God's blood! The damned man with his slowly blinking eyes and his calm demeanor merely gazed at Crispin, certain in his pronouncement. Of course he could be lying and Julian might have been missing for longer periods of time. But then again, where would he have performed these deeds?

"This does not sufficiently explain away his guilt." But even as he said it his stomach swooped unpleasantly. It was explaining it away very nicely, as a matter of fact. "You could be lying to protect him," he snapped. Only after it left his mouth did he feel a slight twinge of loutishness.

Jacob lifted his chin and his cheeks darkened to a dusky hue. But his lips firmed and he spoke not a word.

Their silent joust yielded nothing. The man was formidable and his sharp gaze never wavered. This was no certainty of the man's veracity . . . but it was close enough.

With a growl, Crispin spun away from both father and son and shoved his knife hard into its sheath. He found himself staring at the table, watching that god-awful *thing* floating in its jar. He hated like hell to be wrong. He hated still more to admit it. But there *was* something about that youth that irritated the devil out of Crispin, got under his skin like a rash. There had to be something he could blame him for—oh yes. With a sly grin, Crispin turned back toward them. "There is also the little matter of a dead servant who was about to inform me of a very interesting fact regarding your parchments, Master Jacob. A servant who made an appointment to meet with me . . . an appointment overheard by Master Julian."

Relaxed, Julian's lids drooped over his eyes and a brow arched. It galled Crispin that he did not seem to fear him or God's retribution. "Yes, I heard that servant when you were talking to him. But I was not the only one in the corridor. There were several men behind me. Any one of them could have heard. You should have closed the door."

"How very convenient. And impossible to prove. Give me your sash."

Julian started and his hands went instantly to the scarlet sash at his waist. "W-what? Why?"

"I'll give you exactly to the count of three."

Those droopy lids snapped open. Whatever expression Crispin wore, it certainly convinced him. Julian hastily grabbed at the silken sash and unwound it. He held it forth and Crispin snatched it and stomped to the hearth. He held it to the light as he carefully untied the thread from his money pouch and laid it upon the silky cloth.

The colors were not even close.

Crispin braced himself. He almost tossed the sash into the flames for spite but held himself in check. Instead, he studied it. No tears, no sweat stains, no wrinkles as one would find had it been used as a garrote. It was in perfect order.

Without looking back, he thrust the sash behind him until someone took it from his fingers. He tied the thread to his pouch again. His shoulders winced when he heard Julian's throaty laugh. "Are you satisfied *now*?"

"No." His arms were firmly crossed over his chest. "What do you know of these secret Jews?"

It was Jacob's step he heard approach and then the man's shadow quivered beside his. "Secret Jews, *Maître* Guest? What tidings are these?"

"I have encountered the unlikely habitation of a secret enclave of Jews, descendants of those Jews supposedly exiled from England. These were supposed to be converts, but they forsook their oaths and their baptisms." He spat the last, disgusted by anyone whose oaths meant nothing.

Jacob made a snorting sound and pressed his hand to his mouth. "Interesting. But . . . I have nothing to do with them, if these tidings are true. And my son is also innocent of congress with them." Jacob's face was lit from the hearth, half in light while the other surrendered to shadow. The stark line of light served to emphasize the deep creases and wrinkles carving the man's features. "*Maître* Guest, it is late. You have had strange encounters today. And these murders are vexing and horrifying. I have not heard these details before. I only knew of the murders. I did not know of these . . . other matters." He appeared worried, but he did not look at his son. "I will offer a prayer, for it is all I can do." He gave Crispin a steady look. "And I offer assurances about my son. He is a man of science with a superb mind. But he is not a murderer. Nor is he any of the other things you would ascribe to him. Come back on the morrow, and we will talk of it. Perhaps he can tell you of the other men in the corridor."

"No. I do not know who they were," the boy retorted. Crispin wanted to strangle him. But then he realized the context of his thoughts and felt slightly ashamed. There had been far too much strangling of late.

He raised his eyes instead to Jacob. He wanted to offer an apology, an explanation, but it withered on his tongue. Holy saints, but he was tired. Bone weary and melancholy at all these events. Perhaps, just perhaps, he had not been thinking as clearly as he could have done. He was hungry and in need of wine. It was too late to patronize the Boar's Tusk, but perhaps not too late to call upon Gilbert and Eleanor.

12

CRISPIN ESCAPED THE PALACE without incident, vowing to return in the morning to further question Julian. When he had looked at the boy to make this avowal, the knave had the nerve to sneer at him.

The fog was no better at this late hour, but it served to hide him from the Watch and he was grateful for that relief at least. Back to London, Crispin was grounded in the familiar as he made his way down Newgate Market until it became the Shambles. He cast an eye to his window above the tinker shop and frowned at the absence of a candle glow piercing the shutters. Perhaps Jack had gone to bed, tiring of waiting for Crispin to return.

He traveled down Cheap and turned the corner at Gutter Lane, and because of the dense fog, he had to travel by rote to the shuttered Boar's Tusk. He was no stranger to this trek, drunk or sober.

The Boar's Tusk was a blocky edifice with a stone foundation and lime-washed walls slashed by dark timbering. Some of its roof slates hung precariously over the street, but Crispin viewed all its flaws as a besotted lover disregards the wrinkles of his paramour. The place was as poor as he was and perhaps just as flawed. He felt a kinship with that old building as much as he felt a warm stirring of friendship for those within.

The door was shut and no doubt barred. The entry was a large expanse of old oak, fastened with heavy iron hinges. He pounded upon it and waited a beat before his fist offered a few more.

A voice from within called through it, "Peace, friend. The tavern is shut for the night. Come back on the morrow."

"But I would have my wine now," said Crispin as loudly as he dared.

A pause. "Crispin?"

"The same. Open up, Gilbert. I'm cold."

A heavy beam clunked as it lifted from the door and the way was suddenly opened, revealing Gilbert's smile and a shadow of a beard on his round face. "Crispin, do you know the hour?" he chided, even as he ushered him in. He closed the door again and replaced the beam to bar it.

"My apologies," he said with a cursory bow. "But I was hungry. And I need my wine. It has been . . . a day."

"And perhaps you wanted your friends to offer a comforting ear?" He rested his hand on Crispin's shoulder and steered him toward the hearth.

The place seemed more solemn without the usual raucous crowd. Forlorn. The shadows hung in the corners like cobwebs. Even the hearth, still glowing from a few good-sized logs, seemed dispirited. But it was warm. He sat, easing a sigh from his lips as Gilbert leaned over him. "I will bring wine and a bit of cold fish. Will that do?"

"Gilbert, you are a saint."

Gilbert guffawed and rubbed the back of his reddened neck. "That I am not." He trudged back toward the kitchens, and Crispin heard him call to his servant Ned for some fish.

Crispin leaned back and kneaded the ache in his shoulder, not realizing until he sat down how taut and gnarled his muscle was. Sitting before the fire, he thawed, glad of this small pleasure.

A few moments passed and Gilbert returned. He had a tray

with two stacked bowls, a jug of wine, and a trencher with several fish and a wedge of cheese.

Crispin reached for his money pouch but Gilbert waved him off. "No, Crispin. Tonight you are my guest. It is a rare thing indeed when you come to us as friends."

Crispin ducked his head as Gilbert set the table. He could feel his cheeks warm from more than the fire. It was true. He had neglected this friendship, using the Boar's Tusk as a convenient tavern and selfishly taking advantage of the kindness of his hosts. They had befriended him when few would. He owed them far more than an overdue tavern bill.

He mumbled his thanks, too embarrassed to say more.

"So Crispin," said Gilbert, settling into his chair. He stretched his thick legs, wiggling his pointed-toed shoes toward the fire. His own wine was half gone as he settled the bowl on his ample belly. "Tell me about this terrible day that has you creeping about into taverns well past curfew."

How much to tell? He eyed Gilbert, knowing the man was oath-bound by friendship never to reveal something Crispin told him in confidence.

"There have been foul murders in the city, Gilbert. Perhaps you have heard—"

"Oh aye," he said. He suddenly snapped forward, catching his wine bowl in time. His earnest face searched Crispin's own. "The boy. I heard of it. You are searching for his killer?"

Crispin nodded and drank down the rest. Gilbert quickly refilled it from a round jug. He licked his wine-slickened lips. "God be praised. I know that since you are on it, you will not give up. That child shall find justice."

Crispin slurped another gulp of wine. He wiped the rest with his hand and took up a fish. It was cold but it didn't matter. He pulled the meat from the bones and chewed. "*Four* children," he said quietly.

"Four?" Gilbert muttered a prayer and crossed himself. He did not move or speak for some time. Crispin finished two fish and two more bowls of wine. He was feeling warm and soft.

Gilbert finally looked up at him. His brown eyes flickered to gold in the hearthglow. "And today. What happened today?"

Crispin sighed around the bread in his mouth. He tore off another hunk, dipped it in his wine, and sucked up the soggy dough. "A man who might have told me the culprit was himself murdered."

"Oh!" Gilbert jerked in his chair. He shook his head in disbelief. "Crispin, this is unbelievable. Unheard of in all of London's history! How can such a thing be?"

"You do not know the half of it, Gilbert. But I am too much of a friend to fully share the horrors with you."

Gilbert shuddered. The Langtons had no children. Perhaps this was why they so took to Crispin, forlorn and very like a child in his naïveté when he had first lost everything. Though Gilbert and Eleanor were a scant few years older than he, they still often treated him like their own. For the most part, he ignored it. But today, for the first time, *he* felt like the parent, protecting his charge from the evils of the world. No, he would not tell Gilbert the gruesome details.

"I do not know what London is coming to," said Gilbert, his voice slurring. The both of them finished the jug in no time. Fortunately, Ned had poked his head out earlier, and now approached with what looked like another full jug.

"Ned, my boy," said Gilbert. "Bless you. You know us too well."

"As does Mistress Eleanor," said Ned. He wore a patched cap and a stained apron. "She warned me she'd box me ears if I didn't send Master Crispin home soon."

Crispin eyed the jug critically. "I think much can be accomplished in that time, Ned."

It was Gilbert who took up the jug, saluted to the retreating Ned, and poured more into each of their bowls.

"Now, I've always said. . . ." said Gilbert, leaning precariously toward Crispin as he poured. The jug's spout barely teetered over the bowl. Crispin pulled his leg out of the way to avoid a drenching. Gilbert laughed. "Whoops. Perhaps this shall be my last bowl."

"Perhaps it should be," said Crispin, though his own words weren't as crisp as when they'd started.

Gilbert thumbed the rim of his bowl. "What was I saying?" He stared at Crispin with a lopsided expression. "Oh yes!" His eyes suddenly brightened and he sloshed his wine when he sat up. "I've always said what a clever man you are. You will not let this murderer go free."

"I thought I had found him tonight. But it might be that I . . . I was wrong." Even the drink did not take the sting out of it. He drank but it did not numb the irritation he felt for Julian. But it was more than irritation. His emotions seemed all over the map. He could not reconcile his feelings in this instance. He wanted to throttle the young man, to be sure, but there was something else about him.

He laughed at himself and drank. Too much of this had softened his well-earned frustration with the youth. He had not wanted relief from that but from the other strange tidings today: of the secret Jews and the murdered servant, plainly killed by the same monster that slew those boys.

Monster. Was there not a monster on the loose? That strange being that was more demon than man? Had he not seen him with his own eyes? And Jack. He had seen it, too. Dare he call it a Golem?

He raised his head. It felt muzzier than it had before. With a serious tone that came out a bit more slurred than he would have liked, Crispin said, "Gilbert, be warned. Do not let your own out after dark."

Gilbert blinked at him. "After dark? As a matter of course, we have no cause. Except to the kitchens."

"Even to go outside to the privy. Stay within."

"What? But why?"

"Demons are afoot, Gilbert. And I do not say this lightly. I do not know what prowls London's streets these nights, but I fear for its citizens. Do not go out after dark."

Gilbert stared at him, his jaw hanging. It took a moment, but he slowly closed it and nodded, fear shining though the wine glaze in his eyes.

Crispin leaned in. "There is no reason to tell Eleanor. I would not cause her undue anxiety."

"Anxiety about what?" asked Eleanor.

Crispin jumped three feet at least. He pressed a hand to his racing heart. "God's blood, woman! Must you creep up on a man?"

She smiled and folded her arms over her generous bosom. "Sometimes it is the best way." She eyed the wine jugs sitting before them. "The hour is late, Gilbert. I think the two of you had best bid your farewells."

"Can't a man gossip with his friend, Eleanor?" He swung his arm over Crispin's shoulder, an overfriendly gesture he would never have attempted when sober.

"Now I am certain you are in your cups. Come now. Up, husband. Let Master Crispin to his bed."

"I'm not sleepy, Nell," said Crispin and then stifled a yawn.

"Indeed not." She pulled the large tavern keeper to his feet. "And neither is this fellow. Which is why his lids droop and his step slackens. The two of you! Adolescents. Go home, Crispin."

"Home," he muttered and stood. As soon as he did his vision slanted. *Ah. Just right.*

Ned arrived and Eleanor surrendered Gilbert to him. She took Crispin's arm and escorted him to the door. "Mayhap you will come to Christmas dinner this year. Do we have to serve it in such an ungodly hour for you to accept our invitation?"

"Christmas." Crispin was not so drunk that he would capitulate so easily. "I will think on it," he said with no intention of doing so.

"Aye. I'll wager you will." Eleanor was not fooled. Damnable woman.

She propped him against the wall as she lifted the beam that barred the door. She made to open it but the door slipped out of her hands. She gave a little shriek just as Jack Tucker poked his head in. He stuck dirty fingertips into his ears. "Hold, woman! You'll make me deaf!"

"Jack," said Crispin, relieved. He needed someone to lean on for the journey home.

Jack looked Crispin over and smirked at Eleanor. "Right drunk, ain't he?"

She nodded. "As a pickled crabapple."

Crispin's foggy brain tried to feel affronted. All he could summon was, "What are you doing here, Jack?"

"Looking for you."

"I would have come home anon."

"I ain't been home."

Crispin struggled out of the boy's grasp. Eleanor placed a hand on her hip. She seemed to be wrestling with the notion of pushing them out or hustling them back in.

"Jack! I sent you home hours ago!"

Jack smiled. It was the most insincere thing about him. "I didn't go. I got a notion. About that Golem, sir."

Eleanor frowned at them but Jack's words seemed to decide it. She closed the door and replaced the beam, then shooed them toward the fire. "Well, you might as well sit down if you are to have a discussion. And what, pray, is a 'Golem'?"

Jack sat but then shifted forward on his seat. "Oh Mistress! It is a foul monster!"

"Jack," warned Crispin.

"A fiend who stalks the night. We seen him. Master Crispin and me."

"Jack. . . ."

"He was huge and awful. Murdering boys and such with his bare hands—"

"JACK!"

Jack turned mildly toward Crispin. "Aye? What is it?"

The worst had been done. It couldn't now be unsaid. Crispin sat back. "Never mind."

"Well then." Jack licked his lips, staring anxiously at the discarded wine bowls. Eleanor pushed the jug decidedly away toward the other end of the table. With a sigh, Jack gripped the table's edge. "There is this Jew physician at the palace—oh!" He turned a sheepish expression toward Crispin. "Was I supposed to keep that part a secret?"

Crispin waved his hand and settled back, resting his chin on his chest. "I have no secrets, apparently."

Jack blinked. "Well." He looked at Eleanor who urged him on with a gesture. "And so, there is this Jew and he lost some parchments. But they were magical parchments because some whoreson—beggin' your pardon, Mistress—used them to summon this demon."

She gasped. "Oh Crispin! Is this true?"

With eyes closed, he waved his head as vaguely as he could. Eleanor took this as an affirmative and Jack as a cue to continue. "They're made out of clay, these Golems, and the demon somehow goes into the clay body, see. And then it tromps all over London at night, killing what he wills."

Crispin snorted, barely awake at this point. "Jack, you're getting it quite wrong."

"No, I ain't. It's killing boys is what it is. And *worse*!"

Eleanor planted her chin on her hand. "What do you mean by 'worse'?"

"Eleanor!" said Crispin. "For Christ sake."

"Very well," she said, waving him off. "Did *you* encounter it? How did you get away?"

"It was a fair pace from us. We tried to follow the beast but it was a slick piece of work. Got clean away every time Master Crispin chased it."

Her eyes flicked to Crispin. "You gave chase?"

"He did," answered Jack proudly. "He don't fear nought, does Master Crispin."

"Only your loose tongue," he grumbled.

"And so, this night, when Master Crispin sent me home—"

"Where you should have gone!"

"I got m'self an idea. This Golem is made of clay, ain't it? And me and Master Crispin saw the bits of clay for ourselves, didn't we? So I thought to m'self, 'Where can a body get that much clay?'"

Crispin suddenly sat up. Not quite sober but not quite as drowsy as before, Crispin stared dumbfounded at his charge. "Jack! You are a genius!"

Jack sat back with a wide grin and laced his fingers behind his head. "I know."

13

IT TOOK SOME TIME for Jack to convince Crispin to come home to sleep and see about the clay on the morrow. Climbing the narrow stairway to their lodgings, Crispin had almost tumbled down the stairs, but Jack's steady arm prevented his breaking his neck. He was grateful in the long run to settle into his bed, the scratchy blanket tucked under his chin, while Jack covered the embers with ashes. Crispin imagined himself to be warm, but he knew it was only due to his inebriated state.

But now that the morning had come, and with it the sharp lance of light piercing the shutters and the raucous clang of iron kettle against clay cauldron, he could no longer appreciate his perceived comfort. Not when his head felt leaden, swollen, and like a pot on an anvil, being beaten upon by an unsteady tinker.

"Jack," he moaned. "Can't you be quiet?"

"Sorry, Master," said Jack heartily. "But it is morn and you said last night that we must get an early start. The water is almost hot for your shave and the peas porridge is ready when you want it."

He offered Crispin a wooden bowl of ale. Crispin sat up and glared at it. "Where did you get this?"

"Master Kemp brought it up this morning. He heard how you were feeling poorly and said this was a good remedy."

"I have only just awakened. How did he know I would be feeling poorly?"

"Well, when I came across him this morning I might have mentioned about how you were . . . last night."

Crispin did not question it further. He downed the ale and smacked his lips. It wasn't enough to take off the edge but it was better than nothing.

Jack took Crispin's cloak and draped it over his master's shoulders as he hunched in the bed, trying to keep warm. The boy next pressed the bowl of porridge into his hand and Crispin drank the warm liquid. He wiped his mouth and handed the bowl back to the boy, who scooped up a helping for himself and sipped at it. "Your water, sir."

Crispin muttered to himself as he slid out of the bed, the straw in the mattress crunching under him. He wrapped the end of his cloak over the kettle's handle and poured some of the steamy water into a basin and took that to the shelf under a bit of shiny brass nailed to a post. He lathered his chin with a soap cake and hoped the razor was sharp enough. He ignored his shaky hand and did the best he could. He scrubbed his teeth with a finger and the leftover water, and spit it back into the basin.

Jack took the basin from his hand, swished open the back garden shutters, and tossed the water out.

"How do I look?" asked Crispin blearily.

Jack studied him and cocked his head. "As well as can be expected."

"High praise," he muttered and pulled the edges of his chaperon hood down over his cloak.

Jack fingered the book that lay on the table. "What is this, sir?"

He had quite forgotten about the book. Did he have time to look it over now? His hand inched over the leather cover and he found himself sitting before it with both hands at the leather ties.

He opened the cover, tsking at the water damage done when Giles's cousin tossed it into the mud, and settled down to read.

Jack tinkered with the fire and rambled about, finally settling down in his corner to brush the mud vigorously from Crispin's cloak hem.

Crispin read, and it wasn't long before his ire pricked the back of his neck. The more he read, the angrier he got. He had thought little about Jews before, but that they would scheme to kill an innocent boy for their strange rituals was unthinkable. Yet it was all there, inked on this parchment. Yes, well. He'd have a thing or two to say to Julian about this!

Crispin got unsteadily to his feet. He wasn't certain if it was still the effects of drinking or of his anger. "Jack, if we go we had best go now. While I am still upright."

Jack mumbled something that Crispin did not care to hear and waited for the boy to don his own cloak and hood. There was much he needed to relate to Jack about the happenings of yesterday.

As they made their way down the icy steps, Crispin began his tale, and Jack listened wide-eyed to all its ups and downs, particularly when he came to the part about the dead servant. Several "God blind me" exclamations later, Jack drew silent.

There was slush upon the ground but the sky held no snow. It was washed in a mottled gray like the ocean after a storm. They moved south toward the Thames, making their way to Salt Wharf in Queenhithe. When they arrived, they hired a ferryman to take them across, and Jack stood at the bow like any other child excited to be making the trip. Crispin leaned on the side, looking out across the choppy, gray water. Skiffs speared the water beside them, their pilots glaring as if Crispin were invading their territory. Possibly, he was. He paid them no heed and pulled his hood down as far over his head as he could, trying to shield his face from the icy wind and spray. His mind was on death and blood and the treachery of Jews.

The Bankside suddenly loomed out of the mist. As they drew closer to the dock, fishermen mending their nets took shape out of the gloom.

He thought he could make out the smoke from the kilns though it might just be suspended fog. But perhaps it was only cooking fires from the row on row of houses and shops lining the riverfront. Crispin seldom traveled to Southwark. Not if he could help it. The stews did not interest him. At least that's what he told himself. The truth lay more in practicalities. A tumble with a Bankside whore seemed less critical when one's purse was empty.

As he stepped out onto the wharf and handed the ferryman a halpen, he could not help but feel surrounded by the low speech of Southwark such as came from Jack's mouth. In his exile, Crispin had decided early on that he would not live in Southwark, no matter what it took. It was bad enough living on the Shambles, but to live on the Bankside with whores and thieves . . .

His eye fell upon Jack springing forth from the ferry's unsteady rolling bow and landing squarely on the wharf. The boy smiled up at him; a grin that was as wide as the Thames. So much for not living with thieves.

He raised his chin and took in the busy wharves and street above. The potters were not far, for indeed that *had* been smoke coming from the hardworking kilns of London. He could smell it now.

He followed his nose while Jack ran back and forth at his heels like a pup. He was quite proud of Jack for coming up with the notion. The boy was sharp, no question about it. It surprised him that a creature of such low beginnings could be so clever, but with a bit of gloating, he owed much of Jack's shrewdness to himself and his careful tutoring.

Jack raised his arm and pointed. "That's the potters," he said. "They're the ones I seen yesterday. I watched them for a good long time, Master. I talked a fair bit to one of them apprentices, a boy named Wat. He told me about their trade. They make jugs and cooking pots and such. But business is getting poorly, so he says. His master is worried that they might have to find another vocation."

"Business is that bad?"

"Oh aye. So he said. But he *is* just an apprentice."

"I find the word of apprentices more and more valuable these days."

Jack missed the compliment. His attention was taken by the many ovens as they cleared the corner, of the young men carrying buckets of clay hanging from yokes over their bent shoulders, of young boys balancing vast bundles of sticks on their heads.

It was hard to believe that this industriousness might all be for nought. Crispin watched silently from across the lane, staying in the shadows. Jack fairly vibrated beside him, no doubt impatient for Crispin to do something. But Crispin had no need to do anything as of yet. He, too, wanted to watch the work, especially the men and even women he could see through doorways, their feet pushing at a wheel while they worked their alchemy on a shapeless slab of clay. With hands drenched in murky water, they brought forth tall hourglass-shaped jugs and squat, round-bellied pots. Decorations were daubed onto the sides in diamond patterns and basket weaves, or merely rolled on with small wheeled instruments.

Quick as a wink, a pot was done, pulled from the wheel, and placed on a shelf. Another blob of clay was thrown to the wheel, and the potter began again, something new emerging from his clever hands.

"Aye, Master," said Jack. "I could watch them all day. I nearly did. It's a right fine skill, that is. But I ain't clever with me hands. I'd best settle on using me mind and becoming a Tracker, like you."

He snapped a sidelong glance at his young charge. "I know it is a step down from a potter, Jack."

But Jack suddenly straightened and speared his arm outward. "There's Wat now!"

A stick-thin boy with gaunt features and straw-colored hair staggered under the burden of a bundle of fuel a donkey might have balked at carrying. It was not an unusual sight to see such young boys working harder than beasts, but Crispin felt a strange sensation in his belly watching this lad. It seemed he noticed all the young boys in London now, seeing them as potential victims and wondering how on earth he was to protect any of them.

"Wat!" Jack sprinted toward him and immediately took the sticks from his shoulders, carrying them himself. Wat's look of relief was heartbreaking.

"Jack," said the boy. A smile spread on his face, stretching the chapped skin to a shiny sallow color. But when his eyes lifted to Crispin, the smile vanished.

"Wat," said Crispin mildly. "I am pleased to make your acquaintance."

Wat looked uncertainly at Jack. "This is me master, Crispin Guest. Worry not. He's a good soul."

The boy seemed disinclined to believe this and remained standing beside his stick bundle.

"This business of pot-making," said Crispin, sweeping the row of ovens casually with his arm. "It is fascinating work. Your master must be very skilled."

The boy said nothing. His hollow-eyed stare was becoming unnerving.

"And so," said Crispin, trying like the devil to think of something to say to draw the boy out, "I am most interested in how it is done. Perhaps you can enlighten me."

Wat's glassy stare rested on Crispin for a long while before he turned it back toward the workers. "There ain't much to tell," he said in a slow, careful voice. "You get the clay and you keep it in the slip, and put it on the wheel and then . . . you work it."

"So I see." Crispin nodded importantly, not truly understanding. He rocked on his heels. "And the clay. Where does it come from?"

The boy squinted. It ruined his already long face by twisting it strangely, and gave an expression that rather assumed Crispin was a simpleton. He thumbed behind him. "It comes from the Thames, don't it?"

"That it does," he said, feeling a bit foolish. "Perhaps I can talk to your master." Crispin dropped his friendly tone and used one reserved for menials. The boy certainly recognized it. He snatched the stick bundle from Jack and hefted it up to his shoulders.

"I'll take you to him."

Jack scrambled happily beside his new friend while Crispin took up the rearguard. They threaded through the busy path of muddy snow and clay. Freshly fired pots stood in a row in the mud outside a few shops and huts. Women wove through the streets, bringing bread and salted fish to some of the men.

Wat lumbered on, finally dropping his bundle with a great sigh when they came to a hovel at the end of the row. He didn't look back as he entered and Jack followed him right behind. Crispin was a bit more cautious as he ducked his head to enter the low doorway. He looked around, his eyes adjusting to the dark space. The floor was made of rotting planks covered in a layer of dust, except for the places where water had been sloshed or muddy footprints had tramped.

A man, bald except for a fall of ginger hair streaked with gray hanging down his back, sat at a wheel, urging its turning with his toes. He stared at the clay that climbed as he pulled it until it was shaped into a tall drinking jug. It was only then that he looked up and frowned.

"Eh? Wat? Who is here?"

Pained by the fearful look on Wat's face, Crispin stepped forward with a slight bow. "I am Crispin Guest, good Master. And I have come to examine your wares."

"My wares?" The man slowly rose and glared from Crispin to Jack. "*My* wares? They are just like everyone else's."

"Indeed." Crispin looked idly at the tilting shelves of pipkins, bowls, and small jugs. They might not even be as good as some of the other wares he had seen, but he certainly did not voice this opinion. "Well, truthfully, there are a few things I am most interested in knowing. For one, if a man should want a large quantity of clay, how should he acquire it?"

Jack, who had been trying to chat with Wat, suddenly fell silent. His face was turned anxiously toward the potter.

The man rose to his feet and dipped his hands in a basin of clear water, washing away the layers of dried clay up his forearms. The water instantly turned brown. His sagging stockings seemed to have a perpetual splatter of wet clay. His back was to Crispin when he spoke. "I am only a poor potter, sir. I do my job, make my wares. That is all."

"Yet if a man should want such a thing. . . ." urged Crispin, stepping closer.

The man turned. His wide-spaced teeth bit into his lower lip. "It is a strange request. I remarked upon it the first time I heard it."

Crispin felt a surge of excitement burn his chest. "The *first* time?"

"Aye." The man reached up slowly and scratched his bald pate. "A man—oh, it was a good long time ago now—asked for bucketfuls of clay. Not from me, you understand, but from some of us. I remember hearing it. 'Bucketfuls of clay?' I asked. What would a body be doing with that? And him a gentlemen, so they said."

"A gentleman? Who?"

He stuck a finger in his ear and reamed it good before pulling it out again. Crispin ignored the finger the man stared at before wiping it down his tunic. "He didn't say. Now I ain't the suspicious kind, mind you. But I did wonder, as did my fellows here. And there was only one scheme we could reason out."

Crispin leaned in, curious. "And that is?"

"That whoreson wants to take our business!" He stood up properly and squared with Crispin. "And if you have the same intention, sir, you can be on your way. We potters aren't getting wealthy here, but we'll take no more money for our own clay."

"He paid, did he?"

"Aye. But don't be getting notions. I'll not take a farthing."

"You mistake me, Master. I do not wish to buy your clay. I have no use for it."

The man looked Crispin up and down suddenly, as if registering him for the first time. "Truly?"

"Indeed. Did the man indicate that he was going into business?"

"I don't rightly know. It wasn't me talking to him, was it."

"I suppose not. When did you say this was?"

The hand returned to the head again and rubbed slowly, back and forth. "I reckon it was before Michaelmas. I remember because I sprained me ankle and Wat here had to turn the wheel for me. You recall that, Wat?"

Wat nodded and offered nothing more.

Michaelmas. That was when the murders began, when the Jewish physician arrived from France. "I must know who talked to this man. Will you tell me which of your fellows it was?"

The man suddenly became reticent. He glanced at Wat before he turned distractedly toward his wares drying on a shelf. "I mind me own business, good sir. I don't wish to cause trouble for any of my fellows."

"No one is in trouble. I am not the law. I am merely here to see to these matters to make certain . . . to make certain . . . er. . . ." He had no wish to go into specifics. He blurted the next thing that came to him. "That the guild is not being impinged upon." It seemed like a poor excuse but it made the man ponder.

He brought up his head. "Aye. The guild, did you say?" He

looked at Crispin anew. Yes, Crispin supposed he might look more like someone who might speak on behalf of the guilds. "We did not know this man who wanted the clay," said the potter thoughtfully. "And we know many of our competitors. The Oxford men and the Kingston men. These Londoners," he growled, "that they would buy the wares from far away over the good pottery we make right here in the city! It's a shame, it is. There's no loyalty at all anymore, is there?"

"Very little," Crispin agreed. "But can you direct me to someone who spoke to this man?"

He nodded. "Oh aye. Come with me, then." He ambled toward the door in a stooped posture that spoke of his years over the wheel and motioned for Crispin to follow.

Many eyes followed Crispin and his little company. The potter took the lead, hailing his fellows through their doorways as he passed. Crispin strode behind him with Jack in the rear, trying to urge a contrary Wat to follow.

After the man greeted what seemed like every potter in London, they finally arrived at their destination. Just another potter's hovel, in Crispin's estimation. The white daub had long ago turned gray. The thick mist could not hide the unnatural slope of the roof whose clay tiles were mostly broken or missing.

"A cobbler's children," Crispin muttered.

"Eh? What's that, good sir?" asked his guide.

"Nothing," said Crispin. "Is this the place?"

"Aye. But Bert does not look to be within. We will have to wait." And then the man proceeded to push open the door.

Crispin stood on the lane as the man disappeared into the shadowed doorway and didn't reappear again. He had time to share a look with Jack before the man poked his head out again. "Coming?"

Jack gave a shrug and gestured for Crispin to go first. Manners appeared to be a little less formal on the potter's row. Crispin girded himself and stepped over the threshold, ducking his head under the lintel.

It was little bigger than Crispin's own lodgings and as sparsely furnished. A cot, a potter's wheel, and some makeshift shelves were all there was to it. The room itself was smoky from a neglected fire situated in a ring of stones in the middle of the floor. This particular potter did not appear to have an apprentice to keep the fires stoked and the rest clean.

"Should be nigh at any moment, I reckon," the man said, pouring what looked like ale from a decorative jug into an equally decorative ceramic beaker. He drank up without hesitation as Crispin eyed the doorway. At length, a woman stepped through and Crispin straightened.

"Bert!" The potter wiped his mouth and set the beaker aside. The woman entered and stared suspiciously at Crispin.

"Dickon. What mischief is here?" She was carrying a heavy bundle and set it down by the smoky fire ring. When she rose she brushed back a lock of brown hair. Her face was plain, drawn. A small nose perched above chapped lips. Her squinting eyes, what Crispin could see of them, were light in color.

"This man is from the guild, Berthildus, and he would like to talk about that knave who bought your clay."

Her head snapped up but her face did not lose its suspicious glint. When she crossed her arms over her chest and clutched her elbows, Crispin could see the dark clay imbedded under her nails. So this woman must be "Bert" the Potter.

"Damosel," said Crispin, dipping his head in a slight bow, "I am investigating whether certain men are bypassing the guild to make and sell their own wares. Can you tell me what this man looked like?"

Slowly, she bent to her sack and withdrew her shopping; a stringy-looking pullet, some eggs, and a bundle of onions tied together by their dried stems. She set them into a basket under her cot. Wiping her hands on her skirt, she looked from Dickon to Crispin. She had a shrewd look in her eye. More so than the gullible Dickon.

"'Bout time our guild fees showed for something," she said with a nod. "Aye, I recall him right enough. He was a short man, bird-like. Very young. A gentleman. All golden. And foreign."

Crispin's breath caught. He certainly knew this man. "And so. He wanted a quantity of clay?"

"Indeed he did. Six bucketsful. And he paid well for it."

"Did he say what it was for?"

"Alas, no. I was suspicious at the time, but what is a poor widow to do?"

"Indeed. What did he pay for this bounty?"

"Two shillings. I wish I had those shillings still. Business is poor."

"Did you, by any chance, catch his name?"

"He did not offer it and I did not ask it. It is rare indeed that a gentleman comes down to the potter's row to buy anything at all. When I discovered he wanted clay and not pots, I wasn't keen on it. But coin is coin."

"Coin is coin," echoed Crispin. How well he knew that particular chant. "How did he transport this clay? Surely he did not carry it himself. Did he have servants?"

"No servants. I sent my boy after him."

"And where did your boy deliver these buckets?"

"To Westminster Palace. The boy had a lot to say about it, he did. Took him three trips."

"Where is the boy now? I would speak with him."

Berthildus gave a proud smile and her hard face softened. "Hugh, that's my boy, he was told that he had promise. A gentleman of the court, taking him on as a page to teach him to read and write? I could scarce believe it. I gave my consent at once. You never saw a boy more excited than my Hugh."

Her words settled in and a chill of realization rippled slowly up

Crispin's flanks. God's blood! Was it as easy as that? Rather than snatched, were these boys lured away with the promise of a better life right under their parents' noses? By all the saints! How diabolical! They would never be reported missing. They had been given away! And these simple folk could not expect a letter they could not read. Nor any other message from so far away. These boys were gone, never to be seen again. But for all their parents knew, they were simply in a better place. Little did these trusting parents know that that better place was Heaven.

Crispin glanced at Jack to see if he had caught on, but apparently he didn't. Crispin licked dry lips. Should he tell her? Could he dash her hopes and bring the roof down upon her? On any parent?

"Master?" Jack was at his elbow, touching his sleeve. His voice was soft. "Master, what is amiss? You are pale."

"Nothing," he said hastily. He raised his head and nodded to the woman, saying slowly, "Life as a page is difficult. He will have much to learn but it will be rewarding. He . . . he will have little time to communicate with you. There is the possibility that you will see him no more. . . ."

She nodded and wiped at her eye. "Aye. But it's a small price to pay for a better life, I say."

Crispin gritted his teeth and couldn't help but offer a bow. "I thank you for your time." He thought of offering her a coin and wondered if it might seem more like blood money. In the end, he could not leave her without offering something. He dug out two farthings and handed one each to both potters. "For your time," he said lamely and staggered out of the hovel. He walked quickly over the clay-slick lane. Jack ran raggedly behind to catch up.

The boy seemed to sense his mood and said nothing until they were well away and on the Bank, hurrying back to where they could catch the ferry across. When they reached the wharf they had just missed it and had to wait for its return.

"Master," said Jack soberly. "You know something, don't you?"

"Yes, Jack." With a sigh, he leaned against the damp pier jutting up from the wharf. "Did you not hear what she said? She gave her boy away, thinking it was for the good of him."

It took only a moment. "Oh! Oh my God!" Jack began to tremble and Crispin almost wrapped an arm around him. Jack was not an infant. He was nearly a man, having lived as a man for some years. He could deal with this knowledge as a man.

"You don't think—" Jack struggled with the notion. "Why did you not tell her, sir?"

The sick feeling would not leave him. "What would be the use in it? Her child was gone. Dead. Worse than merely dead. It could not help her to know the truth. It might even destroy her."

"'Slud! That's a sore, sore thing." He chewed on his fingers and stared out onto the gray water. Perhaps Jack was thinking the same thing as him: that had Jack consorted with the wrong man instead of Crispin, then he, too, might have been found floating in the Thames.

"Do you know who did it?" he said after a long pause. His voice was roughened by anger.

"Yes. It is Julian." The satisfaction that he had *not* been wrong settled in his chest.

"Aye." There was recognition in the one word. "That was his description right enough. What are you going to do now?"

"I'm going to haul him to Newgate before *I* do something."

Jack made an affirming sound. They said nothing more as they waited for the ferryman slowly making his way across the choppy river.

CRISPIN DID NOT ALLOW Jack to accompany him. He didn't want Jack anywhere near Julian. It was nearly Sext when he reached the gates of Westminster. He still wore his livery from Lancaster over his cotehardie but his hood was drawn low over his face, as always. A light dusting of snow helped to disguise him. He joined a group of pages filing in through the great hall like a pack of sheep.

Westminster Hall was nearly as grand as a cathedral. It was as wide as a row of infantry lined up shoulder to shoulder. The roof reached upwards on columns into a ceiling of wooden beams and trusses. A remarkable space, to be sure, and one that Crispin had enjoyed at many a feast when he was still in the good graces of the old king, Edward of Windsor.

Crispin kept his head down, well acquainted with the high ceilings and hanging banners and shields. He recalled all too well the last time he had been in this hall facing King Richard. It was an event he did not willingly wish to repeat.

He'd gotten halfway across the hall when he heard Giles's voice hailing Lancaster. The hall was crowded with those begging audiences, clerks, servants, pages, and lords. One more liveried servant would be beneath Giles's notice, and, Crispin hoped, Lancaster's.

The duke turned a narrowed-eyed gaze toward Giles. "De Risley."

Giles was with that thin, wheat-haired man, and the stockier dark fellow, Radulfus, who had taunted Crispin in the courtyard.

"Your grace," said Giles with a deep bow. His compatriots followed suit. "I wondered. Had you had an opportunity to look into the monies the king promised to me from my uncle's estate?"

Crispin could only see the back of him, but he recognized well the stiffening in Lancaster's shoulders and the growl undertone to his voice. "I was not aware, my lord, that I was your personal banker."

"No indeed, your grace," he said. "It is just that you have the ear of the king, and since these funds were promised to me—"

"You throw the term lightly, my lord. 'Promised?' I know of no such promise from his Majesty. Your relations had the greater right to your uncle's funds and lands. I think, rather, that you should take it up with them."

"But your grace! That is impossible, as you surely know! They have turned their backs on me, foreswearing their oaths as kinsmen—"

Lancaster yawned. "That *is* troubling news. Then I am at a loss, de Risley."

"But your grace—" Giles reached for Lancaster's arm. The scowl the duke delivered was monumental. Giles slowly unwound his fingers from Lancaster's sleeve.

The duke said nothing more, did not even grace de Risley with a look, before he swept away.

Giles grimaced after him. His fellows crowded closer and spat an oath. He talked in bitter whispers to his companions. "And so you see my dilemma."

"The bastard," said Radulfus, sneering after Lancaster. Crispin felt an unnatural rage, but held himself back from knocking the man's head with his dagger hilt. "So our little games continue."

"As entertaining as they are," said Giles, worriedly, "they are not working!"

"I have told you, my lord," said the birdlike, fair-haired man. "These things take time."

"I spent everything I had on the Guest Manor," he growled. Crispin stiffened. He could not help taking a step closer. "And some money I took that was not my own," he said, voice lowered. "It was supposed to be temporary. I was supposed to be able to pay it back without notice. You *promised* me—"

"I told you, my lord, that the planets were not yet aligned. We should have waited until the next new moon—"

"You and your star charts!" Giles looked around and Crispin turned swiftly, feigning a search across the crowded hall. Giles clutched the man's arm. Crispin surmised this small fellow to be his astrologer. The man always did have a soft spot for such foolery. But what was this about borrowing money? Had Giles paupered himself buying Crispin's lands? It warmed Crispin's heart that Giles somehow wished to preserve his estate from other snatching hands. But Giles should not have overextended himself.

He took a quick glance at the cousin, Radulfus, who was adjusting the long liripipe of his scarlet hat. Perhaps he had put Giles up to it. Giles always was gullible about certain things, especially about money. More often than not he took up with the wrong sort, making the wrong choices.

Carefully, Crispin backed up until he could hear them again. "I must do this thing. We must be able to call upon our lord. Only He can help me. Our funds are dwindling."

So Giles had a patron? That would explain where he got the extra money for the lands. But had he borrowed a little too much? Apparently, Giles had wagered on this uncle's funds that had not been bequeathed to him. Foolish. What was Radulfus urging Giles to do?

Crispin shuffled as close to them as he dared.

"I think you are a fool, Cornelius," said Radulfus to the astrologer. "What have the stars to do with it at all? You are a liar. You have always been a liar!"

The young astrologer ruffled like an affronted guinea fowl.

"Now, now, dear cousin," said Giles. "Keep your voice down. You know his Majesty barely tolerates us. And for that, I lay the blame at your feet!"

Radulfus snorted. "Blame me all you like, but it does not change the fact that we have not been invited to Christmas in Sheen."

"But fear not, coz. We will be at my home at the Guest Manor."

"When will you stop calling it the 'Guest Manor'?" spat the man. "Is it not the de Risley Manor now?"

Giles made some sort of noise and Crispin smiled to himself. *It will always be the Guest Manor,* he chortled inside.

"Of course," said Giles, recovering. "The *de Risley* Manor. We will be a stone's throw from his Majesty. We will be close enough when the festivities begin and he will not notice one more lord at his feast."

"Two, you mean," said the cousin.

"Th-three," ventured Cornelius, glaring at the two of them.

"Of course, my dear Cornelius," said Radulfus. "What would we do without you?" His hand slid around the man's collar.

The young man did not seem pleased by this knowledge. Perhaps it was the odd tone that Radulfus invoked or the leer he gave him. Cornelius pulled his furred collar and looked around. "At any rate," he said angling away from Radulfus, his Flemish accent growing stronger the more agitated he grew, "The Feast of Saint Nicholas will be the time. I am absolutely certain."

"You were absolutely certain the last time, too," said Giles.

"And the time before that," said the other man.

Giles hooked his thumbs into his belt. "And there is no new moon on the feast day."

"No," said the astrologer. "There is no need. The stars are in the proper position. It will work."

"It had better. I have risked too much as it is."

The cousin chuckled. "And a great strain it has been."

Giles sneered, broke away from them, and crossed toward the exit. They moved on and Crispin watched them go from under his hood. What mischief was here? It worried him that Radulfus seemed to be drawing Giles into his schemes. What could he do to warn Giles? He did not trust this cousin.

He'd have to think on it. There was nothing to be done now. He had other business to attend to.

DOWN THE LONG CORRIDOR he went, lowering his face when he neared others wearing the duke's livery. The young pages, too young to recognize him, praise God, stared hard at him as he passed, but he skirted by, hoping to escape another encounter with the duke.

The Jew's door stood at the end of the corridor in the gloom of oil lamp smoke. Crispin flipped his knife from its sheath as he strode toward it and rapped on the door with the hilt.

Julian answered and appeared to be alone.

He pushed his way in and before Julian could shoot him an impertinent remark, Crispin grabbed his collar with his free hand and pushed his knife up to his face. "You are under arrest in the name of the king. I suggest you go quietly, for I do not mind in the least shoving this down your throat."

Julian stared cross-eyed down at the blade and stammered in French. Even as Crispin dragged him toward the door he dug in his heels and began to struggle. He grabbed the edge of the door and it slipped from his fingers, slamming shut. He wriggled completely out of Crispin's grasp and ran behind a chair.

Crispin laughed unpleasantly. "You wish to play games. You will not escape me."

White fingers clutched the chair back. "Why are you so determined to accuse me? I did nothing. My father—"

"Doesn't know you as I do. Doesn't know you are a lying, murdering sodomite!"

He shook his head furiously, his brown hair wisping over his angular cheeks. "I am *none* of those things! Why won't you believe me?"

"You went to the potters to buy clay to make your own Golem. *You* stole your father's parchments."

"No! I do not know what you are talking about."

"Still lying. It will avail you nothing. The sheriff does not abide liars any more than I do."

The young man looked down and bit his lip, leaving it red. "But *you* are lying to make me seem guilty. Why? Because you dislike Jews? You took my father's hard-earned silver! He trusted you. He was only worried about your countrymen; men who would just as soon spit on him than help him."

"Is that why you killed those boys? Because you hate Christians so? Or was it to experiment on them in your vile ways? Oh, I know about you Jews and your Passover sacrifices. The lots that are drawn to determine which town will do the slaughter. The drinking of blood. The eating of human flesh."

"*Seigneur Saint!* I would *never*—!" His eyes flew open and his mouth slackened. For a moment, Crispin thought he might finally see a flicker of honesty on the man's face. But the door closed quickly and Julian raised that pointed chin of his and pressed his trembling lips together. "Who has told you these lies?"

"They are not lies. This is evidence written down from reliable sources."

"Reliable sources. And what are these 'reliable sources'? Christians?"

"Of course! Who else would they be?"

Julian measured Crispin steadily, his eyes narrowing to slits. His nostrils flared and his chest rose and fell in quick succession. "What an absurdity! I do not know from what source you say you read such nonsense, but it certainly is not the Scriptures. Do you even know the word of the Lord?" He waved his hand impatiently. "Never mind. I know that you must. A man who troubles himself to quote Aristotle would take the time to know Scripture. If you want evidence to the contrary, then you had best go there."

"You waste my time." He made a move toward the young man, amazed at the coolness of the boy's demeanor, even as he seemed on the verge of bolting. Julian raised a steady hand and for some reason unknown to Crispin, the gesture made him pause.

"Scripture," said the boy, voice trembling. "Let us take Leviticus. The Law. It is in Leviticus that the Lord says to Moses, 'It shall be a perpetual statute throughout your generations in all your dwellings, that ye shall not eat neither fat nor blood.' And so, consuming blood, any blood, is one of the greatest prohibitions. 'Whosoever it be that eateth any blood, that soul shall be cut off from his people.'"

Crispin listened in spite of himself. He dearly wanted to grab the boy by the neck, but he hesitated. And he listened.

"Do you need more?" said Julian, inching closer. "Hosea. 'They that sacrifice men kiss calves.' But we cannot forget the last instance that a Jew even tried to sacrifice another living man. That was in Genesis and it was Father Abraham laying a blade to his son Isaac's throat. 'And the angel of the Lord called unto him out of heaven, and said: "Abraham, Abraham, Lay not thy hand upon the lad, neither do thou any thing unto him; for now I know that thou art a God-fearing man, seeing thou hast not withheld thy son, thine only son, from Me."'"

Julian shook his head, tearing his eyes away from Crispin who stood dumbly before him. "We draw lots, do we? Such fascinating organization. Across seas? Across borders? How do we accomplish this feat, we who are watched wherever we go? It is decided that this year a boy in . . . in London, is it? . . . is to be sacrificed, no? For the Passover? Is your Michaelmas near Passover, our feast held in the spring?"

"That is all very well," said Crispin. "But an angry youth will kill in the foulest of ways for his own vengeance. Murder is against God's law as much as this blood prohibition you so passionately plead."

Julian returned a scathing glare. "You're not even listening. You, a man of facts. A man of logic. Is it logical to kill four boys, to sacrifice them far from the paschal season, if sacrifice it was? They were crucified, I suppose, as your libels say? You did not mention that. For I have heard of these foul lies before." He threw up his hands and stalked to the fire. "I weary so of Gentile lies. You claim to be holy and then unjustly slaughter my people to satisfy your own superstitions. Because you do not have understanding. These facts are in the Hebrew Scriptures that even your people consider holy. And yet you do not understand them."

Julian stared into the flames. The fire played over his cheek. A flicker. A shadow. His skin seemed to glow warm with the fire. Crispin watched and felt a strange clenching in his gut. He did not like these tangled emotions that Julian seemed adept at wrenching from him.

Julian turned to Crispin suddenly, realization awakening in his eyes. "You do this to hurt my father. You steal his money and then extort him for more. This is your plan. I knew it was foolish to hire some outlaw!"

Crispin bristled. "Do not accuse *me*, whelp. You do not know me. I am not an extortionist."

"And I am not a murderer!"

"I am done arguing with you. I have witnesses who took your money for their clay. Golem or no—and I still do not believe in your Jewish magic—you were intent on foul deeds. Was your false Golem designed to lure these boys? To ensnare them? You tricked them with your ghastly tales and they were enticed to see this monster that you made, is that it? And after you had entrapped these boys, how did you murder them without your father knowing?"

But Julian's features suddenly became surprised again. He even took a step forward, putting himself within Crispin's reach. "You . . . you are serious? I thought my father was exaggerating the case, worrying over some foolish parchment. But . . . This is horrible." He grabbed Crispin's tabard, shaking him. "You must stop these killings! I swear I will help you prove it has nothing to do with Jews."

He grabbed both the boy's wrists in one hand. "You do not play the fool well," he snarled.

"I play at nothing," he beseeched in a startlingly sincere fashion. His eyes were strangely luminous and very green. But then his earnest expression slowly changed to one of resignation. He sighed deeply. "Your heart is like a lion, to be sure, to protect those weaker than you. Even these slain boys. I . . . I suppose, after all is said and done, my father was wise to trust you."

Crispin's grip loosened. "What?"

"You tear at the truth like a dog on a bone. There are few men as tenacious or as clever as you. You must be very clever, indeed, to have discovered all this for yourself."

He shook out the confusion in his head. "Yes. I discovered *you*."

"No. These things. These secret things. *You* discovered them. This is the sort of thing you do to earn your coin? It is very unusual. Surely you see that. You would seem to be a very intelligent man. For a Gentile."

"Hmph! Useless flattery. And now you will come with me."

Julian did not resist but Crispin was not moving. His fist was still wrapped tight around both the boy's thin wrists. But Julian's expression no longer held fear or anger. Instead, it was suffused with awe. His manner had transformed to one of curiosity and composure. He studied Crispin with disquieting steadiness.

"I've never met anyone like you."

"Ha! You mean someone who would arrest you?"

"No, *imbécile*. Someone who uses their mind as their sole vocation." Julian stepped closer even with Crispin still griping his wrists. "You must know that I am not guilty," he said softly. "Your logic tells you."

"The witnesses—" said Crispin halfheartedly, compelled by that gaze.

"The witnesses are wrong." He looked down at his sash, the red cloth wound about his waist. "You thought I had used my sash for some vile purpose. But when you looked at it I could tell you knew it was a lie. Why do you believe that lie now?"

"Because of the witnesses. The . . . the witnesses who described someone like you."

"Someone Jewish?"

"No, you fool! Why would they know you were a Jew if you did not tell them? She said you were small, foreign, all golden—" Crispin pulled up short. *Golden?* What had she meant by that? That he was wealthy? Because of the yellow rouelle on his chest and the gold jewelry around his neck? Yes, of course. What else could it mean?

But Julian had grasped at his words. His hands slipped easily from Crispin's yielding grip and he picked up his lank hair in his fists. "Golden?" he asked, shaking his brown locks, locks that could not by any means be mistaken for golden. Julian chuckled, but for once, it was not sarcastic. "You *are* mistaken." Crispin's chest began burning with undirected emotion, even though Julian was not even goading him. The boy nodded almost sympathetically. "I can see where you might have misread it all. What a grand jest. My journals, the jars, the strange nature of the parchments . . . my father's unusual request. And then that description of this purchaser of clay. Logically, it all seems to fit. And yet, it does not."

Julian did not act in the least like an accused murderer. He had the appearance of a man who knew himself justified, and Crispin was seized by a sinking feeling. He had been so certain of his guilt, but when laid out logically, it did not seem to fit. He had *wanted* the boy to be guilty. But why? Because he was a Jew? Despite Julian's earlier demeanor, he had seen the intelligence in the youth's eyes, his determination . . . and even saw a bit of himself there.

Crispin blinked and looked at the boy anew. Julian had perched on the edge of the table, rubbing his smooth chin and studying Crispin with bright eyes. "This curious vocation of yours. 'Tracker,' you call it. I can see why a man of intelligence would find his place in such a profession. Are you truly good at what you do?"

Crispin's arms swung flaccidly at his sides. "I am beginning to wonder." Either Julian was an extremely clever killer or . . . or . . . dammit! There was no denying it. Julian might just be innocent. The sash—that perfect murder weapon—had not been used as such. There was no evidence on the cloth itself. And Julian's manner. Crispin had never seen the like. He exuded confidence and, frankly, lack of guilt. These things of themselves were not proof of innocence. But Crispin had not been at this vocation for four years for naught. He recognized when he had made a fool of himself.

He stared hard into the flames until he was blinded.

"No," said Julian. "I can see you are good at your vocation. And Father said he had heard of you from many sources. You seem to be well respected. I . . . I apologize for treating you so foully before. I thought you were just another greedy Gentile out to ruin us." His voice grew weary when he said, "I have met so many, you see."

Julian slid off his perch and strode forward. Crispin turned to him. He could not speak, either to offer an apology or another accusation. Neither seemed appropriate.

"You know," said the boy thoughtfully, "I now recall those men behind me in the corridor, overhearing you and that servant. There was one man who might very well fit your witness's description. He, too, is slight, like me, and foreign. And . . . he has blond hair."

Was this merely a ruse? The boy could be making it up. *Checkmate, Crispin. The game is over.* And yet he could not stop himself from saying, "Prove it."

"I do not know his name. But he is one of three men who make themselves a nuisance at court. There are more whispers about them than there are about my father and me. I surmised that they are not well liked."

A stirring in his chest was almost like a tickle, warring with a darker sensation. "Who?"

"As I said, I do not know his name. But the man he is always with; his name sounds something like . . . 'rizzy'?"

It sprang off Crispin's tongue without a second thought. "De Risley?"

Julian nodded slowly. "Yes. I think that is the name, but I cannot be certain. I try not to listen too much to those around me at royal courts. It is never wise to mix too much with court politics. We do our task and hide in our chamber."

But how could that be? Was Radulfus a murderer and sodomite? God's blood! Right under Giles's nose! But wait. Giles had mentioned "our lord." Perhaps he was speaking of a nobleman, one above him in rank who would secure him wealth in exchange for pandering. Someone like a lord in a mysterious carriage. A lord who wanted those stolen parchments.

How could Giles be involved except as a dupe? Crispin felt a miserable sense of guilt that one of his acquaintances could be used so, even though he couldn't possibly have known or done anything about it.

Well, that was before. This was now. He could certainly help Giles now. After all, the man was living on Crispin's old estates. Under his jealousy, he was grateful it was Giles.

But this Radulfus was another matter. Crispin would see him hanged or worse for what he was doing. If it was him. For as cruel as Radulfus was to him, was he capable of such acts as stealing boys for profit? The astrologer certainly fit the description that Berthildus the Potter offered. But even if they were stealing boys by treachery, what did that have to do with clay and a Golem?

Julian spoke again and Crispin started, not realizing how close the boy had maneuvered. He was right at his elbow, looking up at him. "Did you truly see the Golem, *Maître*?"

Suddenly the boy used a respectful title. Well, the entire tone of their exchange had taken a turn, to be sure.

"I don't truly know what I saw. But there was clay. . . ." It could not be denied. He had seen the clay on Jack's fingers but the clay could have . . . could have . . . No. It couldn't have. He lowered his head. "I do not know."

"An intelligent answer from a man who does not believe. Tell me, *Maître*. Do you believe in such things at all?"

It was his turn to lean back against the table and slump. He ran his fingers through his thick hair, letting his hand fall back to his thigh. "I have seen . . . many curious things. But I do not know whether I believe in them or not. Mostly, there is an explanation that is plain and simple. But this situation. There does not appear to be anything simple about it."

Julian fell silent for a long time. The silence grew uncomfortable, in fact, and Crispin was deciding whether or not to simply depart when Julian raised his face. "Why don't you like me?"

Crispin gazed at him sidelong, surprised by the sudden question. "I wasn't aware by your manner that you aspired to be liked—by me or anyone else."

That seemed to throw the lad and he looked thoughtfully into the corner. Crispin studied his profile with its angular nose and sharp chin.

"I don't aspire to be *dis*liked," he said softly. He turned. "I . . . have had to fight for everything in my life. Because I am a Jew, even in Avignon, my opinions are less than that of other men. Am I not clever? You seem the sort to appreciate cleverness."

"An open mind can fascinate," Crispin found himself answering, "but I do not know if I find you open or not."

"Because I am a Jew."

"I don't—" Care? But he did. He knew he did. And he knew it mattered to Julian. "You care that I am a Gentile."

"True. But these truths can be overlooked in the throes of intelligent discourse."

Crispin couldn't help but laugh. It bloomed a wounded expression on the young man's face and he was surprised he regretted causing it. "You would seem to prefer to argue with me."

"And you would seem to prefer to manhandle me and accuse me of murder."

Well played. "Then tell me, what do *you* make of these murders?"

Julian tapped his lip. "It would be difficult to comment knowing little of the facts," he began. But that one statement impressed

Crispin like none other. God's blood! Was he in danger of *liking* this youth?

"Do you believe I am innocent?" Julian suddenly blurted.

Crispin stared. The young man gazed up at him with intense eyes. How Crispin had wanted him to be guilty! But it was not as simple as that. William of Ocham be damned.

Julian drew closer. His face seemed to know the answer before Crispin spoke it.

"I . . . suppose . . . so."

Green eyes sparkled with sudden delight. "A man of honor!" he breathed. "I knew it!"

Crispin was going to comment, planned on saying something noncommittal and vague, perhaps even scathing to put the youth back in his place. But he never got the chance. Julian grabbed him suddenly, pulled him forward, and kissed him hard on the lips.

Crispin pushed him off as if he were on fire. Julian staggered back and lifted a hand to his mouth, horrified.

Crispin lurched back. "You *kissed* me!"

"I'm sorry," he said behind his fingers. "Please don't tell anyone."

"You . . . you *are* a sodomite!"

"Please, you don't understand—"

Crispin drew back his balled fist and swung. The smacking sound of knuckle hitting flesh should have been more satisfying. Julian went down, hitting the floor on his backside. He quickly scrambled backward until he was almost under the table. Blood oozed from his lip and a bruise was slowly forming on his jaw.

Crispin charged toward him, bent on more violence, but those widened, frightened eyes made him hesitate. His face felt suddenly hot. He looked around the room in a daze and pushed his way toward the door. He had to get out. He couldn't breathe. Yanking open the door, he stumbled into the corridor, leaving the Jew's door far behind. He did not stop until he was out in the cold air of the courtyard, where he inhaled great mouthfuls while leaning hard against a plinth.

"God's blood!" Julian had kissed him. *Kissed* him!

And God help him. But for a fleeting moment, the tiniest of flickers that lasted only the blink of an eye . . . Crispin had liked it.

14

CRISPIN BREATHED, DID NOTHING but breathe. His back felt the chilled stone permeate through the layers of his tabard, coat, and chemise. Staring at nothing, he tried to feel the same nothingness, but couldn't. He *had* felt something. Something . . . wrong. So wrong.

He stayed as he was for a long interval before he bent slowly at the waist, scooped up a handful of dirty snow, and smeared its gravelly ice into his face, rejoicing in the hard pain of it like a penance. Once he'd ground it into his numbed cheeks, he tossed the slush aside and straightened. He had to rid himself of Westminster, leave the shameful emotions of it far behind.

The gate was open to him and he trotted forward. Hurried steps took him back toward London. He tried not to think, tried to concentrate on that astrologer who had bought the clay from the potters, on this strange scheme that now seemed to surround Giles de Risley and the mysterious stranger. He could not think how warm Julian's lips were. *Would* not!

It was this case. It was all too much. These Jews and child killings and strange Golems. It was a wonder he wasn't driven mad!

And he had been too long without the warm arms of a woman.

He hefted his coin purse and felt enough coins. Yes. He would go to the stews today. Now!

He fled to the river's edge and searched along the wharves for the nearest ferry and ran toward it, tossing his farthing to the man in hopes of hurrying him.

Instead, the ferryman waited until his craft was full before he pushed it away from the wharf. A man with a horse on a lead stood off to the side, but the horse's flank kept pushing into Crispin. Crispin didn't mind. Its tangy warmth kept him from shivering as the beast blocked most of the wind.

He barely waited for the ferry to dock before he leapt away and hit the dock running, heading for the darker streets where the brothels huddled together like old whores.

He slowed as he wended his way down a narrow close. The light was dim, but Crispin could make out the shape of a woman facing a wall, leaning her hands on it, her gown hiked up to her thighs. A man stood behind her, rutting, and she cried out in little sighs and rocked with each thrust. Crispin did not turn to leave. Instead, he watched for a few moments, not in the least embarrassed. It took a few moments more for recognition to set in and his eyes rounded in horror. "John Rykener!"

The man jerked up his head. Hastily, he pulled up his braies and before he was fully covered, he fled into the dimness, his feet slapping harshly until he disappeared completely into the mist beyond.

The woman slumped against the wall and let her skirts fall back into place. "Dammit, Crispin!" She turned. Her face was round with a small chin and a petite mouth, a mouth that was twisted with ire. "You frightened him off before he could pay."

"John," breathed Crispin. The very last person he wanted to see. Today of all days.

"It's Eleanor," he said in his soft voice, "when I am garbed so. How many times have I told you?"

"For God's sake, John. Must you continue to do"—Crispin waved an arm at him—"this?"

"You do what you do and I do what I do. It is simple finance." John turned around and leaned with his back against the daub wall. He pulled his cloak about him. "That cost me my supper, I'll have you know. Now you owe me."

Crispin said nothing. He never liked the familiar manner Rykener insisted with him.

He felt the man's eyes on him but refused to look. He couldn't stand the notion of a man in women's clothing. It was indecent. Ridiculous.

And it annoyed him still further that he didn't know why he suddenly felt guilty that he had cost the man his supper money.

John fiddled with the looped braids hanging over his ears. "And what are you doing here, Crispin? As if I didn't know. It's been ages since I've seen you in Southwark. I know you hate it here."

"Nothing," muttered Crispin. "I'm doing nothing." And it was true. This whole adventure was becoming God's little jest. He had wanted the first whore he could find to prove his manhood. To prove to himself that a desperate kiss from some feminine youth could not unman him. As it had.

Naturally, the first whore he encountered would be that madman John Rykener, yet another sodomite. God's jest indeed!

Hugging himself, he joined his companion by leaning against the damp wall beside him. The gray light angled down the alley against the opposing wall, smudging the already vague line between shadow and light. It smelled like a pissing alley and probably was. How often had he spent a halpen in such a place with a whore?

Crispin slanted a glance at the man in women's clothing and shook his head. "They'll arrest you again."

He shrugged. "I know."

"There are better ways to make a living," said Crispin. "Believe me. I should know."

"And yet none could be quite as satisfying."

Crispin snorted.

"Do not snort at me, Crispin Guest," he said, cocking his head in the very likeness of a woman. "We all have our roles to play. We all get by as best we can."

"John . . ." He didn't know what to say. He was in a strange enough mood as it was. To encounter John Rykener just now seemed to be more than Fate. He dropped his face in his hands and breathed through his fingers. Suddenly a hand was on his shoulder. He did not look up.

"Crispin," cooed the man. He pushed away from the wall and drew closer. "What troubles you? I have never seen you like this."

"I have never been like this," he muttered between his fingers. Finally, he raised his head and leaned back until his head rested against the clammy plaster. John was wearing some sort of flowery scent that clashed with the alley's acrid smells. "What makes a man . . ." He stared upward into the slice of gray sky caught between the buildings. "What makes a man . . . want another man, John?"

John studied Crispin silently for a time before he turned his gaze. He stared at the wall facing him a scant few feet away. "Would that I knew the answer to that." He sighed and dragged himself forward, giving Crispin's shoulder a friendly cuff. "Come along. I'm cold. And I have wine at home." John beckoned but Crispin hesitated. "Come along. I don't bite. That costs extra."

"You are a pig," spat Crispin.

"Very likely," he agreed.

Reluctantly, Crispin followed him down the muddy lane, trying to keep his distance, afraid someone might think he had hired the man.

They turned down another tight alley and up a short flight of stairs to the narrow door of John's lodgings.

Inside, the room was cold. The hearth had burned low and John rushed in to stoke it back to life. He dropped a bundle of sticks and a square of peat on top of the burgeoning flames and stood back, rubbing his thighs to warm them. "It was cold in that alley with my bum waving in the wind."

Crispin sneered in his direction but joined him by the fire. "You said something about wine." Anything to change the subject.

John smiled at him and curtsied. "Where are my manners?" He took a drinking jug from a shelf, removed the cloth covering, and offered it first to Crispin. Grateful, Crispin took it and drank. It filled his hollow belly. He knew he should be hungry. It had been a long time since he'd eaten. But he didn't feel the least like having food right now. He drank a bit more before handing the jug to his companion.

John drank with a loud exhale and lowered the jug. "It was a harsh day, Crispin. And a long, cold night to come. Would that I could find a nice man to keep me warm at night."

Crispin ignored the man's leer. "Why must you be so disgusting? You know I hate that kind of talk."

"And yet you befriended me anyway. One has to wonder why."

"I just . . . did. God knows why."

"So far, He hasn't told me."

"Would you add blasphemy to your many sins?"

"Why not? If I'm for Hell then I might as well make it a fast journey." He pulled a stool over and sat, offering the other to Crispin. The room was small and spare, not unlike Crispin's own, though it was considerably more dilapidated. The sky was clearly visible through a hole in the roof where a shaft of gentle snowflakes softly fell. Crispin edged his chair to the side to avoid the snowfall and scooted closer to the fire till his toes nearly burned.

He couldn't help stealing glances at his companion. "Must you continue to wear that?"

John put a hand to his breast. "Would you prefer I remove it?"

"Er . . ."

With a smirk, John snapped to his feet and wriggled, loosening laces, until it slid down his slim form and pooled at his feet where he stepped out of it. He scratched luxuriously at himself over his shift. "Better?"

Crispin gestured to his braided hair and the man sighed elaborately. "For a man who is paying me nothing, you are certainly demanding." He sat and began to unbraid his hair, pulling his fingers through the loosened strands until they fell in kinked waves to just below his jaw. When he was finished he posed with an inquiring brow.

Crispin drank from the jug again and nodded. "At least you look like a man again."

"I *am* a man, you know."

"Then why not look like one? Why do you insist on this?"

John paused, rubbing his hands for warmth. "I don't whore all the time. Sometimes I work as an embroideress and so I must go on as Eleanor. But I *have* lain with women. Nuns mostly."

Crispin spit his wine across his chest.

"Careful there, Master Guest." He pounded on Crispin's back. "That is all the wine I have."

Crispin wiped uselessly at the front of his coat. "You are telling me tales again," he choked out.

"No. Women of all sorts pay me. I do not discriminate. One hole is like another."

"God's blood!"

"Enough of this!" He settled on his stool again and plucked the drinking jug out of Crispin's hand and took a swig. He wiped his mouth and settled his gaze on Crispin's squirming form. "You asked me a very provocative question before. 'What makes a man want another man?' Wasn't that it, Master Guest? And just why should you be so interested in my answer?"

There was nothing for it but to drop his heated face in his hands again. Crispin turned his head from side to side. He couldn't forget

Julian. It would take a very large dose of wine indeed for that to happen. "Just tell me!" he hissed through his fingers.

John slouched. He set the jug down between his legs and rested his long fingers on his knees. "I wish I knew," he whispered. He cast a glance to the gown on the floor and a wash of uncertainty changed his expression for only a moment before it was lost again in the room's shadows.

For the years Crispin had known him, John seemed to be a merry fellow. John had helped Crispin when he had first come to the Shambles, showed him how to stay alive on the streets, where the best almshouses could be found for food, prevented him from losing his way. He had never tried his wiles on Crispin except for his occasional seductive banter. Crispin felt slightly ashamed that he had done little to return John's charity and instead offered the man scorn. It seemed ungrateful, but it was always difficult for Crispin to reconcile John's kindness with his predilection for dressing as he did and laying with men.

But now John's usual merry demeanor seemed swallowed by his thoughts.

Rykener settled on his stool and never looked at his friend as he spoke. "When I was a child," he said softly, "I adored my mother's things. Her gowns, her veils. I wanted so much to wear them. I knew such thoughts were wrong, but I would steal away from my chores to merely touch them. But it wasn't until I was a lad of thirteen. I was working in Madam Elizabeth Bronderer's stew as a scullion when she dressed me in women's clothes for the first time. It was a scheme of hers, but . . ." A look of bliss passed over his face. "Ah Crispin, it was wonderful," he said at last. "I was no longer a scullion after that."

"A woman's gown is one thing. But playing the mare—"

"I tried, Crispin," he said wearily. "Truly, I tried. Madam Bronderer had me lay with women, too. But . . ." He shook his head. "A wife and children at my knee. What man does not want these things? And yet . . ." He rubbed his arms absently. "Have I not prayed enough, done enough penance? Even as a child I denied myself food and drink in recompense for my sinful thoughts. Even Madam Bronderer would admonish her 'girls,' as she called us, to pray. But there was never any joy with women. Only with men. Why should that be so? Alas. I continue to sin. And pray. I do not know which is the stronger."

Crispin shrugged. "I know not either, John. We each have our burdens."

"Yes, that is so." He sniffed and clapped his thighs with his hands. "Well, did I answer your question, at least?"

The discomfort returned. "Erm . . . I suppose."

John smiled. "I wish I could be more like you, Crispin. You're very brave."

In the face of it, Crispin was beginning to think that this wasn't quite true.

"I have shared my tale with you. Now you must tell me why you ask, Crispin. Come now."

"There were murders, John," he said carefully. "Vile murders of boys. And they were . . . sodomized."

John dragged his cloak from the floor and pulled it about him. "Oh." He rose and leaned over the small hearth. His face, usually so pliable, seemed to harden before Crispin's eyes. "And so you come to me. Do you accuse me, then? I am a man who indulges in the pleasure of other men so I *must* be a defiler of boys as well, is that it? Am I also a murderer?"

It was the furthest thing from his thoughts and yet his thoughts had been so jumbled he hadn't quite known what he said. He had never seen Rykener so angry before. He slowly stood. "I am not accusing you, John. That was not my intention. Forgive me if I have offended you."

John knotted the cloak at his throat with a fist. "It is a vile thing to call me, Crispin. I thought better of you. And here I have shared what little wine I have. Perhaps . . . perhaps you should leave now."

What was there to say? Crispin moved uncertainly.

John sighed and tapped a foot, trying unsuccessfully to avoid catching Crispin's gaze. Finally he rolled his eyes and waved at the room. "Don't be absurd." He blinked at him to show his hurt and Crispin did feel genuine remorse.

At last, John sat again and adjusted his cloak and shift over his legs, rubbing them for warmth. Crispin returned to his stool. "I don't lie with boys," said John harshly. "I lie with *men*. Especially priests. They're more profitable."

"John! God's blood! Will you be serious!" But at least he seemed to have forgiven him.

"I *am* serious!" he said, his demeanor changing again to the merry soul Crispin remembered. "For it was they who told me what a grave sinner I was . . . before they dropped to their knees before me. The hypocrites."

Crispin cringed. The man loved to taunt him with such tales. Could any of them be true? He conceded that they could be.

"But despite your misstep," John went on, "I can see you are greatly troubled. So I shall try to speak plainly to you." He cleared his throat and took on the look of some of the preachers Crispin had seen near pilgrim sites. "Though there are some men who seek out boys, I do not truck with them. They are . . . vile. Twisted." Crispin gave him a look and John wagged a finger at him. "I know what goes on behind your eyes, Crispin Guest. But I am not vile or twisted. I am a gentle soul, as you well know. I do not seek to hurt. My weakness is for grown men, not boys. This damns me as it is. Have I not been threatened with terrible tortures by the sheriff? I am condemned enough when caught in women's clothes. The fines! Last time I spent a month in Newgate." Crispin refrained from telling him "I told you so." "But that is no matter. The truth of it is, I have no interest in children. None of my fellow whores do. Perhaps you do not see the difference, but I do. If I were of the sort who violated children, then I should be obliged to hurl myself from the highest tower."

Crispin grunted in reply. Perhaps there was a difference. Perhaps not. Such things were difficult to fathom. Especially in the face of his own strange situation.

"I have been told there are secret stews of boys," Crispin went on, staring into the fire.

"Vile panderers," said John, swiping his hand absently across his knee. "I have heard of them. To use these boys . . ." He shook his head and seemed to be genuinely appalled. It relieved Crispin. He had always liked Rykener. Though he did not approve of his doings or his choice of laymen, he had seen beyond the women's clothes to the man beneath. Rykener's petite features did not belong on a man, nor did those slanted and all-knowing eyes. But he wasn't a bad sort, even with his insistence at being called Eleanor.

They both fell silent. After a time John ticked his head and turned to face Crispin. "You mentioned murder."

"Yes. Horrific. Four boys in the same way."

"Why murdered?"

He shook his head. "I do not know. To hide their crimes against these children perhaps. But there is more. I—" He recalled that John was not a man to enjoy blood. "I am reluctant to share the details with you. It is not . . . pleasant."

The man wrinkled his nose. "Then don't. I'd rather not know." He offered Crispin the jug again and he took it. "But if there is more of a violent nature involved"—he tilted his head to verify it and Crispin confirmed with a gesture—"then it seems that perhaps this is less about the sodomizing of boys and more about murder. Perhaps if you reason the why you can reckon the who."

"Yes. Very astute of you, Master Rykener. I thought I knew the who and then . . ." He felt his face heat again and he took another swallow of wine to hide it. But John was more astute than he would have liked. The man's gaze stuck to him steadfast.

"The who was not the murderer?"

"No. Well, at least I do not think so. I mean—dammit." He clamped his mouth shut before he condemned himself further.

John shook his head with a chuckle. "Crispin, I have never seen you this discomfited. Verily, you are the most unflappable man I know. And yet something seems to have, well, *flapped* you. These murders are horrible, yes. But I do not think it is that."

"Leave it alone, John."

"Oh now! You know that is an impossibility." He scooted his stool closer to Crispin until their knees nearly touched. "Now then, Master Guest. You will tell me what has happened to bring such a faint glow to your cheek. Come now. Out with it!"

"No, I—" He reached for the jug but John snatched it from his hand.

"No more, Master Guest. Tell me and I shall see if you are deserving."

Crispin used his harshest glare but it did no good against the gleeful expression of his companion, all former rancor forgotten.

Very well. Get it over with. Like scratching off a scab.

He positioned himself to fully face Rykener and dug his fist in his thighs. "A young man kissed me. And I liked it."

The jug crashed to the floor. It took several moments for the gape-mouthed John to realize he had dropped it and he jumped to his feet to retrieve the shards.

Crispin morosely watched the spreading wine puddle. After all was said and done, he felt he truly deserved that wine.

John tossed the shards into the fire. "Bless me!" he gasped, searching for a rag to mop up the wine. "Bless me, bless me. I never expected you to say that!" He stole a glance at Crispin and couldn't seem to help a small smile. "I wish I had been there to see that. Better, I wish it had been me."

"Don't be ridiculous!" The blush to his face only grew more furiously warm. He threw himself from the stool and tried to pace in the small room.

On his knees and sopping up the mess, John sighed. "Alas. He is fairer than me, then?"

"No, he is— I am *not* having this conversation!"

"He is young. Is that it? Is that why you ask about boys? Do you worry you will be wanting—"

"God's blood, John! No! A thousand times *NO*!"

"Then what? It was a kiss. A little kiss. It took you off guard. Perhaps you were a bit in your cups. Perhaps he reminded you a bit of a woman. You lost your head. It means nought."

Could it have been those things? Crispin grasped at the notion. Grasped so hard he'd throttle the notion to death.

John tossed the rag to a corner and Crispin was reminded briefly of the bloody rags he had seen in Julian's rooms. There was so much yet to be explained. Was the boy entirely innocent? His experiments, his notes. Dammit, but the boy was clever in his distractions! Did Crispin truly believe him about the astrologer? He certainly could have made that up.

John found another jug and brought it forth. "Ale," he said, raising it. "I have a feeling we are not done drinking, you and I." He raised his chin and drank a heavy dose, his knobbed throat rolling with several swallows. Crispin watched him for a moment until—

"My God! John!"

The jug was pulled away and John stared, swallowing before he choked. "What now?" he rasped, trying to clear his throat.

"Julian," he said wonderingly. "I'll be damned." He clutched his friend's shoulder. "I thank you for your hospitality, John. But I must take my leave."

"What? But you haven't finished your story! I want to hear about this kiss—"

"Later. For now, I must return to Westminster. There is something I must do."

John stomped his foot. "You are the most maddening man I have ever met, Crispin Guest!"

Crispin smiled. For the first time, he was feeling much better. "And you are a good friend, John. God keep you."

"He always does," he sighed, reluctantly allowing Crispin to leave.

CRISPIN HURRIED, ANXIOUS TO test his theory. But he did not make it more than a few paces from Rykener's lodgings when someone familiar passed him on the other side of the lane. The mist, as always, grumbled along the way and made even close objects difficult to discern, but there was little mistaking Matthew Middleton, the goldsmith.

The Jew.

Crispin watched him hurry along under the eaves, trying to escape the lashing of wet snow sloppily winging on the wind. His furtive movements and the unmistakable glances over his shoulder urged Crispin to cast aside his earlier quest. Westminster could wait. His instincts told him to follow.

If Middleton was trying to be subtle, he was making a poor job of it. He seemed clearly too distracted to hide his movements. He bumped absentmindedly into the whores and thieves making their way to shelter in the dim afternoon. Whatever his mission, he seemed to know where he was going, for he never veered from a direct path before him, never stopping to assess the way. He knew it.

The Jew soon followed along the Bank and took the strip of mud overlooking the Thames, heading for the territory of the potter's kilns.

There were few along the same path but Crispin managed to pace himself behind a cart, following in its shadow even as Middleton glanced quickly over his shoulder. He had not seen Crispin, and with a hand on his sheathed dagger, Crispin hurried away from the cart to slide into the darkness of an alley, peeking out to watch Middleton disappear into the potter's village of kilns and hovels. Moving slowly after the man, he kept his distance and watched his quarry stride down the row. He passed Dickon's hovel and picked over the muddy way, until he reached a familiar hut.

Crispin hung back, keeping his back against a wooden post upholding a rickety canopy. Middleton knocked at the door of Berthildus the Potter and waited until someone answered. When she appeared in the doorway, her face bloomed into shock. She looked urgently both ways down the busy avenue before pulling him inside.

Crispin moved. He was under her window in an instant.

"—did you come here?" he heard her say. "That was foolish, especially in the daytime."

"No one suspects," he said, exasperated. "Don't be a fool."

"They had best not! What would I do if they made me to go to the Domus? Who could live off the pittance the king supplies those poor sots?"

"One wonders if the king truly wishes to support his converts or to starve them."

"Aye. I do not wish to see for myself."

"I did not come to talk to you of this." Crispin heard the man's shuffled step move closer to her and his voice dropped. "I came to talk to you of . . . Odo."

"Not him again! Why must it be me?"

"I've told you before, Berthildus. There is no one left of our people here. It must be you."

"I can't control him anymore than you can."

"But you must. That Tracker has been sniffing about."

"Tracker? I ain't seen no Tracker."

"He's been asking things. You must keep an eye on Odo."

"He's his own man, as you well know."

"But he has been to the northbank. To Westminster."

"What? How do you know that?"

"There was trouble. Tell him he must stop whatever it is he is doing or it will be the ruin of us all."

There was silence for a moment. Crispin listened hard before he heard the door creak open. He scrambled to the other side of the hut and pressed against the wall.

"I'm counting on you, Berthildus. We all are. Here. I know it has been difficult for you with Hugh away."

There was the soft clink of coins exchanging hands.

"God grant that he returns soon," she said.

"Yes. God keep you." His slushy steps moved away and Crispin waited, wondering if he should question Berthildus, if anything could be gained by it. Clearly he had prodded a nerve when questioning the Jews in London. But who was this Odo and why did they both seem to fear him? Something clicked in Crispin's head, and he thought he might just know this Odo after all.

"Master Guest."

Crispin whipped around. Blindsided, he stared into the face of the stranger from the carriage.

"I hoped I would see you again," said the man. And before he could answer, a fist snapped hard into Crispin's face. Stars exploded in his vision and he fell to his knees, blood rushing down his nose and over his lips. The taste of copper flooded his mouth.

A shadow glided over him. Crispin looked up blearily into the face of the carriage driver.

The man looked down at Crispin, drew back his arm, and finished the job.

15

CRISPIN KNEW HE HAD been dragged away. He just wasn't certain by whom or where he had landed. The blow had not knocked him out completely. There had been vague images of alleys, ditches, and people, but he had been powerless to make any resistance. Instead, he had hung lifeless in their arms and dragged a long way.

He felt cold damp under his back when he was roused enough to care. His face hurt and his mouth was sticky from drying blood.

Raising a hand to his face, he heard the stirring in the dark room. Someone moved across the floor. He turned his head in time to see a boot jabbing toward him. A soundless cry opened his mouth as the boot sunk into the flesh between his ribs, not hard enough to break bones but enough to garner his attention.

Breathing became the first priority.

The thickened voice above him gave a mirthless chuckle. "That is for stabbing me. A man, after all, must know his place."

Gasping seemed to work. Coughing ached his already bruised ribs so he tried to avoid it. Wrenching open his eyes, Crispin glared at the silhouette above him. "You have me at a disadvantage," he rasped, adding with vinegar, "your Excellency."

That seemed to satisfy the man, and he drew back, enough to show Crispin he wouldn't kick him again. For the moment.

Slowly, Crispin rolled to his side and gingerly pushed himself upright, wary that the man would lash out at him again. Once he was standing, his eyes quickly took in his dim surroundings. A stable. Disused by the look of it. There was straw under his feet and the stench of moldy hay permeating the air. A place whose walls might well swallow his cries. But when his hand brushed against his scabbard, he was surprised to feel the knife still there.

"You have my attention," he said guardedly, wiping his mouth with his sleeve. Where was that damned driver? "What is it you want of me now?"

"I was very disappointed with our last encounter, Master Guest. Very disappointed. When I encouraged you to continue your investigations, I did not intend for you to follow *me*. That was very . . . discourteous."

Crispin made an abbreviated bow in apology, but never said the words. "I cannot help, your Excellency, if my investigation led me to you."

"Nonsense. Your insatiable curiosity led you to follow me. I've no doubt that this will someday be your downfall."

"My lord, may I remind you of my current circumstances in London? I met my 'downfall' ages ago. And I have arrived . . . intact. More or less."

"Less, I should think." The man cocked his head. Crispin saw the briefest of shimmer in the blond locks. Golden, one might even call them.

"What were your intentions with that child?"

Crispin was used to the dark by now. He saw the gleam of teeth with the man's smile. "My intentions were my own."

"Then you can understand why I was reluctant to let you escape with him."

The man nodded and lowered his head. He contemplated the floor for quite some time. "I suppose your intentions were noble and could therefore be forgiven. In time." The man limped a little to reach a stool and sat with a grunt. He regarded Crispin with a shadowed face and glittering eyes. "What an unusual man you are. Perhaps I underestimated you. A dangerous thing to do."

Crispin shrugged. He looked around the room pointedly, what he could see of it. "So what now? I have apologized. May I be on my way?"

"One wonders what you could possibly be doing here in Southwark."

Still in Southwark, then. "Come, your Excellency. A man makes many a pilgrimage to the stews without this much fuss."

He thought he could see the man's face wrinkled in distaste. "Blessed *Jesu*. More sin, Crispin? May I call you so? We seem on more intimate terms now, you and I."

"And yet I still do not know *your* name, Excellency."

"You seem to be making little headway. Why have you not found my parchments?"

Sudden thoughts of Julian flooded his mind. He needed to get back to Westminster, but there was some question as to whether he would be escaping this stable at all. He gave it another inspection but the dimness made the edges of the walls disappear. It smelled of rat piss. An unpleasant place to spend his last hours.

"It is difficult finding a murderer," said Crispin. "Find the murderer and find the parchments. But I think I am closer than you think."

"Don't try enigmatic with me, Master Guest. I invented it." He rubbed his thigh, the one Crispin stabbed. "No doubt you think me too young to have such authority—"

"I was lord of my manor at quite an early age. And the king gained the throne when only ten years old. How can I begrudge you your authority? Whatever that authority is."

The man looked at Crispin as a cat studies a mouse. "Just so."

"You wish for me to continue my investigation? Or rather, are you hindering it? And to what purpose? These are the things that keep me up at night."

"Are they?" The man bent forward and rested his clasped hands on his knees. "So I must conclude from your words that you suspect me of the heinous crime of murder."

"And sodomy."

A brow arched. Slowly, he sat up, easing his hands apart. "A grave charge, indeed."

"Convince me. Why were you trying to steal that boy?"

"That is none of your concern. Yes, I see how that can be misinterpreted. But it is of no concern to you. Or your case."

"That judgment I reserve for myself. Test it. Tell me."

He chuckled again, that lifeless sound. "A most unusual man. You are a man who has been touched by the hand of God and yet you do not see what lies before you."

"This again," he grumbled. "I little believe in such things, Excellency."

"Tut! My dear Crispin, you do not believe in the holy objects that grace your path?"

"I've had little reason to."

He shook his head and his blond hair fell behind him. "But you should. You should be grateful for God's protection from the devil, for he strides amongst us into every facet of our lives." The accent that Crispin now recognized as Yorkshire, deepened as his voice intensified. "We must use every tool at our disposal to conquer the devil, Crispin. To shun God's gifts is unforgivable."

"I do not shun God's gifts, for He has given me the gift of insight and discernment. What has he given you?"

"Authority."

"Are you a cleric, then? You do not garb yourself so. And you are young."

"A cleric? Perhaps. And my youth . . . is beside the point. I am accomplished with what I do."

"And just what is that?"

The man smiled. "Rooting out the devil, of course." He chuckled at Crispin's expression. "Are you surprised?"

"Few things surprise me these days."

"Then let us talk of your investigation."

"Certainly. My Lord Odo," Crispin tested.

The man smiled but said nothing. "Your investigation. You must know it has little to do with murder and more to do with the devil."

"Does it? Is this what you, too, are investigating? Shall I guess further?"

"It will do you little good."

"Indulge me. Perhaps you are seeking to discover the number of Jews living in secret in England."

The man shot to his feet and stormed toward him. *A hit,* thought Crispin.

"What do you know of it, Master Guest? Come, come."

"Me? You want me to be forthcoming when you have been less so? I think not."

A sigh. "I thought not to have to resort to this. Stephen!"

A door opened and with it a sharp lance of light that temporarily blinded Crispin. Footsteps hurried forward, and then a fist sank into his gut. He dropped to his knees, hitting the dirt floor hard.

He let out a gasp, ringing his belly with his arms. But the man, Stephen, did not move to strike him again. Crispin squinted up at the two shadowy figures now hovering over him.

"Well?" said Odo as calmly as before. "Have you nothing to tell me?"

"You haven't asked me anything of worth."

He squatted to face him, and Crispin edged back slightly, not knowing what to expect. "What do you know of the Jews living in London, Crispin?"

"There are two at Westminster Palace. Do you mean them?"

"No. What do you know of the Domus Conversorum?"

"Nothing. Converts live there. They are protected by the king. That's all anybody cares to know."

"But not you. Not the Great Tracker. You know more than that, do you not? Tell me. It will go easier."

"Easier." He laughed, recalling the torture inflicted upon him seven years ago. They had asked questions, too. Questions they also already knew the answers to. And like those long ago days best forgotten, Crispin remained silent.

Odo drew circles in the dust on the floor. Or was it in Crispin's blood? He stopped and hung his hands limply from his bent knees before he straightened and rubbed his thigh again. "A pity. You could have helped me. And then likewise, I could have helped you."

"What do you mean? Do you know something of these deaths?" He leaned forward even at the risk of another onslaught. "This is no game. It's murder. These boys—these *children*—suffered abominably. Can't you see that there will be more deaths? Whether a man or the devil, I do not care who is the cause only that it must stop!"

The man limped to the stool and sat. His driver stood stoically behind him. "There may very well be more deaths."

"It's not the Jews. It can't be. They have a biblical prohibition against drinking blood. It can't be them."

"Curious indeed. Who has schooled you in this, I wonder? It couldn't be Abbot Nicholas."

The idea that Crispin had been spied upon slammed his gut harder than the driver's fist. "How do you know about—"

"So many things I have been watching. So many people in so many places. You say that little surprises you, Master Guest. But I'll wager you'll be surprised by what I have seen."

Crispin got one foot under him. "If you know something about these murders you are *morally* obligated—"

"Morally? A strange term coming from you."

"Never *mind* me! Children are *dying*. Innocent children!"

"Innocence. Such a vague term, is it not? A man might plead his innocence in one respect and be quite guilty in another. Where lies the guilt then? Where the innocence? But you are right. For the most part, children are innocent. Even these that you would protect. They are in the hands of God, no matter their sins."

It was Crispin's turn to sneer. "Surely you are not suggesting that they had any part in the sins against them?"

"I suggest nothing," he said in such a way as to suggest much.

"That is a foul supposition. And you claim to be doing God's work."

The man frowned. "As I said. You have not seen what I have seen. You have not imagined the things I have encountered. It even stretches the bounds of my beliefs. Who could have expected such utter sin and blasphemy?" He turned his face away. Through his outwardly cool exterior, Crispin saw his body tremble with taut emotion he refused to show. "The Jews, for one. They live where they do not belong and take the charity of good Christians. Better that they were wiped off the face of the earth—"

A booming noise stopped him and he jerked around. The door crashed open and a man stumbled in. Blinded again by the light, Crispin fell back, covering his eyes. What now?

"Who are you?" the lord demanded.

"Get away from that man!" cried the voice in the doorway.

Crispin squinted. All he could see were silhouettes of three men. One had a club of some kind. Behind them he saw the vague shadows of others, heard their murmuring. But that voice had sounded terribly familiar.

"Rykener?" Crispin said, shielding his eyes with a hand.

Stephen, the driver, drew his sword with a metallic hiss and everyone froze.

John Rykener was the first to move and pointed at Crispin. "Release that man!" he said, in a voice slightly higher than before.

"You said there was to be a fight," said a gruff voice behind Rykener.

"Well . . ." John turned to the men flanking him. They had uncertain looks on their thin faces.

"Fight!" said the gruff voice. "Fight, fight!"

The chant was taken up by the rest of the crowd, which Crispin could now see was considerable.

What the hell was John doing? Was this a rescue? Crispin rolled his eyes. Well, at least he was armed. He drew his dagger.

Odo moved behind his driver, who directed his sword toward Crispin.

"You do not know what trouble you are in, friend," said Odo to Rykener and his companions.

"Nor you," said John. He nodded to the men on either side of him. They were slight men with features as delicate as John's. A sick feeling began roiling in Crispin's gut. Were these more of John's "friends"?

"You're holding captive a very important man," John went on. "The Tracker is not a man to be trifled with."

Odo took a step forward. "Neither am I."

"Perhaps it's a fairer fight now," said Crispin, falling into a crouch.

Odo sneered. "Do you truly think so?" He turned toward the noisy crowd in the doorway and waved his hand. "Disperse! You are interrupting an important interrogation—" But he never got to finish his sentence. The crowd overwhelmed with their guffaws and taunts. Even a few crusts of bread were tossed forward. It was plain that a Southwark crowd was not intimidated by his fine clothes and courtly bearing. He cut his gaze to Crispin.

Crispin grinned. "A fair fight."

Odo gestured to the driver. Stephen turned to face Crispin, his sword looking too long compared to Crispin's shorter dagger. He tightened his grip. A fight with a dagger against a sword *could* be won. He'd done it before. Once. But his head still felt a little woozy. He gritted his teeth and began to circle.

Stephen raised his sword, ready to chop downward, when John Rykener made a howling cry and suddenly burst forward. Before the driver had time to turn, Rykener had clasped his arms about his neck and jumped onto his back, limpetlike. The man spun in place, clearly at a loss as to what to do. He clawed at the arms choking him and then tried to use his sword to dislodge his attacker, but Rykener swung his body back and forth, keeping the driver unbalanced. Stephen turned his blade flat and whacked away at John, until John leaned forward, took the man's ear between his teeth, and bit down.

The driver howled and ran backward full tilt into a beam. John smashed against it and cried out. He slipped off and tumbled to the straw-littered floor.

Winded, his ear bleeding, Stephen whirled back toward the room, his sword poised.

"Fight, fight!" the crowd continued to chant.

"Blessed Mary," Odo murmured, clearly flummoxed.

"They want their blood," said Crispin cheerfully. "Shall we give it to them?" He raised his dagger.

By now, John's timid companions strode haltingly forward. One had a club in his hand. The other had what looked like a drinking jug. He swung it back and forth threateningly.

Odo signaled Stephen—and suddenly darted into the darkness. The driver soon followed.

That was it for the crowd. They all surged forward, squeezing through the narrow doorway, pushing Crispin and Rykener aside to stumble into the dark, searching for Crispin's captors.

A groan of disappointment arose when a back door was discovered. Odo and his driver had escaped.

Crispin could scarce believe it. He felt a waft of disappointment, too, and slammed his knife back into its scabbard.

And then the noisy crowd returned and glared at Rykener and his two companions.

"We came for a fight," said a tall, square-shouldered man with a grizzled beard. "You promised us." He slapped his fist into a palm. "And a fight we will have."

"You're right," said Crispin. He took in the crowd and then the large man before him, looking him in the eye. Then he swung his foot up and lodged it hard into the man's groin. Down he went without another sound. Everyone stared wide-jawed at the man as he writhed on the ground.

"Anyone else?" asked Crispin.

The crowd seemed considerably more subdued, casting glances at one another before, as one, they shuffled guardedly toward the entrance, looking back only hastily at the man helped to his feet by two of his fellows.

When they had all dispersed, Crispin breathed a sigh of relief.

"Come along, Master Crispin," said John. He seemed surprised at his sudden victory. "Let us make our escape while the going is good."

John's companions looked disapprovingly at their own weapons—a club and a jug—and tossed them to the stable floor.

When they all ventured outside, Crispin saw that they were before an inn. The blood-lusting crowd had, apparently, come from the inn and was now returning to their ale.

Crispin licked his lips, thinking a short delay was needed, but John was already pushing him out of the inn yard, his two companions shouldering him.

"Crispin, these are my friends," said John as they walked. "We all share the same vocation."

Crispin glanced over the men warily but it seemed disingenuous to complain since they rescued him. At least they wore men's garb. "For your help, much thanks."

A thin man with wispy blond hair smiled a toothy grin. "Any friend of John's is a friend of ours."

"I am not that sort of friend," he insisted.

"Be at ease, Crispin. They know who you are."

"How did you find me?"

"Well!" said John. "After you told me"—his eyes took in his companions and he lowered his voice—"what you told me, I couldn't let it lie. It took about three heartbeats for me to get dressed and rush out the door. I followed you to the potter's row and then I saw that man hit you." He reached tentatively for Crispin's nose but Crispin batted his hand away. "It's not broken, praise God. You have a perfect nose, I'll have you know. It's a shame you keep bruising it."

"John! Get on with it."

"So I fell back and followed as they dragged you off. Here, in fact."

Crispin looked back at the ramshackle stable.

"And then I gathered my friends to assist me. I promised those whoresons in the inn a fight in the hope they would help. But we rescued you anyway!" His voice became shrill with delight.

"God be praised," Crispin mumbled.

He allowed John to take him back to his lodgings. John's friends bid their farewells and left Crispin and Rykener to climb the steps to his room alone. Once inside, Rykener gave Crispin a basin and a jug of icy water. He washed the blood from his face and assessed the damage.

"You'll be bruised right well," said John, tsking and peering far too close at Crispin's face. "You'll have two black eyes for a few days, but you are whole at least."

"Thanks to you and your friends. I hope . . . I was not too rude to them."

"They can forgive a great deal because you call yourself my friend." He patted Crispin and brushed off his tabard, eyeing it but saying nothing. "Who were those cowardly men who captured you?"

"I am uncertain exactly who they are, but I have my suspicions." Thoughts like fallen leaves tumbled in his mind. Odo, the Jews, the Golem, and a murderer. But foremost in his mind, though it shouldn't have been, was Julian.

He cleared his throat. "Well, I did have some unfinished business before I was waylaid. I must get back to Westminster."

"Is that where your interesting problem is?" he asked with a wink in his voice.

Crispin actually smiled at that. "Yes, and I must hurry to him to discuss the matter forthwith."

"Oh!" John was so shocked he failed to follow Crispin to the door. But he awoke in time to clutch the jamb as Crispin passed through it. "Godspeed! I expect a full report."

"You shall be the first to know," he said over his shoulder as he trotted down the steps two at a time.

HE KNEW HE SHOULD be on the trail of the murderer and, better still, the man from the carriage, though that trail was presently ice cold. It was a confusing hash of facts. Was this Odo the one who bought the clay? It did not sound like it. If he did not create a Golem, then why did he so desire these parchments?

In fact, there was much to absorb, from the fact that Berthildus was another secret Jew to this Odo they were so afraid of. Yet if Odo was this mysterious man who was apparently welcomed at Westminster, then he did not know that Berthildus and Middleton were secret Jews. Or did he? The pieces to this puzzle were baffling and out of sorts. The devil was behind it, the stranger insisted, and it had to be so. For what could bring such opposing persons together but the Tempter himself?

Was this Odo working with the Church or was he merely a madman that the Jews were trying to control, as Middleton had said? He *was* admitted to Westminster. That's where he had followed Crispin. It was not unlikely Crispin could encounter him again there, be the one spying instead of the one spied upon and find out what he was truly doing at court.

Who was he trying to fool? Crispin was at Westminster to see Julian. He could no longer deny it.

He passed through the Great Gate at Westminster Palace, determined to find the lad. He had much to say before he moved on with his investigation. Much indeed.

Passing through the Great Hall, he skirted trunks and furniture. Clearly court was ready to take its leave to the country for Christmas. All of the court would be going, except for Radulfus. That warmed Crispin's heart. The man intended to admit himself to the king's party. Good luck to him! Good luck to them both!

Down the corridors he went, barely mindful to keep his face down. He passed Bill Wodecock and he was damned if the man did not turn toward him with a disapproving scowl. Crispin did not acknowledge him. Better that way. Instead, he followed the winding passageway to the queen's rooms and beyond to where the Jews resided. With any luck, the physician's son would be alone.

The way was deserted. He reached the door at the end of the corridor and knocked. The boy answered it and fell back from the door, wide-eyed. Before he recovered and slammed the door in Crispin's face, Crispin took a hold of it and forced it open. When he entered the room, he slammed it closed. Searching over the boy's shoulder, he saw that they were, indeed, alone.

"Now then," said Crispin.

Julian held his hands out, trying to fend him off. The bruise on his jaw was somewhat satisfying. "Forgive me! *Forgive* me! I did not mean—" But Crispin lunged forward and clasped Julian's arms and practically picked him up. Crispin's eyes raked over that face;

prominent cheekbones, dark green eyes. His hair was a mousy brown and hung to below his bruised jaw line.

Crispin loosened his hold on one arm and clutched the boy's chin, causing Julian to wince. His eyes slid over the abrupt planes and angles of cheek and jaw, sliding further to that long, smooth neck.

So it was true. The feelings that threatened before suddenly erupted within him. The confusion, the crossed emotions, the anger. It all made sense to him now. He felt his heart thrumming, his breath quickening, and a distinct tightening in his groin. How could such a thing excite him?

By all the saints. He hoped he wasn't about to make an arse of himself.

Slowly, he lowered his face until he could feel Julian's rasping breath against his chin. "Tell me something," he said, his voice a low rumble in his throat. "The truth now."

Julian opened his lips. "What?" It was not so much a word as a breath. His eyes locked on Crispin's.

Crispin leaned further, his nose almost touching the other.

"Tell me . . . are you . . . a woman?"

Was it relief he saw in her eyes? She said nothing and the merest of smiles began at the edges of her swollen mouth. She nodded.

"God be praised," he sighed. And then he leaned forward and closed his mouth hungrily over hers.

16

SHE TASTED LIKE EXOTIC wine. His tongue traced her swollen, cracked lips and then he sucked, tasting a renewal of coppery blood. His hand left her arm and tucked beneath it, finding the swell of a bound breast. She was leaning her whole weight into him now, but when he cupped her breast, she sighed a soft moan.

He filled her mouth once more before he drew back a little, lips still teasing hers. "Tell me your name."

"It is . . . *Julianne*."

He smiled against her mouth, kissed her again, and nibbled his way across her cheek. He pulled her smaller body against his, feeling his stiffening groin come up against . . . nothing. He truly didn't need further proof but it was nice to have it. "Ah," he whispered to her soft skin. He ran his stubbled cheek against her smooth one before finding her mouth again. He lingered over hers before her tentative tongue slid past his lips. A rush of emotion stiffened his whole body and he let her explore for a moment while his hands found her backside. Strange how he had somehow known all along. Relief mingled freely with his awakening desire.

"Was this your father's idea?" he asked breathlessly. She seemed a novice in the art of kissing, but she was a ready student. He wouldn't mind spending time tutoring her.

"We . . . we came upon it together." Crispin found her throat—that smooth, feminine throat—and licked and bit at it. She moaned for a moment before continuing in a staccato. "I wanted t-to learn the art of the physician. He w-wanted to protect me from Gentiles on our travels. It seemed to be—oh!—th-the perfect solution."

His mouth found her ear and he sucked slowly on her lobe. Her knees seemed to give way and if he weren't holding her with one arm wound about her waist, she would have slumped to the floor.

Still so wrong. Crispin chided himself for choosing so poorly when it came to women, but his tastes were never satisfied by those found on the Shambles.

"Are you . . ." He kissed her jaw and left a trail to her mouth with his tongue. "A maiden?" he said to her lips.

"Yes," she gasped. "But I have wanted you. I have never met a man like you: intelligent, thoughtful. You are my . . . equal."

He pulled back and looked at her. "Equal?"

"For a Gentile." There was a sly smile on her lips as well as in her eyes.

"Indeed." He studied her face again and gently touched the bruise on her jaw. "I'm sorry for this."

"You were justified, I suppose. You thought I was a man." She reached up and ran a finger down his nose. "You seem to have had your own encounter."

He smiled. "Trouble manages to find me." He swept the cap off her head, running his fingers unfettered through her stringy locks. "Your hair . . ." he said regretfully.

She ducked suddenly out of his reach. "It is only hair," she muttered. "I am a woman in every other way."

A bit of hysterical laughter tried to bubble up in his throat. The irony! She in her boy's clothing and John Rykener in his woman's garb. Was anything as it seemed?

His hands lighted gently on her shoulders. She leaned into it to chin his hand affectionately.

"Julianne," he said, enjoying the slightly different accenting of the name. He kissed the top of her head, feeling a surge of need well in his chest. But just as these warm feelings crested, they were slashed with a rush of dejection. He saw their situation in one sweep, like figures on a tapestry. This was not just any woman. Not only was she masquerading as a boy—something that was enough to get her landed in Newgate—but she was a Jew! And Jews and Gentiles did not mingle. Was he to toy with her affections merely to satisfy an itch? He knew there was a fine line between the raw emotions of anger and lust. He had crossed over that line with her numerous times. But he couldn't take what he wanted. He owed her father more respect, if not as a father at least as a client.

She seemed to draw the same conclusion. "What's to be done?" she sighed.

Her hand covered his for a moment before she turned, looking up at him with sorrowful eyes. He wondered now how he could ever have been fooled.

"This is foolish," she said. "You are a Gentile. That would seem to be the end of it."

Crispin nodded. She was right, of course. He shouldn't be touching her. But it had been so long without the touch of a woman, even a woman in men's clothing. Even a Jew. He should stop. "We are both fools." His hands traveled up her arms. "You must eventually go back to France. I . . . must remain here. Nothing can come of this."

"But why? The king exiled you from court. You have no ties here." He stiffened and pulled away, but like some irresistible pull, he swung back and looked at her. Yes, she had a face that could not be entirely characterized as feminine, but the look she returned was as coy as any maiden. "I asked around court about you," she said quietly. "I learned many . . . interesting . . . things."

He raised a finger to toy with the collar of her man's gown. "While it is true that I no longer have ties to court, I feel obligated to remain in London. Call it penance, if you will."

It was her turn to frown. "You owe no further allegiance to his Majesty. You are no longer his knight."

The words were like a slap. "I owe my allegiance to the *crown*. And to the people of London."

"Bah!" This time *she* pulled away from him and strode across the room in her distinct, manly gait. Her every mannerism was male. He wondered how long she had been masquerading as a boy. Since childhood?

"Allegiance to people who scorn you?" she said. "It is a foolish enterprise."

"I could say much the same to you. You serve Christian monarchs who do not even allow you at the same table—"

"We would not sit with a Gentile at table! To do so is against the Almighty's law."

"And yet," he said gently, striding toward her. He slipped his hand around her waist again, feeling now the gentle swell of the hip below. His other hand curved under her jaw. "You would kiss me. You would . . . lay with me." He kissed her trembling mouth. A promise. He pulled her against him and she laid her head upon his chest. He stared down at the part in her hair, at the dark tresses scored by the whiteness of her scalp, smelled the fragrance of her, a combination of herbs and balsam. He wanted to kiss her again. Wanted to do much more. He reached for the nape of her neck when the door flung open.

There had not been time to break apart. They merely gaped at the figure in the doorway.

Jacob stared at them for a moment, that moment stretching longer and with it the realization on his face. He shut the door and threw the bolt.

"Julian! Get away from him!"

"*Mon père!*"

"And you!" His finger jabbed. Crispin backed up until he jolted against a table with nowhere else to go. "What have you done?"

"I . . . I . . ."

"It wasn't his fault, Father," she said. "*I* kissed *him*."

"You *what*?" But instead of a further explosion, his voice deflated and he sagged against a chair, sliding into it.

"And then . . . he reckoned that I was a woman."

"We are lost," he said, shaking his head. "They will seize you and throw you into prison."

Crispin straightened. "Sir, I would never divulge what I have learned. Your secrets are safe. I would see no harm comes to Julianne."

"You must not use that name," rasped Jacob, as if he had said it a thousand times before. "She is in danger every moment she is in England."

"Then dammit, man! Why did you bring her? Why this charade? Are you mad?"

He couldn't help but notice the smug half-smile on the woman's face even as he rounded on the physician.

"*You* do not tell *me* what to do!" It was the first time Crispin had seen Jacob act in this manner. Always, the subservience was foremost, but now he was the very portrait of a father. Crispin gulped and took a step back. "You will not touch her, do you understand? It is forbidden."

His glance slid toward Julianne, who did not look contrite in the least. In fact, she was openly leering at Crispin. He swallowed again.

"Master Jacob—" But he did not know what he wanted to say. He could promise the man he would not touch her, but he knew that to be a lie.

Before he could open his mouth, a scream broke the twilight.

Outside.

Crispin lunged toward the window and cast open the casement. A woman huddled with a cluster of other ladies in the garden near Lancaster's window. She was sobbing and pointing toward the garden wall. Without thinking of his own well-being, Crispin leapt out the window and landed on the dead grass below. He gathered himself and rushed to the gate toward the women.

"What's amiss?" he asked.

The woman merely pointed toward the wall.

A long smear of gray clay swathed a portion of the wall from top to bottom. His heart gave a jolt, but he did not hesitate to leap forward and grab the top of the wall with his hands, hauling himself up.

The narrow path along the Thames was deserted but there were large indentations in the muddy snow leading down the bank. Crispin scrambled after it.

In the dim light, a large figure loped away, swaying with each long step. Crispin ran, skidding on the loose stones of the embankment at the low tide. He followed the hulking frame, even as it hurried with remarkable speed up the steep slope. Chasing after it, Crispin fell forward, catching himself with his hands on the sharp-edged rocks. Stumbling to his feet, he crested the slope and searched. A shadow ducked into an alley and he followed.

The alley drew narrower as the buildings on either side leaned in, their eaves sharing secrets mere mortals were not privy to. The damp smell overpowered as Crispin took cautious steps, unable to see much as the shadows converged and swept through, obliterating details. A chill shot down Crispin's back when one particularly deep shadow . . . moved.

He froze. It moved again. A sliver of waning light dimly outlined a head and broad shoulders before the shadow tilted back and disappeared again.

But it did not run.

"You there!" said Crispin. The waver in his voice was from being out of breath, surely.

A grunted reply.

Crispin felt a shivering wind sweep up from the Thames, pebbling his skin. "What . . . who are you?"

And then a voice. The frostiest midnight could not have chilled his heart more than this slice of voice, both gravel and mud slurred together. "Must . . . protect," it said.

Crispin was tempted to cross himself. "Holy Mother of God," he muttered. He slid his knife from its scabbard and felt the comfort of the hilt in his flexing hand. "Protect? Protect what? Who?"

"Pro-*tect*," said the unearthly voice again. And then a shoulder caught the light as the figure turned. Crispin felt the heavy tread of footsteps lumbering away. He girded himself and pursued.

The creature ran. For his size, he could run well and knew the alleys even better. He quickly outstripped Crispin, seeming to have no end of energy. Crispin ran solely on the hot blood in his veins, but he was a man and a man tires. His muscles screamed at him and his lungs burned. The creature was relentless and clever and though he pushed and pushed himself, Crispin could not catch up.

His steps slowed and he finally had to stop. Bent over his thighs, he wheezed in the cold air by the lungful. He listened with a heavy heart as the steps drew farther away and finally dimmed altogether.

Raising his head, he blinked into the cold and licked his dry lips. "I don't believe it," he told himself. "I don't *believe* it." But even as he tried to convince himself, he could not swear that he had been in conversation with a human man. Surely this was what Odo had been speaking about. If he had tried to abduct that boy, perhaps it was for information about this creature, for Crispin, as implausible as it seemed, was now convinced that he had encountered a Golem.

17

CRISPIN TRUDGED BACK THE long way to the palace courtyard, but as he suspected, all was barred due to the late hour. There was no point in going in. Except that Julianne was there and he suddenly ached for the feel of her, to wash away the fear and uncertainty that had grasped his heart for the last several days. The world was not as it seemed. Tonight, he had seen something darker, from the pits of Hell. Unnatural. And it made him long for the comfort of a woman's arms.

But a Jewess? As much as she teased he could not oblige, either her or himself. A quick tumble would yield him some relief but afterward, for her . . . No, he could not do that to Jacob, who seemed an honorable man. He rubbed the back of his neck before he jostled his hood up over his head. Was it the fact that she was forbidden that so enticed? Or that she was clever? "Leave it alone, Crispin," he told himself. Jews were scorned by society, not even allowed legal residence in England. Yet there were Jews hiding in secret but living openly as Christians, and still others who had converted and lived silent lives like monks in the Domus. Who were these Jews? Where did they come from? Why did they not leave the confines of the Domus? Was it they who had created that hulking creature, bent on the destruction of London's Christian inhabitants? There were answers to be had and one man might very well know them. In fact, that man had to answer for much.

Instead of turning toward London, he turned again toward Westminster Abbey.

CRISPIN PULLED ON THE bell rope at the abbey gate. Likely, the monks were in Vespers, but there had to be a porter still roaming nearby.

Just as Crispin was about to pull the bell rope a third time, a monk with a hurried step emerged from the shadows. The disgruntled look on his face was illuminated by the lamp he held aloft.

"Peace!" he grumbled. He was an old man and his thick, white brows furred over the tight band of his eyes. He looked Crispin up and down with a watery gaze. His toothless mouth was wrinkled like a dried fig. "Young man, do you know the hour?"

"I do," he said with an apologetic bow. "But I have need to speak with Abbot Nicholas. Tell him—"

"I will tell him nought. Young men should know better than to tramp about when Vespers have struck. Begone. Get you to your own home. It is late."

He turned to go when Crispin grabbed the bell rope and gave it another hard pull, pealing the bell in a harsh jangle of metal on metal.

The old man cringed and swiveled back, waggling a finger at Crispin's raised brow. "Miscreant! Do I set the hounds on you?"

"Nicholas would scarce appreciate his hounds used in such a manner. Besides, they know me."

The old monk cocked his head in a gesture of disbelief. "Eh? Who are you then?"

"As I was about to say, I am Crispin Guest. If you tell him so, he will see me and you can spare yourself much grief."

"Crispin Guest? Why didn't you say so?" he grumbled into his cowl and trudged back the way he came.

Crispin sighed and waited for an escort to open the gate. He did not wait long. Brother Eric arrived and with a quizzical tilt to his cowled head, unlocked and opened the entry. He did not scold Crispin but it was there in his manner. Crispin followed him silently to the abbot's quarters and waited alone until Vespers were done. The fire was the only light and he warmed himself before it, sighing in contentment at the amount of heat radiating from the generous flames.

The door swung opened and Nicholas entered. He seemed glad to see Crispin though he wasn't smiling. "Master Guest, so late?"

"Forgive me, Nicholas. But this could not wait."

Nicholas took his chair by the fire and Crispin took the other. He studied the face of the man, his old friend, and wondered how to begin. Nicholas took the task from him.

"Has the book been useful to you?"

"It has been . . . instructive. But mostly because I now question its veracity."

"What?" The monk leaned forward. He pushed his cowl back. The fire painted his features gold, cutting deep shadows into the ridges of his lined face. "Thomas of Monmouth has always been regarded highly for his scholarship."

"But I wonder how his scholarship was schooled. Who told him the details of these tales?"

"The Jews themselves, I imagine."

"Under torture? Yes," he said, recalling his own. "A man will say much under those circumstances."

"Crispin," said Nicholas, "I am surprised. You have always taken my word before."

"Not this time."

The monk shot to his feet. "Indeed! And what have I done to deserve such treatment at your hands? We have been friends!"

"And I have no wish to jeopardize that friendship. But this is more important than friendship."

The monk's face was stricken and Crispin was awash with guilt. For a moment, Nicholas hovered uncertainly. Would the monk demand he leave? He would reluctantly acquiesce, of course, but feared tearing a rift between them that could not be crossed.

Instead, the monk slowly lowered to his chair again, sitting back against it with a frown. "Very well," he said sourly. "My curiosity has gotten the better of me. What is it that is more important than friendship?"

"The truth. Thomas of Monmouth made his accusations against the Jews, citing their mission to kill a Christian child at the Passover . . . with a communication system so vast it staggers the mind. But the Scriptures themselves, the Old Testament, prohibits this shedding of blood, especially of drinking it. Why, if they demark themselves so much from our society because of these strict laws, would they break them for this? And why have there not been more stories of such boys throughout the ages? One a year?" He shook his head slowly. "Tell me you recall a record of it." He watched the old monk's face carefully, saw the eyes search fathoms deep, his lips twitch. "And yet more strange," Crispin went on, "why are there still Jews on English soil?"

Those old eyes flicked toward him. "There are those who live in the Domus Conversorum, but they are now Christian."

"I am not speaking of them."

The monk fell silent. His steady gaze finally turned toward the hearth. "So you know."

Crispin gritted his teeth. "And so did you, though you did not deign to tell me."

"And why should I? Does it have a bearing on this situation?"

"It might! How long have you known?"

"Some of us have known a long time. But little has been said. There has been an inquisitor on the matter looking into it."

"An inquisitor? Who?"

"I do not know his name."

"Have you met him?"

"Yes."

"Is he young, blond, from the north?"

Nicholas stared. "How did you know?"

"I have met him, too. What is his purpose? Surely Canterbury can take care of its own issues."

"It was the Archbishop who requested he come. Apparently, he is an expert on these cases."

"*What* is his *purpose*?"

"I beg you to remember to whom you speak, Master Guest," he said with quiet dignity.

Crispin took a deep breath and let it out slowly. The old man's hands twitched on the chair arm. "My apologies, my Lord Abbot. It is just that I have been entertained by this inquisitor to my peril and I would simply like to know—"

"*What!*" He launched from his chair again and pressed a hand to Crispin's with concern. "Are you well? Did he . . . did he . . . ?" He seemed to notice Crispin's swollen face for the first time, and reached forward.

Crispin leaned away. "Very nearly. And I am well, though a little hungry, truth be told."

"How neglectful of me." He hurried to his door and spoke in low tones to his chaplain, Brother Michael, returning to his place by the fire. He fidgeted now, snatching guilty looks. "Why did he wish to do you harm?"

Crispin stretched out his feet, feeling warm for the first time today. "I stopped him from performing an unseemly act. He was about to steal a boy. A Jewish boy."

"Why would he do that?" asked the monk.

"At the time, I thought it was for some nefarious purpose. But now . . . I think it was to question him. Which, come to think of it, might have been just as nefarious. Why did you not tell me about this man?"

"I did not think it important for you to know. Crispin, there are some things you may not be privy to. I know your curiosity is insatiable, but there are times when you need to curb it."

"This man is dangerous, Nicholas. He means these people harm."

"Why does this concern you? Jews are, by law, prohibited on English soil. They must convert or leave."

What was it to him? Green eyes and a boy's barbered hair. That was far more than it should have been.

Brother Michael brought a tray and set it on a small table between them. The abbot silently prepared the bread and soft cheese with much ceremony, then served Crispin a generous helping.

They both ate in silence, occasionally sipping from their goblets. It would have been a pleasant repast, with the fire crackling and the ordinarily good cheer they shared. But words had been said, feelings exposed. Crispin had needed to utter them, much to his regret.

An apology poised on his lips. But no. He could not allow these ideas about Jews to poison his investigation. He was a man who loved the truth, and if these words had been lies, then they could not help his case or his disposition.

Bells suddenly tolled and Nicholas rose wearily, wiping the crumbs from his cassock. "Compline. I must go. And so must you."

"Nicholas." He reached out and touched the man's sleeve. "If my tone was harsh, I did not mean . . . I would not put our fellowship at risk."

Those old eyes searched his, flicking back and forth. "I know," he said, patting his hand. "You do involve yourself so."

His thoughts fell to Julianne once more. "That I do."

HE FELT THE WEARINESS in his bones. Trudging back to London was a chore he had not desired, especially as the icy night swept over him. He hunched in his cloak and hood, breathing hard clouds into the air. The Shambles seemed a world away, and he could not help but glance over his shoulder from time to time, thinking that nightmare of a creature might appear again and seize him with those large, clay hands.

Once he passed through Newgate and plodded down Newgate Market, he looked over his shoulder again, only a bit more secure that the walls of London would not be breached. Newgate looked back at him, implacable and rigid, its portcullis grimacing with ice-slicked teeth. Crispin *had* to solve this. And soon. Exton and Froshe could not be patient forever. That vile Odo had given Crispin some clues, even as he had battered him. He said that the devil was at the heart of it, and that may be so, for the devil surely whispered his vile lies to the bastard who had committed these crimes. But if this Golem were real, and Crispin had to grant the nature of his own eyes, then this monster was certainly not innocent. It was up to no good that he could see. But when it spoke to him, and he shivered again at the thought, it had told Crispin that it was trying to protect something. The Jews, he supposed. But why go to the palace? Did it need to protect Julianne and her father?

The thought made him stop in his snowy tracks. Might someone be after them? That mysterious man, that Odo. But he was the abbot's inquisitor, wasn't he? Yes, he meant the Jews harm, but surely he would not dare touch the queen's physician! Except . . . The man wanted those parchments and might do anything to get them.

Suddenly, he found himself at the foot of his stairs. He dug into the icy steps and forced himself upward. Inside, he noticed the hearth was cold and Jack was nowhere to be seen. Damn that boy! He would be the death of Crispin yet. He grumbled as he tossed some peat into the hearth and bent toward it with his flint and steel. It was too cold a night for Jack's mischief. If the boy didn't get himself killed, Crispin would do the job for him.

He blew on the smoldering tinder and a few bits of lint helped it catch and soon the peat was burning with a small flame, enough to begin to thaw his toes and cast some light into the room.

So, Jacob and this Odo wanted the Jewish parchments. Jacob to protect London, and Odo to . . . what? His motives were to rid London of Jews. A strange request, then, to possess parchments that could create a Jewish protector with Jewish magic. Perhaps, but it would be diabolical, create a Golem to wreak havoc, blame the Jews, and roust them out. Crispin shook his head. No, there was little need to stir the populace against Jews. Only an excuse, a rumor. Odo would not truly need to *do* anything.

Crispin lifted the tabard and untied the red thread. He held it up to the firelight, turning it. Someone entirely heartless had killed the servant and those boys. Someone with some ungodly motive. Someone vile and twisted, John Rykener called it.

Red thread. Some red cloth had been used. He divorced Julianne's sash from consideration, though it was difficult once thought of. But something else had snagged in his mind. He knew this color. He had seen it recently. His thoughts fell to a rondelle hat with a long liripipe tail, certainly long enough to use as a garrote. And it did belong to a man who was, indeed, heartless and perhaps even bloodthirsty enough to commit these atrocities. Once the idea was in his head it stuck fast like a nail in a shoe. But he needed iron-clad proof.

He tossed the thread into the fire. It curled quickly and became ash.

Yes, he had gotten to know this man in the last few days. That cousin of Giles de Risley.

Radulfus.

THE MORNING COULD NOT come soon enough. He had sat up in his chair all night, staring into the small fire, demons dancing before his eyes and in his head, telling him awful tales of broken boys and greedy, lascivious men.

Radulfus. Yes, he was capable. But as a lord, Radulfus was nearly untouchable. When Crispin accused him and brought his name before the sheriff, he would have to be very certain of his guilt. Crispin might even suffer the backlash and be slain in the streets as Radulfus had intended. A lord versus someone like Crispin? There was no contest. Crispin would lose and there would be nothing he could do. The sheriffs would suffer, too, and they wouldn't likely stick their necks into a noose for him or anyone.

He hardly blamed them.

No, he had to find hard proof, something the sheriff would accept without question, something that could be taken to the king. Perhaps even Giles could be persuaded to help Crispin. Surely he had no knowledge of these doings. Yes, it seemed plain from their conversation that Giles might be up to no good, but he could be forgiven by helping Crispin now. He knew if he could talk to Giles he would have an ally. After all, the man owed him.

He had to get into their rooms and find that evidence. The last crime had been committed at Westminster. He was sure of that. There might still be something he could find, something that would tie Radulfus to this.

He glanced again to the weak rays of light spilling from the cracks in his shutters. It had to be Prime, or thereabouts. Time to head toward Westminster.

He rose, adjusted Lancaster's tabard over his coat, gave a brief thought to the absent Jack, and cast open the door.

WHEN CRISPIN ARRIVED TO the Great Gate, there were already many horse-drawn wagons and carts assembled, with bustling pages and servants loading them with supplies for the country. Boats, too, were secured at the docks. The king would likely travel up the Thames to his Christmas destination with wagons carrying the lesser courtiers. Court was leaving, perhaps that afternoon.

Crispin would have to work fast. But first, he needed to know where Giles's quarters were.

He swept the courtyard with a glance. No help here. He pushed his way in, either the tabard or the crowds making it simple for him to pass through to the great hall. More people jammed the space. But when Crispin turned his head, he spied the two people he never expected to encounter together.

Radulfus was leaning on a column and his hand was closed over Julianne's shoulder. Clearly she did not enjoy his proximity and her eyes darted, looking for a way out.

With his hand on his dagger hilt, Crispin strode toward them and stopped himself in time before he ruined all.

He threw himself against a pile of trunks, breathing deeply to get himself under control. He could not let Radulfus see him.

Radulfus raked his gaze over the boy he thought Julianne to be. And what Crispin saw on his face was unmistakable. He *coveted* him! His body leaned in and his smile was that of a crocodile. Yes, Crispin *had* been right about him.

And he was wearing his signature rondelle hat with the long liripipe tail.

"There is no need to rush off, so," Radulfus was saying. His eyes took a deliberate perusal of her boyish form from top to toe. "I have never had a chance to speak with you, young friend."

"There is little need. Unless you are in need of a physician."

"Oh, I do have an ache."

"Then I shall send my father to you."

"I doubt he will be able to heal me as well as you can."

"I am not a proper physician, my lord. My father is better qualified—"

"And I tell you"—Radulfus tightened his grip on Julianne's shoulder so harshly that Crispin saw her wince—"that it is *you* I want."

"My lord. Please."

Radulfus cackled and pushed. Julianne fell from his grip and nearly stumbled to the floor.

Crispin was a hairsbreadth from revealing his hiding place. But he drew back in time and tightened his grip on his dagger, though little comfort it offered.

Julianne straightened and adjusted her gown, the yellow rouelle clearly visible.

"I changed my mind," said Radulfus, looking down his nose at her. "Take yourself away, Jewish dog. Remove that pretty face of yours back to France. God knows why *they* accept your like." Others had taken notice and turned to look. Radulfus, sensing his audience, looked around and gestured toward her. "Jews. Why should the king trust them with the queen's health? Better to use good English physicians, eh?"

There were mutterings, but Crispin could tell what Radulfus could not, that the crowd seemed reluctant to naysay the king, even over this troublesome matter.

"The lot of them should be slaughtered," Radulfus went on, oblivious. "I've a mind to gather some men to go to Chancery Lane and save the king's treasury by burning down that House of Converts. Converts, indeed! How can you ever trust them? Who can believe their avowals, especially at this sacred time of year?" The murmurings became more directed. Perhaps they were not willing to harm the king's physician, but the idea of Jews, even converts, obviously did not sit well with the men of court.

Was a riot fomenting before his eyes? Crispin searched for help. He had promised the secret Jews to protect them, but if Radulfus brought down all of court to the site of the Domus, how could he hope to come between them and a mob?

A short, beefy servant suddenly pushed his way forward. The king's colors on his chest and back assured him that the crowd would part, and part they did. Bill Wodecock approached Radulfus and bowed deeply. "My lord, Master Cornelius wishes to see you. He has sent me forthwith."

Radulfus seemed perturbed that his rant was interrupted, but it was enough to foil the concentration of the crowd, who went back to the business of seeing to their baggage and goods.

Wodecock gestured to a page and instructed him to take Radulfus to that astrologer, Cornelius. Wodecock watched them go, dusting his hands together at a job well done. Crispin approached and stood behind him. "That was well played, Wodecock."

The servant stiffened and barely turned toward Crispin in acknowledgment. "Sometimes a distraction is what's needed."

"Did Master Cornelius truly request to speak with Radulfus?"

Wodecock paused before he twisted round to look at Crispin with his tiny eyes. "He might have done."

Crispin smiled and bowed. "Your servant."

"Hmpf. Indeed." Wodecock was on his way but Crispin stopped him.

"Master Wodecock. I wonder if you would further serve the king by directing me to Radulfus's apartments."

"And how can that serve the king, pray?"

"You know I cannot tell you."

"You're up to mischief, Master Guest. I cannot abide it."

"Not mischief. But it also serves the king, I assure you. Can you not put your trust in me, Master Wodecock?"

Those eyes studied him and Crispin felt them like hot coals burning through his clothes.

"I find it hard to do so, Master Guest, and you know the reason why."

Crispin had no more words. He allowed the other man to gage his character by looks alone. He felt very self-conscious with his patched stockings and shabby cloak, but there was nothing to be done.

At length, Wodecock turned away and strode through the great hall, leaving Crispin behind. He had walked a good length of the hall before he stopped and pivoted. He cocked his head impatiently and gave a short gesture for Crispin to follow.

THEY WOUND THEIR WAY silently through the crowded corridors. It seemed only ghosts were to remain behind at court when the king's retinue journeyed to Sheen. Twenty days from now, Christmas would be a grand affair. Crispin remembered many of those feasts and gatherings from years past. Garlands of greenery would festoon the hall and the smells of meats and pies would inhabit the tapestries for days. Warm fires, good wine, even better companionship. It was a relief from the cold winter without.

He dusted the memories aside and stopped when Wodecock stopped. The servant gestured to a narrow door at the end of the corridor nearest the stables.

"That is the door, Master Guest. But it is locked as it should be. Do not," said Wodecock, raising a hand to Crispin's opened mouth, "ask me to unlock it, for I shall do no such thing. If you wish to speak to my lord Radulfus, you must wait for his return."

"And how long will that be?" How much time would he have to look those rooms over? He looked back at the narrow passage. There was no one there.

Wodecock seemed to know what Crispin was thinking and he wagged a finger at him. "No tricks, Master Guest. If anyone should ask, I did not see you."

"Of course. Thank you, Master—" The servant turned on his heel and was already halfway down the corridor when Crispin finished, "Wodecock."

Alone in the corridor, he hurried to the door and tested the latch. Locked, just as Wodecock said. He hadn't much time, so he set to work. He flipped his dagger from its sheath and reached into the collar of his tabard and coat to pull out the lace to his chemise and its sharp aiglet. With knife tip and aiglet, he manipulated the pins within the lock until they released the latch. Sheathing the dagger and stuffing the lace back under his clothes, Crispin rose and gently pushed the door open.

The room was dark with only the faint, red glow from the ashes in the hearth. He slipped inside, closed and locked the door, and waited for his eyes to adjust, then lit a candle. A modest room, larger than the Jews' quarters but much smaller than Lancaster's. There were several chests still in the room. Crispin remembered that Giles and Radulfus were not invited to court for Christmas, but he would still be traveling to Sheen for the feast. Traveling to Crispin's manor.

He tried the lid of the first chest and found it open. Setting the candle above on the nearby table, he rummaged inside, but found nothing of worth.

He went to the next, opened it, and looked inside. The third chest was locked. He used both aiglets this time. It took longer than the door, but the lock finally clicked and he lifted the lid.

He could smell the blood immediately. Dried, but the coppery scent lifted up to his nostrils, nonetheless. He pushed past the gowns and plate when his fingers lighted on the rough weave of a small tunic. He pulled it forth and shook it out. It was a boy's tunic. With blotches of dried blood. Crispin stared at it, trying to detach himself from what it meant.

His fists curled into the small garment that had once belonged to a young boy. Which one had it belonged to?

He cast the tunic aside and dug deeper, pulling out more; a ripped stocking, a shirt, another tunic. Far more than could have belonged to four boys.

He ploughed further and came away with parchments rolled together. He set the clothing down and unfurled the skins. It was Hebrew with the strange drawings accompanying them.

Evidence at last! But was it enough? A few torn shirts, some with dried blood, and an indecipherable parchment? The sheriffs would laugh in his face.

A key turned in the lock.

He looked toward the door and froze for a heartbeat before pinching off the candle flame and retreating to a curtained alcove.

A figure entered and stood in the doorway for a moment, a brazen silhouette against the dancing fire of the rushlight without. The door shut and darkness swelled around them. Footsteps crossed to the hearth and a log or two were tumbled in. A spark and then flames tickled the tinder. The candle was relit and the man stopped, staring at the clothing tossed about, the formerly locked chest lying open. When he gasped, Crispin moved. His hand clamped hard over the man's mouth and his blade pressed against his throat.

"Don't move," Crispin hissed in his ear.

The blond man wriggled uncomfortably and squeaked but stilled himself.

"You are the astrologer. Nod your head."

Shakily, the head nodded.

Crispin was breathing hard. His knife was at the man's throat and he'd like nothing better than to shove it in deep, choking the man with his own blood. Instead, he kept the blade steady and spit the man's hair from his lips.

"I will remove my hand and you will not cry out. Do you understand? Nod again if you do."

Slowly, he nodded.

"Good. You will tell me things. Things about these parchments and about these pieces of clothing. Now, I am removing my hand."

Crispin steadily pulled his palm away from the man's mouth. With the blade still pressed to his neck, he closed his hand tightly around the man's upper arm and manhandled him into a chair. He came around to the front of him, his knife still in his face. "Your name?"

"C-cornelius van der Brooghes. Please, what is it you want?"

"Answers. You are de Risley's astrologer. For what purpose does he need an astrologer?"

Sweat speckled the man's face. He licked his lips, eyes wide. "His f-fortune. He follows the stars to f-find his fortune."

"Indeed." He scooped up the parchments and held them under the man's sharp nose. "And what of these?"

"They are . . . important to his star charts—"

Crispin backhanded him with the stiff skins and held them before his dazed eyes again. "*What* are they for?"

"Important star charts. To help find the best days for—"

Crispin used his knuckles this time and the man fell back, nearly toppling from the chair. He whimpered.

"Tell me what these parchments are for. Did you steal them from the Jews?"

"They are only Jews. They do not know the power these parchments wield."

"Are they for creating a Golem?"

Cornelius's pale eyes lifted and searched Crispin's. "A G-golem? What is that?" he whispered.

Crispin drew back his arm to strike again and the man cringed, holding his hand protectively over his face. "I do not know what you are talking about? Please! I don't know!"

Lowering his hand, Crispin glowered. He leaned forward. "Then tell me this." He bent to retrieve the bloodied tunic and fisted them into the man's face. "What can you tell me of these?"

The eyes widened before he crushed his lids closed, shaking his head from side to side. "No. He'll kill me."

"I'll kill you if you don't. Tell me!"

"Oh God! Oh blessed *Jesu*! What have we done?"

He backhanded the man anyway. He felt the blood and spittle on his knuckles. The man began to shake and hug himself. "Holy Mother," he whispered hoarsely. "He made me do it."

"Damn you! DO WHAT?"

Crossing himself, he muttered in a foreign tongue that Crispin did not understand, rattled on and on before Crispin grimaced at him and knocked him in the side of the head.

"English, you cur!"

The astrologer barely acknowledged the cuffing. But his mutterings switched to heavily accented English. "I lured those boys. I brought them to him. Holy Mother grant me mercy, but I promised their parents that they would learn to read and write, that they would be gentlemen. Instead I brought them to *him*. Oh God! The blood!" He dropped his face in his hands and wept, snorting loudly through his bloodied nose.

Crispin grabbed his hair and jerked his face upright. A crimson smear painted the man's cheek. "*What did he do*?"

"Oh God forgive me!"

"He sodomized them. He murdered them."

Cornelius's eyes were almost all whites now. "How did you know?" he gasped.

Crispin barely believed it. But if he allowed his emotions to come into play, he could not deal with the astrologer as coldly as he needed to. With some measure of satisfaction, he realized that this was his evidence. "You must testify that Radulfus forced you to bring him these boys."

Cornelius looked up with bewildered eyes. "Radulfus?"

But in the next moment, the door burst open, and Crispin realized how fragile his predicament was.

18

RADULFUS AND GILES PUSHED their way in and stopped when they spied the situation.

Crispin leapt back and held his dagger uncertainly.

Eyes flicking back and forth between the weeping astrologer and Crispin, de Risley motioned for his cousin to close and bar the door. "What goes on here?" His gaze encountered the clothes and parchments now strewn across the floor.

"Much," said Crispin.

Giles reached for Cornelius, hauling him to his feet. "What have you done, you whoreson!"

Cornelius blubbered, trying to speak through his sobs.

"Your cousin, Giles," said Crispin. "Vile things he has done right under your nose."

Giles looked back at Radulfus. "Has he now?"

"The testimony of this astrologer will most certainly condemn your kinsman. I am sorry, Giles. But you must learn the truth."

"Testimony? I do not know what you are talking about, Crispin."

"The murder of boys. Murder and sodomy, it grieves me to say. I will make certain your name does not come into it, Giles."

Giles's steady gaze on Crispin might have been unnerving, but Crispin could see his mind working like a millwheel. "Radulfus?"

He looked from Cornelius to Radulfus. "Murder and sodomy? There must be some mistake."

Radulfus glared.

Giles shook his head. "It's unbelievable. This can't be true. Cornelius? Did you know of this?"

Cornelius turned away from him and sobbed.

Giles blinked hard at the man and then spied the bloodied clothing on the floor. He stooped and gingerly took up a tunic in his hand, turning it over and over. "Horrible. You would give testimony against my cousin here? Yes, surely you must." He took Cornelius's arm again. "Except for one thing."

Cornelius jerked and gurgled, twisting like an eel on a spit. He fell to the floor with a flood of blood and bile rushing from his side. With a dispassionate flick of his brow, Giles looked down at his own bloodied dagger and sleeve.

Cornelius choked and writhed, face wet with blood and tears. He reached his hand toward Crispin, tendons straining against his pale hand, eyes beseeching. It had happened so fast. There was nothing Crispin could do. He watched in horror as the man sunk down, twisting as death took hold. He bled out, his cheeks growing pale, until his eyes rolled back.

Giles coldly wiped the blood on the child's tunic and dropped it to the floor. "So much for your witness."

"Giles!" The horror of it finally reached him. Cornelius had been surprised that Crispin thought Radulfus was the culprit.

He had not meant Radulfus at all.

Giles sheathed his dagger and shook his head. "Crispin, Crispin. Why could you not leave it alone?"

"Giles." It was a nightmare. How could it be true? Friendly rivals they had been, even stubborn rivals. Giles had stolen away Crispin's lover and there had been words and fists exchanged. But that had been young men out to best the other. Surely Giles was not capable of this horror. He was not that man.

Was he?

Giles strode up to Crispin and grabbed him by the tabard, twisting the cloth in a fist. His bloody hand imprinted the material even as his breath ghosted over Crispin's face. "Why couldn't you leave it alone? We must have no witness, Master Guest. And no arrest."

"But Giles. For God sake. Why?"

He took in his pale-faced cousin to his right. "Why? Oh Crispin. So much has happened over the last seven years. So much. When Margaret died in childbed, there was much to think about. She had brought a fine dowry to the marriage, as you know. But gold seemed to slip through my fingers. My coffers emptied. There was ruin around every corner, until—"

"Cousin," warned Radulfus.

Crispin lunged forward. "Giles! I beg you. You must stop these vile crimes! To kill these innocent boys! To . . . to do the things you are doing to them—"

"But I *like* doing what I am doing to them!" he screeched, his voice slightly hysterical. Gone was the innocent mask he had worn. Crispin saw him as he now was. Something had changed him. Something had rotted him from the inside. He was not the man Crispin had known, and the fearful realization of that stilled his heart and sickened his belly.

Giles drew himself back and barked a laugh, bringing his cousin into his shared laughter. "The quivering flesh of these young, fresh-faced creatures. It is like taking a maiden, Crispin. Better. You should try it. I think you will find it pleasing."

"You disgust me!"

"And the blood. No, I never thought to find such enjoyment in it. The young boys, yes. I have had that proclivity for some time. Even before Margaret. Oh she was a prize, indeed. Something to best you at. I never thought to find such success. I had finally beaten you at something. How it burned me to fail again and again.

But Margaret was a willing sacrifice. And I saw how it hurt you." He smiled. "Did she die in childbed? Did she?" Crispin tasted the bile in his throat but he could not lose himself to retching. He had to stay alert.

Giles chuckled. "I suppose you'll never know. There was much blood in the bed that night. Blood. And I found the idea of it . . . pleasing. The battlefield was never as pleasing as this." He strutted now, walking up and down before the still body of the astrologer. "Do you know why I cut out their entrails?"

"Giles!" hissed his companion.

"No, no, Radulfus. I think Master Guest should know. At least some of it. After all, he's worked so hard to get this far." He stepped forward and Crispin, a bubble of horror filling his chest, took a step back. "Have you ever held the quivering entrails of your enemy in your hand, Crispin? No? I know you have killed many men. And surely you have seen it. But to never have held them? Such a pity. Do you know that viscera is not merely warm, it is *hot*. It holds such heat that steam rises as the hot blood oozes over your fingers. That's because the boy is still *alive*. You can feel the blood pulsing through the viscera. It is fascinating, truly. They are drugged, of course, so they cannot ruin my fun."

Crispin could not look away. Even as the slick blood of the astrologer filled his nose with a metallic scent, his eyes met Giles and he saw demons within.

"And witnessing the moment—that very moment—that life leaves them," Giles continued, his voice drifting dreamily. "It's the eyes, Crispin. They dull. Their gloss seems to fog over, as if a veil shrouds them. It is at this moment that I like to feel the slick entrails in my fingers as they cool. And then I cut them out and save them in jars for my own amusement. Later, I can look at them."

Crispin thought desperately. What could he do? This monster could not be stopped! If these boys had been the sons of wealthy merchants perhaps something could be done. But no one would come forth for these boys. De Risley was unreachable. Crispin snatched a glance at the dark-eyed cousin, Radulfus. Both were looking curiously at the cooling body of the astrologer.

"I suppose we shall have to call someone about Cornelius," said Radulfus. He stepped back, trying not to soil his boots with the pool of dark blood. They both looked up at the same time. "We could blame him for it," he offered.

"I could not do that to an old friend," said Giles. "Even if we weren't truly friends." He gave Crispin a chilling grin. "Hurry you now, Crispin. We will tell them that we caught Cornelius stealing from us. Consider it a debt paid. But I might just as easily change my mind."

Throat dry, Crispin made one last frantic attempt to think of something, but Radulfus shifted toward him. "Out, Master Guest," he said, sliding his hand seductively over the hilt of his sword.

Crispin cast a sorrowful glance at his dead witness, and with a feeling of disgust at himself, could do nothing more than stumble through the door. He shuffled like a dead man through the crowded corridors, scarcely marking the chaos around him. When he made it to the Great Gate he looked back at the bustle of oblivious servants and noblemen, turned to the wall, and vomited against it.

He held the wall to steady himself, and when his belly was empty he wiped his mouth and pushed away. "Margaret." He had not loved her, had not thought of her in years, in fact. They were paramours, exchanging favors in the others' bed. But he could have fought harder to keep her, to save her. Had Giles truly killed her or was that more taunting? Crispin didn't know him at all. Hadn't ever known him. How could he have been so wrong about someone? Was nothing as it seemed?

The cold was even worse now. The chill wind slashed against the rawness of his cheek. The futility of it all. What good was being this damned Tracker if he could not protect the citizens of London? He could go to the sheriffs, he could explain it as clearly as he could, but he knew, he *knew* there was nothing the sheriffs would do. Not against a nobleman. There was no evidence against him for murder. True, if the sheriffs could arrest both Giles and his cousin Radulfus, torture could extract the truth, but neither sheriff would do such a thing on Crispin's say-so.

And these victims. A beggared victim was little good to him. There would be no one to pay the bribes to the sheriffs, no one to put forth the accusations that would hold any weight.

With a frustrated cry, Crispin wrestled the tabard from his body and heaved it to the dirty snow, ignoring the strange looks from those milling outside the gate on the street. A waste! What good were the duke's arms to him? None of it was any good to him. If he had only been a knight he could have properly faced Giles, could have accused him. But Giles was right. He was nothing. Less than nothing. If he could not bring criminals to justice then what was his purpose now?

He left the tabard in the snow, paying little attention as a half-starved urchin pounced upon it and slipped it over his shivering shoulders. Better to give it to beggars. It did more good on them than on him.

He plodded back toward London, bypassed his lodgings completely, and turned up Gutter Lane. When he pushed open the doors to the Boar's Tusk and sat by the fire with a bowl of wine in his hands, he felt safe to surrender to his despair.

HIS FACE WAS PRESSED to the table. There was drool wetting his cheek where it rested against the rough wood. Crispin licked his numbed lips. Something had awoken him but in the haze of alcohol, he wasn't certain what.

A voice. Two voices. They were talking to each other over his head and he heard his name. He raised a finger to his flaccid lips and sent a sloppy "shhhh" their way.

The talking ceased and he sensed eyes upon him.

"He's been like this for hours," said the deep male voice above him. "He would not speak when he arrived. He ordered his wine and he had a look about him like death but he would say nothing to me."

"Bless me," said the young voice in the harsh accent of the streets. Jack. Must be. And the older was Gilbert. But he wouldn't open his eyes. Keep them closed and don't move. Moving would remind him why he was here.

"And you say he's been like that for hours?"

"Yes. I wish I knew what was troubling him."

"It must be this case," said Jack softly.

Crispin feared they'd let slip something. With supreme effort, he opened his mouth and uttered a slurred, "Be still!"

Jack crouched low toward him. Crispin could smell him; adolescent sweat and hay. "Master! Master Crispin! Tell me what happened. What is amiss? Is the sheriff on his way?"

"No!" he bellowed. "No! Don't talk about it!"

"But Master! The murderer. We cannot allow him to get away. You said—"

Damn that boy! He *had* to insist on opening the floodgates and letting the memories flow in. Damn him, damn him, *damn him*!

"NO!" Crispin lurched up, spittle trailing in a long iridescent tether from his mouth back to the puddle on the table. He wiped unsteadily at his mouth with his hand. "Damn you, Jack! Can't you let me forget?"

Gently, Jack laid a hand on his shoulder. "But Master Crispin, what happened?"

He felt the bench creak behind him and the warm presence of Gilbert blocked his other escape. There was nothing for it now. He straightened, tried to focus his eyes on the table, and reached for the wine jug. He sloshed the red liquor over his hand and into the waiting bowl and drank it greedily. "Jack," he said, doing his best to enunciate. He swayed and turned his head. "Gilbert. My friends." He dropped his head and sighed. "I fear the name of Justice is no more in the city of London."

The man and the boy exchanged looks. Gilbert rested a large paw on his arm. "Crispin, what can you mean?"

"I mean," he said, shaking off the man's hand and climbing precariously to his feet, "that Justice is damned, along with everyone else in this stinking town!" He used Gilbert's shoulder as leverage to step out of the bench and lurched toward the hearth. Jack launched himself to his feet to prevent Crispin from pitching headlong into the fire. But he shook Jack's hands off of him, too.

"Le' me be!" he growled. He leaned unsteadily over the flames, letting them roast his thighs and knees. It didn't help. He still felt cold and numb. Dead. He was a corpse already. Should have let Radulfus kill him in the street. Then the pain of that unspeakable ache in his chest wouldn't feel so bad now. "Let me be," he whispered.

"What happened at court, Master?" asked Jack, positioning himself beside him.

"What happened? You wish to know what happened? Very well. I was emasculated, that's what happened."

Jack's eyes made a quick glance down over Crispin before the expression on his worried face cleared.

"Degradation was nothing compared to this," Crispin went on. "That, at least, was physical. Taking my sword, my arms. But this long, slow, stripping of my ability to *do* anything . . . I am not a man, Jack. Not a man."

"Of course you are, sir! You are more man than half of court! Is he not, Gilbert?"

"Aye, that you are, Crispin! A finer and more honorable man I have never known, I assure you."

"Empty words," he snorted. "What do you know of it? What do either of you know of it?"

They fell silent. The three of them stood, merely looking into the flames. Crispin felt his bones begin to thaw. His knees gave out and both Gilbert and Jack grunted as they grabbed an elbow to prevent him from falling on his backside. They wrestled him onto a stool.

"I went to Giles de Risley's apartments." He leaned toward Jack, nabbed his collar, and pulled him close. He could see every freckle on the boy's pale face. "It's him, Jack. My old friend. *He* is the murderer and vile sodomizer. That astrologer confessed it. I had him, Jack. I *had* him! I had a witness. He confessed it all. And then de Risley arrived. And he confessed it, too. But then . . . to prove that he was untouchable, he killed the astrologer, killed our only witness." He heard Jack's gasp but ploughed on anyway. "Killed him in cold blood before my eyes in the company of his vile cousin. And then he told me all, Jack. Every disgusting, horrifying truth. How he killed them, how he enjoyed it, how he cut out their entrails and held them in his hands . . ."

Gilbert drew back in horror, making a sound of retching.

"He *told* me, Jack," he whispered. "And I couldn't lay a finger upon him."

Silence. Crispin nodded. What could be said to that? The evidence of his final humiliation, his uselessness was now before them. For four years he had only played at a man who honorably served justice. Four years out of the thirty miserable years of his life.

"He's a dog. A horrible, mangy dog!" said Jack, his tone vicious. "But dogs are trapped when they are dangerous. If we could only lay a trap for him."

"It isn't possible," murmured Crispin. "The sheriffs would have to discover him and they won't even entertain the idea. Not a lord like de Risley. There is nothing we can do. Nothing!"

Jack nearly quivered with rage. His white fists grew whiter, crumpling the hem of his tunic with twisted emotions. And then, as Crispin watched, he grew thoughtful and suddenly the boy looked up at Gilbert. "Master Gilbert, could you see that my master gets home safe and sound? There is something I must see about."

As soon as Gilbert nodded, Jack, whey-faced and solemn, darted out the door.

Crispin looked up at his friend and scowled. "Tomorrow is the Feast Day of Saint Nicholas," he mumbled. "Christmas is not far behind. Another wretched Christmas on the Shambles."

"Don't be alone, Crispin. Stay with us. With Nell and me. We've asked you so many times. Accept our invitation this year, Crispin. Of all years."

"No." He pulled away and staggered to his feet. "No. I'm going home. To the only home I deserve. Maybe I'll break my neck going up those stairs. It will be a fitting end."

Gilbert gathered his cloak about him. "I'll take you."

"No!" he said mulishly. But Gilbert drew himself up and barked in Crispin's ear.

"Be still, Crispin Guest! If I were a better friend I should backhand you for the sorrowful fool you are!"

Crispin blinked at him, mute.

"Can you not see the good you have done to this old town?" Gilbert went on. "Can't you see the countless lives you have saved, the innocent souls you have protected? Bah! You are drunk, but such foolish prattling comes out of your mouth even when you are sober. Wake up! This may be your lot, but a man can make the best of any situation. I have seen you crawl forth from the very gutter and make yourself anew. Who else in this town is a Tracker, eh? No one. If a man needs someone to help him find a lost necklace or a stolen parchment, they have no one to go to. The sheriff? Not unless they had the money to bribe them. But you'd do it. You'd say it was for the coin, but I know you better than that. It's for the honor of the thing. Yours and theirs. What man can ferret out a puzzle like you? These wretched sheriffs? They are only aldermen. Merchants. What do they know of men's hearts and the cunning therein? Who amongst them can look at a corpse and know the nature of his death and the manner of it? None, I say. None but you. But you would wallow in your own pity until it sucks you down like a peat bog. Well, Master Guest." He grabbed Crispin's arm and hauled him to the door, kicking it open until they were both slapped in the face by the cold. "I'll hear no more of it this night. I'll get you home where you can sleep it off. And the next time I see you I had better see a humble face and an apology for such churlishness on your tongue. And then no more will be said of it."

Crispin wanted to say much, to refute Gilbert's bald derision. But even in the muddiness of his wine-soaked mind, he could discern the truth of it. He clapped his mouth shut instead and allowed Gilbert to drag him home, push him up the icy steps to prevent him from breaking his neck as he desired, and dumped him on his bed. Crispin vaguely recalled him banking his coals before the door shut and all was quiet again. In the haze of drunkenness and sleep, he wondered if he would remember any of this come morning, hoping that it was, perhaps, all a dream.

BUT IN THE MORNING, his head felt cracked open with a pike, with the added accompaniment of devils poking at his eyeballs with pitchforks. His belly told him to get up quickly and empty it into his chamber pot before he soiled his linens, and he jerked to his feet, pulled the pot from its place beneath his bed, and did just that. When it seemed he was hollow again, he pushed the disgusting pot away and wiped his lips. He sat back on his bum, resting his wrists loosely on his upraised knees, and tried a shaky sigh. His head still pounded but not as badly as before, and the perspiration on his face cooled his fevered brow.

He almost questioned why he had allowed himself to get this way when his memories returned to him, and along with it, his feelings of helplessness. But strangely, a tirade from Gilbert began to filter through the self-pity and he took stock. Yes, he supposed he could succumb to futility, but Gilbert was right. He could not solve all of London's woes, but he could find a way to stop Giles. He merely had to think it through. He could make the sheriffs see reason. Giles would slip in some way. The arrogant always did. Crispin tried not to think that more innocent lives might be sacrificed to it, but in the end, Giles would get his.

He pushed himself forward and used the bed to rise. He waited a moment to see if his stomach would churn again and was pleased that it did not appear to do so.

So Giles's astrologer—*dead* astrologer, he corrected—had stolen the Jews' parchments. But when he questioned him on the fate of the Golem, he did not know what Crispin was talking about. Surely it was no lie. He had spilled his guts about everything else. There would be no need to lie about this. And if this was the case, then they had nothing to do with a Golem. But if that were so, who did?

Crispin cast an eye toward his wine jug on the windowsill. Dare he? At least to get the sour taste of vomit from his mouth, surely. He took up the jug and drank from its lip. That was better. It helped to clear his head, at least that's what he told himself.

Now what was the next step? Plan what to do about Giles. Giles had been waiting for the stars to align or some such nonsense. To what end? He was planning something. Did he murder because of the position of the stars? Tonight, at the feast of Saint Nicholas, something was supposed to happen. Then perhaps Crispin had best return to Westminster—

He touched his cotehardie and searched the small room for sign of Lancaster's tabard. And then he remembered. He had tossed it to the ground in a fit of anger and some beggar had made off with it. Well, good for him. He would go without. Perhaps Bill Wodecock would help him enter the palace regardless.

But something on the table caught his eye. A small scrap of parchment. He recognized Jack's weak scrawl. The boy was learning his letters, and his writing was no smooth scribe's hand, to be sure. Yet as he read, his heart stopped.

Goode Master Cryspyn,
Synce you wyre out of sorts last night, I got it in me head to set a trap. I haff made m'self known to Lord de Risley and lyke the curr he ys, he has agreed to take me to Sheen and we will be leeving early the morn of the Feest of Nickolas. But do not fret. I know what he is about. Just make certain to bring the sheriffs so we can cotch hym!

I am your devout servant,
Jack Tucker

19

CRISPIN STARED AT THE letter. For how long, he did not know. His hand shook as he let the parchment slip through his fingers. The first word from his mouth was a whispered, "No."

Jack. That fool, Jack. God in heaven. What had Crispin done?

He flung open his door and raced down the steps. Blindly, with snow smacking his face and eyes, he ran up the street toward the frosty edifice of Newgate. He didn't quite remember crossing the threshold, or pounding on the door, or just why that great oaf William was pushing him back and why the man suddenly had a black eye.

But Crispin seemed to come to his senses when he was standing in the sheriff's chambers, breathing hard and raggedly, heard but did not feel the fat logs crackle in the hearth, and the scowl on Exton's fish face and the nervous finger drumming of Froshe's stubby little digits on his bejeweled belt.

"You come here, thrashing your way through our men," Exton was saying, but Crispin cut him off by slamming his hands on the table.

"I need a horse!"

"What, by the blessed Virgin, do you mean barging in here?" Froshe suddenly grew some backbone, only it was entirely the wrong time. Crispin glared at him, which made Froshe take a step back.

The Fishmonger narrowed his eyes. "You had better have information on that child killer, Master Guest. Or this tirade of yours might be better served in a cell."

Exton, too, seemed to have learned a thing or two, except now there was no time! "Will you listen to me! I need a horse. I must rescue my servant Jack. He has been abducted by that very child murderer."

Exton came swiftly around the table. "And who is the murderer?"

"Giles de Risley. Now will you give me a horse?"

"Giles de Risley? You mean Lord de Risley? Of Sheen? Are you mad?"

"He confessed it. His man confessed it. It is he. Only there is no proof. But he will kill my servant if you don't give me a goddamned horse!"

Froshe rustled his considerable jowls. "There is no need for blasphemous language, Master Guest."

"Help me. Come with me to Sheen and see this despicable dog for yourselves."

Exton took his seat and Froshe followed suit. They were more concerned with studying the contents of their table with its many parchments and seals. "I am certain this all seems quite urgent to you. But you must understand. We have only been in our office for two months and to accuse one of the king's courtiers in his own house? No, no. That would be intolerable."

"It occurs to me, Master Nicholas," said Froshe, his small eyes darting to his companion, "that we have yet to pay Master Guest for his services. Perhaps some gold might appease this sudden bout of urgency."

"No, you fools! I need your help, not your gold!"

Exton rose and raised his small, pointy chin. "Sir! May I remind you of your rank? Must I bring in one of my sergeants to tutor you?"

Crispin blinked at them. They weren't going to help him. They were going to sit there like a couple of toadstools and let a good lad die. The horror of it struck him like a blow to the face and he stepped back. Pivoting on his heel, he pushed his way out the door and stumbled down the chamber stair.

Out into the cold of the bustling street, Crispin felt lost and helpless. The king's retinue was no doubt halfway to Sheen by now if not there already. The king himself must have taken his barge. The others would be on the road following the twisting Thames southwest.

Crispin needed a horse and damn the consequences. He did not have enough coins to hire one. He'd steal one, then! But perhaps . . . The thought came to him like a thief in the night, creeping slowly upon him.

He had to try.

He ran, dodging carts and people. He found the street of well-kept shops and houses, and pursued the sloping lane to the large shop at the corner with its own wide courtyard. He hustled to the entrance and wondered if he shouldn't have gone to the servant's entrance instead. But it was too late. He stood knocking, praying he would not be turned away.

When the door opened and the servant eyed him he thought of pushing him aside and searching for the master himself, but instead, he took a deep breath and bowed. "Is Master Wynchecombe here?"

The servant said, "You are Crispin Guest, are you not?"

"Yes. Please, I must see him."

The servant, bless him, was more understanding than most, and motioned Crispin into the warm entry. The man led him to the parlor and told him to wait. Wynchecombe would either have him thrown out or come to investigate out of curiosity.

It wasn't long until he heard a clatter and the heavy footfalls of his former rival, and then the man was standing at the threshold.

"Crispin Guest. What the devil are you doing in my place of business? Haven't I seen the backside of you for the last time?"

Crispin was almost grateful for that familiar and grating tone. He bowed and when he rose again, Wynchecombe looked surprised. "Master Wynchecombe, I am in urgent need of your help. The sheriffs of London will do nothing."

"Ha!" Wynchecombe stepped into the room and made himself comfortable in his chair. "How I have longed to hear you say that. You are now someone else's problem. I do not see why you come sniveling to me—"

"Simon, for the love of God! Please listen to me."

Wynchecombe seemed to take in Crispin's desperation for the first time. It made him squirm a bit on his chair. "Have your say, Guest, and then get out."

Crispin paced, drawing his fingers through his snow damp hair. "My servant, Jack, is in trouble. Desperate trouble. He got it in his head to trap a child murderer by being the bait. I need a horse and your help to arrest the murderer."

"And why is it the sheriffs will not assist you?"

"Because the man I accuse is a courtier."

"Goddammit, Crispin! And now you would draw me into your foolish plots? And have *me* arrested? No! Get out!"

"My lord! You know I would not be here if it were not the direst of circumstances. Jack Tucker is an innocent lad. He will be used most foully and then slaughtered like a spring lamb. Help me, Simon. Help *him*!"

Wynchecombe stared. Clearly he was not used to such emotions from Crispin and Crispin was certainly not used to showing them. He would rather cut his own throat than expose himself so to Wynchecombe, but he had little choice.

Simon rubbed his hand under his bearded chin. "God's teeth," he muttered. "Where have they gone?"

"To my . . . my old estates in Sheen. Giles de Risley purchased them for his own. It is not far from the king's court. I will return the horse in good order. You know I will. Simon—"

"I have given you no leave to use my name," he muttered, thinking. "You have proof?"

"I had a witness. But Giles killed him with his naked blade before my eyes. He is a cruel man without a shred of mercy. He told me how he likes to kill them, likes to make them suffer while still alive. I cannot let that fate befall Jack Tucker!"

"All you want from me is a horse—"

Silence. How long did they face one another? Crispin's rapid pulse beat out the time as precious moments slipped away. How long would Jack Tucker have?

Simon rose and scowled at his table. "Damn you, Guest." His voice was low and deadly. "If you are wrong, I shall have you skinned alive and hang your worthless hide over my hearth." He strode from the room and bellowed over his shoulder for a servant.

WYNCHECOMBE WOULD NOT COME with him but at least he gave Crispin a horse, and a fine one it was. Crispin wanted to urge the beast faster, but he feared to tax it. He stopped late afternoon to water and rest it.

He paced beside the river, unable to rest himself. The day was drawing late. It wouldn't be long until nightfall and he *had* to be in Sheen before then!

The landscape was pearly white with snow. Black, barren trees veined the white expanse, scraping a gray, overcast sky. Once or twice, Crispin thought he heard something just beyond the dense thickets lining the road and verges. Possibly a deer or even an outlaw. He had the oddest sense that someone was following him, but each time he turned his head to the place he thought he heard a sound, there was nothing there but cold and snow.

He mounted once again and took on a harder pace. Hours later as the sun was near setting, he rounded a bend in the river and took a sharp breath. He had not seen his estates in some seven years but there they were. A handsome stone manor house surrounded by walls with a gatehouse nearest the road. In the distance and through the mist, he could just make out the shape of the mill perched at a turn in the brook. He had spent many a day as a boy at that mill, vexing the miller with his questions . . . No. As much as he might wish to, he knew he had no time for revisiting the past.

Lights in the manor's windows meant that Giles and his retinue were there.

Jack was in there.

But how to approach it? Giles would need someplace quiet, secluded and undisturbed. The only place Crispin could think of—"The mews." Vaults lay below the house's foundations. Nothing was stored below, at least not in his day. It could be locked away from prying eyes. And there was access to the river. A convenient way to dispose of a body.

HE TIED HIS HORSE in the dense copse above the grounds and crept down from the woods to the walls. In the icy darkness he thrashed through the dried reeds and found the disused door near the riverside. Disused in his day, perhaps, but here, the threshold had been dug away to make the way smooth and the hinges had been newly oiled.

Crispin listened, putting his ear to the door. When he heard nothing he pulled the door ring. Slowly he opened it and peered around its edge. Nothing but the gray passage, though a light shone ahead around the corner.

With the knife comfortably in his hand, Crispin made his way forward. Dusty barrels filled one arch and old beams lay stacked in another. Besides the mildew smell of the river, Crispin detected the slight scent of incense. A strange place for it, but he followed his nose and the light.

Shadows played on the columns and low vaults. Crispin slithered against a column and listened. The echoes played with him and though this place should have been familiar, he thought it had been too long since he had been here and things had changed—

"Don't move, Guest."

Hot blood swirled through his veins and he turned. Radulfus nodded the tip of his blade toward Crispin's chest. He chuckled low. "I do not know why, but I had the strangest feeling you'd be here. Must be the devil whispering in my ear."

"He'll be doing more than that soon." Crispin gripped his dagger until Radulfus glanced at it.

"Drop it," he said. He poked Crispin with the sword tip. "I said drop it."

Crispin did. It clanged on the floor and echoed the deed over and over. Crispin backed up, until he was against a column. "Does he have the boy?"

"How the hell did you know—" He shook his head and smiled. "You amaze me. I have often heard Giles speak of you. He told the most atrocious lies. Oh, I never believed him. I can tell a jealous man when I hear one. He always wanted to best you. I suppose, in a way, your degradation should have pleased him no end, but he's the type of man to want to have done it for himself."

"And so he bought my manor."

"Yes. And can barely afford to run it. He's a fool."

"Then why do you condemn yourself with him and his doings? Why not flee?"

He smiled. It was the smile of a snake with the cunning of a scorpion. He ran his tongue over his lips. Was it forked or was it just the light? "I . . . enjoy what he does. We share in it. All of it.

That boy in there," he said, nodding with his head to the faint glow too far away from Crispin's reach. "We shall both partake of him before he is slain. Or perhaps . . . even after."

Crispin grimaced but Radulfus leered. "He has not told you all, has he? It matters little now since you will be dead." He gave a great sigh of satisfaction. "Have you ever given much thought to your religion, Guest?"

"Is this your feeble way of telling me to pray my last?"

"No, you misunderstand me. We are baptized, catechized, eat communion bread, do penance, repeat. But where does it lead? Tell me, Guest. How often are your prayers answered?"

Crispin tried to keep his mind on point. It was useless to ponder the man's words, for in truth, Crispin prayed very little. But this was definitely not the time to consider that!

"I thought not," the man continued. "But Giles and I have found a better way. A better master. One who does not merely answer prayers on a whim but who grants our deepest desires."

"More blasphemy? Your souls are already in peril—"

"But our souls are our bargaining chit." His eyes gleamed in the dimness. Crispin studied him now, wondering how these two had found each other. "I am talking about the other Lord."

Crispin raised a brow. "The . . . *other* Lord?"

"The Prince of Darkness. The Devil himself. We have found a way to summon him to our bidding. And in such a way as to indulge our own . . . *habits* . . . as well."

"What are you saying? That . . . that the killing of these boys is some sort of unholy mass?" The scent of incense wafted toward him again. It smelled bitter to him now.

"That is *precisely* it! That wretched Cornelius first proposed it. It was he who had the knowledge of Hebrew, he who first suggested the idea from scrolls he had read. I do not believe his mastery of the language was all he said it was, but that is no matter. He gave us what we needed. But the poor fool had no stomach for the rest of it.

He was weak, wanted nought to do with it. His greed kept him close." A blaze of light from behind painted the vaults with temporary gold. Radulfus smiled. "Giles is preparing. That boy should be incapacitated by now. Unable to move but aware. Tonight, Giles will say the words, the final stroke that will open the Gates of Hell. Riches, power. All of it will be ours."

Crispin was beyond horrified. "You are both mad."

Radulfus blinked and slowly nodded. "That is, indeed, a possibility. But it doesn't matter. Oh the rush of it! With each killing we grow stronger, closer to our Lord!"

Struck speechless with revulsion, Crispin covertly looked about, trying to find a way of escape. But his back was to the room where Giles was and Radulfus stood before him with a sword.

Crispin couldn't help but look back toward the light as it flared again. "But . . . an innocent life, my lord," he said, stalling. "These crimes. You cannot expect to escape justice forever."

"Don't I? Giles has made quite a study of this. With the help of that dog Cornelius. He needed my help. And my money. But I've gotten my money's worth. I don't believe I have ever enjoyed myself with a woman as much as I have enjoyed those dear, struggling boys. He's been doing this for years, you know. Dropping the bodies into a dried-up well on his old estates. He's been getting a bit sloppy of late, letting those boys turn up so easily along the Thames. But it makes no matter now."

Crispin gritted his teeth. "It *must* come to an end."

"My dear Master Guest, who's to stop us? You?" And he poked him again with the sword blade to emphasize it.

A hand as wide as a ham lanced out of the darkness. Crispin gasped as it suddenly closed over Radulfus's face from behind and yanked him back into the gloom, his sword skittering across the stone floor without him.

Crispin jolted back, his heart thundering. Muffled squeals and shuffling of feet went on just a few feet from him in the blackness.

Then silence.

Never taking his eyes from the place Radulfus disappeared, Crispin leaned down and took up his dagger in his trembling hand. "My lord?"

A shuffle. Out of the gloom a large figure, larger than Radulfus, stood at the edge between light and shadow. Its small head nearly touched the low vaulted ceiling.

"Pro-tect," said the gravelly voice.

"God's blood," he whispered, breathless.

"Pro-tect."

"Yes," he said, voice steadying. "Protect. Are you here to protect the boy?"

"Protect boy," it said, before it swung an arm out, slamming Crispin in the head. He whirled and collided with a column. He slid down in a haze of blood and pain. A dark shape lumbered past him, but he heard no steps.

Dizzy, Crispin raised his eyes, searching for the hulking figure but saw nothing move out of the darkness. Where had it gone? Had it been a figment of his imagination?

From behind, the light whooshed again and Golem or no, Crispin knew only that he had to reach that light, had to save Jack, and despite the sweet darkness straining to pull him under, he heaved himself up and staggered toward it.

"Radulfus? Is that you?" came the voice from the light. "Come quickly! We are almost ready!"

Crispin pushed himself from column to column. Everything around him was blurry from the pounding ache in his head. Blood trickled into one of his eyes. But the thought that his knife was still miraculously in his hand spurred him on and he was at a doorway. Carefully, he slid inside and leaned against the arch. Braziers burned brightly against a far wall where strange markings were etched on the stone, much like he had seen on Jacob's parchments. At the other wall were tables engorged with food and drink, while pillows and furs lay strewn about on the floor, fit for a Saracen. Among the many pillows lay a pale, ginger-haired figure, devoid of shirt, his stocking-covered legs splayed lazily, his head lolling drowsily to the side.

"Jack!" he hissed.

Crispin stumbled forward only to be stopped by Giles's voice behind him.

"You! Damn you, Guest! You *won't* ruin my plans." He swung and Crispin ducked.

Giles grinned, getting a good look at Crispin's bruised face. "I see Radulfus took care of you." He laughed and gestured back toward Jack. "You know this boy, Crispin? I *knew* you had the predilection."

Jack was breathing, he could see that, but he was obviously drugged. "What did you do to him, you bastard?"

"Had I known he was *your* plaything, Crispin, why . . . I would have been *certain* to steal him sooner." Giles laughed.

Crispin steadied himself. "I'm taking him home."

The man sighed. "That would foil my plans considerably. Tonight is an extraordinary night."

"Afraid the Devil won't come? I have an inkling he'll make a special journey just for you."

"Oh, so Radulfus told you." He seemed disappointed. He snatched a glance behind. "I wonder where my cousin has gone off to."

Crispin put a hand to the side of his aching jaw. It did not help his throbbing head. "I imagine he's explaining a few things about now."

"Explaining? To whom?"

"Saint Peter." *Stall!* "I may not look it, but I did not lose our fight."

Giles frowned and looked behind again. Crispin took that moment to reach toward Jack but Giles stuck out his foot and easily tripped him. He barked his chin on the table and tumbled to the floor. Head spinning with stars and the edges of his sight fraying with blackness, he could not rise any higher than his knees.

Giles was beside him and grabbed his hair, yanking his face up. "I'm glad you are here, Crispin. You can witness my triumph. Always you were snatching victory out of my hands. Not this time."

Crispin's bleary eyes slid to the helpless form of his servant, half-naked, prepared for an unspeakable act of violence.

Giles laughed again, seeming to read the patter of Crispin's mind. He left him and moved to Jack, lifting him. The boy whimpered and writhed, trying to fight off the potions. Giles carried him to a table before the brazier and laid him upon it. He took up a stack of parchments, showing them to Crispin. "You see these? Magic and secret incantations worked on over many years. Do you see the ink? It is blood, Crispin. The blood of my boys. I dipped my quill in their still warm and running blood and I wrote out the words so I could read them aloud at this triumphal moment." He turned away from Crispin and spoke his words to the strange markings on the wall. The braziers on either side of him seemed to flush and spurt with an unnatural glow. Crispin tried to shake out the dizziness in his head and climbed to his feet, bracing a hand on a table. He saw a flash of silver, the knife in Giles's hand as he waved it over Jack.

Through his hazy vision, Crispin saw the flames rise and cast wavering shadows on the wall. The flames took shape. One looked like a dragon while the other was the image of a figure rising slowly from the flames.

"It's working!" cried Giles over the roar of fire. He whirled back toward Crispin, a smile of victory on his face. "Ha! You can never stop me. I will be wealthy and powerful! And you, my poor, poor Crispin. Look at you. Bloody. Bruised. Helpless. You can't do a *thing*!"

Helpless? He cut his glance to Jack but his vision was darkening. Blacking out. He had to hold on. He had to do something.

Giles laughed and it was that maniacal sound that gave Crispin a sudden bout of strength. He shook out his glazed head, gritted his teeth. Leaning against a pillar, he slowly pushed his way upward. His legs shuddered, no longer willing to uphold him, but from his will alone and the desperate blood surging through him, he thrust himself away from the pillar and stood upright. He took a long breath, braced himself, and leapt on Giles, spinning him around.

Giles's face opened in surprise, but before he could react, Crispin growled, "Think again, you bastard!" and shoved his dagger deep into the man's gut.

Giles grunted with the impact, but it wasn't nearly enough for Crispin's vengeance. He yanked the dagger upward, ripping open the cloth and flesh. Gore oozed over his hand and he remembered Giles's taunt about how he enjoyed the feel of viscera in his hands. With a cry of bloodlust, Crispin yanked the blade all the way up to the man's sternum. Giles's wide, astonished eyes finally turned to fear. He choked a red cough, spattering his chin.

Crispin thought he heard the sound of something screaming, and the flames wavered wildly behind him. The smell of sulfur and puffs of angry black smoke choked the air before settling down to a gentle flickering of light.

Crispin yanked back his blade and watched the man sink to his knees. Gurgling, Giles reached his bloody hand toward Crispin, beseeching though he could no longer speak.

Awash in wet crimson, Crispin watched dispassionately through the smoky haze as Giles struggled, life slowly ebbing, his guts now steaming in the light. Hot blood dripped from Crispin's knife hand, down his fingers, over the hilt, and slithered along the blade to the floor. "Here's your sacrifice," he growled. "Let the Devil take *you*."

The flames twisted around the logs in the brazier and a candle sputtered. Giles breathed his last in a terrible rattle of groaning and the twisting of his body. A sudden whoosh of stale air whirled about him, riffling his hair. In his last throes, his leg jerked and toppled a brazier. The burning log rolled along the straw floor, leaving a blazing track. The fire jumped and wrestled with the furs and pillows. The stench of burning hair filled Crispin's nose as the flames climbed, reaching the low rafters and burst into life.

Jack was suddenly surrounded by flames. The throbbing in Crispin's skull finally overwhelmed him and he fell to his knees. *No! Not now!* He pulled himself forward, tried to crawl toward Jack when something large loomed over him. He could no longer see from the smoke and ash, but someone was lifting him by his waist, swinging him around, and suddenly he was moving, held like a sack against a hip. He felt the heavy footfalls as they left the smoke behind.

"Save the boy!" he croaked and then coughed uncontrollably.

Carried further until he felt the cold on his face, they climbed.

He was suddenly released into the snow where he groaned and slowly rolled to his back. He breathed the fresh, cold air, filling his lungs with relief, but even that was small comfort to the anguish that stabbed his heart. "Jack," he whispered.

"M-master!" came the weak cry beside him.

Crispin turned. Jack lay in the snow beside him. He gathered the shirtless boy in an embrace, unable to speak for his gratitude. Below him, he was vaguely aware of fire licking into the starry sky. His ancestral home was engulfed in flames and smoke, and its sturdy walls were beginning to crumble.

His still hazy mind was filled with jumbled thoughts. Jack, alive and safe. Giles dead. How were they saved?

The sound of timbers falling stole his attention at last and though he knew he was far from safety, he couldn't tear his eyes away from the sight below. As each wall fell, as each arch toppled, a bit of his heart was ripped away. So final. The home of his ancestors, the manor house given to them by a king so many centuries ago, nothing but blackened rubble. This was the end, then. No going back. No returning to better days. While the house still stood, there always seemed to be that one slim chance, that possibility that the world could be righted again and everything could be put back in its place.

But not now. Not ever again. A frost colder than the snow chilling his face and hands clutched at his vitals. His time had slipped away. He would never be master of Sheen again. Never.

A shadow swooped above them and a feeling of panic gripped him. A figure blocked the starry field. He swung his cloak over Jack's bare shoulder before he slowly faced his savior.

20

"HOLY GOD!" JACK SCREAMED. "The Golem!"

Crispin curled his arm protectively about Jack.

The creature moved forward and the moonlight washed his face and chest in silver light. His head was small on wide shoulders, but perhaps it was only a trick of the eye, for his shoulders were unnaturally wide, piled as they were with pelts and hood. Crispin looked up at the face of the creature . . . and saw clearly that he was only a man.

"My God. Who are you?"

The man shuffled, peeking at Jack burrowed deep into Crispin's cloak. "Odo," he said in his gravelly voice.

"*You're* Odo?"

The man nodded. He fumbled at his tattered cloak. His fingernails were crusted with dirt and something lighter, like white dust. No. Not dust or dirt. Clay.

"You're one of the potters in London."

The man nodded again.

"But . . . what—?"

"Hugh was my friend," he rasped. "I followed. Bad, bad men hurt Hugh." His voice winced higher and a sob escaped.

"Hugh? Berthildus's son, you mean?"

Odo nodded.

"You . . . couldn't protect him."

He shook his head sorrowfully.

"So you took it upon yourself to protect other boys."

He nodded.

"You followed me here."

Odo nodded.

"Now you understand that I am not one of the bad men."

He bowed. He reached a hand forward as if wanting to pet Jack, who cringed back, but then Odo let his large hand fall to his side. "Bad men not hurt boy?"

"No. We stopped the bad men once and for all. They won't hurt anyone else ever again."

Odo considered this and turned his face toward the burning house. Crispin looked, too. Watched flames lick at the stones and timbers that had once brought such joy to his young life. Home. But that such evil had occurred in his beloved manor . . . He was glad to see it in ashes. Better that.

Odo turned back to Crispin. The man smiled. "You are friend."

But before he could speak again, they heard shouts closing on them. Odo looked up and with a fearful face, quickly disappeared back into the woods.

"Wait!" Crispin stared into the darkness of tangled boughs and listened for his footfalls but could hear nothing. As big as the man was he was as silent as the night itself.

"Unbelievable," he said to the icy air.

"Then . . . he's not a Golem?"

Crispin hugged the shivering boy tighter. "No. There is no Golem, Jack. Only that poor hulk of a man."

"He . . . he was only trying to help them boys, then?"

"Yes, it appears so."

"Merciful Jesus. What a world is this!"

"Verily," he murmured.

The sound of shouting and of many feet slogging through the snow reached them and suddenly, figures clambered up the hill and stopped, looking at Crispin and Jack in bewilderment. Crispin didn't even try getting to his feet. In his best courtly manner, he said, "If you would be so kind as to take us to the king's manor. I urgently need to speak with his grace the duke of Lancaster."

DURING THEIR BRIEF JOURNEY, Crispin glanced back at what was left of the manor, his heart wrenching with the dying glow of it. The smell of smoke in his nose would not soon leave him.

When they reached the king's manor, the king was mercifully abed. That meant Crispin would not have to face him. But facing Lancaster was no better. After much pleading, Crispin and Jack were ushered none too gently to the duke in his royal chambers. And when Lancaster's eyes fastened on Crispin, his face darkened. He studied Crispin's singed and bloody clothes and Jack's nakedness. "What happened?" he asked of his guards.

"There was a fire, your grace. At the Guest . . . I mean, the de Risley Manor."

Lancaster glared. "Was it contained?"

"No, your grace. It looks as if . . ." He flicked an awkward glance toward Crispin. "It . . . it burned to the ground."

"Is this your doing?" he growled at Crispin.

"No, your grace. But I was there."

"And what of Lord de Risley?"

The guard shook his head. "Many died, your grace. We believe de Risley was amongst them. He was in the mews where the fire appears to have started."

"In the mews?"

"No one knows why he was there, your grace. The servants said that he often . . . entertains there."

Lancaster's sharp glare never left Crispin's face. "Very well. Leave Guest here."

"What of his servant, your grace?"

His eye fell on a cowering Jack who was wearing Crispin's cloak. "Leave him here, but bring him some clothes. A shirt and a cloak, at least."

The guard bowed and left. Lancaster himself closed the door to his apartments and walked slowly toward the fire. Crispin felt the heat melt the permanent chill but he would not take his encircling arm away from Jack.

Lancaster did not speak for several moments. The anger in his eyes told Crispin why and he waited for his lord to do the talking first.

"Not your doing but you were there."

"It . . . it is difficult to explain, your grace. De Risley was the murderer I sought. Now he is dead. He started the fire."

"Is there proof of this?"

Crispin shook his head.

"Master Crispin saved my life!" cried Jack, startling both men.

Lancaster gave him a look of incomprehension. Crispin supposed it wasn't often that the lowliest servant ever dared speak to him let alone shout. Though Jack always seemed of a mind to confront Lancaster.

Gaunt approached the quivering boy and bent at the knee to look him in the face. Crispin could feel Jack trembling where he clutched at his cotehardie. "He saved your life? Tell me."

Jack did, starting with the body of the young boy Crispin found and how Jack decided to lay a trap but never expected to become trapped himself. With comical gestures using Crispin's cloak like a costume, Jack made it sound as if Giles and Crispin had fought hand to hand, that it had been a chivalrous battle to the death. It sounded to Crispin like the most heroic tripe any minstrel had ever croaked.

When Jack was finished, Lancaster slowly straightened. He rubbed his beard like a carpenter sanding it smooth. "Giles de Risley toyed with boys, did he?"

"As did his cousin."

"Did he kill that astrologer, Cornelius van der Brooghes?"

With an unpleasant smile of satisfaction, Crispin said, "Yes. I witnessed it."

"May he rot in Hell."

Crispin vaguely recalled a strange fiery figure rising from the brazier. "I think that a safe wager."

"What will you do now?"

"We need a place to rest for the night," he said wearily. "We will leave for London at sunrise. But Jack, here, has been through much this night and he is in need of a dry place to sleep."

"And just where did you intend this quiet place, Master Guest? This is no inn."

"With your permission, your grace, if we may stay with your . . . your servants." It had taken the rest of his courage to mouth that aloud. To beg to sleep with Lancaster's servants! Surely the duke would accede to that.

His dark eyes studied Crispin's reddening face for some time. "I see. And then?"

He raised his chin but not his eyes. "I must go to the Jewish physician. He hired me to recover something for him that is now lost. I must inform him of that fact."

"Before you inform *me*?" asked a voice behind him.

Crispin whipped around. The stranger from the carriage stood in the doorway to Lancaster's inner chamber. Crispin was instantly on his guard. He longed to unsheathe his blade but there had been enough mayhem this night. Instead he said, "What is *he* doing here?"

"Your betters, Crispin," warned Lancaster. "The Bishop Edmund is my guest."

"Tut, your grace," said the man. "Master Guest and I have met before. Under trying circumstances, to be sure, though never formally. I am Edmund Becke, a humble bishop from Yorkshire, on a mission." He bowed. "Am I given to understand you have been successful in your trials? Did you, by any chance, obtain the object I desired?"

"The parchments you wanted?" The man frowned at Crispin's deliberate release of information. Too bad if he had wanted to keep it a secret from Lancaster. "They didn't belong to you. They should go to their rightful owner."

"Rightful owner?" Becke seemed genuinely puzzled. "*I* am the rightful owner."

"I beg to differ. Parchments in Hebrew? Could those possibly be yours?"

The man's face darkened. "Yes. They would certainly be mine to confiscate. The parchments you speak of are illicit, smuggled into England for the purpose of its *secret* Jews to continue their unholy worship from their Scriptures."

Crispin felt the tiniest of twinges in his gut. Somehow there were too many parchments afoot. And he was beginning to feel as if he had been duped.

"What the devil are you two talking about?" bellowed Lancaster.

"Master Guest knows." The bishop stepped closer and looked Crispin in the eye, holding his gaze captive. "Give them to me." He held out his open palm.

"*That* was what this was all about? The Jews' wish to *worship*?"

"These Jews do not belong on English soil. *Give them to me!*"

"Give them to him, Crispin."

Crispin gave an angry grin. "They burned. All of them."

Bishop Edmund looked aghast before his expression changed. He chuckled. "That shall save me the trouble of burning them myself, at least. We shall soon purge these Jewish creatures from the land as easily as burned parchment."

Creatures. Crispin could not help but picture that boy, John, in his mind, innocently thinking that Crispin could protect their secret. Well, he had, for what it was worth. Not that it would do them any good in the long run.

"May I go?" he spat. He refused to meet Lancaster's gaze.

Becke waved his hand. "I am through with him. For the moment. But I suspect Master Guest and I shall meet again." He offered Crispin a last smile. "I am supposing you wish you had taken my gold now, eh?"

"You would suppose wrong." He looked to Lancaster once more. "May I go, your grace?"

Lancaster swept the two of them with his glance. "Yes, Crispin. It appears you are done here. But when you are through with your other business, you and your servant may find rest in yon alcove. Let it not be said that I was uncharitable this Advent season."

"Let it not be said," he grumbled. He instructed Jack to stay, even though there was a pleading look in his eye. It wouldn't do for Lancaster to see how indulgent he was with his own servant. He decided he would be safe enough in Lancaster's care.

Once in the corridor he asked a sleepy servant where he could find the Jewish physician and was directed to a door at a far end, away from the other chambers.

When Crispin knocked, it was some moments before Jacob opened the door. "Surprised?" The man's shocked face did not stop Crispin from shoving his way in.

He gave the room a glance before turning on the physician. "I found your parchments."

Julianne was pulling on her dressing gown as she rubbed the sleep from her eyes with one hand and carried a candle with the other. She smiled upon first seeing Crispin, but her face took on a look of shock. Bruised, with clothes singed by fire and covered in another man's blood, he must look less and less like a proper suitor, even a Gentile one. As much as he wanted to fall relieved into her arms, now was not yet the time to rest.

But Jacob, too pleased with the tidings, surged forward. "Where are they?" His eager hands opened, waiting to receive them.

"They were destroyed," he said with a certain amount of satisfaction. "But even had I recovered them, I would have been forced to hand them over to a Yorkshire bishop. He seems to think they are smuggled Scriptures to be given to the secret Jews of London."

The color drained from Jacob's face and he slowly sank into a chair. "Oh."

"Father, what is he talking about?"

A shaky hand reached up and touched her arm. "My dear child. Forgive an old man for his folly. For the pages of Creation were indeed stolen. But I used that as a ruse to hire this gentleman. I knew of his education and sought to arouse his curiosity by citing their strange provenance. For along with them were the parchments I was truly most concerned about. These were a portion of the Torah. A Torah I brought from France to give to a small band of Jews hiding in London."

"*Mon père*! Why? Why risk such a dangerous move?"

"You are not blind, my child." His body spoke of a deep weariness, but his voice took on a harder edge. "You have seen the persecutions. Our life in Provençal has been good, but it hangs by a thread. The whim of a monarch can send us into certain poverty and sorrow. When I knew I was coming to England, I made preparations." His eyes blinked once at his disguised daughter before he turned them to Crispin. "My apologies for deceiving you, *Maître*. I could not very well tell you my mission here without putting lives at risk. As a physician, it is my task to heal. And if that healing is merely spiritual, well. Then that is also my task. And a blessing."

"You placed me in unnecessary danger without full disclosure. That is unacceptable."

"Yes. Yes, for that, too, do I apologize. But I am only guilty of the sin of omission. The parchment to create a Golem was missing, but I did not worry over its loss as much as I let on."

"You waited two months to hire me."

"It took two months before I first heard of you."

"There seems a great deal of deception about you, Master Jacob." And he looked pointedly at Julianne. She pulled her gown tight about her and raised her chin insolently. "Do not fret over the loss. I do not think they will fall to the wrong hands in this instance. I rather think they were also destroyed."

Jacob nodded. "Perhaps a better end to them. The loss of the Scripture, however, is of great sorrow. It is only that my people wished to worship in the tongue of their forefathers. Why is this so wrong?" He shrugged and stared at the shaky candle flame in Julianne's grasp. "I will still pay you for your efforts, of course." He pushed himself up from his chair and ambled slowly toward an iron chest. Withdrawing a key from a ring on his belt, he unlocked it and pulled out a small pouch. "I think this silver will cover your fee."

Crispin did not allow pride to get in the way of his taking this money. It was certainly well earned. He stiffly bowed his thanks and then turned to Julianne. "I would speak with your daughter, sir. Alone."

"No."

"Father, please."

Jacob did not look as if he would relent, but after a moment of reflection he shuffled toward the inner chamber, pulling the door after him but leaving it ajar.

He gazed at her, small and solemn in the light of the one candle. "I had to see you. I . . . wish to continue to do so."

She took a step closer. "That is madness."

He pushed a hand through his crusty hair, thinking of the last few hours. "I *am* mad."

When she set the candle down she touched the blood on his clothes and face. "Crispin. What happened to you this night?"

"Much. *Jesu,* but I am weary."

"But . . . you are unhurt?"

He nodded. A hand lifted and touched a lock of her hair. "I have been thinking about you a great deal."

She shook her head, but gently so as not to dislodge his caressing hand. "We can do nothing, you and I. The best thing we can do is forget each other."

He stepped forward and engulfed her in his arms. The candle flickered in those glistening eyes. "I am afraid I cannot do that." He bent his head and took her lips. Even as she tried to shake her head, her mouth responded, opening. The kiss lasted until he needed to take a breath. "Julianne," he whispered to her forehead, kissing the warm flesh. Maybe something good could come of this horror. Maybe . . .

"But Crispin." She pushed him back. Worry lines replaced the kiss he had bestowed there. "What of the Golem? You must first see to that."

"That was no Golem," he said, pulling her back against his chest. How he liked the feel of her there. He wondered what her hair would look like grown out and down to her hips. "It was a man. A potter. A strange man, true, but—"

"No! There *is* a Golem!"

He clutched her tighter. "Julianne, there is nothing to fear. You heard your father. I tell you there is no Golem. It is only your fanciful imagination. It was a man. I spoke with him."

"But there *is*!" She shoved him back hard. Wildness radiated in her eyes. "There is!" she insisted. "*I* made it."

His head. It must still be throbbing from the thrashing he'd gotten. "I . . . I don't understand."

She sighed with both shoulders. "When my father's papers were stolen, it gave me an idea. I stole the parchments of Creation myself and studied them carefully. *I* went to the potter's row and bought the clay."

"But . . . when would you have had time? Your father says—"

"I was in my menses. For a Jew, a woman in her menses is unclean. It was a good excuse to hide away. I created the Golem in the unused mews at the end of the stables at the palace."

The shadows played with her face, changing her angelic features to those of a darker angel. His gut felt as if a stone now sat there, hard and solid. "You . . . you can't have."

"*I* spoke the words of Creation." She turned her hands, looking down at them. "I carved the word on its chest, gave it life. It moved for me, did as I bid. But when I returned the next day, the Golem was gone. And the murders began."

"A man murdered those children," his voice said dazedly.

"I never meant for children to die."

"Then who *did* you mean?"

"Christians, of course." He took a step back. The cold stone in his gut grew heavier. "My revenge," she was saying, though her voice sounded far away. A ringing started in his ears. "You do not know, Crispin. You do not know what Father and I have endured over the years. The Golem was to teach them a lesson."

"I see."

"Do you? Oh . . . but Crispin. *You* are not like them. You're different."

"More like them than you seem to realize."

She studied his face, squinting from the faint light. "Crispin?" She reached for him but he pushed back those hands, hands he had desperately wanted to caress him a mere few moments ago.

"How could you have done such evil? And then to allow me to—"

"Evil? Like the evil that has been done to us!"

"An eye for an eye, is that it?"

"Yes!"

He shook his head. The cold stone made the bile rise to his throat. "You don't know me at all."

"I know you are a fool for helping those people when they do you wrong. But I can overlook that."

"Can you? And yet I cannot overlook this evil you would set upon London. Where is this Golem now?"

"I don't know. It vanished. But you said you encountered it."

Crispin tried to think, tried to distinguish the times he had seen the Golem. Had it truly been Odo *all* those times? What of that clay-smeared wall in the palace? Was it Odo who killed Radulfus? He hadn't seen its face at the time.

"It's no matter," she said. "When it rains he will wash away. Without the symbols etched on his chest he will cease to exist. You don't have to worry. He will melt into the pile of clay from which he was made." She reached for him again but he slapped her hands away.

"Don't touch me!"

"Julianne!" cried Jacob, standing unsteadily in the doorway, his white face older by some years. "Is this true? Did *you* let loose the Golem?"

"Father, you don't understand—"

"Let the man go."

"No! Father! He's not like the others. Make him see—"

"Julianne! No. Go to the chamber."

"But Father!"

"GO!"

Julianne hung her head. Wringing her hands, she obeyed Jacob at last, retreating sullenly into the darkened room.

Jacob silently closed the door. With his trembling hand laid against it, he did not turn to Crispin. "I have committed many sins, it seems," he said brokenly. "To raise a daughter like a son was a grave sin indeed. I am just now paying the price. That I see with clarity. There is no need to regret this episode, *Maître* Guest. We will leave England as soon as possible. I will send my regrets to the queen. It was a mistake to come here. I was only trying to do my countrymen a *mitzvah*. A good deed. But I see now that I have only cursed them all."

Crispin had no words of comfort. If he opened his mouth, he did not know what would come out. Instead, he turned away, tight-lipped, and left.

THE NEXT DAY CRISPIN and Jack returned to London with Wynchecombe's borrowed horse, neither of them speaking of Jack's harrowing experience. The days passed, and Crispin tried to forget short-cropped hair and green eyes. He thought of venturing back to the potter's row to tell Berthildus the fate of her son, but he could not bring himself to do it. It was by mere chance that the astrologer had chosen Berthildus from whom to buy the clay, and her poorer luck that she had a young son. No, he could not tell her.

He did send an anonymous message to Matthew Middleton the goldsmith, warning him that the Church knew of their secret. A fortnight after that, there was a sudden selling of many properties near the Domus and several of London's most successful citizens had departed the city for parts unknown.

Advent passed and Christmas day dawned, just like any other. He went through the motions of the day, shaving, brushing down his cotehardie, taking turns with Jack adding fuel to the fire. He admonished Jack to go to mass, but the boy would not leave his side. When the bells tolled for Sext, Crispin reminded Jack that he was expected at Gilbert and Eleanor's table.

Sullenly, Jack adjusted his cloak and rested his hand on the door ring. "Master, I think you should come."

"I believe we've already had this discussion, Jack."

"But Master, of all Christmases, don't you think you deserve a little cheer? Some reward?"

"My reward is that, apparently, I won't hang for Giles's or Cornelius's murders."

"But Master Crispin—"

He laid his hand on the boy's shoulder. "Jack, I appreciate your concern. But I cannot go with you. Give them my greetings."

Jack scowled and grumbled to himself, but he pulled open the door and stumped noisily down the stairs.

The smells of good cooking soon wafted up the stairwell. His landlady, Alice Kemp, was doing her best for the tinker and their daughter, Matilda. All around him, in fact, people were gathering for their Christmas feast, whether it be humble or not.

After a time, the brooding silence began to aggravate. Crispin threw on his cloak and hit the stairs. He made it to the street and tucked his hood over his head. Snow was falling in feathery flakes and mist made midday seem much later. He felt the cold nip his face and was grateful for it, grateful to be alive, though he couldn't put the image of the burned-out shell of his ancestral home out of his mind. Well, there was nothing to be done about it. Gilbert was right. They had been lost to him for years, and now they were gone for good.

He watched as people tramping in the street dragged greenery behind them, some even carrying large Yule logs. For a moment, Crispin wished he hadn't been unreasonable and turned down the kind offer of his friends at the Boar's Tusk. Why didn't he just go? They had certainly asked him often enough. With a sigh that turned to a puff of gray, Crispin had no real answer. Only that, for the last seven years, he did not feel fit to join in with the celebration of others. Call it part of his personal penance.

The people on the street were thinning to just a few here and there. The trampled snow told him that the processions had ceased and all had been blessed by their parish priests. Shops were closed and it began to feel lonelier. *As it should,* he reminded himself. A traitor such as himself had no right to feasts and joviality, but wallowing too much was also uncalled for, at least that's what Gilbert had told him. *God loveth a cheerful giver.* He snorted at that before he nearly ran into a woman idly walking near the closed shops.

"Pardon me," he said with a bow, and when he looked up, a familiar face looked back out of the hood. "God's blood! John Rykener!"

"Crispin! Oh this *is* my lucky day! My Christmas blessing." He scooped up Crispin's arm before he could protest and began to walk with him.

"Let go of me," he hissed, trying to wrench his arm away.

"I worried over you, Crispin. There were rumors of all sorts."

"What are you doing on this side of the Thames?" he asked, still struggling.

"I fancied a change of scenery. I do like it better here. I imagine I will find myself living on this side from now on."

"Too many arrests?"

"Alas. I am known there."

They walked on in silence for a time, the snow crunching under their feet. Crispin did not try to push the man away after a few more unsuccessful attempts. He may like to dress like a woman, but Rykener had a strong arm.

"You shouldn't worry over me," said Crispin, hating the silence. "I always seem to survive."

"Like a cat. You land on your feet every time."

"Not every time."

They passed a house where the smoke from the chimney slithered down the stone wall. John sniffed the air. "Mmm. Smells like Christmas. Where are you bound, Crispin? Some fine feast with your companions?"

"No. I make it a habit of spending Christmas alone."

John stopped, bringing Crispin up short. "Crispin Guest! How abominably morose of you. Do you also wear a hair shirt?"

Crispin frowned. "No. This is none of your business, John."

"Of course it isn't. That is why it so intrigues me."

"Then what of you? Do a bit of whoring before you gather around the Yule log, do you?"

He jabbed Crispin hard with his elbow. It took the wind out of him for a few moments. "Don't be crass. But as a matter of fact, yes. I find myself woefully without funds." John jerked to a halt and turned his head, squinting down a gloomy alley. "What was that?"

"What was what?"

"I thought I saw something. Something . . . large."

Crispin looked with that familiar tingle scraping across the back of his neck. "Like a man?"

"Couldn't have been a man. It was too big."

It was quite possible it was the potter Odo skulking about in London. And yet. It was also quite possible . . . No. No, he refused to entertain the notion.

John had a stark look on his face, even under the curls of hair just at his temple.

Crispin glanced in the other direction down the gray street. They weren't far from an alehouse. And a warm fire and wine did sound pleasing. "John, would I embarrass myself too much by buying you some Christmas cheer?"

John's face brightened. The hulking figure was forgotten, though the tingle at Crispin's neck remained. "I thought you spent Christmas alone?"

"Perhaps . . . that is a tradition I can do without this year."

John smiled. "They don't know me here. They will think I am a woman."

"Then . . . *Eleanor* . . . shall we?" Crispin always suspected he was a bit mad but he didn't know how much until he held the alehouse door open for his unusual companion.

Afterword

It is a wild notion indeed to write about a medieval serial killer, and especially one who murders and defiles children, using their blood and entrails for summoning demons. This surely is the stuff of gothic horror fiction of the most melodramatic kind.

Unfortunately, it might have *inspired* gothic horror fiction, but this was definitely *not* fiction. This is the retelling of the very real and very strange tale of the fifteenth-century serial killer, Gilles de Rais, in all its horrific detail.

De Rais lived in France about one hundred years after the action of this novel. He was a contemporary of Joan of Arc. In fact, he served with her in her army. Too bad he wasn't influenced enough by her life to follow in her saintly footsteps. He and his cronies indulged in their perversions by using the excuse that they were summoning demons to do their bidding, mostly for riches. De Rais sought his wealth and status through his own special *grimoire,* written in the blood of the hundreds of boys and girls he slaughtered. If he had not run afoul of the Church he might never have met his justice.

Eventually, he did meet a grim and well-deserved end.

A medieval serial killer is one thing, but to include a medieval cross-dressing male prostitute? John Rykener did, indeed, exist in Crispin's London. We know little about him except what is found in one court document when he was arrested in 1395. What he explained in the story is strictly from those documents: He used the name "Eleanor" when he dressed as a woman and was arrested for his attire as well as soliciting sex. He confessed that his clients were made up of priests, scholars, monks, women, and nuns, but he preferred priests because they paid him more!

Homosexuality was certainly little understood in the Middle Ages, though Rykener appears to have been more vilified for his gender-bending attire than for his interest in men. According to historian John Boswell in his book *Christianity, Social Tolerance, and Homosexuality,* the penalties for homosexual behavior were erratic. More often than not, punishments came in the form of ecclesiastical penance rather than civil penalties, but these actions by the authorities were by no means universal or unduly obsessive. The idea that the Church or civil authorities were "getting medieval" on homosexuals in the Middle Ages might have come to us from criminal records in the seventeenth and eighteenth centuries, when harsher punishments and prison time was meted out for acts of sodomy. "Homosexuality," says Boswell, "is given no greater attention than other sins and, viewed comparatively, appears to have been thought less grave than such common activities as hunting." Still, between the law courts and the Church, it was best to keep a low profile.

As for the tale of the Jews in England, Edward I exiled them in 1290, but those that remained—the converted—were scarcely received with open arms. Many were ghettoed in the Domus Conversorum for their entire lives. Others did strike out on their own and eventually blended into the society at large, marrying Gentiles and disappearing from sight. Did many convert in name only, remaining secret Jews? In the 319 years that Jews were officially barred from England, the documents of the Domus record a regular succession of Jews arriving on English shores. According to those documents, there were still thirty-eight men and ten women admitted into the Domus even after expulsion, but more, surely, had entered England than had converted and lived in the Domus. There are no exact records to document it, but there had to be many Jews who remained, even forsaking their dietary restrictions in order to blend in. Some continued to live as secret Jews and some even lived openly as in the case of Nathanael Menda of London and Johanna and Alice of Dartmouth, though they eventually ended up in London's Domus.

Records of the Domus inhabitants end in 1609. The Master of the Rolls actually continued to receive his stipend for being Keeper of the Domus well into the nineteenth century. In 1891 the post of preacher of the Rolls Chapel was finally abolished by Act of Parliament and the buildings in Camden were used as a storehouse for the rolls of Chancery.

Jews were not officially allowed back into England until 1655 under Oliver Cromwell (even though they were residing in England openly as Jews at this point, and performed bravely in the Jacobean conflict), but it wasn't made law until the Jewish Naturalization Act of 1753. That act was repealed the next year, but it didn't stop Jews from immigrating back to England.

The bishop in this piece is modeled on the later Spanish Inquisition of 1478 (and, of course, according to Monty Python, no one expects that!) that made its mark by rousting out the converted Jews still secretly practicing their faith, leading up to the 1492 expulsion of the Jews from Spain. The northern countries of Europe seemed mostly spared from Inquisitions, including England, which only had a Templar trial (perhaps because they had already ousted their Jews). But anti-Semitic sentiment was certainly fired up in the medieval world, especially the blood libels that seemed to easily stir the rabbles. Yet there were still staunch men who protected Jews from the mobs, including the sheriff of Norwich in the days of Saint William of Norwich. The sheriff gathered the Jews in Norwich castle and refused to allow any trial that he well knew would end in Jewish bloodshed. Despite Thomas of Monmouth's writings, there were many such men who did not believe that Jews were responsible for the deaths of children. Blood libels reached such a peak—insisting that Jews ritually crucified a Christian child and drank their blood and ate their flesh during the Passover—that in seventeenth-century Poland, only white wine was served at Passover so there could be no suspicion that the wine was instead blood!

Anti-Semitism had its proponents in the Middle Ages, even from the highest of authorities. Quotations from such worthies as Pope Innocent III ("The Jews, like the fratricide Cain, are doomed to wander about the earth as fugitives and vagabonds, and their faces must be covered in shame. They are under no circumstances to be protected by Christian princes, but, on the contrary, to be condemned to serfdom. . . .") and Saint Thomas Aquinas ("Since the Jews are the slaves of the Church, she can dispose of their possessions. . . .") fueled expulsions until Jews either remained in the Muslim world, or fled to the farthest reaches of eastern Europe.

However, Avignon was a place that allowed Jews to flourish, many becoming physicians and enjoying any number of trades in crafts and the arts, some even welcoming the patronage of the popes who had moved their residence to Avignon during the fourteenth century. This was not to last, and though they became wealthy in their many vocations, they could not buy chateaus outside the Jewish streets called the *carriers* that soon became their ghettoes.

Crispin's early attitude about Jews reflects medieval sensibilities from outright hatred and mistrust, to the more thinking-man's approach, much as Saint Bernard and many other contemporaries expressed. Exploring this aspect of his personality as well as the Jewish influence on the Middle Ages was interesting and refreshing.

Crispin and Jack have more murder and some new surprises to contend with when they leave London for a trip to Canterbury in the next medieval noir installment, *Troubled Bones*. In the meantime, I invite readers to keep abreast of Crispin's doings on his very own blog at www.CrispinGuest.com.

Glossary

AIGLET the metal point of a lace to make it easier to thread through the lace hole.

ARRAS a tapestry.

CANONICAL HOURS also called the Divine Office. Specific hours for certain prayers by monastics, though the church bells to call to each canonical hour helped divide the day for the laity as well.

CHAPERON HOOD a shoulder cape with a hood attached.

CHEMISE shirt for both men and women, usually white. All-purpose.

COMPLINE last canonical hour of the day.

COTEHARDIE (COAT) any variety of upper-body outerwear popular from the early Middle Ages to the Renaissance. For men, it was a coat reaching to the thighs or below the knee, with buttons all the way down the front and sometimes at the sleeves. Worn over a chemise. Sometimes a belt was worn at the hips and sometimes the belt moved up to the waist. This is what Crispin wears.

CRESSET an iron basket used for holding wood, coals, or oil, and lit for illumination, mounted on a post as a torch in a sconce, on feet, or suspended from a pole as a lantern.

DEGRADE when knighthood is taken from a man, usually because of treason or other crimes against the crown.

GARROTE a cord wound around a stick used to strangle.

HOUPPELANDE fourteenth-century upper-body outerwear with fashionably long sleeves that touched the ground. As fashion changed, so did the collar, growing in height.

LIRIPIPE the long tail on a hat or hood.

LISTS field for jousting.

MATINS, LAUDS canonical hours, about sunrise.

NEWGATE a city gate as well as a prison.

NONE canonical hour, three p.m.

PIPKIN small clay pot or drinking vessel.

POULAINES long, pointed-toed shoes.

PRIME one of the canonical hours, about six a.m.

RONDELLE HAT broad-brimmed cloth hat.

ROUELLE a circle used in heraldry, but also a round piece of yellow cloth sewn to the breast of a gown or tunic designating the wearer as a Jew.

SENNIGHT a period of seven days, a week.

SEXT canonical hour, midday.

SHRIVE/SHRIVEN to make confession in the penitential sense.

STEWS brothels.

TERCE canonical hour, about nine a.m.

VESPERS canonical hour, evening.

VILLEIN peasant.

WHELP young dog.